RESISTING THE SINGLE DAD

KATRINA CUDMORE

A NEW LEASH ON LOVE

MELISSA SENATE

MILLS & BOON

First Published in Great Britain 2019
by Mills & Boon, an imprint of HarperCollinsPublishers,
1 London Bridge Street, London, SE1 9GF

Resisting the Italian Single Dad © 2018 Katrina Cudmore
A New Leash on Love © 2018 Harlequin Books S.A.

Special thanks and acknowledgment are given to Melissa Senate
for her contribution to the Furever Yours series.

ISBN: 978-0-263-27205-5

0119

MIX
Paper from
responsible sources

FSC
www.fsc.org

FSC™ C007454

This book is produced from independently certified FSC™
paper to ensure responsible forest management.

For more information visit: www.harpercollins.co.uk/green

Printed and bound in Spain
by CPI, Barcelona

RESISTING THE ITALIAN SINGLE DAD

KATRINA CUDMORE

To Harry, my night owl.

CHAPTER ONE

THE EXACT SECOND her office clock hit midday, Carly Knight grabbed her laptop bag and the yellow cardboard box jammed with the natural sleeping aids she brought to all her parent talks. She was about to leave her office when the angry blare of a car horn from the road outside had her pause by her office window to watch a taxi driver angrily weave past a silver car that had pulled in on the double yellow line.

The driver's door slowly opened. A tall, powerfully built man climbed out. He moved to the other side of the car. Wasn't he worried about getting a parking fine? But then, given the car he was driving, a parking fine would probably be nothing more than pocket change to him.

He came to a stop at the rear door of the car and bowed his head for the briefest of seconds before sending his gaze heavenwards. There was an aloneness, a heaviness of spirit in how he stood stock-still, his feet firmly anchored to the ground, staring upwards. The man's lips moved briefly in speech as though he was talking to someone.

She needed to leave or she'd be late for her talk, but she couldn't drag herself away from watching him. She moved closer to the window, placed her palm against the cool glass.

Opening the rear door, he leant into the car for a moment before reappearing with a little girl in his arms.

He kissed her forehead, tenderly smoothed her soft brown curls and attempted to place her down on the footpath. But the little girl, dressed in a yellow jacket and blue pants, and who Carly guessed was about two years of age, refused to let go.

The man shook his head and then began to pace the footpath, the little girl in his arms, glancing all the while down the street. Who was he waiting for?

Carly soon had her answer when a petite, dark-haired woman, holding hands with a similarly dark-haired boy of four or five, rushed towards him. She hugged the man warmly, stroked the little girl's cheek. They were a beautiful family. Carly's heart tightened at their intimacy. But then the man attempted to pass the little girl to her mother, but she clung to him, refusing to let go. In the end, he was forced to remove her baby stroller from the boot of his car one-handed, refusing the mother's offer of help. When he lowered the little girl into the stroller, Carly could hear her cries of protest. Kneeling before the stroller, the man stroked the little girl's curls, but her leg smacked against his forearm and pushed him away.

The woman said something to him and hugged him again before rushing off with both children.

Fists tightly bunched at his side, the man stared after his family for a long while before turning in the direction of Carly's building. Carly's head jerked back at the desolation etched on his face. She stepped back from the window, out of his view, feeling like an intruder on his suffering.

Should she go down and ask him if everything was okay?

The man's chest rose heavily and when he exhaled, the torment in his eyes disappeared. An aloof, guarded expression took its place. He removed his phone from his pocket, answered a call and strode in the direction of her office block.

Carly frowned. Could this be Mr Lovato? Her client who was supposed to have been here half an hour ago? But why didn't his wife come in with him?

Locking the office door behind her, she went out onto the stairwell and was on the turn of the stairs when the door to the reception area burst open.

A blur of dark wavy hair, a phone pressed to hard jawbone, an expensive grey suit, the jacket spilling backwards as he climbed the stairs two at a time, raced towards her.

Carly's heart lurched; it was rather disconcerting to be faced with such male perfection on a Tuesday lunchtime on the concrete stairs of an office block desperately in need of refurbishing.

Light, misty green eyes flicked in her direction as he passed her by.

Turning, she saw that he had already reached the turn in the stairs. 'Mr Lovato?'

He came to a stop and looked down towards her. Standing still, he was even more devastatingly handsome than when he had been in motion. He considered her through a serious gaze, his mouth shaped like a soft wave, turning ever so slightly downwards at the corners.

He rolled his impressively wide shoulders and gave a nod.

'I'm Carly Knight, the sleep consultant you made the appointment with. Is everything okay?'

His eyes narrowed. 'What do you mean?'

There was a defensiveness to his tone that had Carly wavering. She wanted to ask if she could somehow help in whatever had been troubling him outside, but the proud tilt of his head told her he would not welcome her intrusion.

Instead she climbed the stairs to stand a few steps below him. 'I'm sorry but I have another appointment that I have to leave for. If you speak to Nina on reception she will schedule another appointment for you.'

He considered her for a moment, the ever so slight tightening of his jaw the only indicator of his unhappiness. 'I apologise for my lateness. I promise I won't delay you for more than ten minutes.'

His voice was deep and—okay, so she'd admit it—*really* sexy. Where was his accent from? His surname, Lovato, was that Italian or Spanish? His smooth tanned skin and dark hair suggested long, sun-kissed Mediterranean days in whitewashed villages with views of a glistening sea.

For a moment, a deep longing for some sunshine and freedom washed through Carly. After a long icy winter, spring in London had proved to be cold and miserable. And it felt as though she hadn't seen daylight for years thanks to the ongoing task of establishing her fledgling sleep consultancy business, which entailed working late into the night on far too many evenings.

'I'm sorry, Mr Lovato, I really have to leave for another appointment.'

'It's important that I meet with you *now*.'

Carly attempted to give him a sympathetic smile, but in truth her earlier irritation with Mr Lovato, which had temporarily disappeared in the face of his upset, was quickly reappearing at his insistent tone. Only this morning, he had somehow managed to sweet-talk an appointment with Nina, the office-block receptionist who provided a diary booking service for all the tenants, despite the fact that Carly's diary was already full for the day. Nina usually guarded the diaries like a Rottweiler on steroids.

When Carly had questioned Nina on why she had given him an appointment, Nina had given her a soppy smile that was alarming in itself and said he had been referred by Dr Segal, a paediatrician who was increasingly referring patients to Carly, and that she hadn't had the heart to turn him away; that he had sounded so lovely and sincere and such a concerned dad for his daughter who wouldn't sleep at night. Tough-as-nails Nina had obviously fallen for that deeply accented voice that no doubt had the potential to melt granite.

'It's now close to ten minutes past twelve, you're over half an hour late for your appointment,' Carly pointed out. From his expensive suit, glistening black leather shoes and a car even her stepfather couldn't afford, Carly guessed that Mr Lovato was rich. Seriously rich. And no doubt used to getting his own way. But not now. Not with her. She had spent her teenage years being manipulated by a stepfather who had used his wealth to get his own way regardless of the consequences to others. If Mr Lovato was anything like her stepfather he would have no problem in making Carly late for her appointment with a group of other parents, as long as his own needs were met. Money talked for some people and it gave them an inflated sense of entitlement. 'My receptionist shouldn't have given you an appointment today. My diary was full. She tried calling you back to make alternative arrangements but you didn't answer her calls.'

'I was working from home today—between taking care of my daughter and client calls I never managed to call Nina back.' He shrugged, gave her a hint of an apologetic smile. 'When it was time to leave I couldn't find my daughter's shoes. And when we were finally on our way I realised that I had left her changing bag in the hallway so I had to turn around. You know how it is when you have children—time seems to disappear into a void of chasing your own shadow.'

Carly cleared her throat, ignoring the nudge of pain in her chest at his not unexpected but incorrect assumption she had children of her own. It was a common assumption many clients made. 'I don't have any children of my own but from working with them for the last decade I agree that you have to be very organised around them.'

His gaze narrowed. Carly pressed on, knowing she had

to leave for her meeting despite a nagging feeling that she should give Mr Lovato some time. 'Nina should be able to schedule you in for some time next week, after the bank holiday.'

Moving down the steps towards her, he came to a stop directly in front of her. Carly tilted her head to meet his gaze. He was tall. Very tall. At least six feet four, and over eight inches taller than herself.

He carried himself with a smooth ease, which, combined with his prominent angular features and soul-searching eyes, had the effect of making you forget all that you were thinking, and everything you were about to say.

'I want us to speak now.'

Carly blinked at the smoothness of his tone, at the bluntness of his words. 'That's not possible. I'm giving a talk to a parent group in Kilburn at one. I have to leave now or I'm going to be late.'

His eyes narrowed but did not move from hers for a moment. Carly had to force herself not to look away, hating the heat that was growing on her skin at his nearness, the strange feeling of undoing that was unravelling in her insides.

'How are you getting there?'

Carly frowned. 'The underground.'

'I'll drive you.'

Carly stared after him as he moved to the reception doors. He held one of the scruffy blue doors in need of a repaint open for her. Carly followed him down. 'That's not necessary, Mr Lovato.'

His beguiling mouth curved upwards into a hint of a smile. 'My name is Maximiliano but you can call me Max. We can talk on the journey there. It's the least I can do considering my lateness for our meeting. Can I carry your box out to the car for you?'

Irritated, Carly shook her head. 'No…and I don't think it's appropriate you driving me. After all, we have just met.'

To this he let out an amused exhalation before saying, 'I'm a seriously sleep-deprived father. I can assure you that you have nothing to fear from me.' He looked towards reception where Nina was staring in their direction and added in a teasing tone, 'Nina, I'm driving Ms Knight to her appointment in Kilburn. Should anything happen to her you have my address and telephone number, which you can pass onto the police.'

Unbelievably, Nina giggled at this. Carly eyed her with exasperation but Nina was too busy ogling their visitor to catch her annoyance.

'I really don't think—'

Before she could add anything else, Max interrupted her, his voice low, the intensity of his proud gaze flipping her stomach. 'I urgently need your help, Ms Knight…as does my daughter.'

Carly Knight's cornflower-blue eyes disappeared in a slow blink behind her long and lush eyelashes as she considered his words.

Max wanted to walk away. He hated asking for help. It wasn't in his nature. He found it degrading—a sign of weakness. He valued his privacy, disliked having to expose himself and his family to the scrutiny of an outsider. From a young age he had understood the importance of self-reliance. His mother, a strict disciplinarian, had constantly told him that to be dependent on others made you weak. And growing up in a tough suburban neighbourhood of Rome, he had quickly learned that to survive he had to be strong, resilient and, most important of all, never show weakness.

Carly Knight was not what he had expected. When he had reluctantly called the number his paediatrician had given him, he had imagined meeting an older woman, a grandmother perhaps, with sensible hair and sensible shoes to match her sensible personality. A woman with years of experience dealing with strong-willed toddlers hell-bent on testing their parents.

He hadn't expected a woman who hadn't experienced first-hand the exhausting reality of parenting. He hadn't expected sparkling white trainers under ankle-length faded blue jeans, a white blouse covered in red stars. He hadn't expected tumbling blonde hair or creamy skin so smooth he wanted to touch his thumb against her high cheekbones. He hadn't expected the attitude that said he was an inconvenience in her life.

He wanted to walk away; to tell her he didn't want her help after all. But that would be a lie. He did need her help. And so did Isabella, his beautiful, inspiring, contrary-as-a-hungry-goat daughter. They could not go on as they were. As much as he hated to admit it, they were both miserable. He clenched his jaw as the constant slow burn of guilt for failing his family intensified under Carly Knight's critical gaze.

Her brow wrinkled but then something softened in her eyes. She let out a deep breath. 'Okay, I'll take the lift.'

Torn between the relief that she had said yes and the deep wish that he had never needed to ask for her help in the first place, he took hold of her box, which she released reluctantly, and guided her out to his car.

She had resisted even taking a lift from him. How on earth was she going to respond when she learnt of everything he wanted from her?

Outside she folded her arms and stared pointedly at the double yellow line his car was parked on. He opened the passenger door for her, and nodded down towards the box. 'Do I smell lavender?'

'As part of bedtime routines, I recommend to parents

that they use aromatherapy creams and oils in baths and in massaging their children—lavender and camomile being just some they can use. I take samples along to my talks to give to parents.'

He placed the box in the rear seat of his car, beside Isabella's car seat, sure that Isabella would never tolerate him massaging her. Thankfully.

When she got into the car, Carly's gaze flicked over the leather and walnut interior, her head twisting to take in the rear seat. 'This must be the cleanest family car I've ever seen. Most of my clients' cars are covered in toys and crumbs and empty wrappers.'

'I'm away with work a lot. My daughter isn't in my car that often.'

She frowned at that. Max punched the buttons of his satnav, wondering not for the first time if he had done the right thing. Was Carly Knight about to judge him, to confirm that, yes, he was an inadequate father? Knowing your inadequacy was one thing, allowing someone else to see it, exposing yourself to their criticism, was another matter.

Carly gave him the address of her appointment and he pulled away from the kerb, following the instructions of the satnav voice.

Beside him Carly asked with a hint of surprised amusement in her voice, 'Is your satnav speaking in Italian?'

'Yes… I like some reminders of home.'

Her bee-stung mouth carved upwards into a light smile. 'I wondered if you were Spanish or Italian.'

Despite himself he smiled and faked indignation. 'How could you confuse the two? I'm Italian and very proud to be.'

'So why are you in cold and damp London? Why not the Amalfi coast or somewhere as gorgeous as that?'

'I like London, the opportunities here. I've a home in

Italy too—on Lake Como—but my work commitments mean I rarely get to visit there.'

'I've never been but I would love to one day.' She gave her head a small shake and, sitting more upright in her seat, she clasped her hands together. 'Okay, tell me how I can help you and why it was so urgent that we talk today?'

Her voice had returned to its formal professionalism. Max waited for a break in the traffic to turn right out of Rowan Road, fighting the reluctance to confess the problems in his family. Eventually he forced himself to admit, 'My daughter Isabella is twenty-two months old. She's a terrible sleeper. The worst in the world. I thought as she got older it would improve but in recent months it has only worsened.'

Carly twisted in her seat and he glanced over to find her studying him carefully. 'What do you mean by a terrible sleeper?'

Her tone held a hint of censure, as though she didn't quite believe him. Frustration tightened in his chest. 'She won't go to sleep—it can take hours and has tried the patience of even the most chilled-out nannies that I've managed to employ. She wakes frequently at night and refuses to go back to sleep. It's causing havoc. She's tired and irritable during the day and my job is very demanding—her sleeplessness is killing my concentration. I can't retain nannies. They all walk out eventually. My neighbours have a boy of a similar age who's been sleeping through the night since he was five months old.'

'No two children are the same. Don't compare Isabella to other children—on this or anything else. Trust me, it's the quickest route to insanity for any parent. Studies vary in their results but some say that fewer than half of all children settle quickly at night and sleep through. Isabella is in the majority by waking.'

Max shook his head, picturing Isabella's brown eyes

sparking with anger last night as she stood beside her bed and shook her head each time he told her it was time to go to sleep. *'È ora di andare a letto, Isabella.'*

His daughter's word count was slowly increasing but her favourite word continued to be a defiant, 'No.' And last night she had used it time and time again, her chestnut curls bouncing about her face as she dramatically shook her head.

He had been so tempted to crawl into bed beside her, to hold her in his arms, sniff her sweet baby scent, listen to her soft breaths when she eventually fell asleep. But to do so would be to do Isabella a disservice. She needed to learn to go to sleep on her own, learn to be independent of him.

He rolled his eyes. 'I bet she's an outlier though; I bet she's in the top one per cent for waking at night. My daughter doesn't do anything by halves.'

She smiled at that. He felt a surprising pleasure that she got his attempt at humour. 'Waking at night is normal. Children wake for a variety of reasons: shorter sleep cycles, hunger, being too hot or cold, their room being too bright, or the need for comfort and assurance. I find that unrealistic expectations cause parents the most stress. How does Isabella's mother feel about her sleeping?'

Max cursed under his breath at a car that swerved into his lane on the Hammersmith flyover without indicating. The tight fist of guilt that was his constant companion these days squeezed even fiercer. Would talking about Marta ever get easier? Would the guilt of her death—how they had fought in the hours before—ever grow less horrific? 'Isabella's mother, Marta, died in a car crash when Isabella was three months old.'

'I thought…' She glanced in his direction, confusion clouding her eyes. 'I saw you from my office window earlier…'

Now he understood her confusion. 'My wife's friend

Vittoria agreed to take Isabella this afternoon so that I could meet with you.'

He waited in the silence that followed for her response to hearing of Marta's death. Most people responded with panic, a keen urge to change the subject or preferably, if circumstances allowed it, to find an excuse to get away.

'I'm very sorry to hear about your wife. It must have been a very difficult time for you.'

Her softly spoken words sounded heartfelt. He glanced in her direction and swiftly away again, not able to handle the compassion in her eyes.

'Do you have other children?'

'No, just Isabella.'

'Have you family or friends nearby, who support you?'

'I have some friends, like Vittoria…but they have their own families to look after.' Max paused, pride and guilt causing him to add more fiercely, 'Anyway, we don't need support.'

'It can't be easy coping on your own since Marta died.'

He didn't answer for a while, focusing his attention on merging with the traffic on the Westway, but also thrown by all her questions, what she was saying…how easily she said Marta's name. Most people skirted around ever having to mention Marta's name, as though it was taboo to say it out loud. He swallowed against a tightening in his throat, suddenly feeling bone tired. At work he deliberately kept a professional distance from those who worked for him. The few friends he had in London, friends that in truth had been Marta's friends and had probably stayed in his life out of duty and respect to Marta, had stopped asking him about how he was managing a long time ago. In the early months after Marta had died, he had made it clear it wasn't up for discussion.

He saw a gap in the traffic open up in front of him and he pressed on the accelerator. He needed to get back to the office and he was keen to get this conversation over and done with. He wanted Carly Knight to show him how to get Isabella to sleep, not ask all these questions. 'I grew up in a one-parent household, my mother raised me single-handedly. It's a fact of life for a lot of people.'

'Yes, but it's not the future you had envisioned, and losing that must be very hard.'

He wanted to thump the steering wheel hard with the palm of his hand. Carly's words were resonating deep inside him. He didn't just miss Marta, he missed the future they had mapped out together, he missed the support of co-parenting, he missed having someone to talk to. All selfish things that only added to his guilt that Marta had died so young, that she would never see Isabella grow up. Marta would despair over just how out of sync he and Isabella were—their relationship was more often than not a battle of wills, and at the moment Isabella was winning. Of course he adored his daughter but he worried deeply about how dependent she was on him, which only seemed to be worsening in recent months, given her tendency to cling to him and her refusal to be cared for by others. How would she cope if anything ever happened to him?

'Isabella's nanny walked out yesterday. Dr Segal referred me to you this morning when I took Isabella to see her. She said you have helped some of her other patients.'

'Your nanny walked out on you because of Isabella's sleeping?'

'Yes.' He glanced over and saw that she had an eyebrow raised, not buying it. He shifted in his seat, gripped the steering wheel tighter. 'The fact that I'm away a lot of the time is probably a factor too.'

'How often are you away?'

'Two…sometimes three nights a week. When she was younger I took Isabella with me but the travel was too much for her.'

'She's probably missing you a lot—and the fact that you are coming and going means she has no consistency, which will have an impact on her ability to sleep.'

Her voice was calm, matter-of-fact, which annoyed him as much as what she had to say. 'It's the nature of my work… I don't have a choice.'

'I've never come across a situation that doesn't have alternative choices, or solutions. What is it that you do?'

Maybe she should try living his life some time. In architecture, you were only as good as your last design and winning bids was a never-ending cycle of late nights and client meetings. 'I'm an architect and property developer— my main office is here in London with other offices in Milan and Shanghai. My clients are worldwide, as are my properties.'

'My guess is Isabella needs more stability and routine to sleep better at night.'

Reluctantly he nodded. She was right. And he needed Carly's help in establishing that routine. It was time he started broaching his plans with her. 'I have to leave for my second home on Lake Como later this week. My in-laws live there, and my father-in-law is celebrating his sixtieth birthday on Friday evening, and on Sunday my brother-in-law, Tomaso, is marrying. I have no choice but to go— Isabella is a flower girl at the wedding. I've no idea how she will behave. I need her to sleep in the nights before— that way hopefully she might not throw a tantrum, which she's prone to do at the moment.'

Along Harrow Road they came to a stop while the driver of a concrete mixer ahead in the road tried to manoeuvre into a narrow construction site entrance. He turned to her and asked, 'Will you work for me for the rest of this week, come to Lake Como this weekend, to help me in getting Isabella to sleep? I'll pay you generously.'

* * *

Carly looked at him and then turned to stare at a nearby billboard advertising happiness via a deodorant, trying to contain her irritation. He was a client, clearly in need. But seriously! She turned back to him, cursing once again that he was so distractingly handsome, and tried to keep her voice calm. 'I'm a sleep consultant, Mr Lovato, not a nanny.'

'I know that.'

She forced herself to hold his gaze, even though his misty green eyes did something peculiar to her heartbeat. 'Do you?' She waited a pause before adding dryly, 'I'm busy with other clients all of this week and have my own plans for the weekend.'

'Nina told me earlier that you were on annual leave Friday—can't you at least come to Lake Como with us?'

Nina! What had got into her this morning? 'No—I've rented a cottage in Devon; I like to surf. I've been planning this trip since the New Year.' Why was she telling him this? Why did she feel she had to justify saying no to him?

'I'll pay for you to rebook.'

'I don't provide the type of service you are looking for. Yes, I visit clients' homes but I don't stay overnight or get involved in childcare. I provide a bespoke plan that parents follow over a period of months. Isabella is not going to be sleeping through the night any time soon—it doesn't work that way. My approach to your child sleeping contentedly takes time, patience and consistency.'

The traffic ahead of them began to flow again. Max eased his car forward, the expensive engine barely making a noise. 'I'm not asking you to get involved in the child-care.' His tone was one hundred per cent exasperation. 'Isabella barely slept last night. I flew in from Chicago yesterday. She's exhausted. I'm jet-lagged.' He rubbed his brow and continued to stare forwards. 'We need help.' His voice was so low, Carly had to lean towards him to hear him. 'This weekend…with Marta's family, the wedding… it's going to be trying. I want them to see that Isabella is happy and well cared for.'

Carly dropped her head and studied her hands, thrown by the honesty of his words. 'I've bookings all of this week. I can't—'

'Come to Lake Como with us this weekend.'

She closed her eyes to the soft appeal in his voice. The image of him standing alone on the street staring after Isabella's stroller, looking so alone, and then the anguish she had witnessed when he had turned towards the building had her tempted to say yes. But she needed to think this through. How many times had she believed others only to find out a very different truth? Not only did she have a stepfather who used his wealth to keep her at a distance, who thought throwing cash at her made up for a lack of love and affection and his poorly disguised belief that she would never be as good as his own three daughters, but Carly had trusted her own father when he promised he would visit her when her mother had ended their marriage. That promise had lasted all of twelve months until he decided to emigrate to New Zealand. Men had a habit of smashing her trust in them—her ex, Robert, had told her he loved her only to break off their engagement weeks before their wedding, telling her that he couldn't marry her because he was still in love with his ex. Carly had learned never truly to believe or trust in others, always to dig deeper to find out the truth.

She needed more facts and details before she made any decision…and Isabella's father needed to understand that she provided no magical cure for disturbed sleep. She buzzed down her window, needing some air. 'I don't sleep train. I don't give you any magical formulas. I just assist in building a routine and developing the correct expectations in parents as to how children sleep. There's no instant cure. There's just slow improvement over weeks, if not months.'

'I will take on board everything you have to say.'

'Yes, but will you actually implement what I suggest? It takes a lot of time and patience.'

His jaw worked for a moment. 'It depends on how persuasive you are.'

The hint of humour in his voice was matched by a glint of defiance in his eyes when he glanced in her direction.

Despite herself, Carly found herself having to fight the temptation to smile. 'That sounds like a challenge.'

'Lake Como is beautiful. You said earlier that you'd like to visit it some time. Why not now? The forecast is great for the weekend. Unlike here in England where rain is predicted. Surfing in the rain or boating in the Italian sunshine on Lake Como…there's not much competition, is there? I promise you lots of free time. Isabella and I will show you around the area, even take you for the best ice cream, not only in Italy, but in the entire world.'

She folded her arms, telling herself not to fall for his promises that were so, so tempting. 'That's some claim.'

He shook his head, clearly amused. 'What's your favourite flavour of ice cream?'

'Dark chocolate.'

He nodded. 'Good choice. I meant it when I said I'd pay you well. I'll quadruple your fees.'

Carly closed her eyes, disappointment slamming into her. Why did he have to ruin it all by mentioning money again? 'I don't want your money,' she said sharply.

He gave her a quizzical look. 'It was not my intention to insult you.'

'I don't like people who use their wealth to get what they want in life regardless of the consequences and how they affect others.'

'And what are the consequences of you coming to Lake Como with me?'

Carly held his gaze for a moment too long, felt heat travel up along her neck at his softly spoken words. She grabbed her phone from the central console where she had placed it earlier, checking the time, trying to ignore a deep instinct that in going to Lake Como with Max Lovato her life would never be the same again. It wasn't a rational feeling, yet it sat there in her stomach like a long trail of worry beads. 'I'll be cancelling my holiday. And I don't know you—for all I know you could be an axe murderer.'

Before Carly knew what was happening, Max had his paediatrician, Dr Segal, on the loudspeaker confirming that he wasn't a danger and, worse still, enthusiastically agreeing that Carly's intervention was badly needed. Then he put a call through to Vittoria, who laughed when Max asked her to give him a character reference and proceeded to say that, though he was much too stubborn when it came to letting others help, she admired him greatly for how he was coping on his own. Max quickly ended the call with Vittoria, looking uncomfortable and taken aback by what she said.

By the time those calls had ended they had reached the offices of the family support group that was hosting her parent talk.

Outside the car, Max lifted her cardboard box from the rear seat. She went to take it but he wouldn't let it go. Instead he held her gaze and said softly, '*Vieni con noi.* Come with us.'

Carly swallowed hard, hating the effect his voice, his gaze had on her. Max and Isabella clearly needed some help but something deep inside her was telling her not to go. 'I need some time to think about it.'

'When will you give me an answer?'

'I'll call you tomorrow.'

'Isabella is bright and intelligent—you'll really get along.'

Carly could not help but laugh at the mischief sparkling in his eyes. 'Are you trying to bribe me with a little girl?' Not waiting for his answer, she walked away, saying, 'I'll call you with my decision tomorrow.'

CHAPTER TWO

It was late Wednesday afternoon and instead of chairing his weekly major projects review meeting, Max was sitting on a much-too-small chair in a Montessori school, surrounded by other similarly exhausted-looking parents.

Early on in his career, Max had been shortlisted in a prestigious competition for the design of an art gallery in Seville. He had been certain he'd win. His design had been stronger than all his competitors'. Winning the competition would not only have brought much-needed finances into the fledging practice but, more importantly, would have brought his name to international attention. But another practice had won. He had sought out the chair of the selection committee after the announcement, desperate to understand why his design hadn't been selected. The chair had revealed that his competitor had brought the committee out to see their other completed projects and had organised for them to meet the building contractors who had vouched for their ability to flex to the ever-changing nature of big projects but still bring those projects in on budget. In short, his competitor had chased the business and had anticipated every issue the client would have concerns over. Max had learnt that, no matter how great the design, it was no match for the trust and reassurance that came from the strong connections face-to-face meetings brought.

Which was why he was here, listening to Carly Knight give a talk to parents on helping their children to sleep.

When he had entered the room, ten minutes late, she had done a double take. He had smiled, apologised for being late and explained that he had spotted on her website that she was giving the talk here this afternoon.

He had waited all day for her call and when none came he knew he needed to take matters in hand.

Carly spoke with a professional enthusiasm to the group, explaining her approach to sleep with the aid of an overhead presentation and a detailed account of some of the previous families she had successfully worked with. Max listened to her talk, realising it would be so easy to believe in everything she said. But Max knew that life wasn't so simple. He raised his hand when she spoke about the importance of initially staying with your child as they fell asleep.

Her brow furrowed. 'Yes, Max?'

'Shouldn't we be encouraging our children to be independent? Everything you are saying will make them even more dependent on us.' Max was gratified to see some of the other parents nod in agreement.

'The most independent and contented people are those who are secure in their love—isn't that the gift we want to give our children?' Without waiting for him to answer, Carly continued her talk.

Max shook his head. Didn't she understand the importance of making a child independent? All of her *tenderness* and *comforting* talk was nonsense. Children needed to learn to cope on their own. Just as he had done growing up. His mother had rarely been around when he was a child as she had often worked a double shift in her job as a hotel chambermaid. Being independent hadn't done him any harm…how many other people were running a billion-euro business at thirty-three? And he had coped when his mother had died when he was nineteen. He'd got on with his life. Isabella was without a mother too. She was at a greater disadvantage than other children so it was important that she learned to be strong. Not to rely on others.

What if anything happened to him and Isabella was completely reliant on and attached to him? How would she manage? One thing was for sure, Carly Knight's tenderness and comfort would be of little help then.

At the end of the talk Carly patiently answered the other parents' questions. Begrudgingly he admitted that some of what she said made sense, especially the need for routine and consistency. He knew he needed to revise his work commitments, but his clients expected him on location to personally present at design bids, and with a workforce of over five hundred staff, it was his responsibility to make sure that work continued to flow into the practice. And as loath as he was to admit it, sometimes a hotel room was preferable to facing the emptiness of his house late at night when Isabella had eventually fallen asleep. The loneliness that engulfed him in those late hours often felt as though it were eating him up from the inside out.

As the other parents drifted out of the room, after giving Carly enthusiastic applause, he stood and approached her as she packed away all the sleeping aids she had shown around the group.

She raised one of her perfectly arched eyebrows. 'It was an unexpected surprise to see you here.'

Hidden in her teasing tone was a hint of scepticism. He shrugged, leant against the wall next to a table filled with pots of tender, newly sprouting plants, name stickers haphazardly applied to the terracotta-coloured plastic. 'I thought it would be a good opportunity to get a head start in understanding the techniques you'll use with Isabella.'

Carly placed the lid on the yellow cardboard box. 'In other words, you're here to try and persuade me to come to Lake Como with you.'

'Yes.'

She shook her head. 'At least you're honest, unlike a lot of other people.'

Surprised by her jaded tone, he said, 'I thought in your line of work you'd see the positive in everyone.'

Today she was wearing a knee-length, primrose-yellow summer dress. She rested her hand against her upper chest, where the top buttons were undone to reveal smooth creamy skin. 'I try to be…' She eyed him carefully as though trying to weigh up just how much she could trust him.

He hesitated for a moment, but decided to go for broke… no matter how humiliating it was to be practically begging this woman. He cleared his throat. 'I'm a proud man who doesn't like to admit when he's getting things wrong…' he paused, taken aback by the sudden need to unburden himself in the face of Carly's attentive blue gaze '…but I've been getting things wrong with my family for far too long. I need help. I need *your* help. Will you come?'

'I don't usually—'

He stepped forward, handed her the paper sheet he had folded into his jacket pocket earlier this morning. 'Isabella created this drawing yesterday with Vittoria, I thought you might like it. I think she has an artistic flair.'

She took the sheet and smiled at the tiny pink handprint that had then been covered in a rainbow of assorted Pollock-like paint drips. 'Considering your profession it's no wonder that Isabella would have an artistic flair too. What type of projects is your firm involved in?'

'We mainly specialise in large commercial contracts.'

She nodded and lifted her laptop bag. 'Any that I would be familiar with?'

He went and picked up the cardboard box. 'The Ayer building in New York, Yumba International Airport.'

She held the classroom door open for him to pass through, her eyes widening. 'The Ayer building—wow, I've seen photos in the press. It's a stunning building.'

After she said her goodbyes to the owner, who was in her office, they walked out into the school garden and then to the road beyond the security gate. 'What did you think of my talk?'

'You have a flair for public speaking—really engaging.'

His answer seemed to amuse her, but then with a more serious expression she said, 'I meant the content, the substance of my approach.'

She had said earlier that she liked his honesty. He didn't make it a habit to talk about his past, or anything to do with his family. But he knew he had to open up to Carly if he wanted her support. He lowered the box to the ground, shrugged on his jacket against the chill in the evening. 'It's very different from how I was brought up—I had to be independent from a young age. I can see the benefit to a lot of what you say…but I need help implementing it.'

She gestured for him to pass the cardboard box to her. Nodded down the road. 'My underground station is in that direction. I have to go—I'm meeting a friend later.'

'Can I give you a lift?'

She shook her head. 'The underground will be faster.'

'So, have you made a decision about this weekend?'

She frowned and indecision shone in her eyes. Why was she so reluctant to go to Lake Como with him? His instinct told him that there was more to it than just her planned weekend away. She didn't trust him. He smiled. 'Honestly, the ice cream in Lake Como is really good.' He gestured to the dull day surrounding them. 'And you can't say that you'd prefer to stay here with this weather.'

Her eyes narrowed. 'What time is your flight tomorrow?'

'My plane has a slot for five p.m. at London City jet centre.'

'I've a full schedule tomorrow until three.'

'A driver from my office can collect you if you give me your address. We can board immediately, so provided you are there by four-forty we can go. Will that work for you?'

Carly inhaled a deep breath. Looked down at Isabella's painting she was still carrying in her hand. 'I'll go because of Isabella. You can pay me my standard fee but also make a charitable donation to the family support group I gave the talk to on Tuesday. They do incredible work helping disadvantaged parents—please make sure your donation is generous.'

She turned away from him and walked quickly towards the station, the low heels of her summer sandals clipping on the footpath, her loose blonde hair shimmering in the sudden burst of sunshine that broke free of the cloud mass.

For a brief moment he felt elation.

And then he remembered what it was he was facing this weekend.

Isabella asleep in his arms, Max stared out of the jet's window, his thoughts clearly far, far away, which Carly supposed was a welcome change from how he had longingly been eyeballing his phone, which was lying on the coffee table sitting between them. After Isabella had fallen asleep, he had asked her to pass it to him but she had whispered, 'No, it will disturb Isabella. Use this time to enjoy holding her; giving her the comfort she wants.' He had thrown her an exasperated look but she had just shrugged and returned to pretending to read the magazine the jet's hostess had passed to her along with the best Americano Carly had ever tasted.

The implications of Max's words yesterday that his plane had a slot at five for take-off hadn't fully registered with Carly until she had seen his private jet sitting on the runaway. He owned a plane. Max Lovato was even wealthier than she had first guessed and that wealth made her uncomfortable and extra cautious around him. It made her want to push him to prove that he was a good father to Isabella. To figure out what his real priorities in life were—wealth or family?

Soon after take-off Carly had suggested that Isabella should have a nap; from her eye rubbing and yawns it was clear she was tired. Max had questioned whether they should instead keep her awake in the hope she would sleep through the night but had accepted Carly's explanation that they needed to avoid Isabella being overtired and taken her into the jet's bedroom. But Isabella had refused to settle and had clung to Max instead. Guessing that Isabella was picking up on her father's stress, lying down in the middle of the day clearly not being his thing, Carly suggested that they come back out into the lounge and cuddle. Within five minutes Isabella had fallen fast asleep.

Now, Carly tried to focus on an article about the benefits of superfoods and whether they were superfoods or not, but her attention kept being drawn back to father and daughter.

Isabella had her father's mouth, the soft wave now relaxed in sleep from its earlier unhappy jutting out. When Carly had boarded the plane, Isabella had eyed her warily before burying her face into her father's chest, her little hands bunching the light blue material of his polo shirt. Isabella's complexion was lighter than Max's—her skin was the colour of golden honey, her hair adorable chestnut curls. Her eyes were molten chocolate brown and could easily break your heart with the defiance that sparked in their depths and spoke of a toddler struggling to understand her world.

Alongside his polo shirt, Max was wearing navy chinos, his sockless feet in loosely laced navy boating shoes. Carly's gaze time and time again was drawn to his bare ankles, the smoothness of his dark tanned skin over the ankle bone oddly compelling.

He had started off sitting upright, his reluctance to

relax, to spend downtime with his daughter obvious. What was holding him back from fully engaging with his daughter? Was his job that pressurised? Was it the need for success and even more wealth and power? Or was he simply struggling like so many other parents? She thought back to that torment she had witnessed the first time she had seen him and winced. She wanted to help him in his grief for his wife, in his struggle with understanding and connecting fully with his daughter. That was why she had agreed to this weekend. Even after he had shamelessly turned up at her meeting Wednesday afternoon in a bid to persuade her to go with them to Lake Como. But to give him his due, he had listened attentively to her talk, which she had delivered in a more faltering than usual style, thanks to his unnerving concentration that had his gaze follow her every movement. After, out in the street, she had heard the sincerity in his voice when he said he needed her help.

But, despite all his well-meaning pledges, she wasn't yet convinced he really was prepared to put the effort into what needed to be done.

As Isabella had relaxed in her sleep, as though by osmosis, Max too had visibly unwound. He had shifted forward in his seat, his legs moving outwards, his shoulders dropping, his right hand relaxing to gently rub against his little girl's bare leg where her pink denim dungarees had ridden up from her bare feet.

Isabella's earlier hot cheeks from fighting both sleep and her father had now cooled and Carly smiled at the little girl, already taken by her strong spirit.

Her gaze shifted back up to Max. His eyes were closed. Was he asleep too? Carly sank further into her chair and tried to ignore just how attracted she was to him. He was a client. She was here to do a job.

Carly knew only too well how workplace romances derailed life. Her parents had once owned an accountancy practice…until her mother had fallen for one of their clients. Carly, then aged eleven, could still remember to this day the elation that had shone in her mum's eyes when she had spoken every evening at the dinner table about her new client. She had relayed with awe the details of his holiday home in Sardinia, his corporate jaunts to sports events and conferences in exotic locations. How devoted to and proud he was of his three high-achieving and beautiful daughters. How miserable his ex-wife had made him.

All this her mum would recount with great animation, her voice bright, which only emphasised the dislike that settled on her features when Carly's father would interrupt with some story of his own.

Carly had been devastated when her parents split but she had held out hope—after all, her dad promised that she could stay with him at weekends and she was gaining three sisters. Carly had always wanted siblings. But with the business collapsing amidst a bitter divorce, her dad had left England for a new life in New Zealand where his sister lived. And Carly's three new sisters, all much older than her, showed little interest in her on their visits home from university other than to make it clear that they considered her nothing other than a nuisance who would never be welcomed into their tight circle. They idolised their father and jealously guarded their relationship with him.

Carly shivered. The air temperature in the cabin had dropped. She smiled as Isabella snuffled, turned her cheek into her father's chest and sighed. Carly's throat tightened at the sight of Max's strong forearm lying so protectively around Isabella's tiny waist.

Then Max stirred, his head shifting to the left. But he continued to sleep, his chest rising and falling regularly. Even sitting four feet away, Carly could see the long dark length of his eyelashes. His eyebrows were thick and expressive; his nose was at a perfect angle to complement his high cheekbones; his chiselled jawline travelled down in a perfectly defined curve from his ears to end in a cleft chin that gave his face a devastating beauty.

Standing, she tiptoed across the cabin and picked up a lemon-coloured wool throw from the lounge sofa. Tucking the blanket around Isabella, she pulled back, lifted her eyes and looked straight into Max's gaze.

'You think of everything.' His voice was low, croaky from tiredness. And so, so sexy. Her feet curled in her trainers. Her stomach did a little flip. She was not going to blush. She was going to brazen this out.

She inhaled a scent that reminded her of the summer she had gone Interrailing as a student and camped in a Croatian forest next to the Adriatic—sea mist and earthy pine combining to produce a potent sense of vitality and adventure. 'All part of the service.'

He raised an eyebrow.

She stepped back. 'Can I get you anything else?'

His lips twitched. He nodded to the table behind her. 'My phone.'

'Not until Isabella wakes.'

Carly sat back in her chair. Aware of his gaze on her, she picked up the magazine and tried to develop an interest in a berry favoured by sub-Saharan goat herders.

'Are you sure that sleeping like this won't teach her bad habits?'

She dropped the magazine. 'Isabella needs to feel secure with you. This will teach her that you will spend time holding her, comforting her when she needs it. Being with her, responding to her needs—this is the starting basis of developing good sleeping technique. In the next few days hopefully you will start to appreciate that.' She leant towards him, determined that he understood the main message of her sleeping technique—that parents learn to allow themselves to be tender with their children and themselves.

'We all need physical touch. We all need to have someone hug us and tell us that everything is going to be okay.'

His expression hardened. A tense silence settled between them.

Confused, Carly stared at him, slowly realising what she had said. 'I'm sorry—that was insensitive of me. With your wife—'

He interrupted her with a quick shake of his head. 'It's okay.'

Carly's gaze shifted down to Isabella, her arms suddenly aching with the desire to hold her. 'Trust me on this, Isabella won't want your cuddles in a few years' time... and when she's a teenager she won't even want to know you. So you should enjoy it while you can.'

His gaze dropped down to consider Isabella for a moment before he asked in a low voice, 'Were you like that with your dad when you were a teenager?'

'My dad moved to New Zealand when I was twelve. I didn't get the chance to...'

'You miss him?'

Carly's heart fell. She spoke to her dad occasionally but there was so much time and distance between them now that their relationship just consisted of the polite conversation of assuring one another that all was well in their lives, and a hollowness when she ended the call that would stay with her for hours. 'Sometimes.'

'Have you other family?'

There was a gentleness to his tone that stirred unexpected emotion in her—a loneliness, a longing for a family of her own that she was usually so good at burying. 'No—my mum remarried. It was messy.' She gave a shrug, trying to dredge up her usual acceptance of her situation but there was something about Max's intelligent gaze that was stopping her doing so. 'I'm not close to my mum and her new family, but I have good friends, people I trained with. We all live close to one another in London.'

'Were you going away with them this weekend?' He paused for a moment. 'With a boyfriend perhaps?'

'Six of us were heading away together…all friends.'

He nodded to her answer and shifted the arm that was resting on Isabella. 'Thank you for agreeing to come with us this weekend. I realise it was a lot to ask of you.'

She studied him for a moment, thrown by the sincerity of his tone, the restrained pride in his expression. Maybe he was different from her stepfather, who would always somehow twist everything he did for people, whether they wanted it or not, into the fact that he was doing that person a favour. He had insisted that Carly attend boarding school and signed her up for endless residential courses during half-terms and summer holidays. He had claimed that he wanted her to be more adventurous, more ambitious, more accomplished, just like his daughters. The unspoken truth was that he hadn't wanted Carly around.

She nodded in acknowledgement to his thanks and said, 'Most of the parents who come to me find it difficult to talk about their child not sleeping. They think they should instinctively know how to get their child to sleep, that they are somehow failing as a parent. Which of course is not true. The parents I meet are doing their best in their individual circumstances. I try to help them see and understand that…to learn to be tender with themselves.'

Carly laughed when Max's smooth forehead creased at her last sentence. 'You don't like that expression "be tender with themselves"?' she asked.

'I can't see any man buying into it.'

'You'd be surprised.'

He shifted in his seat, his expression sceptical. 'Is this going to work?'

'If you allow it to—if you give it the time and patience needed.'

'You think I'm impatient?'

'I get the feeling that you like to be on the move a lot. With children you need to slow down, to connect with them.'

He looked down at Isabella and shook his head. 'With this firecracker I've no option the way she clings to me.'

There was such weariness to his voice. Understanding the positives in Isabella's personality might help him in dealing with his daughter. 'At least you know that Isabella will fight for what she wants—she's determined. It will stand her in good stead in life, having that strength of character.'

For a long while he stared at her, considering what she had said. 'I hadn't thought of it that way... I guess you could be right. Do you want children of your own some day?'

Carly smiled at his question, while inside it felt like a soft swift pinch to her heart. She had envisioned herself and Robert having children quickly; they had even spoken about trying to have a baby soon after they married. 'Some day hopefully I will. I love being with children. Before I set up my sleep consultancy business I was a Montessori teacher, but I have to meet the right person first.'

'That hasn't happened yet?'

Carly paused, a heavy weight lodging in her chest. 'I thought it had. A few years back I was due to marry. But three weeks before the wedding my ex broke it off.'

Emotion continuing to whirl in her chest, Carly grabbed the magazine and again pretended to read it.

'I'm sorry.'

Carly nodded but refused to look up from the magazine, hating how exposed, how humiliated she felt having told him. She flicked through the pages of the magazine, trying to understand why the publishers thought their readers would be interested in the weight gain of a soap-opera actress. Hadn't they heard about emotional eating? Carly might have binned her wedding cake but that hadn't stopped her from eating her own body weight in ice cream and her favourite comfort food, Brazil nuts, in the weeks that followed. It had taken her months to return to her normal weight. A weight that wasn't particularly impressive in the first place. But Carly had long ago accepted that her body would never be lean, no matter how much she dieted or exercised.

'Tell me about your ex—what happened?'

'I'd prefer not to.'

'It clearly upsets you.'

Carly raised her eyes. She knew she should change the subject. Not answer even. But there was a genuineness to his expression, as though he really wanted to understand what had happened to her that had her blurt out, 'He told me he was still in love with his ex-girlfriend.'

Max's eyes softened. 'That must have been heartbreaking for you.'

Something popped in Carly's heart. She had expected pity, perhaps even outrage from him. Just as her friends had been outraged on her behalf, calling Robert every name under the sun, telling her she needed to be positive, that there were plenty of other guys out there. Her mother meanwhile had fretted over what people would think while her stepfather had simply asked why she could never get things right in life. Nobody had got just how sad it all had been. Until now. Carly's throat closed over; she felt undone by the understanding in his eyes. She shrugged.

'I'm sorry you had to go through that,' he said gently.

Carly nodded, not trusting herself to talk.

Max considered her for a while and then, with a gentle

smile, he added, 'I bet he's regretting it now, letting some-one like you slip away.'

Carly grimaced. 'Not really. He's married his ex since.'

He tilted his head. 'But I bet he's not on the way to taste the best chocolate ice cream in the world.'

Carly laughed, something lightening in her. 'That's true.'

They smiled at each other for the longest while. Carly felt the heat grow on her cheeks. Max's smile disappeared to be replaced by a tension in his expression that reflected the heavy beat of disquiet that was drumming in her heart.

She tore her gaze away, picked up her magazine.

The sun had set when Max turned his car into the drive-way of Villa Isa with the beginnings of a throbbing head-ache about to take hold.

The narrow road cut into the hillside and, surrounded by woodland, hid well the exquisite beauty about to be revealed.

'Wow, oh, wow—now that's what I call a view.' He winced at Carly's excited exclamation as Lake Como in all its magnetic night-time beauty of shadowy mountains and fairy-tale villages with twinkling lights opened up to them.

He pulled the car to a stop in the carport and looked to-wards the brightly lit villa with a heavy heart. His house-keeper, Luciana, had turned on the lights in many of the downstairs rooms to welcome them before she left for her home in nearby Bellagio. He knew he should be feeling pride in the renovations he had commissioned to restore the mid-twentieth-century villa to its former glory. So many would have knocked it down, but Max had loved its quirkiness, its tall ceilings, exposed stonework and vast open-plan living spaces. But instead of pride he just felt a numbness, a detachment from the villa that was once sup-posed to be his primary home.

'Papa, out!' Isabella's call was accompanied by her feet banging against the sides of her car seat. Since they had landed Isabella had been truculent, running away on the tarmac, refusing to sit in the car that had been waiting beside the runway on their arrival. And once in the car she had immediately begun to grumble, unhappy at being restrained in her car seat.

Carly's pert nose had wrinkled when he had admitted that he didn't have any nursery rhyme CDs he could play for Isabella. So they had spent the journey from the airport with Carly leading a sing-along and insisting he join in. Unfortunately Isabella became fixated on 'Three Blind Mice' and insisted they sing it time and time again.

He had known it was a bad idea to allow Isabella to sleep on board the plane.

'Out!' Isabella shouted again, her foot furiously hammering her car seat.

He had work to do. It was going to take him for ever to get Isabella to settle.

He turned and regarded Carly. 'Are you so certain of the benefit of allowing her to nap now?'

Carly glanced back at Isabella, gave her a smile. 'You just want to run around, don't you, Isabella? Why don't you play with Papa?'

'It's beyond her bedtime. She should be asleep by now, not bouncing off the walls.'

Carly shrugged and got out of the car. She went to unlock Isabella's belt but Isabella shook her head and then buried it into the side of her car seat, refusing to allow Carly to lift her out.

The headache gripping his temples ever tighter, Max pushed open the driver door and lifted Isabella out of her seat. His phone, in his trouser pocket, buzzed once again.

'I'll say it again, the views from here are spectacular. And it's so warm, even at this time of the night. I've missed the heat so much. What's the nearby town called? It looks so cute.'

Distracted by an email from a client in Taiwan, he glanced over to see Carly at the edge of the driveway, looking beyond the brightly lit terraced garden that sloped down to the waterfront and his private jetty, and vaguely answered, 'The town is Bellagio...' This was unbelievable—how did the client expect the new train terminal to open in time if at this late stage they wanted to make changes to the roof design?

'I have a call to make.' He attempted to pass Isabella to Carly but Isabella clung to his shirt, her legs wrapping even more tightly around his waist.

Carly folded her arms. 'No calls. You must settle Isabella first.'

'This is important.'

'I'll sort out the luggage. Isabella needs some exercise to wind down. I suggest you take her down to the garden, let her explore for a while. In the meantime, I'll prepare her a small snack.'

He was about to argue that she should take Isabella down to the gardens instead but before he could do so, Carly had popped open the boot of his car and was walking towards the front door, carrying two heavy suitcases with ease. There went his excuse that it made sense for him to look after the heavy luggage instead of playing with his little girl.

He glanced down at Isabella. She frowned back at him. His daughter might not have many words but she sure seemed to understand every word spoken around her.

How did a twenty-two-month-old possess the capacity to make him feel like a completely lousy dad?

He was still standing by the car when Carly returned to retrieve more luggage.

She steadily ignored him but gave Isabella a smile.

Isabella tucked her head into his shoulder.

He yelped when her fingers pinched his skin as she gripped onto his shirt sleeves.

Carly ducked her head, laughter threatening on her lips.

He stared after her once again retreating back as she carried more suitcases into the hallway, before he climbed down the steps and headed in the direction of the playground that had been constructed to the side of the terrace. He went to place Isabella onto the swing but she clung to him. He tried not to sigh and instead sat on one side of the sprung seesaw. He bounced up and down, feeling ridiculous. He was about to climb back off but then he heard Isabella chuckle. He bounced again, his heart lifting to hear her chortle again. His serious-minded daughter rarely laughed.

He bounced and bounced, feeling an unexpected happiness. And he remembered some of the things Carly had said during the past few days—that it was natural for children to wake, that Isabella wasn't alone in doing so.

A movement inside the villa caught his attention.

Carly was inside the open-plan kitchen searching through the cupboards, taking out some items, pausing to stretch her back, roll her head side to side as she studied the contents of the fridge. She had tied up her hair into a loose ponytail and rolled up the sleeves of her blue blouse that was tucked into slim-fitting, navy, ankle-length trousers. Her body was curvy. He supposed some men would say sensual.

He slowed in his bouncing and winced at the realisation that it felt good to have her around. Yes, he had employed nannies, had some support. But Carly was different. She had the strength of conviction to tell him things he didn't want to hear but with an empathy that had him struggling to argue back. He admired her for that. As much as he hated to admit it, he was enjoying her company.

And earlier, in the tight confines of the plane, when Carly had placed the blanket on his lap, when he had woken to see her staring at him, as they had spoken in low voices to one another, he'd known he could no longer ignore the kernel of attraction for her growing inside him.

This was not supposed to be happening.

Isabella squirmed in his arms, began to protest at the lack of movement.

Her once again serious eyes glared up at him.

Fresh guilt slammed into Max. He had no right to enjoy the company of another woman.

CHAPTER THREE

AFTER PREPARING A snack for Isabella, Carly had unpacked both her own and Isabella's suitcases, carried out a recce of Isabella's room and returned to the kitchen to find Isabella sitting in her high chair, munching on a banana, her gaze firmly fixed on her father, who was typing on the keyboard of his phone.

Carly came to a stop beside him and waited until he finally looked up. 'I chose a bedroom for myself close to Isabella's so that I can help you during the night when she wakes.' She pushed on in the hope that if she spoke quickly there was less chance of her giving away just how disturbed she felt to be in the intimacy of his home. 'I left your suitcases in your bedroom.' She didn't add that she knew it was his bedroom because a quick look into the attached dressing room had revealed a row of bespoke suits and expensive casual wear. His whole bedroom, with its accent blue wall behind a white supersized headboard filled with dramatic modern art and pale wooden floor boards, was masculine. Him.

Her own room, next to his, decorated in soft greens, had the same breathtaking views of Lake Como and shared the same terrace that led down to the floodlit outdoor pool. She just hoped that they never bumped into each other out there. The image of Max dressed only in swimwear strolling down to the pool made her pause; she'd happily bet the entire annual income of her business on the guess that he had a seriously impressive body.

'I…' She paused as the image of Max's powerful broad shoulders, narrowing to a slim waist, swam unwanted into her mind. 'I… I…yes, what I was trying to say was that I had a look at Isabella's bedroom to ensure that it's the right environment to promote sleep. I suggest you install blackout blinds in addition to the curtains that are already there.'

Max considered her for a moment, his raised eyebrow the only hint of mischief in his otherwise deadpan expression. 'I take it that you're wanting some company in bed tonight?'

Carly stared at him; only after a long few seconds did it dawn on her that her mouth was gaping open. She snapped it closed. 'What? Certainly not!'

Max's lips curled upwards before he nodded towards the toys in her arms. 'I meant the soft toys…are you taking them to bed with you?'

Carly shook her head, trying to rein in her embarrassment. She hit him with an unimpressed glare and went and placed the three stuffed toys on the long sleek white kitchen table that complemented the steel and pale wood of the super-modern kitchen.

Turning, she moved back to him, held out her hand. 'Okay, for the next hour we're having a phone-free zone.'

He pulled his phone out of her reach. 'Please tell me that you're joking.'

She shook her head. 'Phone on the kitchen counter, where I can see it.' Then she wiped Isabella's hands free of banana mush and cleaned the tray of her high chair with some wipes. She placed all three toys onto the highchair table—Sami the white long-eared rabbit, Skye the blue bear and Sunny the grey elephant. Isabella eyed the three toys dubiously but then lurched and grabbed hold of Sunny, squashing his long trunk in under her armpit.

Carly smiled at Isabella and touched her fingertips against Sunny's grey velvety fur. 'This is Sleepy Sunny, Isabella. He and his friends here, Sami and Skye, live together in Sleep World. They love nothing more than lying in bed, being all snugly and warm and falling asleep.'

Isabella looked at her doubtfully and held onto the heavy-eyed and tiredly smiling Sunny even closer.

Carly turned to Max. He was propped against the kitchen's central island thick slab of white marble countertop, arms crossed with a bemused expression on his face. 'And tonight your papa will read to you a story about Sunny in Sleep World, won't you, Papa?'

He eyed Sunny and the other animals. 'Will I?'

Carly decided to ignore his dubious expression. 'You mentioned at the parent talk on Wednesday that Isabella has no particular toy she uses as a comforter.' She had shown the group the story book she had written and published to encourage sleep, *Sleepy Heads in Sleep World*, and the three main characters that were available as soft toys, Sami, Skye and Sunny. 'As Isabella clearly has taken a shine to Sunny, for the next few days we're going to include him in all of Isabella's activities until she identifies with it as being something of comfort and reassurance.' Max's sceptical frown only intensified when she added, 'Starting now. I found a toy teapot and teacups in Isabella's room. I've left them on the rug there—I want you to take Isabella and Sunny to her room and for all three of you to have a tea party.'

'I don't have—'

Carly interrupted Max, choosing to ignore his horror at her suggestion. 'Give the tea party ten minutes. I want Isabella to associate her bedroom with comfort, that it's a nice safe place for her to be in.' Moving to the door that led to the main hall and stairs, Carly added, 'In the meantime I'll run a bath for Isabella. You can bathe her after your tea party—make sure to bring Sunny along to take part. Then it's into bed and you can read *Sleepy Heads in Sleep World* to her. After that it's lights out. If Isabella is still restless I have a lavender massage cream that you can use with her.'

'I've calls—'

With a bright smile Carly interrupted him. 'Let's go. Think of this as the new, exciting beginning of you and Isabella spending some fun time together.'

Max's expression grew incredulous.

And as though to make her position clear, with one mighty throw, Isabella threw Sunny towards her father, the drowsy elephant hitting Max square on the shoulder.

Carly fled the room, her initial amusement at Isabella's amazing aim giving way to disquiet as she climbed the polished concrete stairs. Would she ever manage to get Max and Isabella in tune with one another? And more to the point, would she manage to get through this weekend without embarrassing herself by revealing that, rather foolishly, she was attracted to him?

An hour later, Carly stood at Isabella's door, hearing Max speaking in low whispers to his daughter as he sat on the side of her bed. Isabella's room was in darkness, the only light coming from the faint moonlight twinkling through the roof lights that ran along the corridor.

Max was whispering in a mixture of English and Italian, his voice deep, gentle.

Carly closed her eyes, suddenly tired after such a long day, her shoulder dropping against the doorframe.

Max's whispers continued.

Carly inhaled the lavender massage cream Max had at first reluctantly massaged into an equally reluctant Isabella. Max had used unsure strokes on Isabella, who had slapped his hand away when he had first begun to massage her forearm as Carly had suggested. But slowly and rather miraculously father and daughter had eventually given in to the soothing pleasure of the massage.

'You're tired.'

Carly jumped. Her eyes shot open to find Max standing directly in front of her. Unnerved at having him stand so close, unnerved by his height, the force of the bone-melting energy that oozed from him, the darkness enclosing them, she edged back into the corridor.

Max followed slowly closing Isabella's door, but leaving it slightly ajar.

He nodded when she asked if Isabella was asleep.

She gave him a smile, trying to focus on being professional. 'You did a really good job tonight. Well done.'

In the faint light of the corridor she saw a gleam of amusement light in his eyes. 'Apart from bath time, you mean.'

Carly laughed softly. 'I'm sure Isabella didn't mean to soak you.'

'You reckon?'

Carly tried not to react to the lightness, the teasing in his eyes, all the while doing her best not to recall how gorgeous he had looked as he knelt beside the bath earlier, his damp hair slicked back, his tee shirt soaked through, his exasperation towards Isabella's splashing giving way to amusement and shared laughter.

'I've an office downstairs—I must go and make some calls. My housekeeper, Luciana, has left food in the fridge. Please help yourself.' He went to walk away but, pausing, he added, 'Thank you for your help tonight. It was calmer than usual.' He rubbed a hand tiredly at the base of his neck. 'It took for ever, though. I won't be able to spend so much time settling her every night.'

For a moment Carly considered Max. He was so loath to relax, to allow himself to enjoy being a parent. Sometimes, a lightness broke through his intensity. She needed to help him appreciate the joy of being a father. 'You know, with time, you might grow to enjoy spending your evenings with Isabella.'

He shook his head, clearly unconvinced. 'Why did no one warn me just how exhausting and time-consuming being a parent is?'

'But it's rewarding too.' Carly waited for a response from Max but when none came she asked, 'Don't you agree?'

Rewarding. That was not the term Max would use for being a parent. Bewildering. Frustrating. Exhausting. Those were better words. But what parent could admit to those feelings?

He winced at Carly's calm gaze.

And then her hand was reaching out, touching his bare forearm. 'Things will get better, Max...you've been coping for far too long on your own.'

He swallowed at the gentleness of her tone. He should step away, tell Carly that he would see her in the morning. But for the first time since Marta's death he wanted company, he wanted to be able to sit down and eat a meal with another human being. Apart from work dinners, he ate alone, mostly snacks taken at his desk.

He wasn't sure what madness was taking him over, and quickly he rationalised to himself that, as it was at his insistence she was here this weekend, the least he could do was be hospitable. And after this weekend he would rarely see Carly Knight again, so what was the harm in sitting down and sharing a meal with her?

'You know, I'm hungry. Let's go and have dinner. We can sit outside on the terrace, where you can take in the view—you haven't seen much of Lake Como since you arrived.'

Carly edged away from him. 'I...' She wrapped her arms tightly around her waist, her fists bunching against the red wool of the jumper she had earlier pulled on. He could tell she wanted to say no. Was she this wary of all men thanks to her ex? A desire to somehow make it up to her in some small way saw him offer her his arm. 'Luciana makes the best pasta in the whole of Italy…she'll have left some in the fridge for us to have tonight.'

Carly eyed his arm warily but then with a disbelieving eye-roll she placed her hand on his arm.

In the kitchen he told her to take a seat on one of the stools at the kitchen island.

He caught her gazing about the room, taking in the artwork and the furniture.

'I'm guessing the villa was recently renovated?' she asked as he swung open the fridge door.

He rifled through the contents of the fridge, reading the labels of the containers Luciana had left, finally settling on one lidded bowl, which he laid on the countertop. 'It was renovated last year…' Pointing to the bowl, he asked, 'I've chosen *ravioli di zucca e ricotta*, pumpkin and ricotta ravioli, for us to eat—is that okay?'

Carly nodded, her gaze once again shifting around the room. She tilted her head back to gaze up at the modern chandelier he had commissioned a local artist to make, the almost translucent ceramic pieces engraved with images of the villa at different stages of the renovations. 'It's such a beautiful villa. Were you in charge of the renovation designs?'

Max busied himself filling a large pasta saucepan with water, pleased with her words, but unsettled at the truth that despite all his best efforts to make this villa a home— the endless hours he had put into the designs, the daily calls to the renovation team, the meticulous sourcing of just the right furniture and artwork—he felt nothing for it. 'I wanted to keep the uniqueness of the existing villa intact so most of the original features were retained but some new windows were added to take advantage of the views, internally the walls of some of the smaller rooms were knocked through to create larger spaces. We also built a new boathouse down by the waterfront and the pool was made bigger.'

Carly stood from her seat and wandered around the open-plan dining room, taking in the décor and the nooks and crannies of this unconventional villa. 'The renovations are beautiful—you're seriously talented. What's the history of the villa—has it been in your family for many years?'

Putting the saucepan on the hob to boil, he inhaled a deep breath before admitting, 'No, we only bought it two years ago. When Marta became pregnant she decided that she wanted to move back here to Lake Como to be close to her parents. She found the villa when she was six months pregnant with Isabella.'

He waited for Carly to smile awkwardly at what he had said, to change the subject, but instead she nodded and said, 'Marta clearly had good taste.'

He could not help but smile at that. 'Well, she did agree to marry me.'

His heart lifted to hear Carly's laughter. Shaking her head, she asked gently, 'What was Marta like?'

Taken aback, he turned away from Carly, busied himself with taking oils and condiments from the pull-out drawer next to the hob. For so long he had pushed all thoughts of Marta away, the grief of recalling her too intense. But now, for some reason he found himself wanting to tell Carly about her. 'She was smart...really smart—she was the only student in her law-degree year to be awarded maximum marks on a difficult course. And she was ambitious; she was specialising in intellectual property law. She loved being pregnant, being a mother.'

Emotion tightening his chest, Max took a tray from a cupboard and started to load it with glasses.

Carly stood and moved next to him. 'You take care of the cooking, I'll set the table out on the terrace. I know where everything is from preparing Isabella's snack earlier.'

With the water boiling in the saucepan, Max turned the temperature down. When the water was simmering he carefully placed the handmade ravioli into it. He turned as Carly lifted the tray now loaded with cutlery and glassware. She smiled at him, a smile full of warmth and kindness. 'You know, it sounds like Marta was an incredible person. And she was right to want the support of her family. Have you considered moving back here to Lake Como to get that support yourself?'

Max considered for a moment shrugging off Carly's question with some vague answer but there was something about her open gaze that had him admit, 'It's Marta's family who live here. I grew up in Rome. I've no family of my own since my mother died when I was nineteen. Marta's family...they have never approved of me.'

'Why?'

Trying to focus on keeping the cynicism from his voice, aware that he was speaking about Isabella's grandparents, he answered, 'My in-laws, the Ghiraldini family, own one of the biggest pharmaceutical companies in Italy. They've always been suspicious of my reasoning for marrying Marta.'

'But you're wealthy in your own right.'

'Now I am. Not when we met at university. Back then I was nothing but a kid from the wrong side of the tracks with a mother who worked as a chambermaid and a deadbeat father who had disappeared from my life when I was three.'

Carly lifted the wooden tray closer to herself. 'But now, with your success and having got to know you, Marta's parents must approve of you.'

Max turned away to check on the pasta. He waited with his back to her, expecting to hear her footsteps as she went out to set the table, but after a while he realised she wasn't going to leave until he answered her. Swinging around, he stared at her, his arms folded on his chest. Inside, he was on fire with emotion, but his answer came out in an icy tone. 'Their daughter died when married to me. Why on earth would they approve of me now?'

'But it was a car accident.'

The guilt inside him exploded in the quietness of the villa, in his jet-lagged exhaustion, in reaction to Carly's softly spoken words, at the compassion in her eyes. Without meaning to, for the first time since Marta died he spoke out loud some of the torment living inside him. 'I should have taken better care of Marta, made sure she wasn't out driving late at night.'

He whipped around, grabbed the saucepan…but the handle was too hot. It scorched his palm. But he bit against the pain and continued on to the sink where he drained the pasta.

He tried to ignore Carly, who had come to stand beside him. 'What happened on the night Marta died?'

He lowered his head, wanting to keep that night inside himself. But he was so tired of hiding it. He turned around, placed his back against the sink. The act of turning to face the villa for which he and Marta had cherished such dreams caused him almost to back out of speaking. But Carly's steady blue gaze, the softness of her expression, brought him to say, 'Isabella had woken just after midnight. Marta had fed her but Isabella wouldn't settle. I took her downstairs, walked her in my arms. She would fall asleep but the moment I took her back upstairs and laid her down she started crying again. Marta got up and told me to go back to bed. I had an early flight to Munich later that morning. Marta left a note on the hall table saying that she was taking Isabella out in her car for a drive in the hope that she would settle. It was three in the morning. I was asleep. An hour later our intercom rang. It was the police. A taxi had driven through a red light and smashed into Marta's car. Isabella was uninjured…but Marta…'

For long moments Carly closed her eyes. 'I'm so sorry.' She stepped even closer, her hand reaching against the countertop, inches from him. 'It must have been such a horrible shock. You can't blame yourself for it though.'

Carly was wrong. He was to blame. If he and Marta hadn't argued that evening then everything would be different. He struggled to breathe against the shame filling his chest. No one knew of their argument. No one knew that Marta had died when they weren't speaking to one another. Max hadn't had the opportunity to say he was sorry, to hug her, to ask for forgiveness for not being there enough for her and Isabella. 'If I had managed to get Isabella back to sleep, Marta wouldn't have been out driving.'

'If your roles were reversed, if it had been you who had gone out and been in an accident, would you blame Marta?'

'Of course not.'

She tilted her head and gave him a sad smile full of care. 'Why are you any different?'

Heat burnt on his cheeks. Her question, that until now he had never considered, hit at the core of his guilt. He had seen his mother struggle his entire childhood after his father had abandoned them and had sworn he would always protect his family. 'It's a husband's job to care for and protect his wife, the mother of his child.'

Carly considered him for a moment. 'Would Marta have agreed with that?'

He could not help but smile. 'No. She would have yelled that she was a strong woman perfectly capable of taking care of herself.'

Carly smiled back. He knew he should end this conversation now. Already he had divulged too much personal information. But Carly's compassion, her humour and intelligence in the midst of all he was telling her, was proving hard to walk away from.

'I'm sure your in-laws will appreciate how well you're caring for Isabella.'

At the mention of the Ghiraldini family again, he realised just how badly he needed a drink. 'Yes, I'm caring for Isabella so well that I've been forced to employ a sleep consultant.'

Carly pushed the sleeves of her blouse further up her arms, clearly unamused at his attempt at dark humour. 'There's no shame in asking for help.'

She was wrong. He should be able to father Isabella without help. Frustrated with his own incompetency, frustrated at the thought of facing his in-laws tomorrow, at having to sit through Tomaso's wedding which would bring back so many memories of his own wedding day, he turned and studied the pasta, which was now dried out and cold. He grimaced and looked towards Carly, who was scrutinising the pasta too.

A grin broke on her mouth. 'I don't think we're going to be able to rescue our dinner. I saw some sourdough bread in the cupboard—how does a cheese and pepperoni toasted sandwich sound to you?'

She had to be kidding. 'In a word, horrible. I'm Italian, we love our food…proper food.'

She popped a hand on her hip. 'You haven't tasted my toasted sandwiches. They were legendary with my friends when I was at college.'

He raised his hands in surrender to the playful indignation sparkling in her eyes. Grabbing hold of a corkscrew, he said, 'I'll open some wine.'

In the midst of raiding the fridge, Carly popped her head out. 'Not wine, you need beer with toasted sandwiches.'

'This is sacrilege—your first night here in Lake Como and you want toasted sandwiches and beer.'

'I can't think of anything better.' Now armed with a selection of cheeses and cold cut meats, Carly added, 'You go and set up the table outside, I'll make the sandwiches.'

Ten minutes later, Carly popped the already toasted sourdough bread, now loaded with pepperoni, mozzarella and goat's cheese, under the grill and then began to clear the counter top.

Her hands were trembling. She pulled in some deep breaths, trying to relax, but the heartbreaking emotion in Max's voice when he had spoken about Marta, how he blamed himself for her accident, continued to upset her. He had clearly loved Marta greatly.

Carly felt a deep need to reach out and help him. He had been trying to manage on his own for far too long. But to help him properly, she knew she had to put aside any feelings, any attraction, she had towards him.

The food ready, Carly took it out onto the terrace. Max soon returned from checking up on Isabella, nodded that she was still asleep and popped the baby monitor on the terrace table.

Once they were both seated at the table, Max bit into his sandwich and chewed slowly, his forehead bunched sceptically. Carly pretended to ignore him but could not help but smile in relief when he said, 'These aren't too bad.'

Carly lifted her beer glass. 'Especially when washed down with a good cool beer.'

Max toasted his glass against hers, amusement dancing in his eyes, 'Tomorrow, I'll introduce you to proper Italian food.'

'Don't forget about the ice cream.' Taking a bite of her own sandwich, the melted cheese tasting sensational, Carly sat back in her chair, trying to focus on keeping the conversation light, trying to ignore how disturbingly good it felt to be sitting across the table from Max in the peace of the Italian countryside. The night was balmy and overhead stars and the faint moon, the lights of the villages in the distance, all contributed to a gorgeous setting. *Romantic, you mean?* Carly pushed that thought away.

'It's so peaceful here, you must enjoy visiting the villa with Isabella.' Pointing towards the playground with its swings and slides and sunken trampoline to the side of the terrace, she added, 'That playground is most kids' idea of paradise.'

'This is Isabella's third time in Villa Isa.'

'Really? It's so perfect here—I thought you'd visit regularly.'

In the shadows of the night, Carly saw Max's chest rise and fall heavily, his expression tighten. 'It's not easy coming here. Marta had so many dreams for this villa…and then there's Marta's parents…' He paused. Carly's heart flipped to hear the emotion in his voice he clearly was trying to disguise. 'They're still deeply upset by her death.'

So many dreams cut short, no wonder he found it hard to come here, and if he wrongly blamed himself for Marta's death then facing her parents must be incredibly difficult and something he would be keen to avoid. But in doing so he was isolating himself and potentially cutting off a source of support in raising Isabella.

'With time, the more you visit here, you and Isabella can create wonderful memories and dreams of your own for summers on the lake. And I appreciate that things haven't always been easy between you and Marta's parents but you've been through a lot. Maybe Isabella's grandparents could support you, especially as you have no family of your own—'

With a shake of his head, Max interrupted her, clearly

not wanting to discuss Isabella's grandparents and his need for support. 'Why did you decide to be a sleep consultant?'

Carly considered for a moment pushing the point about Isabella's grandparents but decided that was a conversation for another day. So instead she answered, 'I trained originally to be a Montessori teacher. In that work, I heard from many parents who struggled to cope when their children didn't sleep.'

Taking a sip of her beer, Carly waited for Max to say something, but he didn't. Instead he considered her with his head tilted, an intelligence in his eyes that told her that he had picked up on the emotion in her voice as she remembered the catalyst that led her to training as a sleep consultant. She knew she shouldn't get into explaining her decision any further, she knew she should keep this conversation impersonal, but there was something about Max's gaze, the silence of their surrounds, knowing just how much Max was struggling to understand Isabella's disturbed sleep, that had her admit, 'One of my pupils in particular got to me—Mikey. He was gorgeous.' Carly smiled in remembrance of Mikey's wild blond curls and how he used to suck his thumb, his huge baby-blue eyes staring into hers when he used to sit on her lap for a cuddle. 'His sleep became very disturbed when his parents split up. I guess he reminded me of myself when my parents divorced. Even though I was eleven, I found it really hard to sleep. I used to stay awake worrying about my dad. Worrying about everything, in fact. If somebody had stopped to reassure me, to spend time with me, I think I wouldn't have been so confused.'

Max considered her words for a while. 'Do you really think that's key to Isabella's sleep, for me to spend time with her?'

'Yes. It doesn't have to be twenty-four hours a day. Just

some good quality time and a regular bedtime routine should really help her sleep better. It will help you too.'

'What do you mean?'

'You should be enjoying being a father—I sense there's a reluctance in you to do so.'

Max shrugged at that, nudging his now empty plate away from the edge of the table. 'I grew up without a father—sometimes I'm not sure what my role should be.'

Carly's heart tightened to hear the quiet pride mixed with confusion in Max's voice. 'Just love her with all your heart. Give her your time—there's nothing more precious.'

Max's green gaze held hers. He leaned further into the table, his hand reaching into the centre to play with the base of one of the two white ceramic candlesticks there. 'You said earlier that you're not close to your mum—why's that?'

Carly swallowed. 'My stepfather Alan and I have a difficult relationship. It's easier to keep my distance.'

'Do you miss having a close family?'

Carly swallowed again, her heart feeling undone by the understanding in his voice. He had lost people from his life. His mother. His wife. 'Sometimes I do.'

'What happened between you and them?'

'My mum had an affair with my stepfather. My parents divorced and their business collapsed. Soon after, my father moved to New Zealand. I struggled to integrate with my step-family—my stepsisters didn't want me around, the same as their father. He wanted my mother, not an angry and confused teenager.'

'And things haven't improved since then?'

'I decided a few years back to step away for my own peace of mind. It was killing me constantly trying to gain their approval, the disappointment of being excluded. I've learned to have no expectations of them. Life is easier that way.'

Max nodded. He arched his back, considering her for a moment. 'Come to my father-in-law's party tomorrow with me and Isabella.'

Taken aback by his invitation, Carly asked, 'Is that appropriate?'

'It would be nice to have a friendly face there.'

'I thought you considered me a thorn in your side.'

His eyes were green pools of amusement. 'Yes, but so far your methods appear to be working.'

'Does that mean less resistance to what I say?'

A mischievous glint grew in his eye. 'If you come to the party.'

'But I have nothing to wear.'

'There are boutiques in Bellagio.'

Carly shifted her plate to the side of the table, pulled her beer glass towards her. She took a drink. She was here to do a job, not accompany her client to a party. Especially not a client to whom she was futilely attracted. A man still in love with his late wife. 'I don't think I should.'

'My in-laws know how to throw a great party and you get to be in my company for a while.'

Carly laughed at the cheeky glint in his eye. 'I think you need to sell the idea of me going with you a little bit harder.'

Max laughed too and something light danced between them as they held each other's gaze. Their laughter faded into the night. Carly looked away from Max, hating just how hard her heart was beating in her chest.

And then she jumped when a cry rang out from the baby monitor.

Max sighed. 'I guess I spoke too soon about your technique working.'

Carly stood and began to clear the table. 'I told you it would take time. I'll tidy up here. Go to Isabella and talk to her. Reassure her, rub her back, maybe sing her a lullaby.' Seeing Max's doubtful expression, Carly gave him a smile of encouragement. 'Experiment—you'll eventually find a way that settles her. And most important of all, you should consider Isabella waking as being a precious time for you to bond.'

The kitchen cleaned, Carly switched off all the downstairs lights and climbed the stairs in time to see Max leave Isabella's room.

When they met in the corridor she asked in a whisper, 'All settled?'

He grimaced. 'Eventually.'

It felt good to be standing so close to him. To hear his low voice. To see his hand rub against the taut bicep of his opposite arm. He had changed earlier, after Isabella's soaking, into a dark navy tee shirt that pulled tight against his frame. 'You've done well today. Go have a shower...' She paused, disturbed by the image of him in the shower, and added quickly, 'Take some time to relax. I'll listen out for Isabella.'

Max shook his head. 'No, I'll take care of her—as you pointed out yourself, you're not a nanny.'

That was before Carly had learned just how alone he was. Now she wanted to give him some support, even if it was only for a few days. 'Let me do it for you...you need to look after yourself as well as Isabella. Do you have time away by yourself, time for hobbies and your own interests?'

'*Dio!* What do you think? I've multibillion-euro projects to run and a strong-willed toddler who doesn't sleep.'

Carly winced at the tiredness in his voice. She should let things be, tell him to go for his shower, but instead she said, 'Life is a series of choices. Choose well both for Isabella's sake but for your own too. You deserve to be happy.'

Max's mouth tightened for a moment but then his green eyes searched hers softly. 'Are you happy, Carly?'

Carly swallowed hard. She thought she was happy. But looking into Max's eyes, remembering the loneliness she felt when she had gazed at Max and Isabella asleep earlier on the plane, she realised she wasn't quite so certain any more. 'I try to be.'

He blinked at her answer…or more to the point the croakiness of her voice. What was it about Max Lovato that left her feeling so exposed?

His hand reached for her arm. She tried not to react, not to give away just how much pleasure soared through her at his touch. She breathed in, in the vain hope of steadying her pulse.

He tilted his head, shifted in closer. His expression was hard to read. His eyes held hers for much too long. She held her breath, her pulse pounding in her ears. Then lightly, tenderly, he whispered, '*Buonanotte*, Carly,' and turned for his bedroom door.

CHAPTER FOUR

MORNINGS AND CARLY had never seen eye to eye…and after the previous night's broken sleep they most definitely weren't on speaking terms. With a heavy groan she flung her forearm across her eyes wanting to block the day out. Was it seriously time to get up already? Groggily she wondered what it was that had woken her. Her alarm? But why was it no longer beeping? She was pretty sure she hadn't touched the snooze button.

Eventually she dragged up enough energy to locate her phone on the bedside table, in the vain hope that she might be able to squeeze an extra few minutes in bed. She squinted at the time display. And squinted again, but this time even harder. It wasn't seven as she had set her alarm for but an insane five-forty. Five-forty! The last time she'd been awake at five-forty in the morning was during her college days when her gang used to head to a late-night café near Billingsgate after a night out clubbing.

Her gaze moved around the darkened bedroom. Her alarm was set for seven. So what had woken her? She listened hard, but there wasn't a sound to be heard throughout the villa—unlike during the night when twice Isabella's loud cries had pulled her out of a deep sleep.

On both occasions she had found Max already in Isabella's bedroom, holding her in his arms, pacing the floor. She had guided him to tuck Isabella back into her bed alongside Sunny, to rub her back and chat to her quietly.

He had whispered for Carly to go back to bed, but Carly had shaken her head and whispered back that she wanted to observe how Isabella reacted. Which admittedly was only part of the reason why she had stayed—the other being just how wrong it would have felt to have walked away from them both; she had wanted to stay and support them through Isabella's upset…no matter how befuddled her brain had felt at being woken in the middle of the night.

The first time round it had taken Isabella over twenty minutes to drift back to sleep. And three times she had reawakened just as they were about to creep out of her bedroom door. Carly had understood Max's soft sighs of frustration but had assured him that things would improve.

The second time Isabella had stayed awake for less than ten minutes and thankfully hadn't reawakened when they left the room.

Both times outside the bedroom, they had awkwardly said goodnight, the act of whispering in a moonlit corridor, them both dressed in night clothes, oddly intimate and disorientating.

Now, the disappearance of a faint light at the corners of the bedroom curtains had her wonder if a light coming on outside on the terrace had woken her.

Was it a security sensor light?

She eyed the curtains. Should she go and see what might have triggered the light in the first place?

She closed her eyes and sank her head further into her pillow, too tired to move.

But what if there was someone or something out there?

With a groan she clambered out of bed, knowing she wouldn't settle until she was certain that the alien creature who had terrified her dreams during her teenage years, thanks to watching a horror movie late one night in boarding school, wasn't outside the window.

Tentatively she parted the curtains, her already unsteady heart banging even harder against her chest.

Outside, the sky was a deep purple, the stars fading diamonds in the sunrise that was soon to come. The terrace was in near darkness but she could just about make out the faint outline of the terrace furniture and the path down to the pool.

She moved closer to the window, her gaze shifting across to the street and house lights of the villages on the opposite side of the lake. Would she get to visit those villages during her stay? See what secrets lay beyond those lights? She smiled, imagining picturesque villages with houses tumbling down to the lake, magnificent and elegant villas with terraced gardens.

And then she yelled.

Not a quiet yelp.

But a full-on howl.

A hand clasped to her mouth, she stared out of the window, her legs about to give way.

Outside, in full sight of her now that he had triggered the sensor light, was Max, staring back at her wearing nothing but a pair of navy swimming trunks, a towel slung over his tanned shoulder.

He mouthed, 'Are you okay?'

She nodded. But in truth her heart felt as if it were about to launch right out of her chest and fling itself down into the pool.

Max's head tilted. He gave her a smile. An apologetic smile that was rather cute. Then with a pointed finger he motioned towards her bed.

She glanced at it and then she looked back at him and raised a cautious eyebrow; not wanting to give away the wicked thoughts running through her mind thanks to the combination of seeing in quick succession a near naked Max and a rumpled bed.

He laughed, pointed to her and then cradled both hands under his tilted head to indicate sleep. He was telling her to go back to sleep!

She had known that. Of course she had.

With a nod she went to close the curtains and laughed when he gave a wave goodbye that was full of mischief.

She waved back.

They both laughed and reluctantly but with a playful flourish she shut the curtains to his glinting green eyes.

Stumbling back to bed, she collapsed down onto the mattress.

Light-headed, she willed her heart to stop gallivanting around her chest with such merry abandon.

And then she giggled, crazy happiness bubbling in her chest.

It was ridiculous.

But it had felt so good to share that moment with Max. To see his light-hearted amusement. The silent communication they had so effortlessly slipped into.

Her laughter petered out but a smile persisted on her lips. He had looked good—all bronzed skin and gorgeously pumped muscle. She closed her eyes and wriggled in the bed. Her shock shifted to a euphoria she couldn't rationalise away.

She could not help smiling and giggling in remembrance of how his swimming trunks had clung to his thick and powerful thighs. And then there was his chest, broad with a generous smattering of dark hair that screamed abundant testosterone. Yep, she had been right about happily betting her yearly income on his body being particularly delicious.

She groaned.

Then she yanked the pillow over her head, fear slowly threading its way along her veins. She didn't want to fall for a man again. She couldn't take any more heartache.

She must not ogle Max. Time and time again she chanted that to herself, in the vain hope it would eventually have her drift off into an untroubled sleep. But of course it didn't work.

What did have her drift off, as she curled up onto her side and snuggled into her pillow, was the memory of Max's eyes dancing with laughter. How incredible it was. How incredible it was to cause such delight.

'Buongiorno.' Max waited for Carly to look up from breaking an egg into a bowl before adding, 'Again.'

Her cornflower-blue eyes held his for a split second, the charge that ran between them all the more intense because of the brevity of their exchange, before her attention shifted to Isabella, who was in his arms. Reaching her hand across the kitchen counter, Carly touched her fingertips lightly against Isabella's bare leg. 'Good morning, gorgeous, how are you today?'

Isabella shifted her leg away from Carly's touch and buried her head into his shoulder.

For the briefest of moments, Max saw hurt flash in Carly's eyes at Isabella's reaction. Then laying her hand on the counter, the other on her hip, Carly tried to eye him crossly, but the smile threatening on her lips ruined her attempt to appear to be irate. 'What on earth were you doing up so early anyway?'

'Swimming.'

She picked up a fork and attacked the eggs in the bowl with energetic whisking. 'That I know, but why so early?'

'I always get up at five.'

'But that's insane when your sleep is interrupted so much.'

'Hence the need to start the day with a swim.'

Carly shook her head as though he was a lost cause and diverted her interest once again towards Isabella. 'You were fast asleep when I checked in on you a little while ago.'

Once again Isabella turned away from Carly's attention. Max curled his hand around Isabella's head and stroked her hair. Sometimes Isabella's dependence on him didn't scare him but instead sent a warm flush of love through his entire body. And this morning, to his surprise, this tenderness for his daughter was so strong that he felt the compulsion to comfort Carly as well—he actually was tempted to reach out and touch her hair too, soothe the hurt in her eyes at Isabella's rebuff. He walked around to the other side of the counter, and propped himself up next to Carly. He ran his hand along the tiny curve of Isabella's back, inhaling her sleepy scent.

'She just woke. I heard her crying on the baby monitor in my office.' He shifted Isabella in his arms, smiling when she looked up at him with her serious-minded gaze. 'You're not a morning person are you?'

Carly regarded Isabella affectionately, the hurt of Isabella's rebuff easily forgotten. 'Well, that makes two of us, Isabella, I hate mornings too.' Her gaze shifted up to his. 'Have you been working?'

'For the past two hours. I needed to catch up on the calls and emails I missed last evening.'

She shook her head at that, clearly not impressed. 'I'm making scrambled eggs for breakfast. Will you both join me?'

He nodded and went to place Isabella in her high chair. But before he could do so, Carly ran to the high chair, which sat next to the kitchen island, and said, 'Rather than have Isabella sitting out here on her own, let's move her chair in next to the kitchen table.' She removed the chair that sat at the top of the table and had the best view of the lake and placed Isabella's chair there instead.

He cleared his throat, trying his best to sound annoyed. 'That's where I usually sit.'

She did nothing to disguise her glee. 'Yeah, I thought it would be. But now we can both sit comfortably at either side of Isabella and help her eat.' With that she disappeared out of the kitchen, calling out from the hallway, 'I'll be back in a minute.'

Max sat Isabella in her chair and she thumped the plastic tray with her fist and gave a squeal of what sounded like delight.

Max shook his head, sure the two females in this house were starting to gang up on him.

When Carly bounded back into the kitchen he tried to glare at her but, dressed in a thigh-skimming white denim skirt and blue tie-dye tee shirt, holding onto a heavy eyed Sunny, she looked so pretty he had to turn away and busy himself by first popping some of Luciana's frozen pastries into the oven and then switching on the coffee machine.

For a while they worked in silence, Carly at the hob stirring the eggs, him making coffee. Isabella meanwhile eyed Sunny, whom Carly had propped on a chair at the table too, as though Sunny were waiting for breakfast also, and thrashed the rattle that was set into the table of her chair.

Above the noise of the spinning rattle, as she spooned the eggs onto plates for them and into a plastic bowl for Isabella, Carly asked, 'So what are your plans for today?'

He gestured to the now brewing coffee. 'Will you have a cup?'

She grimaced. 'Do you have tea?'

'I'm afraid not.'

She rolled her eyes but then good-naturedly said, pointing to the apple-juice carton he had already used to fill Isabella's drinking beaker, 'I'll join Isabella and have some apple juice. I'm sure it's much better for me anyway.'

'You'll be glad to hear that I've taken on board your advice that I spend more time with Isabella. So the three of us are going cycling this morning,' he said, pouring their drinks.

In the midst of placing cutlery at the seats either side of Isabella, who was busy sipping her juice, Carly said,

'Cycling...the three of us? Don't you want to spend one-to-one time with Isabella?'

He caught the hesitancy in Carly's voice—a hesitancy he understood. Their conversation last night, the closeness that had come from tending to Isabella together in the silent intimacy of the late hours when it had felt as though only they had existed in this world, their laughter this morning when he had woken her...they all added up to an ease, a familiarity arising in their relationship that Max wasn't comfortable with. But he had made promises to Carly, ones he wasn't about to back out of. 'I seem to remember offering to show you Lake Como.'

'You also promised me ice cream...but I'm happy to look around the lake myself.' Carly paused and considered him for a moment. 'Perhaps you should take Isabella to see her grandparents this morning instead?'

Placing Carly's glass and a basket of breads and pastries onto the table, he took one of the seats next to Isabella. He tore off a piece of *cornetto* and handed it to Isabella. He watched her chew on the soft dough, wondering how she was going to behave in the company of her grandparents. He wanted them to see that he was coping, a good father to their only grandchild. 'My plan for the day is that we first visit the Ghiraldinis and afterwards we can cycle around some of the local attractions. I would like you to meet them before the party this evening.'

Bending down to pick up Isabella's beaker, which had fallen to the ground, Carly said, 'About the party... I'm really not sure.'

'We want Carly there, don't we, Isabella?' As he said those words, Max realised just how keenly he meant them. And it was a realisation that was deeply uncomfortable. He shouldn't want Carly there. He was becoming too attracted, too distracted, by her. He could try to pretend to himself that he wanted her there as support in case Isabella became irritable, but in truth, last night when Isabella had woken, he had been blown away by just how calmly encouraging and supportive Carly had been. It had been a welcome reassurance after months of pacing the floor on his own, wondering what it was he was doing wrong. He had long abandoned the practice of having the nanny do night duty when he was at home as it only ever intensified Isabella's upset. It was that aloneness that he struggled most with as a single parent, the responsibility of every single decision you took, the lack of another person's reassurance that you were doing the right thing; the moments when you could laugh together even in exhaustion over something your child did or said.

This morning it had felt so liberating to laugh with and tease Carly over her terror when he had triggered the sensor light. She had stood beyond the window staring at him so wide-eyed that it had made her mussed-up bedhead hair look as though it were standing on end from shock. During the night, in Isabella's room, she had worn a long white cotton robe, but when she had stared out at him, she had been wearing only bed shorts and a skimpy vest top. Despite himself, his gaze had wandered down over her frame, taking in the high swell of her breasts, the voluptuous curve of her hips. *Dio*, he loved her shape. It was so feminine, soft, inviting.

'You can charm the Ghiraldinis if at any point Isabella and I need some time out. It might be overwhelming for Isabella—we have not met them in months. I'm not sure how things will go.'

'Are you kidding me? How exactly am *I* going to charm them?'

He laughed at her incredulous tone. 'You're witty and engaging. The Ghiraldinis will enjoy your company.'

'Really?' She paused and sipped her apple juice, her

eyes over the rim holding his with a dubious gaze. 'I wonder who's doing the charming now.'

He could not help but grin. 'Is it working?'

'You're trying to charm the wrong person.' The laughter in her voice trailed away. 'I'm immune to anyone's charm. Remember that I'm cynical and jaded thanks to my past.'

He shook his head. 'I can understand why you think you are, it's your armour against being hurt, but you're not cynical, Carly. That's not who you are.'

'Trust me, Max, I'm cynical.'

'There's too much kindness and goodness in you. Look at how you are with Isabella, with the advice you give.'

She rose from the table and began to clear away some plates. She smiled at Isabella, who had eaten most of her scrambled eggs by herself, only a little falling to the tray and onto her bib. 'Children are different.' She directed her gaze back to him. All hints of humour had disappeared. 'I reserve my scepticism for adults.'

White sails out on the lake, villas overgrown with ancient vines and secluded terraces, wildflowers tumbling over the pathway, which was a patchwork quilt of light and shade, Carly pedalled furiously past them all, trying not to laugh because it would only slow her down.

She knew he was teasing her. Allowing her to be in the lead.

Daring a quick glance behind her, she saw that Max was gaining on her.

Her calves were yelling in protest; there was no way she could pedal any faster.

Why on earth had she suggested they race in the first place?

Because you wanted to break the delightful pace that you had been cycling at—a pace of easy chatter, warm sun, a soft breeze carrying the perfumes of pine and sweet

*jasmine, spontaneous smiles at Isabella, who stared back
at you with that sharp and perceptive gaze that turned your
heart over, smiles at her father who cycled one-handed
while pointing out local places of interest, his voice melting every bone in your body. You wanted to put distance
between you. In every sense of that word.*

Enormous black-and-gold-painted wrought-iron gates
appeared on the opposite side of the road that ran paral-
lel to the pathway.

High up in the hill beyond the gate, a villa stood watch
over the lake, like a mother looking down on her child at
play.

Villa Fiori. Her pedalling slowed. She was intimidated
by the size and grandeur of the Ghiraldini home—a three-
storey neoclassical villa with an imposing colonnade to
the front.

Max and Isabella sailed by her, Max with a look of quiet
amusement, Isabella with Sunny tucked in beside her in
the bike carrier, frowning as though she was disappointed
in Carly for allowing her father to win.

She pushed down on the pedals, suddenly really wanting to win. Wanting Isabella's approval for reasons she
couldn't even begin to understand.

She gained on Max and together they crossed their finish line—the entrance gates to the villa. They both drew
to a stop just beyond the entrance, the high structure of
the gates towering over them.

She leant on her handlebars and studied him. 'You could
have won.'

Those misty green eyes of his held hers for a moment.
'I guess I could.'

Her heart jigged at the smile that followed. She tore
her gaze away from him to stare instead towards the villa,
thrown by the pleasure she felt at the fact that he had de-

liberately ended the race with them both crossing the winning line together.

'What a gorgeous villa… Does one family really live here, all alone? It's bigger than most hotels.'

Max stared towards the villa and then with a resigned shrug began to walk up the steep driveway. Carly followed, grateful he wasn't going to attempt to cycle any further, as there was no way she'd be able to cycle up the steep gradient.

They passed terraces of olive groves and lemon orchards, and as they neared the villa abundant rhododendrons and azaleas bordered rock gardens and valleys full of ferns, century-old cedars standing guard beyond them. All the while they walked in silence, tension radiating off Max.

Which wasn't surprising given the heartbreaking history of their shared loss of Marta, the often complex and fraught relationship that had to be negotiated when a grandchild became part of a family that was not fully united—and then, beyond all of that, the history of how Max had been received when Marta had introduced him to the family. How must he have felt the first time he came here as a young student? When he'd had nothing to his name, when he'd had no family of his own. How intimidating it must have been for him. Had he longed to be accepted by them, to belong to this family?

A few steps ahead of her, Carly stared at the hard muscle of Max's back visible beneath the bright white polo shirt he was wearing today. Had he longed to belong to Marta's family just as she had with her new step-family all those years ago? Carly sighed at the memory of how she had turned herself inside out in her attempts to be accepted by her stepfather and stepsisters. But instead of being welcomed into their fold she had faced an indifference from her stepsisters that had seen her confidence eroded and her aloneness in the world magnified. She had even home-dyed her hair to be the same shade of brown as her step-sisters and slavishly copied their clothes. All to no avail.

It felt horrible to be an outsider.

She called out to him, 'Max…' and when he slowed and waited for her to catch up she added, 'Why did the chicken cross the road?'

Perplexed, he stared at her.

'Because it was free range.'

His expression went from perplexed to bewildered. But then he began to chuckle.

And together they climbed the last of the ascent, both of them lightly teasing one another until the driveway ended in a vast cobbled semi-circular entranceway with a fountain at the centre. A member of staff rushed out of the ivy-clad main entrance and took their bikes while another member of staff welcomed them to Villa Fiori and led them through a marble and columned hallway, along a corridor lined with paintings and tapestries, through a light-filled living room adorned with gilded furniture sitting on oriental rugs on marble floors and out towards a terrace with spectacular views of the lake.

A woman sitting at an outdoor table with a silver-haired man cried out when she saw them. Jumping up from her seat, the petite woman, dressed in white palazzo pants and a white silk shirt, heavy gold jewellery on her neck, rushed towards Max and Isabella. 'Isabella! *Vita mia!*'

The woman held her arms out, wanting to take hold of Isabella but Isabella buried her head into Max's chest.

The woman looked at Max, her expression crestfallen. *'Non mi riconosce.'*

Max tensed. 'No, of course she remembers you…she's like this with everyone at the moment.'

The silver-haired man approached the woman and placed a hand protectively on her waist. Then he nodded to Max with a guarded expression. *'E bello vederti.'*

Max answered, 'It's good to see you too, Giulio.'

Though Giulio Ghiraldini was much shorter than Max, he bridged the height gap with an aura of self-confidence. Both men eyed each other suspiciously, their chins raised in proud defiance.

But then Giulio's stare shifted to her.

His eyes narrowed before he shot his glance back to Max.

Max stepped back towards her, his arm reaching around her waist to guide her forwards. 'This is Carly Knight. She's...'

Carly smiled at Giulio, trying not to show her shock at how good, but yet so wrong, it felt for Max to touch her, but also trying to hide her unease at how Max was struggling to explain who she was. Was he still resenting having to seek out her services? Did he still dislike having to seek support from others? Had she made no inroads in having him accept that to seek support was a strength?

Max cleared his throat but there was still a catch in his voice when he said, 'Carly is a sleep consultant who is working with Isabella at the moment to help her sleep. Carly doesn't speak Italian so we must speak in English. Carly, let me introduce you to Giulio and Valentina Ghiraldini.'

Carly shook hands with both, who looked at her and then at Isabella with concern.

The heavy tension bouncing between the four of them thankfully disappeared when a man in his early twenties bounded out onto the terrace and with a shout of delight pulled Max and Isabella into a hug.

Lifting off his sunglasses, the dark-haired man, dressed in red shorts and a white and navy polo shirt, spoke rapidly in Italian, his hand affectionately touching against Isabella's cheek and then lingering for a while on Max's arm, his pleasure in seeing them both clear.

Max managed to break through the man's constant stream of happy chatter to introduce him to Carly. 'Giovanni, let me introduce you to Carly Knight. Carly is helping me with Isabella for the weekend.' While Giovanni shook her hand warmly, Max explained, 'Carly, Giovanni is Marta's...' Max paused. A rush of pain, the same anguish she had witnessed in him that first time she saw him outside her office, flashed on Max's expression. Giovanni winced while Valentina bowed her head. For a brief moment Carly saw bottomless grief in Giulio's dark eyes before he pushed on the sunglasses he had been carrying in his hand.

Max cleared his throat and said quietly, 'Giovanni... Giovanni is my brother-in-law.'

Giovanni gave a bittersweet smile and once again embraced Max and Isabella, saying, 'It's been too long, Max. We need to see you more often.'

With that, Giovanni enthusiastically led them all inside the villa, insisting that they immediately see the surprise Valentina had organised for Isabella, promising that refreshments would soon follow.

Valentina smiled in anticipation at Isabella as she slowly opened the door to the room where her surprise was. Isabella frowned and turned her head away from her grandmother. Disappointment flashed in Valentina's eyes. Carly called, 'Isn't this exciting, Isabella?' Isabella looked at her dubiously but then, her curiosity piqued by Carly's enthusiasm, she tilted her body away from Max to gaze into the room.

The room was a child's paradise. An indoor miniature old-fashioned corkscrew fairground slide sat in one corner of the playroom, an array of soft toys in another, an exquisite doll's pram sat alongside a more robust push-along trolley filled with building bricks. One wall held a vast library of children's books, another arts and crafts supplies and various games.

Isabella eyed the room suspiciously.

Valentina looked at her again expectantly, waiting for a reaction. When none came, for a moment Valentina looked dejected but then went and reached up to select some wooden jigsaw puzzles stored high up on a shelf. When she couldn't reach them she turned and asked Max, the tallest in the room, if he could reach them for her.

Max lowered Isabella to the ground and went and helped Valentina, who took the puzzles and, removing her high heels, went and sat on a pink rug imprinted with silver stars by the already open French doors that led back out onto the terrace. Once seated she began to remove the pieces of a wooden car puzzle.

Carly smiled, immediately warming to Valentina and her quiet determination to connect with her grandchild.

Her smile faded however when she spotted Giulio eying her suspiciously, which only worsened when Isabella toddled over to her and, grasping the light cotton of her trousers, hid behind her legs. Carly wanted to clap her hands and give a little shout of triumph. Isabella had come to her! Voluntarily. It shouldn't matter that she did but it made Carly's heart waltz with delight. She reached her hand down and tentatively stroked Isabella's curls, not daring to say anything in case she frightened her away.

'So, how long do you and Max know one another?' There was an accusation to Giulio's tone that had Carly will herself not to blush.

Max, who had come to stand beside her, frowned at his father-in-law. He went to speak but Carly managed to get there before him. 'Only a matter of days. Max contacted me earlier this week when his paediatrician recommended me. Isabella's sleep is increasingly becoming disturbed.' She deliberately paused and shrugged before adding, 'It's very common with children Isabella's age and not a major issue. I must commend Max, however, on being proactive and seeking outside help. Being a lone parent is difficult and he should seek as much support as he can.'

Carly pretended not to see Max's annoyance at her words and she bowed down to gently chat to Isabella, pointing in the direction of Valentina, encouraging her to go and see what she was doing.

Isabella, always her own person, decided to remain clinging to her leg.

When she straightened, Giulio considered her for a moment and asked quietly, 'And do you usually travel with your clients?'

Carly decided to ignore the censure in his tone and answered brightly, 'No. But when Max explained that Isabella is to be a flower girl at the wedding and how keen he was that she be well rested for such a special occasion, I decided I would travel with them.'

Giovanni, who was kneeling on the floor trying to coax Isabella out from behind Carly's leg by holding a rag doll and waving her hand, broke from making playful noises to look towards Max. 'Tomaso and Bianca are arriving later this morning. They'll be so excited to see you,' Giovanni paused, a cloud of sorrow passing in his eyes. 'It really has been too long since we last saw you.'

With Max standing close beside her, Carly could feel his body tense. 'I've been busy with work.'

Giulio shook his head and waved his hands in the air with a disgruntled grumble. 'You must always make time for family.'

Across the room, Valentina looked up at her husband's angry tone and winced. And then her gaze shifted towards Max. She looked at him with such sadness that Carly had to look away.

Isabella cautiously started to move about the room. She paused for a moment by the toy kitchen and picked up a yellow saucepan, before moving on to stand a distance away from her grandmother, who had gone back to playing with the jigsaws, her heavy curtain of jet-black hair cut into an elegant bob, hiding her expression. Carly's heart pulled painfully hard for Valentina—how were you supposed to cope when you lost the most precious thing in the world?

Isabella leant forward to see better what Valentina was doing, losing her balance in the process so that she stumbled forward. Righting herself, she moved closer. Valentina gave no reaction. Isabella landed on her bottom with a bump opposite her grandmother. She stared warily at Valentina when Valentina edged the almost complete puzzle towards her. But when Valentina began another puzzle, Isabella dropped the yellow saucepan and picked up the one remaining puzzle piece and easily slotted it into the awaiting space.

'Those puzzles…'

Valentina looked at her husband and finished his sentence, her tone sad but determined. 'Yes, they were Marta's. I thought Isabella would enjoy them. They're so alike.'

Max moved across the room. Kneeling down, he spoke directly to Valentina. 'Thank you for creating this room for Isabella.'

'In the future…perhaps she could visit us more often? I can go to London and collect her.'

Max tensed. 'At the moment she wants to be with me all the time.'

'But if she spent time with us alone then—'

Standing, Max interrupted Valentina. 'I've promised Carly that Isabella and I would show her Lake Como.'

Valentina looked up at Max with dismay. 'You have to leave? But you've just arrived.'

Max's expression softened at Valentina's upset. 'We'll be back this evening for the party.' Then glancing towards her, he added, 'Carly will be joining us this evening.'

Carly smiled wanly in Giulio's direction and saw he wasn't looking too happy at the news she was coming to his party. 'I hope that is okay with you?'

Giulio blinked at her question and with an abrupt nod of his head said gruffly, 'Of course.'

Passing another jigsaw puzzle to Isabella, Valentina stood and reached out and touched her hand against Max's bare forearm. In a low voice she asked, 'Can Isabella stay here with us? It would be so nice to spend time with her.'

Max shook his head. 'She doesn't stay with others— she gets upset when I leave.'

Carly moved across the room. She knew that Giulio was suspicious of her relationship with Max and what she was about to say might add fuel to that particular fire, but she knew she should encourage Max to leave Isabella in Valentina's care. Standing next to Max, she said in a low voice, 'Isabella looks content here. Explain to her she'll be staying here for a few hours but you'll be back later. See how she reacts.'

Max spoke to Isabella, who nodded. Max stood, explained again to Isabella he would be back soon. Again, Isabella gave a bare nod, her attention fixated on the wooden pieces of a rainbow puzzle.

Max gave Valentina a detailed run-through of all the items in Isabella's changing bag. At one point Valentina caught Carly's eye; both women smiled secretly at Max's anxiety at leaving Isabella.

He stood at the playroom door, watched Giovanni join Valentina on the floor, Giulio sit on a nearby chair, the three of them laughing at something Giovanni said to Isabella, who smiled faintly at her uncle. Max called out to them, 'We'll collect Isabella at three in time for her to have an afternoon nap.'

The foursome on the rug looked briefly in his direction and then away.

Max's mouth tightened. He glanced in her direction, the initial uncertainty shifting to a proud tilt of his head before he walked away.

CHAPTER FIVE

MAX STRODE THROUGH Villa Fiori until he reached the entrance courtyard, where despite wanting to punch something instead he smiled when Hilda, the Ghiraldinis' ancient Labrador, trundled towards him with heavy pants of delight.

Crouching down, he patted Hilda, who offered him a paw by way of welcome. They had always been friends... even when he had been decidedly persona non grata in this household.

A rush of footsteps behind him had him turn to find Carly running towards him. Bending over, she scratched Hilda behind her ears. 'I see someone else is also delighted to see you.'

'They're delighted to see Isabella.'

Her hand came to a stop on Hilda's fur. 'You as well, Max.'

Standing, he gestured towards the gardens of the villa. 'We can walk to Bellagio through the gardens. There's a private entrance that leads out into the town.'

They walked up a flight of steps, the ancient stone mottled and worn with time, and along a pebbled path filled with tall palms and Italian cypresses, towards the sound of a classical piece of music. Carly gave a laugh of pleasure when they came upon musicians out in the internal courtyard of the villa, their playing just about drowning out the sound of the vast catering team also there, busy setting up the tables for tonight's party.

Carly paused to watch the team place gleaming silverware and vast urns of fresh flowers onto the snowy white linen tablecloths. 'Are the tables for this evening's party or the wedding?'

'Tonight's party.'

Carly's gaze widened. 'I hadn't realised it was going to be such a big party—there must be seating for at least three hundred.'

'The great and the good of Italian society will be here tonight. Giulio likes to do things in style. Tomaso and Bianca's wedding reception will take place here too—the ceremony will be in the gardens as the villa's chapel is too small to accommodate all of their guests.'

As they continued along the path, Carly asked quietly, 'Did you and Marta marry here also?'

It was strange—if anyone had asked him about Marta before he would have shut them down. But with Carly it didn't feel wrong; instead it felt natural, respectful. Was it that time had passed or was it more to do with Carly's empathy that seemed completely authentic? 'We married in Milan. Just the two of us and two friends who were witnesses.'

'Because of her family?'

'Yes.'

At the wrought-iron gate that led into the villa's orchards, Carly stopped at his side when he held the gate open for her. 'Did you or Marta mind marrying without your families?'

His heart turned over to see her concern. For a moment he considered not answering her, but something inside him wanted to be always truthful with Carly Knight. 'We were in love…at the time that was all that mattered. But I know it's not the wedding Marta had dreamed of.'

'I'm sure it was still a magical day.'

Surprising himself, he smiled gratefully at Carly. It felt good to remember the happy times he'd had with Marta—up until now it had been too painful to recall those times.

'It was a special day.' Then, remembering her planned wedding, he asked, 'Would your family have been at your wedding—if it had gone ahead?'

'They said they would...'

Max regarded her curiously, 'You don't sound certain.'

Years ago Carly had built a wall around herself when it came to her family. A wall that was easier to maintain when she didn't have to think or speak about them, about how disappointed, how let down, how rejected, how lonely she felt amidst them. She considered changing the subject but she could tell by Max's expression he wasn't going to let her. 'My stepfather Alan has a habit of finding excuses when it comes to anything to do with me. No doubt some urgent business would have cropped up and as my mother is the chief financial officer in his company, he would have insisted she accompany him.'

Max's eyebrows shot up. 'On your wedding day?'

Carly shrugged, desperate to keep up an act of nonchalance, while inside it hurt like hell to talk about all of this. 'It happened on my graduation day, my birthdays. My stepfather's focus in life is his company and my mother. His daughters come after that. Then I'm somewhere down the list.'

With that she walked away, along the path between the blossoming trees. Max soon caught up with her, a hand gently touching against her elbow. 'What about your mother—are you close?'

Her feet threading against the grass at the edge of the clay path, Carly answered, 'My mother tries to smooth things over between us. But she's deeply in love with Alan.'

'Why, when he doesn't sound like a nice guy?'

Carly paused as, not for the first time, she tried to fathom her mother's complex relationship with Alan. 'She was happy with my father but with Alan it's as though he freed something in her. She loves his drive, his ambition, his energy.'

'Wasn't your father like that?'

Carly smiled. 'No, he was soft and gentle. He used to take me fishing to the river that ran through our hometown, and we would go camping.' She came to a stop. Her eyes flickered away from Max's intent gaze, the sadness inside her overwhelming, before she added, 'But sometimes he was distant. It was only when I was a teenager that my mum told me of his depression. How he had struggled at work. My mum ran the business mostly by herself—in the end she grew tired of all that responsibility.'

Max inhaled deeply. 'That must have been very difficult for them both.'

'When I was younger I couldn't forgive my mum. I told her she was selfish for leaving him for Alan.'

'And now?'

'I guess I realise that life isn't as black and white as I thought it was when I was a teenager. We argued a lot back them. Alan used to intervene, which of course only made matters worse.'

'Maybe he was trying to protect your mum?'

Carly blinked at Max's words. She was about to angrily tell him that no, Alan had only been looking to find reasons to create a wedge between her and her mum, but then she paused and admitted, 'At the time, when they sent me away to boarding school, and constantly found me courses to attend during term breaks, I assumed Alan in particular was rejecting me. But maybe you're right, maybe part of his reasoning was that he was trying to protect my mother from our arguments.'

'Would you like to be close to your mum now?'

All the sadness inside her suddenly centred in her

throat. It was beyond painful when she swallowed against what felt like a boulder of emotion stuck there. 'I don't know—it's hard to trust after being let down so often.'

Max nodded, his green gaze swallowing her up with gentle understanding. 'Have you told her how you feel?'

Carly smiled, her sadness dissipating a little in the face of his attention, his empathy. 'About her leaving my dad, yes. But about how Alan treated me, how upset I was when they didn't attend events, no—in truth I was embarrassed at how excluded I was. Somehow it felt as though it was all my fault, as though it defined me as a person—that I was the type of person who deserved to be excluded.'

'You should talk to your mum.'

Carly nodded. Max was right. She *should* talk to her mum. But what if it only led to more disappointment, more times when she was let down?

She raised an eyebrow, happy to change the subject back to Max. 'As you should speak to the Ghiraldinis. They seem very fond of you now, Max. Whatever happened in the past, however hurtful it was, maybe you should embrace this family. You need and deserve their support.'

An unripe fig lay on the path before them. Max picked it up and tossed it into the dense foliage of the grove. 'If Isabella wasn't part of the equation I've no doubt I'd no longer be welcome in their life.'

'I don't agree.'

'You saw how Giulio was—he still has issues with me. And who can blame him after everything that has happened?'

At the wooden bridge that ran over a stream and led to the pine forest, Carly looked down into the lightly flowing water. 'I think right now I'm to blame for Giulio's unhappiness.'

'You?'

'He's worried that there's something between us.'

* * *

'Why would he think that? I've visited with a nanny before.' Even as he said those words, Max felt his pulse quicken. There was an ease between him and Carly that had not been there in his formal and distant relationship with the nannies he had previously employed. An ease Giulio must have picked up on. Guilt caught him by the throat. 'Giulio should trust me better than that.'

Carly's head jerked back. He hadn't meant to speak so loudly, so harshly.

He let out a sigh. 'I'm sorry...'

She gestured towards the path leading through the woods. 'I'll visit Bellagio by myself. There's no need for you to come. It would be...less complicated.'

He cursed himself for her hurt expression. 'I've many faults but the one thing I never do is break my promise. And I promised to show you Lake Como.'

Carly backed away from him, her hand trailing along the wooden handrail of the bridge. 'Well, I absolve you of that promise.'

He followed her. 'I *want* to show you around.' His words were out before he had really thought about them. But they were the truth. He did want to show Carly Como, spend some time with her. Especially after everything she had just revealed. How on earth did this beautiful, intelligent and compassionate woman think for a moment that she deserved to be excluded from anyone's life? And for the first time in years, he was finding it possible to speak to someone, even have some fun. He shoved the guilt that came with that thought deep down inside him and said, 'And I'll even laugh at your jokes.'

After a moment's hesitation Carly turned in the direction of the woods. They walked in silence, their footsteps crunching on fallen pine needles, the warm air thick with the scent of earth and pine, their arms brushing against branches of rhododendrons spilling out over the path.

'Knock, knock.'

He laughed and asked, 'Who's there?'

'Owls say.'

'Owls say who?'

Her eyes twinkling, Carly answered, 'Yes, they do.'

He opened the pedestrian gate from the villa chuckling, a lightness, a feeling of freedom causing him to pause on the narrow road that led into the centre of Bellagio. 'I must remember these jokes for when Isabella is old enough to understand them.'

They moved down the cobbled road, passing ancient ochre and umber-coloured town houses, villas covered in ancient vines. Carly's blue eyes glittered with amusement. 'I used to tell jokes to my Montessori pupils—there's honestly nothing better in this world than to hear a young child laugh.'

Dressed in a white cotton tee shirt tucked into green and navy floral trousers, her hair tied back into a ponytail, Carly smiled at him with such brightness and optimism that for a moment he felt a peace, a belief that life would be okay. A peace that allowed him to admit, 'It feels odd to be without Isabella. Usually I'm either with her or at work.'

The cobbles dipped downwards, and Carly, taking small steps against the steep gradient, said 'You've forgotten what it is to have free time.'

He laughed at that. 'I don't think I ever knew what it was to have free time in the first place.'

Carly paused outside a store selling leather goods and asked, 'Why do you work so hard?'

Her tone was concerned but there also was a hint of misgiving. He had never spoken of his childhood with anyone other than Marta before…and even with Marta he had glossed over some of the detail, ashamed of the poverty and struggle he came from in comparison to her family's vast wealth. But with Carly, knowing of her own childhood, it felt easier to be open.

He gestured for them to move down towards the main square of the town and said as they walked, 'I grew up seeing my mother struggle financially. Even when she was sick she had to work.' Wincing at the memory of his ill mother, thin and frail, but with defiance flashing in her eyes when she came home from work, he admitted, 'She developed cancer when I was in my late teens. Her employer had no sickness scheme. She worked when she could throughout her chemotherapy to support us. I wanted to leave school and then university but she refused to allow me. I had part-time jobs but not enough to support us. She said that I was her future. I guess I never want to go back to that poverty, or let her down.'

Under a plane tree in the square, Carly stopped and considered him, her long slim neck stretching up for her to hold his gaze. 'Your success is for her?'

He swallowed at the gentleness of her tone, the shine of tears in her eyes. 'Yes, and Isabella now too.'

'Know when enough is enough though, Max… These are precious years with Isabella. Enjoy them when you can. I'm sure your mother would want that too.'

He rolled his head side to side, easing out a kink at the base of his neck, remembering the hours he had spent with his mother in the hospital the day she died. She had been unable to speak, had been drifting in and out of sleep but when she'd woken her eyes had immediately searched for his, silently communicating her love. He had stayed holding her hand long after she had slipped away. Later he had gone home to their empty apartment and howled in pain.

He had to protect Isabella from that pain by making her more tenacious and independent than even he had been as a child. Life was unpredictable and unfair and he had to arm her against its cruelty. But now was not the time to point that out to Carly Knight. He was supposed to be showing her Lake Como after all. He nodded to one of the store windows behind her. 'That dress in the window would be ideal for the party later.'

Carly walked over to the window. 'It is beautiful.'

He joined her there in the shade of the store awning. 'It matches the colour of your eyes.'

She shrugged at that and wrinkled her nose. 'It's…a bit daring though, isn't it?'

Max stared at the dress trying to figure out what she meant. The sapphire-coloured knee-length dress with diamantés subtly applied to the flared skirt and fitted bodice was to him elegant. But then he looked at the neckline and realised it was scooped rather low. He swallowed at the tantalising image of running a finger down Carly's sternum, skimming between the valley of her high breasts.

He spoke to her reflection in the store window. 'It will look fantastic on you.'

Carly ran a hand against her neck, touched the lobe of her ear, her gaze in the reflection shifting from him to the dress and back again. 'Maybe I should try it on.'

'Do you want my opinion? Will I go in with you?'

She turned and looked at him. 'I… I'm not sure that it's appropriate that a client helps me shop.'

Max drank in the fluttering of her thick eyelashes cloaking her amazing eyes, the pink in her high and curved cheekbones, the plumpness of her lips. He dropped his head, a delicious burn of attraction humming through him, and spoke against her ear. 'I think we've moved beyond the normal client relationship, don't you?'

Carly arched her back, breathed out a low sigh. 'Have we?'

Max had to fight the urge not to fix the soft blonde hair that had fallen loose from her ponytail behind her ear. And worse still, he wanted to kiss Carly Knight. He wanted to feel her plump red lips under his. He wanted her soft body with all its curves pressed into his. Carly shifted even more to face him square on. A heavy intoxicating charge ran between them. His breathing hitched. His hand reached out, lightly fell on her waist just above the band of her trousers. His pulse upped another notch at the heat of her skin. She smelt of vanilla and citrus; he wanted to kiss her, taste her, explore her body…make love to her.

Thrown, he stepped away. That was *not* going to happen. He wasn't going to open up the potential of Carly being hurt again after all the hurt and rejection she'd experienced in the past. And he certainly didn't need added guilt and complications in his life. He could see the confusion in her expression at his abrupt movement. He nodded towards the boutique window again. 'Can I buy the dress for you?'

Carly's eyebrows slammed together. 'Absolutely not.'

'Why?'

'Because…because…' She stopped and asked angrily, 'Why would you want to buy it for me?'

Why was she so angry? Because he had almost kissed her or because he wanted to buy her the dress? 'As a thank you for coming to Lake Como, of course.' They eyed each other unhappily for a few seconds. But then once again he was drawn in by her soft mouth, by the constant chemistry swirling between them. He stepped back towards her and said, 'As a thank you for agreeing to come to the party later.' His voice dropped another notch as fire slowly licked along his veins. 'For being a good listener. For staying up so late last night with Isabella. As an apology for scaring you this morning. For making me laugh for the first time in years.'

Her eyes widened, she touched a hand to her neck again, her skin now the colour of a cream rose brushed lightly with pink. 'I'm glad I came, Max... I'm enjoying getting to know you and Isabella. There's no need to thank me or want to buy me things.' Pausing, she gave him a tentative smile. 'Seeing you relax and connect with Isabella is enough reward.' Turning, she opened the door to the store. He called out to her the name of the restaurant he would meet her at after she was finished shopping.

Max swung around and closed his eyes, taken aback by just how much he wanted Carly Knight in his arms... in his bed. For a moment he looked about the square, disorientated, but then the colourful summertime dresses in the window of a children's clothes store across the square reminded him that it was his daughter he should be thinking of, not his attraction to her sleep consultant.

Carly moved across the restaurant terrace, trying to act nonchalant, which wasn't easy when Max Lovato's gorgeous gaze followed your every step. It was a gaze so disturbing that it took her a while to realise he was on his phone, yet again. Carly's heart skipped a beat when she recalled how intoxicating it had been when they had stood close together outside the boutique earlier, his scent, the heat from his body, the low timbre of his voice all making her light-headed...and forgetful of her pledges to keep her distance, protect herself from him. They had almost kissed, for crying out loud.

He ended his call and stood as she approached the table. Their table was directly in front of the lake with unrestricted views of the glistening water. Overhead, heavy vines on a pergola gave them shade from the intensity of the early afternoon sun.

Max held out a chair for her, and nodded to the pink suit bag she was carrying. 'Did you buy the dress in the window?'

Carly nodded yes. The dress had fitted her perfectly. She was still a little unsure about how low cut it was but the store assistant had assured her it was entirely appropriate for Giulio's flamboyant birthday party, which apparently was the talk of the town with so many Italian politicians and high-profile screen and sporting stars about to descend on the town later today.

Max called a waiter and asked that special care be taken of the suit bag.

It was only then that Carly spotted a white package wrapped in a blue ribbon sitting on the plate before her. She lifted it up. 'Is this for me?'

When Max nodded she opened the present, hoping that there was nothing expensive inside. All the memories of her stepfather's presents that were bought to impress but with little thought for what the receiver actually wanted made her stomach churn.

Her hand went to her mouth. She giggled—with relief and delight. Without stopping to think what she was doing, she leant across the table and kissed Max on the cheek. Flustered, she sat back down, trying not to react to his surprised expression and then the quiet smile that grew on his lips. 'A box of English tea! Exactly what I needed. Thank you.'

Softly Max muttered, *'Prego.'*

Around them people chattered in an international blend of languages and accents.

The water gently lapped against the quayside.

Carly shifted in her seat, searching for something to say, but touching Max's skin had dulled her brain.

'I called Valentina. Isabella is out happily exploring the gardens with her grandfather and Hilda, apparently.'

Carly smiled to know that Isabella was happy but also at the bewilderment in Max's voice. 'How fantastic for her to spend time with them. And as she grows older that bond will become stronger and stronger.'

Max shrugged at that and the arrival of the waiter meant

they had to focus for a while on deciding what they would order.

Once they had ordered and the waiter had poured them the white wine they had both agreed upon, Carly sipped the crisp lemon-scented wine and asked, 'Why are you so reluctant to accept any support from the Ghiraldinis?'

Max picked up a bread roll from the basket the waiter had left on the table and broke it in two. For a long while he said nothing but then he quietly said, 'Growing up, the area where I lived, you had to be strong, determined. Many of my friends got involved in crime, became addicted to alcohol and drugs. I knew I had to get away. My mother was of the same mind. She wanted more for me. I spent my weekends and holidays working in the hotel where she worked. After school she expected me to study and would test me for hours when she came home from work. She constantly told me that I would only ever be able to rely on myself in life, that only I had the power to better my life.'

Carly watched Max's long fingers tear at the soft dough as he broke the still-uneaten roll into ever smaller pieces. 'Your mum obviously was a very strong and determined woman. But the downside of that is not accepting how sometimes we do need support. We need to be part of a wider community. We can't live in isolation.'

'Maybe it would be easier if we did.'

'Meaning?'

His gaze shifted away to look over her shoulder at something out on the lake. 'Losing someone…losing someone you trusted, someone you had mapped out your life with…'

His gaze moved back to hers. Carly's heart missed a beat to see the pain etched on his face. 'You miss Marta terribly.'

His jaw worked but then he dropped heavily back into his chair and said softly, 'It's not as awful as it was. But… I worry about Isabella.'

'You are doing a good job, Max…yes, I think there are

areas you could improve on, like asking for more support. But you are only human. Don't put unrealistic expectations on yourself.'

His mouth curved upwards. 'You really aren't the cynic you like to think you are, are you?'

Carly's heart kicked at the sight of him smiling. 'I try to be tough, not as easily taken in or hurt as I once was.'

Finally eating some of his roll, which he first dipped into some olive oil, Max said, 'Working hard at being a cynic—is that your motto?'

Carly laughed at the playfulness twinkling in his eyes. 'I guess.'

'Be true to yourself. Don't change or try to be something other than yourself because others have hurt you. Trust in yourself, in how incredible you are.'

Carly was about to argue that she was being true to herself but doubt had her pause.

Max picked up a fresh roll from the basket and, breaking it in two, dipped one piece in the olive oil and handed it to her. 'You should try this. The oil is incredible.'

She took a bite, the oil smooth at first, kicking hard against her throat when she swallowed. Her eyes watered. *'Buona?'*

Her answer was to dip her remaining roll in the oil. She bit into the roll with relish, licking her fingers as the golden oil dripped down. Patting her lips with her napkin, she paused when she saw Max staring at her, his darkened eyes sending a delicious wave of warmth through her body.

'Were you in love with your ex?'

She blinked at his question, at the tightness in his jaw. 'Robert—yes, I did love him. I loved him but I don't think I was in love with him. We were really compatible—it was an easy relationship: we liked the same food, the same TV programmes, we both dreamt of living near the sea one day. He was kind and gentle. But deep down I think I knew he was holding part of himself back. I never really knew the true him. I patched things over, which was wrong.'

'What do you mean?'

Carly really didn't want to get into any of this. 'I shouldn't be dumping this on you.'

Max held off until the waiter who had arrived with their starters had left before speaking. 'You said earlier that you like getting to know me better. Well, the same goes for me wanting to know you.'

Carly's insides melted at his softly spoken words. 'Is that wise…is any of this wise?'

'Maybe this is a weekend we both need…to process the past.' Max paused, his misty green eyes holding a tender hopefulness. 'To enable us to move on.'

Carly speared one of her ravioli pieces blindly trying to force her heart to calm down. She made an attempt to raise her fork to her mouth but knew there was no way she was capable of eating right now. She dropped the fork. 'Do you want to move on?'

Max shrugged and ate some of his raviolini before asking, 'What did you mean when you said that patching things over with your ex was wrong?'

Carly picked up her fork again, dipped the ravioli into the oil and pepper at the bottom of her bowl, trying to ignore how defeated she felt by Max not answering her question about moving on. 'I patched things over for selfish reasons. I wanted love, my own family. I kidded myself that all was well with Robert, ignoring the feeling of disconnect.' Carly paused and, reddening, she admitted, 'That passion that should be there when you're in love.'

'Do you still want love, a family?'

Carly ate some of her pasta, the sweetness of the pumpkin popping in her mouth. 'Maybe…if I ever manage to find the right person.' She speared another piece of pasta, moved it about her bowl, before staring straight into Max's gaze. 'But this time I'm going to make sure that it is an absolute and mutual true love, for us both.'

Something ticced at the side of Max's cheek. He shifted his gaze away, took a drink of his wine. 'Your parents' marriage hasn't put you off?'

'I was oblivious to the problems in their marriage. They protected me from it all. I grew up happy and adored by them both. When they divorced that all fell apart. I guess I'm looking for that again. Being part of a family, knowing you belong and that they will be there for you regardless— my friends have that with their families, so I know it exists. I just have to find it—but not at any cost.' Carly paused as the waiter cleared their plates before adding, 'I'm tired of being second best. I was second best to Robert, second best to my stepfather.' She held Max's gaze and said with a defiance that came from deep inside herself, 'It's not going to happen again. When we first met, my stepfather said to me, in front of my mother and his daughters, that he wasn't sure if he had room in his life for yet another female. He pretended it was a joke, but even as an eleven-year-old I knew he was being serious.'

Looking horrified, Max asked, 'What did your mother say?'

'She laughed it off…which made it all the harder to deal with. I felt I couldn't say anything.'

'You were a child—how could he be so callous?'

'Alan likes to have the upper hand in any situation, for people to defer to him. I tried to indulge him, I so wanted to fit into my new family, but I was also angry and confused and sometimes I stood up to him. He didn't like that.'

Max shook his head. 'In my experience people like Alan, bullies, people with misplaced egos, often are hiding some deep feeling of inadequacy within themselves.'

Carly wrinkled her nose. 'I don't know.' But then pausing, she admitted, 'His first marriage was deeply unhappy.

He's infatuated with my mother—even I have to admit how much he loves her. Looking back, I think my relationship with my mum threatened him.'

'And how is his relationship with his own daughters?'

'I used to think my stepsisters had everything but now I can see how Alan plays one off against the other. It has created this weird insecurity in all three. They are outwardly super-confident but are constantly vying for their father's attention. Adding me to that mix only added to their competition so they never welcomed me into their lives. When I was younger I was sometimes left in their care—they were all at university at that stage. The house would become party central. I thought it would be cool to hang out with them, but in reality I was pretty daunted by the amount of alcohol being consumed. And they weren't too impressed with having their geeky stepsister follow them around everywhere.'

Even though the waiter had returned with their main courses, Max didn't wait to respond to what Carly had said. His voice incredulous, he said, 'You were never geeky—you're way too beautiful.'

The waiter looked from Max to Carly. And nodded in agreement. '*Sì*, you are truly a beautiful woman.'

Carly rolled her eyes, feeling herself blush from her toes to the tip of her head as Max and the handsome waiter shared a wicked grin.

When the waiter had left, Carly eyed him across the table. 'So you do possess the Italian charm your countrymen are fabled for.' Her stomach flipped to hear Max's low throaty laugh. 'Trust me—with glasses, braces, a bad home dye and no clue how to dress... I really did look terrible as a teenager.'

Max took a bite of his swordfish and then sat back in his chair, his gaze not leaving her. Carly cut into her sea bass and forced herself to eat a few mouthfuls, unnerved by the intensity of his gaze. She jumped when he eventually spoke, his voice like a low caress. '*Sei irresistibile…* you're irresistible…you do know that?'

For a moment she considered telling him the truth. Of how she had always felt like the ugly duckling next to her gorgeous stepsisters, how Robert's love for his ex had further eroded her self-confidence. She shrugged off his question with a laugh. 'I'm no supermodel so I try to focus on my inner beauty instead.'

His eyes burnt into hers. 'Most men aren't looking for supermodels.'

Her throat tightened. 'What are they looking for?'

'A woman who's clever, one that radiates beauty through her kindness.' His voice dropped a note. 'A woman who knows how to love.'

Carly's heart spluttered to a stop. She searched for something to say and eventually she blurted out, 'I reckon you should have a conversation with my stepfather. He still grumbles about the money he spent straightening my teeth.'

'Perhaps one day I will.'

Carly dropped her fork at the menace in his voice. And then she laughed, laughed until her sides ached. She could see Max squaring up to Alan, dragging him down a peg or two with his quick intelligence.

Max raised an eyebrow at her laughter, a quiet smile on his lips.

After a while Max pushed his plate away and rested an elbow onto the table, his hand cupping his chin. His eyes held understanding, respect. He didn't say anything for a while, just quietly considered her. Carly knew she should look away but something too powerful, too amazing was passing between them. She couldn't name it but it felt as though something was shifting between them.

'You can always call on me and Isabella when we go back to London. It would be nice to see you.'

Her heart lifted at his softly spoken words. With a shake of her head she asked, 'Are you looking for some free professional advice?'

He gave her a look that said she was incorrigible. 'Obviously,' he said, rolling his eyes. Then after a pause he added, 'We get on…we have things in common.' His voice dipped. 'I find it easy to talk to you.'

Disappointment threaded its way through her at the implication of his words that he wanted to meet as friends. She forced herself to make light of it all. 'You forgot to add that we have the same taste in terrible jokes.'

His eyes danced at that. 'True.'

Carly tried to look away from the fondness shining in his eyes. It would be so easy to fall for him, to believe that there was something more than an odd friendship between her and a billionaire single father still grieving his late wife. Perhaps Max was right when he argued that she wasn't cynical, but she was a realist and resilient. Both traits drove her to say, 'Let's not make any promises we can't keep.' Looking around for the waiter, she added, 'I think we should ask for the bill. It will be Isabella's nap time soon.'

Max nodded, but then he reached down to the side of his chair. Lifting a bag, he removed first a toddler's white full-skirted dress embroidered with silver butterflies and then a pair of matching silver shoes with clipped-on silver butterflies. Carly exclaimed at the cuteness of both. Max smiled in delight, pausing to ask if she thought they were the right size for Isabella. And in his uncertainty, in his keen concern that Isabella would like her new clothes, Carly felt any last vestiges of cynicism ebb away like ice melting beneath a seductively warm sun.

CHAPTER SIX

ISABELLA'S FEET TAPPED proudly on the wooden floor of her bedroom and then, stopping, she once again inspected her new silver shoes, lifting her right foot up, waiting for Carly's approval.

'Oh, Isabella, they're the most beautiful shoes ever.'

Isabella gave a nod of agreement. Carly bit back a smile; Max was going to have serious shoe bills when Isabella was a teenager.

'Now come here and let me do the buttons on your dress,' Carly said from her seat on the side of Isabella's bed, opening her arms out wide in invitation.

Isabella eyed her, seriously at first but then something glittered in her eyes. Carly laughed. Isabella had inherited her father's mischievousness after all.

Backing away, Isabella ran to the other side of the room, an impish angel in her new white shimmering dress.

Carly liked to play fair so, throwing off her shoes, she climbed down onto her knees. Crawling across the room, she took care not to kneel on the heavy skirt of her dress. A quick check told her all was well in the décolletage area—the bra cups of the dress were thankfully holding everything in place, just as the sales assistant had assured her.

Isabella squeaked in delight as Carly neared her. 'I'm going to catch you.'

Flapping her arms, Isabella dashed off giving Carly a wide berth.

Carly swung around. Chased after her.

By the time Carly caught Isabella, her arm wrapping affectionately around her waist and lifting her up, her knees were starting to ache and with a sigh she plopped them both down onto Isabella's bed. Singing a nursery rhyme, jigging her legs playfully, she did up the zip of the dress and then the tiny buttons that ran along the zip seam.

Her heart gave a little quiver when Isabella started to hum along to the tune.

And when Carly set an all-buttoned-up Isabella down onto the floor and Isabella turned and placed both of her hands on Carly's cheeks and playfully squeezed them it felt as if fireworks had exploded in her soul.

Carly let out a playful gasp, pretending to be surprised. And crossed her eyes.

Isabella chuckled.

Carly lifted her back up onto her lap and began to lightly tickle her. Isabella squirmed and laughed.

When the game was over they were both a little breathless and happy to sit for a while to gather themselves.

It was only then that Carly saw Max leaning against the doorframe watching them, a hand in one pocket suggesting that he had been standing there for some time. Carly swallowed, her already unsteady heart doing a few flips. He was dressed in a black tuxedo that emphasised the dark tones of his skin, the broadness of his shoulders, the long length of his legs, his curls tamed by some hair product; his gaze caught hers and something potent whipped between them. 'You two look amazing in your new dresses,' he said in a low husky tone that sent a jolt of pure attraction through her body.

Isabella climbed off her lap and toddled over to him. Carly stood and fixed her dress. Max lifted Isabella into his arms and Carly tried to ignore the burning heat from his gaze, which was still on her. She touched her hair, making certain it was still in the bun she had pushed it into when dressing earlier.

Max, with Isabella in his arms, walked towards her, his

gaze once again sweeping over her. Carly waited for him to speak. There was a hum of attraction…and, okay, she would admit it, sexual tension, in the room. Carly inhaled deeply wishing Max would talk, break the connection that had somehow left her incapable of speech.

Too late Carly realised she was fiddling with the front of her dress, adjusting the neckline a few centimetres. She dropped her hand, blushed when Max's gaze remained there.

She cleared her throat. Scrabbled her brain for something to say. 'Luciana told me you were working so, after her nap, I gave Isabella an early dinner and bathed her for the party. She slept really well.' Carly paused and touched her hand against Isabella's new shoes. 'Didn't you, sweetheart? And you just love the new dress and shoes Papa bought for you, don't you?'

Carly laughed at the delighted squeal Isabella gave.

Max considered Isabella with surprised amusement. 'I'll have to buy you more dresses if this is the reaction I'll get.'

As if to say yes, Isabella buried her head into his shoulder. Max's large hand gently capped Isabella's head. Then his gaze travelled down the length of Carly's body, a low, slow deliberate gaze. 'You're looking very beautiful.' He paused, his eyes darkening. '*Potrei guardarti tutta la notte*… I could watch you all night.'

Startled and with way too many parts of her body about to go into meltdown, Carly grabbed her phone and, calling to Isabella, said, 'Time for a father and daughter photo, I reckon.'

Isabella thankfully turned and, though she was once again serious eyed, she co-operatively stared into the camera as Carly made cooing noises to keep her attention.

Max laughed out loud, his head falling back.

'Isabella is being the perfect subject but you're making it impossible to take a photo,' Carly chided Max.

'It's those noises you make…you sound like a pigeon.'

Carly threw him an indignant look. Max made a valiant attempt to sober but his eyes were still heavily creased in laughter lines in each of the photos.

When Carly declared the job done, Max said, 'Thanks.'

'For what?'

'I can't remember the last time I've had my photo taken with Isabella… It's something I need to do more of.'

'I promise I won't make the pigeon noises the next time.'

'Do, they're cute.' Then, shifting backwards, he asked, 'Are you ready to go?'

'I just have to grab my purse from my bedroom.'

'Meet us outside—on the terrace.'

Uncertain why they were heading to the terrace when they should be heading for the carport, after a quick check on her make-up, Carly joined Max and Isabella out there. In the brilliant evening sunshine, Max was crouched down next to Isabella, chatting to her while Isabella had her nose firmly pressed against a large candyfloss-like white and pink-tipped peony.

When Max heard her approach he lifted Isabella into his arms, and, pulling his phone out of his tux jacket, said, 'I reckon we need a group photo.'

Self-consciously, Carly stood next to Max, her spine stiff. Her unease soon ended, however, when Isabella lunged towards her and, wrapping an arm around her neck, pulled her in tight against Max. Max laughed and Carly tried to smile but it was rather disturbing to have her breast held prisoner against Max's arm, to have her belly pressed against his hip. She tried to pull away but Isabella held on tight.

Max gazed down at her. Her breath held at the dark awareness in his eyes.

He glanced down at his imprisoned arm and her body

pressed against it. 'I hate to break this up, but I can't take a photo now.'

His tone was way too deep and throaty.

She nodded wildly in agreement but Isabella still refused to let go. In the end Max managed to wrap his arm around Carly, pulling her more or less centre of his body in doing so, and Carly smiled into the camera, knowing her cheeks were glowing as Isabella's hold pulled the entire length of her body against the hard muscle of Max's.

Night had fallen and now that the birthday celebration meal was over, couples were out on the dance floor, twirling and twisting under the hundreds of fairy lights strewn across the courtyard.

Beside him, on Valentina's lap, Isabella giggled at Giovanni's disappearing act behind his napkin. Max had been taken aback when Tomaso had told him they were to be seated at the top table along with the rest of the Ghiraldini family. Giulio had stared unhappily at Carly when she had taken her seat beside him. Given Valentina's whispered words in Giulio's ear and his shrug after, Max guessed it was at Valentina's insistence that Carly got to sit with him and Isabella for the meal. If Giulio had had his way, Max reckoned Carly would have been seated in the further reaches of the courtyard…if not in the kitchen itself.

Giulio's mood hadn't improved when Tomaso and Bianca, clearly taken with Isabella's insistence on squeezing Carly's cheeks tight at every available opportunity, chortling in delight when Carly crossed her eyes, had invited Carly to attend their wedding on Sunday.

Max hadn't thought that far ahead. It was the polite thing to do—he could hardly leave Carly at home while he and Isabella attended the wedding. But…this weekend with Carly was getting too intense. He was feeling things for her that he had no right to be feeling. Earlier when he had spotted her and Isabella playing on Isabella's bed he had been torn between joy at Isabella's happiness and guilt that it had taken an outsider to unleash the playful child in his daughter.

When Carly had stood up his pulse had hit the roof. Her dress fitted her like a glove, the deep slash in the neckline revealing a tantalising glimpse of her breasts. He closed his eyes for a moment recalling how good it had felt to have her body pushed against his when he had taken their photo. How her hair had tickled his chin, her light floral perfume doing crazy things to his brain.

Throughout the meal she had chatted to Giovanni about his life in Athens, where he headed up the family's Greek subsidiary, and then excitedly with Tomaso and Bianca about their planned honeymoon trip to Croatia, giving them tips on little-known places to visit. Once or twice she had tried to engage with Giulio but he had shut down her attempts. Each time Carly would tense beside him, growing silent for a while as she absorbed Giulio's rebuttal. Each time Max had glared in Giulio's direction before chatting himself with Carly, wanting to ease her discomfort.

Which made Carly's invitation to Giulio to dance with her all the more puzzling. They were now out on the dance floor, Giulio leading Carly. At first they had danced together stiffly, barely a word passing between them, but now they were talking animatedly. What were they talking about? Max had the uncomfortable feeling it had something to do with him.

When the song ended, Carly returned to the table but Giulio moved to the stage.

Loud applause and whoops of encouragement followed his words of welcome to all of the guests. Max forced himself not to do an eye roll when Giulio gave a long name-check of all the politicians and celebrities present, often adding anecdotes of humorous encounters and experiences he had previously enjoyed with them.

But then he looked towards their table and with deep emotion expressed his love for Valentina and his sons. He tried to continue but his voice caught. He cleared his throat, attempted to continue but it sounded as if a vice were gripping Giulio's throat. Panic stirred in Max. *Please don't mention her.*

Giulio puffed out his chest, gripped the microphone even tighter. 'Great sadness has visited our family in recent years.' Beside him Valentina stiffened. Isabella, sitting on her lap, looked curiously at Valentina as though sensing her upset.

Up on the stage Giulio continued, his gaze not leaving their table. 'At times my wife and I didn't know how we would manage to carry on. But we will, for our beautiful boys, Tomaso, Giovanni…' Pausing, Giulio shifted his attention towards Max. Max's heart came to a standstill. 'And Max.' Giulio cleared his throat. Max felt as if he had been hit by a sledgehammer.

'I'm ashamed to admit that it has taken losing my beloved Marta to fully realise that the only important thing in life is those whom you love.' Once again Giulio's gaze moved back to him. Max shifted in his seat, confounded by what he was hearing.

'We all need to cherish our families, to be there for one another. Support one another. Not hide away, not be too proud to ask for help, to ask for what we need in life.' There was an edge to Giulio's voice now. Max rolled his shoulders, anger stirring in his belly. Was that what Giulio thought…that he was too proud and hiding away?

'And it's important to remember that, however dark the present is, there is always a future.' Giulio's tone lightened. 'A future of weddings and new members in our family. Bianca… Isabella, our gorgeous granddaughter who gives us hope and purpose. Two years ago I didn't think I would be able to stand here and talk to you as I celebrate my sixtieth birthday, but losing Marta has taught me that we should cherish life and each other, to embrace the future.'

Around him, people stood to applaud Giulio, who stepped down from the stage with an extravagant bow of acknowledgement.

'Are you okay?'

He turned at Carly's question, stared at her blankly for a few moments before saying, 'We should head back to the villa… It's beyond Isabella's bedtime.'

For a moment it looked as though Carly was going to argue with him but something shifted in her gaze and she nodded.

After saying their goodbyes to all the family, including a terse thank you and nod towards Giulio, they drove home in silence. A silence that continued apart from forced chatter with Isabella as they gave her a drink before bed.

He attempted settling Isabella himself, but Isabella insisted on Carly being in the room too. Which did nothing for Max's bad humour. What the heck was he going to do if Isabella wanted Carly when they got back to London?

He read Isabella *Sleepy Heads in Sleep World* distractedly, but thankfully she was exhausted by her day and fell asleep quickly.

He and Carly crept out of her room. Outside the door, Carly asked, 'Will you join me in having a drink?'

He wanted to say no. He wanted to clam up.

No, actually, he wanted to say yes so that he could let loose on all of his frustrations with Giulio.

He didn't know what he wanted. So with a curt nod, he led the way downstairs and into the kitchen.

He pulled two beers out of the fridge and passed one to Carly.

Outside on the terrace, they sat on the L-shaped sofa overlooking the pool.

Sitting at an angle from him, Carly pushed off her high heels, swung her body in his direction and, folding her legs under her, asked, 'Do you want to talk about it?'

He shrugged. 'Not particularly.'

Carly took a sip of her beer. 'I'm guessing Giulio's speech upset you. It must be hard hearing Marta's name mentioned.'

'It's not that.'

'What is it so?'

'*Dio*, Carly, you heard Giulio yourself, do you need to ask that question?' He stopped and tried to swallow the impatience in his voice. Carly, after all, had nothing to do with the frustration coursing through him. But years of being looked down on, the guilt of Marta's death, spilled out regardless. 'The assertion that I've been hiding away. Not caring about them. I stayed away because I didn't want to cause them even more upset. They never approved of me. I allowed their daughter to die…why would they want to see me? I invited them to visit us in London soon after Marta died but they never came.'

'But Giulio is concerned for you, Max—he cares for you.'

'How do you know that?'

'His speech…'

He shook his head. 'That was nothing but a veiled condemnation of me.'

'I disagree…' Carly paused and shifted closer to him. 'When we were dancing Giulio asked about you. How you are coping.'

About to take a drink of his beer, Max paused, the bottle hovering in the air, a sinking feeling in his stomach. Quietly he asked, 'Why did you ask Giulio to dance with you?'

'I wanted…' Carly paused, gave him an uncertain look

before admitting, 'I wanted to tell him that you need his support.'

'You did what?'

'But you do.'

Max slapped his beer bottle down onto the glass-topped table in front of the sofa. 'If I wanted Giulio's support I would ask for it.'

Carly unfolded her legs, sat upright and shook her head. 'No, you wouldn't, and Giulio and Valentina are too nervous to ask for your support.'

'*My* support?'

Carly looked at him as though she couldn't believe he wasn't following her train of logic. 'Being closer to you and Isabella would help them in dealing with Marta's death.'

'Why haven't they visited us in London if that's the case?'

'Have you invited them recently? Straight after Marta's death would have been too painful for them.'

He gritted his teeth. 'I do have my pride, Carly.'

Carly frowned. And then after a moment's consideration nodded and said, 'I can understand that, but I think the Ghiraldinis are nervous about getting things wrong in their relationship with you.'

Max threw his head back and stared at the overhead stars. He tried to temper his frustration when he said, 'I'm really not following this.'

'Don't you see, you hold all the power in your relationship. They want to be with Isabella but know that you could stop them seeing her at any point.'

Affronted that anyone would think he was capable of that, he bit out, 'I would never stop them seeing her.'

'I understand why it must be hard for you but perhaps you need to let everything go that happened between you and the Ghiraldinis in the past and focus on where you are now. You need to start talking to them, Max. For all your sakes. I honestly don't believe the Ghiraldini family hold you responsible for Marta's death. Giulio told me tonight that you were a wonderful husband to Marta.' Stopping, Carly cleared her throat, but her voice was still cracked with emotion when she added, 'He said you made her very happy. He's very proud of all that you have achieved.'

Max narrowed his gaze, not buying it. 'You're making this up.'

Her mouth dropped open before she made a disbelieving squeak. 'I most certainly am not.' She gave a little huff, folded her arms and eyed him crossly.

Max swallowed a smile at Carly's outrage; sparks were practically firing from her eyes. 'So are you saying that I should invite Giulio and Valentina to come and visit us in London?'

The sparks in her eyes disappeared to be replaced with shining enthusiasm. 'Yes, and you should visit Como more frequently.'

He picked up his beer bottle. Eyed her over its rim. 'If the Ghiraldinis come to London, I'm going to insist that you visit and you can be the one who has to listen to Giulio's tall tales.'

She threw her head back and laughed. Then, with a satisfied smile, she countered, 'But you'll have no need for me to visit. Isabella will be sleeping perfectly. My work with you will be done.'

Max took a long gulp of his beer. He tried to imagine never seeing Carly again. He took another gulp, thrown by how his heart dipped low in his chest at that thought. He placed his bottle onto the table top again. 'Did you enjoy the party?'

Carly rubbed her hands against her bare arms. 'Of course.' She gave a light laugh that travelled through his body like warming brandy. 'I'd defy anyone not to enjoy such a lavish party.' She wrinkled her nose. 'I was looking forward to dancing more though. You dragged us off home before I got a chance to dance with Isabella as I had promised her.'

Before he knew what he was doing, Max found himself standing and holding his hand out to her. 'Will you dance with me instead?'

For a split second her mouth widened in a brilliant smile but instantly it faded. 'There's no need.'

He kept his hand reaching out, refusing to listen to the voices telling him he was acting crazily, and said quietly, 'How about we forget about reality for a few minutes and pretend we have just seen each other across a room?'

Her head tilted. 'Like in an old movie?'

'Exactly.'

She considered him for a moment. 'Are you the hero or the villain of the movie though?'

Good question. Max stepped closer. Suddenly realising that with Carly he wanted to be a hero as corny as that sounded. He wanted to treat her right, protect her, earn her respect. 'The hero of course.'

Her eyes danced with merriment. 'I like the idea of suspending reality for a while.'

'How about we pretend it's a Viennese ball?'

She stood and playfully bowed. 'I would be honoured to dance with you, Count Lovato.'

'And I with you, Princess Carly.'

He held her at a distance, humming lowly. They danced around the terrace, the stars shining down on them, the still night air whispering against their skin. He felt Carly shiver. He stopped and removed his jacket. Helped her pull it on. Instead of waltzing this time, his hands went to her waist, hers to his shoulders. He pulled her closer, she came willingly. Her thigh bumped against his. He tightened his hold. Her hip touched against his upper thigh. His hand roamed upwards. His thumb ran along the outer side of her breast. She exhaled shakily. Fire raged through his veins.

Her eyes were heavy, mirroring his own need. He lowered his head. Her eyes fluttered closed, her soft plump mouth parted. With a groan his mouth found hers. His arm around her waist, he arched her body against his and she whimpered, her fingers reaching up to press against his scalp. All the while they tasted and nibbled and inhaled each other. One hot mouth on the other, their bodies twisting and bumping against each other. He longed to push back the deep neckline of her dress. To thumb the soft flesh of her breasts.

But then with a shaky breath, he pulled away, knowing it all was about to get out of control. He ran a hand along his jaw. 'Forgive me.' She went to protest but he shut her down. It would be easier if they both pretended that this was something he had got wrong, that he was the only one who wanted this kiss, this fire. He pressed on. 'That was inappropriate. I would like to apologise.'

He stepped back, gestured to the villa. 'I'll walk you to your room.'

Carly removed his jacket and passed it to him. Tilting her chin, she said, 'There's no need.'

She swooped down and picked up her heels.

Max watched her walk away. And closed his eyes when she went inside, a wave of frustration washing over him.

A kiss that was so wrong shouldn't have felt so perfect.

CHAPTER SEVEN

'*UNO...UNO...UNO.*' Her peach shorts covered in a heavy dusting of sand, Isabella picked up one creamy white stone after another from the beach and dropped them into her rapidly overflowing red sand bucket.

Her brown curls peeking out from beneath her white sunhat, she looked adorable sitting on the pebbled section of Max's private beach.

Closer to the water, the beach was made of a bank of fine sand and for the past hour the three of them had played there building sandcastles. Of course, building sandcastles with an architect was never going to be straightforward and they had ended up creating an impressive fort complete with moat, battlements and drawbridge.

Now, as Max sauntered down the steps of the boathouse heading in their direction carrying a laden tray, she lowered her sunglasses from where she had earlier perched them onto her head and bit back a groan. Why were men blessed with such good legs?

Beneath his white shorts, Max's were bronzed and muscular, no doubt as a result of his morning swims. The outside light had triggered again this morning when he had gone down to the pool. She had forced herself not to peek out, which had called for an iron will, given how tempting the prospect of seeing a half-naked Max had been.

Instead she had lain in her bed and confronted some home truths she'd have much rather preferred to ignore.

Number one being the most obvious: her behaviour last night in kissing Max had been totally unprofessional. He hadn't fooled her in his apology—they both knew that they had equally wanted it, but she should have known better.

Two, hadn't she learned anything from the Robert debacle? Max was still in love with Marta. Falling for a guy whose heart lay elsewhere was plain insanity.

Three, Max was a struggling dad trying to negotiate his relationship with his in-laws over an emotionally charged weekend. Was her proximity, the fact that they got on, that there was an attraction between them, nothing more than a welcome diversion for him?

Fourth, and the most crucial truth of all, was Isabella. Carly knew her focus should be in helping develop a stronger bond between Isabella and her dad. Which was why, this morning, Carly had breezed into the kitchen, determined that last night was a temporary blip in the weekend, and suggested they all spend some time together on the beach.

The tray casually hoisted onto one shoulder, Max strolled across the sand in his bare feet. Carly led Isabella by the hand down to their picnic blanket on the sand and, when Max joined them, Carly nodded in the direction of the tray balancing on his shoulder. 'Neat trick.'

Max laid the tray down at the centre of the rug with a flourish and grinned. 'I was a waiter when I was studying.'

Max sat on the turquoise blanket and Carly, sitting across from him, patted a spot between them for Isabella to sit on. But Isabella, as ever, had her own idea and plonked herself firmly down on Carly's lap.

Laughing, Carly glanced in delight towards Max, who looked from her to Isabella with a frown.

Carly placed her hand on Isabella's knee, her forearm lightly preventing her from toppling over. In truth she wanted to wrap her arms tightly around her waist, hug her tiny body in close, but given Max's disquiet she decided not to make a bigger deal out of Isabella's ever growing acceptance of her than was necessary.

All morning Max had been relaxed and courteous towards her. A little too courteous for her liking…he was treating her as you would a colleague you were fond of.

Despite herself she wanted to scream. She wanted to ask if he had felt the same surge of hot hormones, the thrill of something new and wonderful, that same rightness of their kiss. The rightness of two bodies, two mouths and the perfect blend of pheromones all colliding in one incredible explosion of perfection.

But that laid-back vibe he had been projecting all morning was now history. He looked rattled. Why did he have a problem with Isabella sitting with her? Wanting the awkwardness to disappear, she pointed to the tray filled with juices and fresh fruit and delicious-smelling pastries. 'Look, Isabella, at all the wonderful things Papa has brought for our picnic.'

Isabella clapping her hands excitedly seemed to snap Max out of whatever was bothering him. He placed a napkin on his forearm with a flourish and, picking up a plastic beaker of orange juice, presented it to Isabella as though she were royalty. *Signorina Isabella, succo d'arancia per te.*

To Carly he passed a tall narrow glass filled to the brim with iced coffee. 'And for you, Signorina Carly, iced coffee hand-blended by myself.'

Did he really have to talk in such a low sexy voice, which sounded like an invitation to do something naughty?

Isabella drank her juice and munched happily on a piece of a cookie Luciana had baked earlier that morning.

Max's boathouse was a contemporary, two-storey flat-roofed structure. Storerooms were located on the ground floor while upstairs there was a large kitchen and living space with spectacular views out onto the lake and a balcony suspended over the water. A wooden jetty to the side of the boathouse led to Max's powerboat.

Her cookie finished, Isabella began to swing in Carly's lap as she softly hummed a tune to herself. She and Max exchanged a humorous look at Isabella's tuneless humming. Their gazes held. A charge of attraction crowded the air space between them. A shiver ran through her.

Disconcerted by the intensity of the chemistry playing out between them, Carly bowed her head and ran her hand over Isabella's sun hat, wishing she could touch her soft curls instead.

'Isabella is growing very fond of you.'

Carly blinked at the concern in his voice. 'You're worried about it?'

Unease flickered in his expression. 'With Marta…all the nannies who've come and gone… I worry about the amount of loss she's had in her life.'

Her heart almost snapped in two to see the worry etched on his face, the sadness in his voice. Isabella shifted in her arms, her head lolling back against her chest. 'Children are resilient. As long as she knows she can rely on you then she will be able to handle other people coming and going in her life.'

Max's gaze stayed fixed on hers as he considered her words, the intensity of his reflection and deliberation of what she said lifting her heart—he really wanted to do right by his daughter. But it was also his respect for her opinion that got to her. Her stepfather had always disregarded her views. For a long time it had dented her self-confidence and had made her question her abilities and even her right to express her opinions. Dropping her cheek to rest gently against Isabella's head, Carly closed her eyes. Drew in a long breath. Sighed it out silently as her heart took another tumble forwards in falling for Max.

'You're very good with Isabella.'

Carly opened her eyes in surprise at Max's softly spoken voice. Looking down, she smiled fondly when she spotted that Isabella had fallen asleep in her arms. Carly leant back so that Isabella was in a less upright position, a wave of warmth spreading through her as she watched Isabella's long dark eyelashes flicker in her sleep.

She floundered for a moment, knowing she needed to say something, to look in Max's direction, but she didn't want him to see just how emotional she felt. She searched her brain for something suitable to say and eventually managed to ask, 'Has your nanny agency found any suitable candidates for you?'

'They've emailed some profiles through. On paper they look good—' he shrugged '—but so did all of the others that I recruited.'

'If you want a second opinion, I'll happily interview the candidates with you.'

Max looked at her curiously. 'Is that part of your service?'

It wasn't. But without realising it until she'd offered, Carly felt invested in Isabella's future. She wanted to make sure she was well cared for. 'It's not something I usually do…' Carly grimaced down at Isabella, who was leaning heavily against her chest. She leant even further back on her arm that was keeping them both upright. Her bicep and wrist protested with a sharp ache. 'Gosh, she's heavier than I thought.'

Max shuffled over on the picnic blanket to sit next to Carly. His thigh touching hers, he reached over towards Isabella. 'Let me take her from you.'

Their hands met as they passed Isabella between them, their bowed heads almost touching. It was such an intimate act, gently passing a sleeping child, so full of innocence, so defenceless, between them.

Carly's heart missed a beat. And another beat when

she saw Max's tender gaze down onto his daughter as he settled her into his arms.

'You really love her, don't you?' Carly asked softly.

Max's green gaze shifted up to her. Emotion filled his eyes. 'Sometimes…sometimes I'm afraid…' Max trailed off. Carly held her breath, waiting for him to continue.

They both jumped at the sound of shifting pebbles behind them. When they turned they found Valentina staring in their direction, her expression unreadable.

She and Max jerked away from one another, Isabella waking in the process. She gave a little whinge, but then as she grumpily sat up in Max's lap her scowl morphed into a shy toothy smile when she spotted Valentina.

Valentina bent down and held her arms out wide to Isabella. Isabella clambered off Max's lap and tottered towards her grandmother.

Valentina hugged Isabella, pressing tiny kisses against her cheek before taking her hand and leading her down towards the picnic blanket. Carly and Max had already sprung up from the blanket and were standing far apart from one another.

Max stepped towards Valentina, who eyed him cautiously.

Footsteps on the path down from the villa had them all turn to see Giulio making his way towards them.

Max looked at his watch. 'I wasn't expecting you until lunchtime. If I had known you were coming earlier I would have made sure to have been up at the villa.'

Giulio's gaze flicked towards his wife and then upwards, his head shaking as though to say, *I told you so*, but then his expression softened and he crouched down next to Isabella. 'Valentina couldn't wait to see Isabella again. We tried calling you to say we were coming early but you didn't answer,' Giulio said, poking Isabella affectionately on the belly with his index finger. *'Cuore mio, come va?'*

Isabella giggled and held onto Giulio's finger. Giulio made a big act of struggling to get his finger back out of Isabella's grip, much to Isabella's amusement.

Carly stepped back from the group, feeling wrong-footed that Max had not mentioned the Ghiraldinis were calling. Valentina frowned at her movement. Carly bent down and began to tidy their picnic tray.

'The renovations, your new boathouse, all very impressive, Max,' Giulio said a little gruffly.

Max's only response was a quick nod of his head in acknowledgement.

Carly cringed at the awkward silence that followed and only ended when Max said a little unenthusiastically, 'Luciana won't have lunch ready for another hour—would you like to join us in our picnic?'

Giulio eyed the blanket as though it were an alien concept to sit on the hard surface of a beach to eat.

'Thank you for your lunch invitation, Max,' Valentina said in a low voice, 'but if it's okay with you we would like to bring Isabella back to Villa Fiori for the afternoon. The rest of the family would love to spend some time with her…' Valentina paused and her gaze ran between Carly and Max '…and I'm sure you both could do with a break.'

Giulio looked at his wife in puzzlement, obviously only hearing now this change in plans, but his expression soon changed to one of pleasure at the prospect of having Isabella for the afternoon.

Carly willed herself not to blush. Valentina's gaze was a knowing one, giving a whole different meaning to her words. A meaning that had Max work his jaw. 'I'm sure you're busy preparing for the wedding tomorrow. There's really no need.'

Valentina, still holding Isabella's hand, moved closer to Max. She gave him a gentle smile. 'It might be a long time since my children were this age, but I remember how exhausting it is, especially when they aren't sleeping through the night.' Her voice dropped low. 'Let me help you, Max. Please. It's important to me.'

Max's head bowed at Valentina's words but then he slowly nodded his head.

Valentina reached out and held his forearm for a moment. 'Thank you. I will drop her home about seven.' Valentina's gaze shifted towards Carly. 'Has Max taken you to see any of the other lakeside villages yet?'

Carly hesitated for a moment, not sure how to answer. 'No…not yet.'

Valentina looked at Max. 'You should take Carly on a tour of the lake this afternoon.'

Giulio cleared his throat. 'I'm sure Max has work to do.'

Carly added, 'I need to buy a dress for the wedding tomorrow. I'm going to cycle into Bellagio.'

Max picked up Isabella's changing bag from the blanket, clearly wanting to change the subject. 'Why don't we go back up to the villa? I'll need to give you some of Isabella's things and run through her routine with you. She'll need to nap around three.' The four of them walked towards the path back up to the villa. When Max realised Carly wasn't following he turned and looked at her with a questioning frown.

Carly gestured to the blanket and tray. 'I'll stay here and tidy up.'

Giulio gave a nod of approval but Valentina called out, 'Have a wonderful afternoon, Carly…and make sure Max relaxes. He works much too hard.'

She watched them climb the path and sighed when they went out of sight. Carly turned to the lake, stretched her arms out wide, opened her mouth and gave a silent scream. This was all getting too complicated. Valentina obviously thought there was something going on between her and Max. And seemed to be encouraging it. Which was so at odds with Giulio's constant suspicion of her. Admittedly, he wasn't as hostile now that they had spoken last night, but he was still wary of her.

Picking up the tray and folding the blanket over her arm, Carly walked to the boathouse. At least Max was reaching out to his in-laws. Maybe everything would work out for the best this weekend… At the top of the steps to the boathouse, Carly's gaze shifted over the lake and then up to Villa Isa. She doddered on the threshold of the boathouse for a moment, wondering how this afternoon was going to pan out. Then she realised she needed to take control of it. Make the most of her time here in Lake Como. She would go for a swim, cool down, and then cycle into Bellagio. Max no doubt would spend the afternoon working. Which suited her perfectly.

Was he really seeing Carly wearing nothing but a black bikini walking along the jetty? Max edged to the side of the terrace, annoyed at his lack of willpower. Of course, he should turn around and head for his office. But the sight of Carly in a skimpy bikini was way too tantalising.

As she came alongside *Alighieri*, she stopped to give his powerboat a quick once-over. He could see her ponytail swinging from side to side as she ducked down in her appraisal of the forty-five-foot boat.

Then she moved on further down the jetty, walking close to the edge. At the end of the jetty she came to a stop and peered into the water. He waited for her to turn around. When he saw that she was back in the safety of the boathouse or even on the beach then he would go to his office.

Her body swayed. *Dio!* She was going to fall in if she wasn't careful.

She lifted her arms. Max was already running before she dived cleanly into the water.

She surfaced with a yell that echoed up the hill, her arms thrashing the water.

He vaulted over a cluster of terracotta pots and then a low wall, grunting when he hit the path far down on the other side.

He raced down to the beach, all concerns about Isabella becoming too attached to Carly, his discomfort over Valentina's misguided approval of their relationship, his frustration over how keenly he wanted her physically, vanishing.

Nothing mattered.

Other than saving her.

He cursed when the beach house blocked his view of her. He ran past it, his heart tightening in panic.

He bolted down the jetty.

Carly, lying on her back, was motionless in the water.

He dived in beside her, surfaced and grabbed hold of her, pulling her towards the shore.

With a shriek Carly shouted, 'Max, what the hell are you doing? You've almost scared me to death.'

His ears ringing, he stopped and shook his head. Carly pushed his hands away from where he was holding her around her waist.

'You were drowning.'

Sparks flew from her eyes. 'No, I wasn't.'

'Why did you scream and then lie in the water motionless?'

'I screamed because it's freezing...' she flicked some water towards him, splashing him deliberately on the face '...and it's advised that you float when you hit cold water to allow your breathing to adjust. People often drown because they panic and inhale water while hyperventilating.'

'I thought...'

The anger in her eyes disappeared. 'Were you trying to rescue me?'

When he nodded yes she tilted her head, a smile of gratitude lighting up her face. And then she was laughing, and shaking her head, her gaze on his saturated tee shirt. 'You're soaked through.'

Beads of water threaded her long eyelashes, her cornflower eyes even more vivid with her hair sleeked back, the delicate lift of her cheekbones more pronounced. Her lips were plump and ruby red from the cold.

He cursed silently his lack of willpower. He breathed in time and time again, trying not to speak the words that eventually broke free of him. '*Vorrei darti un bacio*... I want to kiss you...again.'

Her eyes widened. It took a long while before she asked, 'Are you asking for my permission?'

Her voice was husky and filled with promises that made his head spin. He touched his thumb against her cheek, and then lightly over her lips. 'I can't promise—'

Her hand landed on his, stilling his progress. 'Don't. I know, I don't want to hear...' She trailed off and then her mouth was on his.

It was a lustful kiss. Hot and passionate. Her hands clasped his neck, deepening the kiss. He pulled her in closer, pressing her body against his. Her pebbled nipples pressed against his chest, her legs threaded in between his. He deepened the kiss, began to edge them both towards the shore, using his free arm to pull against the water.

Even in his testosterone-overloaded state he knew he had to get her to safety.

Her body was trembling and as soon as his feet reached the lake bottom, he lifted her into his arms, ignoring her protests as he carried her to the beach.

There he walked directly to the beach house, where he

grabbed a towel from the stack of them in the utility room and, wrapping her in it, laid her down on the sofa.

She jumped off the sofa the moment he took a step backwards.

A silence full of questions, uncertainty, desire stretched between them.

An angry sigh came from her mouth. 'I didn't need rescuing.'

He should leave, say he had work to do. He shouldn't be so drawn to Carly Knight. He had nothing to offer this woman who'd had her heart broken by another man and needed to learn to trust again. He knew all that but yet he heard himself say, forcing a lightness into his voice even though his heart was laden down with emotion, his body alive with a physical connection to her, and gesturing to his dripping clothes, 'You don't deserve it, but after we shower and change, I'm taking you for an ice cream.'

Carly wrinkled her nose. 'I have to go and buy a dress for tomorrow.'

'I'm taking you over to Mantovana. There's a good selection of boutiques you can visit there.'

Her gaze narrowed. 'I'm buying the dress myself, Max… There are going to be no arguments today.'

'Accepted.' He waited a pause. 'Now, can I suggest that we strip?'

Her eyebrows shot up. *Dio*, even though it was wrong of him, he loved seeing her riled, seeing her blush, seeing the flicker of anticipation in her eyes.

'Strip?'

He went into the utility and gathered up some more towels. He tossed one to her. 'Strip out of our wet things, of course. We can then go up to the villa to change. I'll strip in the bathroom—that is unless you need some help?'

She held the towel tight against herself. 'I'm sure I'll manage by myself.'

He laughed at her sarcastic tone.

He was about to go into the bathroom, when he stopped and said, 'By the way, I've transferred additional funds into your bank account to cover all of the extra expenses you've encountered this weekend.'

She dropped her towel, sighed. 'There was no need.'

He tried to keep his eyes averted from the heavy swell of her breasts beneath the black bikini top. But in the end he gave up and stared at them, desire pounding through his veins. Carly inhaled a shaky breath. 'Are we doing the right thing?'

Her voice was low, gravelly. The burn inside him for her upped another notch. He fisted his hands. No, they weren't doing the right thing, but he could contain this, not allow it all to go too far. He wanted to spend time with Carly. For once forget about all his responsibilities. 'Do you want to stop?'

She shook her head.

'Me neither,' he said.

Taking a lick of her ice cream, Carly threw her head back in pleasure as the intense but oh-so-smooth dark chocolate hit her palette. She closed her eyes to the vivid blue sky, her bones melting under the afternoon sun.

The heat, the ice cream, the lap of the water against the stone wall she and Max were sitting on, their legs trailing over the side, had her thinking of the childhood summers she had spent on the Kent coast with her parents.

'*È buono*…is it good?'

Carly eyed her double-scoop ice cream and shrugged. 'I'm not sure…you really can't beat a Mr Whippy.'

Max looked at her aghast. 'Mr Whippys are nothing but fluff.'

'They most certainly are not! They're creamy heaven on a wafer.'

Max laughed, throwing his eyes skywards. Lake Como suited him. He looked incredible in a suit, but the casual clothes of the lake suited him even better. She could imagine him taking long hikes into the hills, thriving in the outdoor lifestyle. 'Do you think you'll ever come back here, to Lake Como, permanently?'

Max lowered his pistachio single-scoop. 'Perhaps.' His gaze moved across the boats moored in the harbour, out across the simmering lake towards Villa Isa. 'I like London. The culture, the opportunities there.'

Carly squinted against the glare of the sun. 'I want to move to the coast. We spent all my childhood summers in Whitstable on the Kent coast. In a few years I want to move there…perhaps commute to London for work when necessary.'

'What type of house would you live in?'

Carly had imagined herself living in a Victorian red-brick house with tall ceilings and views of the sea from its bay windows. But now she knew differently. 'Your boathouse transported to Whitstable.' In response to Max's surprised look she added, 'It's perfect. Full of light and clever designs that means it has everything you need in a compact space—perfect for cleaning.'

Max laughed. 'You don't like cleaning?'

'Or any type of housework, I'd much prefer to be out surfing.'

'If you find a plot, I'll design it for you.'

Carly laughed, knowing this was all fantasy but enjoying allowing her imagination to run free. 'Have you surfed before?'

Max took a bite of his waffle cone and shook his head.

'You design a house for me and I'll teach you and Isabella how to surf. Does that sound like a fair exchange?'

She was teasing him, of course—a few surfing lessons

weren't exactly a fair barter for the designs from an award-winning architect.

Max pondered her proposal for a few moments as though seriously considering it. 'The boathouse has no bedrooms though…are you going for loft-style living?'

'You can add in a bedroom for me.'

Having finished his own ice cream, Max reached for hers and before she could protest he had taken it from her and was happily licking it. Carly went to grab it but he shifted away. His eyes twinkling in mischief, Max asked, 'Won't you want more bedrooms for a family?'

Carly made another lunge for her ice cream but Max held it away from her. 'If that happens I can extend. Now can I please have my ice cream back?'

Max took another bite, his eyes daring her to stop him. Only then did he pass the ice cream back to her with a satisfied grin. Carly's insides warmed at the light fun dancing between them and she had the crazy urge to kiss his lips, to taste the ice cream on his breath.

'Why not simply add the bedrooms when you're building? It would be more cost-effective and avoids future disruption'

'Because I might jinx it.' Seeing Max's confusion, she added, 'I've stopped hoping for things to happen for me relationship-wise. What will be, will be.'

'You don't believe in a proactive approach?'

'Hah…look where that got me with Robert.' She paused, and, not sure how Max would respond, mumbled, 'We met on an Internet dating site.'

When he didn't respond, she glanced in his direction. 'There are other people out there, you know,' he said softly.

Her stomach suddenly jittery, she handed her cone to Max, who took it and bit into it. 'Maybe.' She shook her head when Max handed her back the cone. 'You finish it.'

He ate it all up in four bites. Carly smiled at his enjoy-

ment. She was going to miss him. That thought slammed
into her. 'What about you? What are your dreams for yourself and Isabella?'

Max stood and tossed their paper napkins from the
gelateria into a nearby bin. 'For now, it's about getting
through each day.'

'What about dating, a new relationship?' Carly asked,
trying to keep her tone light as he sat back down beside her.

'Not for me.'

Her smile wavered at the certainty of his tone. 'Never?'

'Never.'

Carly wanted to tell him that that would be such a waste.
He would make some woman really happy. But she was
not going there. 'You must have other dreams though.'

He stood again and, picking up her shopping bags, gestured that they walk towards the launch that would bring
them back to his boat moored out on the lake. The village was winding down after a busy lunchtime, the locals
heading home for siesta. Beside her, Max seemed deep
in thought and oblivious to the appreciative looks of the
women they passed by. 'Do you think I should move here
with Isabella?'

Carly allowed her gaze to move over the ancient
terracotta-tiled houses of the village. She could imagine Max and Isabella here, the lake becoming their playground, Isabella exploring the countryside when older with
her friends. 'Having family support would be good. The
Ghiraldinis obviously would like you to move here.'

The launch was already out on the water so they waited
on the platform for it to return. Carly could tell Max was
trying to build himself up to say something by his restlessness. Eventually he said quietly, 'Leaving London would
feel like I'm leaving Marta behind.'

Would a man ever love her the way Max obviously had
loved Marta? 'She'll be with you wherever you go.'

He turned and touched her arm, a gentle smile on his lips. 'Has anyone ever told you just how incredible you are?'

Carly laughed. 'Yes, but usually they're drunk.'

Max eyeballed her. 'You *are* incredible.'

Carly playfully gave him a little push on his arm. 'Stop. You're making me blush now.'

'You deserve happiness. Someone who will treasure you.'

Carly gulped, her stomach doing cartwheels at the sincerity in his eyes. Some of the self-doubts that clung to her from Robert's rejection loosened their grip in the pit of her stomach. 'And you deserve that too, Max.'

'*Dio!* I don't have the energy,' Max said, running a hand tiredly through his hair.

'Valentina was right earlier—you do work too hard. You should have some fun in your life.'

Those misty green eyes, already shimmering in the brightness of the day, flashed with a hint of wickedness. 'Maybe I should take you up on your offer to teach me to surf.'

'You'd really enjoy it.'

'If you promise to wear a bikini like you did earlier then I'd definitely say yes.'

Warmth rippled through her body at the heat in his voice. She arched an eyebrow. 'Sorry, but I wear a wetsuit when surfing in England.'

He shrugged. 'In that case…' Pausing, he inched closer, his voice dipping low, 'Although I'd bet you look gorgeous in one.' His head dropped close to her ear. 'I do know how to have fun, Carly.'

Her breath caught at his near growl. She turned her head, answered back, 'Prove it so.'

His gaze darkened. 'Is that a dare?'

A slow sultry smile formed on her lips. 'Yip.'

Max waved to the launch owner, who was nearing the platform, and, turning with a devilish smile that sent shivers of excitement through her bones, said, 'You might live to regret that dare.'

CHAPTER EIGHT

ADRENALINE WAS STILL pumping through Carly as she helped Max tie up the boat to the jetty.

Job done, she high-fived him. '*That*, without doubt, was the best experience I've ever had in my life!'

Clearly entertained by her enthusiasm, Max smiled broadly before jumping back on board *Alighieri*, his bullet-shaped powerboat, with its long extravagant nose.

'What does *Alighieri* mean?'

Grabbing hold of the gold-embossed shopping bag containing the dress she had purchased over in Mantovana, Max answered, 'It's the surname of one of Italy's most famous poets, Dante Alighieri.'

'Did *you* name the boat?'

Lifting his mirrored sunglasses off, he eyed her indignantly. 'There's no need to sound so surprised. I do have a romantic side, you know.'

Carly gave a snort at that, which only doubled Max's look of indignation.

Back on the jetty Max shook his head when she gestured she'd carry the bag and then, reaching up his hand to rub against the corded muscle of his neck, he admitted ruefully, 'Admittedly, I'm a little out of practice romance wise…'

'Well, that makes two of us.'

He gave her one of those heart-melting smiles that spoke of understanding, before nodding back to *Alighieri*. 'You certainly don't scare easily.'

After Carly had taken a turn at driving the boat—and she was pretty proud about how well she had handled the boat given that it was her first time in a powerboat—pushing it hard through the calm waters of Como, Max had taken over, and showed her just what the boat was capable of. She had clung to the hand rail at the side of her seat as the boat had soared through the water, screaming with delight, much to Max's amusement.

Now they sauntered down the jetty towards his boathouse, neither of them seeming to want to end their afternoon yet. 'I have to admit to being a bit of an adrenaline junkie—the higher the roller coaster, the better for me. Anyway, I knew you were in control.'

Max laughed. 'Such trust.' But then drawing to a halt, he asked, 'Do you trust me, Carly?'

Carly's stomach flipped at the heat in his voice. 'That's a big question to answer. I'm… I'm…' She paused, struggling how to articulate the innate caution and scepticism that were still inside her. And then Max's words yesterday that she needed to trust herself echoed in her mind and with them came dawning realisation that it wasn't Max she didn't trust, but herself. She didn't trust herself not to fall for the wrong guy again. Which had nothing to do with Max, who was staring at her with an intensity that was threatening to set her aflame at any moment.

'Yes, I do trust you.' How could she not after he had been so candid over the past few days, telling her things, opening himself up to her in ways she knew were a first for him? In his care for Isabella, in how he was reaching out to the Ghiraldinis despite the hurts of the past.

Something shifted in the air between them. Max's fingers gently landed on her forearm. Sudden and unexpected desire bubbled through her veins. 'Will you join me for a drink in the boathouse?'

The chemistry shimmering between them gave his invitation a meaning beyond the words alone. In going with him she knew she was about to step into the unknown.

Of course, she should say no. But being an adrenaline junkie—albeit suppressed in recent years thanks to her experience with Robert—was pushing her to say yes. That, combined with the delicious intoxicating warmth from his fingers tantalisingly stroking her skin, from the dark promises in his eyes, had her nod yes.

Inside the boathouse, Max folded back the glass doors to the balcony before taking a bottle of prosecco from the fridge.

'I'm more used to having a cup of tea at four in the afternoon,' Carly said, amused when he passed her a glass of the bubbling liquid.

Max casually leant against the kitchen countertop. 'This weekend has been good for me...thanks again for coming with us.'

Carly tapped her shallow champagne glass against his and sipped the deliciously cool wine, the bubbles exploding in her mouth. Her heart was racing like crazy, her insides melting with a slow-burning heat. 'I'm glad I agreed to come.'

'I like you, Carly...'

She swallowed. Finished what he was trying to say. 'But you're not in the right place—I get it, Max. I'm not looking for anything from you.'

'I don't want to hurt you.'

'I'm a grown woman. I know what I'm getting into.'

'You've been hurt before. I don't want to add to that.'

Carly understood why he felt that way but she was tougher than he gave her credit for. 'And I'm equally concerned that you might get hurt, Max... I hope you don't think that I might be using you?'

'Using *me*?'

'As a way of easing myself back into the whole dating scene.'

Max threw his head back and laughed. 'That's the worst excuse for sex that I've ever heard.'

Carly blushed at the sensual way he said sex. Max edged closer to her, his hips mere inches from hers. She inhaled his scent, felt the warmth from his body. 'How about we sleep together because you find me irresistible and because you are everything I look for in a woman—intelligent, sexy, and adorable?'

'I wouldn't use the word irresistible…' Laughing at his knitted brow, she admitted, 'But there's something about your voice… It's pretty hot.'

He gave a nod of satisfaction. 'And you have the best legs ever.'

'I hit you with your most excellent eyes.'

Those misty green eyes twinkled like dew on a blade of grass before he said, 'And right back at you with your mouth—it should be made illegal…' his index finger lifted and for a brief second ran gently across her bottom lip '…your mouth is so sensual.'

Carly let out a shaky breath, hot desire swirling in her belly.

Max's hand landed on the cotton of her tee shirt, the warmth seeping down to her ribs. The age-old story of God creating Eve from Adam's rib sprang to her mind—man and woman were part of the same one. Was that all-powerful need inside her to find someone, to connect with them, to give her heart and soul to them, was that because she wouldn't feel whole until she did?

Of course, she wouldn't give her heart to Max. Her heart she would protect from this man who didn't want a relationship. She would feel fondness, affection, respect for him, but that was all. The road she was on with him was about seeking physical pleasure, and allowing herself some fun for the first time in years.

Her gaze shifted over his face. His features were like a

roadmap to his personality: the soft waves of his lips that at times could be as demanding as any churning sea, but at other times soft and gentle like waves lapping smoothly onto shore; his broad and prominent cheekbones telling of his strength to deal with what life had thrown at him; his long and chiselled nose, his pride, which saw him achieve so much in business but which cost him in seeking out the support he needed.

'You accused me of not being romantic earlier.'

A shiver ran the length of her at the heat in his eyes. 'I wouldn't say accused…'

Taking her hand in his, he whispered in a low growl, 'Let me show you just how romantic Italian men can be,' before leading her out of the boathouse and down the steps to the jetty.

Five minutes later she eyed the long length of the jetty dubiously…anything to distract her from the sight of Max standing next to her wearing nothing but his black form-fitting boxer shorts radiating testosterone and vitality. 'I thought you were going to show me how romantic you are.'

'You're the one who said you were an adrenaline junkie.'

'But the lake is freezing…jumping into it once today was enough.'

'But this time you'll be doing it with me…come on, it will be fun.' His smile fading, Max added, 'This week-end… I'm finally starting to feel alive again. I want to do something stupid, something irresponsible.'

Carly shook her head but she could not help smiling at him wildly. She knew what he meant, understood what it was like to live under a cloud of memories and broken dreams and mistrust. It was a cloud she was starting to burst through, thanks in part to the man she was standing next to, and she wanted to shatter that cloud even further with an act of defiance.

She pushed off her flip-flops and then her shorts. Pull-

ing her tee shirt over her head, she caught Max's glance
down over her body as he took in her white panties and
bra… Her sensible everyday underwear did not appear to
disappoint him given the flare of heat in his eyes.

Taking hold of her hand, he asked, 'Ready?'

Then they were racing down the jetty, their footsteps
echoing lightly against the wood. Carly giggled wildly,
revelling in the freedom of running hard and the kiss of
the sun on her skin.

Her adrenaline soared as the jetty ran out and the vast
expanse of the lake began. She considered slowing, backing out of this altogether, but Max's hand held hers even
tighter, giving her the encouragement to keep going.

They sailed through the air and Carly's heart sailed up
into her mouth.

Max's hand broke away from hers.

She hit the cool water, sank low into the darkness of
the lake. She inhaled some water. Panic rushed through
her body. Her legs flailed. Her arms reached out, searching, searching…after a few seconds she realised it was
Max she was searching for. She wanted him. Needed him.

And then he was there, taking her hand, wrapping his
arm tight about her waist.

They surfaced together.

Carly spluttered, gasping for some air. Her body was
anchored against his, his arm about her waist. She shoved
him in the chest. 'That was the worst idea ever. As for
being romantic, Max Lovato, you've a lot to learn.'

Max laughed. Carly tried to remain angry but his laughter was too infectious. They laughed together, their joined
bodies reverberating with the song of happiness and release coming from deep inside them both.

And when their laughter eventually died, Max gently
smoothed her dripping hair back from her face, and whispered, 'Maybe you'll consider this romantic.'

His mouth touched the tender skin by her ear before running a slow path down along her jawline. She arched her neck, groaned at the deliciousness of his warm lips on her skin. And then his mouth was on hers. She practically whimpered at the beautiful heat of his kiss, his initial gentleness intensifying to an all-consuming, electrifying kiss that had them clinging to one another, her legs threading around his.

But soon the cold of the water forced them apart to swim back into shore.

On the shore, he lifted her up into his arms and headed back to the boathouse. Carly considered saying she could walk but realised that she didn't want to—she was going to embrace this afternoon wholeheartedly, allow herself a few hours of insanity. She knew it wasn't going to lead anywhere, or happen again, so why not for once in a very long time be hedonistic and forget about all the rules?

In the boathouse Max brought her to the bathroom. Perching her onto the side of the bath, he asked, 'So how am I doing on being romantic?'

She gestured around her, grimaced. 'A bathroom…what can I say? Currently I'd give you four out of ten.'

He shook his head. 'I obviously need to up my game.' He went and switched on the shower. Then leading her in, he placed her under the heavy flow of warm water. She closed her eyes, goose bumps popping onto her skin despite the heat, when he began to wash her body with a lemon-scented wash. His hands ran over her arms, along her shoulders, down her back. She arched into him, unable to open her eyes because of the heavy drunken desire flowing through her. Her skin, so cold only a few minutes ago, was now flushed. Every cell of her body felt aroused, her mouth heavy and sensual against the flow of water pushing against it. Her hands reached out and blindly she ran her fingertips over the hard muscle of his chest, down over the taut skin of his abs.

Her legs were shaking and almost gave way when he twisted her around. His hand ran down her back, skimming over her bra, dipping and staying for a while just above her panty line. She arched her back once more. Max ran kisses along her neck.

And then he was washing her hair. The smell of coconut filled the walk-in shower. Carly placed her hands on the wall tiles for support. His hands slowly massaged her scalp. She groaned in pleasure.

'What would you rate me now?'

'Oh…oh, a very impressive seven.'

He rinsed the shampoo from her hair. He stepped closer, pulled her body to his. The hard plains of his body pushed into hers. His arm encircled her waist. 'I love how narrow your waist is…' His other hand landed on her hip bone. 'How your hips flair…everything about you is beautiful.'

She swallowed at the intensity of his voice.

She twisted around. 'My turn to wash you.'

He shook his head, washed himself quickly, his large hands sensually running over the taut muscles and sinew of his body.

Switching off the shower, he stepped out and wrapped a towel around his waist, before passing her one. 'I'll see you out in the living room.' His head dipped down so that his mouth was next to her ear. 'By the way, I'm not going to stop until you give me a ten out of ten.'

Carly drew back. 'I have very high standards.'

His mouth curled upwards devilishly, his eyes darkened. 'Prepare to have your standards blown right out of the water.'

Five minutes later, Max turned to the sound of Carly clearing her throat. Wrapped in a towel, her skin flushed, her eyes bright, she bit her lip. 'My clothes are still out on the jetty.'

He shifted away from the kitchen counter and watched a droplet of water run from her damp hair down along the creamy skin of her collarbone and disappear beneath the towel into the valley of her breasts.

Heat and desire and temptation swirled between them.

He rolled his neck back at the doubts silently but persistently sitting at the base of his skull, pushing them away.

'I promise to fetch them…but only when you give me a ten out of ten.'

She rolled her eyes. 'Don't tell me you're going to hold me hostage.'

He grinned. 'Don't be putting ideas in my head.' He was joking, of course…but the thought of holding Carly Knight captive was rather enticing.

Taking her by the hand, he led her down the steps to the sitting area of the boathouse. Popping open a fresh bottle of prosecco, he filled two glasses and passed one to Carly who was sitting propped against the thick pillows of the sofa, her legs curled up.

Kneeling down before her, he tipped his glass against hers. 'Here's to romance.'

Carly sipped her drink, and then holding up her glass, she eyed it critically. 'It's nice…but isn't the whole prosecco, champagne, whatever you like to call it, a little cliched when it comes to romance?'

Placing his glass down, he lowered his hands onto the sofa, leant in good and close to her and began to recite one of his favourite Dante Alighieri poems in Italian.

After the first line, Carly's skin had flushed even more.

With the second line, a heaviness had invaded her gaze.

By the third line she whispered, 'What…what does it all mean?'

He broke off from reciting the poem, touched his hand

against her bare leg and said, 'Listen to the sounds, the cadence, it will tell you all you need to know.'

By the tenth line she had slipped down against the pillows, and he had propped himself beside her, lying on his side, his hand running along the delicate skin of the inside of her arm.

When he finished the poem, she inhaled a deep breath. 'Tell me at least what the last line means...you said it so quietly.'

He hesitated for a moment, but then decided to translate it, his head dipping close to hers. Into her soft gaze he whispered, '"Tis such a new and gracious miracle."'

'Max.' She spoke with wistfulness, wonder, want.

His mouth sought hers out, the emotion burning inside him for her, playing out in a kiss that contained his soul.

Her body arched into his.

He twisted onto his back, rolling her with him until she lay on top of him.

Her hands captured his head pressed into the vast mountain of pillows behind them. Her fingers raked through his hair, while her mouth, now in control, explored his with unrestrained passion.

Her hips rolled against his, her breasts lifting and dipping, sending his pulse into dangerous territories.

He groaned when her legs shifted to either side of his, her kiss deepening even more. He broke away, breathed heavily, 'Before we go any further...are you sure this is what you want?'

She nodded her head, her eyes bright. 'Yes.'

Flipping them both over so that he was now on top, his pulse was drumming in his ears, his body was demanding that he stop talking but, touching his fingers against her cheek, he said, 'You've been hurt in the past, Carly. I don't want to add to that.'

Indignant resolve sparked in her eyes. 'That doesn't

mean that I'm going to be celibate for the rest of my life.' Her voice dropped to a bare whisper. 'What about you— why do you want this, Max?'

Looking down at Carly, her cheeks blushed, her eyes a mixture of passion and expectancy, he answered from his heart. 'Because I want some joy, some comfort… I want to give you those things too.'

Carly's answer to that was to wrap her arms around his neck and lower his mouth to hers.

Soon their towels had disappeared. He touched her breasts, kissed them, worshipped them, his hand trailing over her curves, his body thrilling to feel her tremble.

The breeze from the lake whispered over their naked flesh when they became one. They both grew silent, stared into one another's eyes, the far-off sound of bird-song reaching them as they blinked and considered each other with wonder.

CHAPTER NINE

TOMASO KISSED BIANCA, one hand cupping her neck, the other wrapping protectively around her waist. The wedding guests clapped and whooped. With a flourish, Tomaso leant Bianca backwards, her veil tumbling down across the ground like a light snowfall, deepening the kiss before swooping back up. With a raised fist Tomaso signalled his delight to the crowd, his wide proud smile springing unexpected tears into Carly's eyes.

She blinked. She was *not* going to cry.

Tomaso turned to Bianca, touched his fingers against her cheek. A look of raw emotion passed between bride and groom. Carly ducked her head and swiped at the tears spilling onto her cheeks.

She angled her body even further away from Max, who was sitting at her side. Her gaze wandered beyond the wedding couple and the garden to the frothy wisps of clouds hugging the mountain tops. Anything but dare look in Max's direction.

The wedding ceremony was taking place on the lawn below Villa Fiori. The air was filled with the scent of nearby lavender and pine. The late afternoon sun was gently bathing the wedding party, the beaded full skirt of Bianca's gown sparkling in its mellow rays.

Max's upper arm came to rest against Carly's.

She waited for him to shift away. When it remained there, the warmth of his tuxedo jacket against her bare arm startlingly intimate, she glanced in his direction.

His gaze was on Tomaso and Bianca, strain etched on his face.

She wanted to reach out to him, place her hand on his leg and ask if everything was okay. But with the Ghiraldini family seated directly in front of them, she couldn't dare to show any level of intimacy towards Max in their presence. Carly wasn't going to make what must be a difficult day even harder by intimating that there might be something between Max and herself.

She leant a hair's breadth closer, waited to see if he pulled away, if his initial touch was unintentional. His arm shifted against hers, applying a minuscule amount of extra pressure, but enough to communicate a silent connection.

The priest performing the marriage ceremony invited Tomaso and Bianca to kneel before him and he began a blessing for them and their marriage.

Carly swallowed. Her heart was heavy. Heavy with joy for Tomaso and Bianca's happiness and love for one another. Heavy with concern for Max—it must be so difficult for him to sit through this wedding, to be reminded of his and Marta's day.

In front of them, sitting on her own chair in between her grandparents, Isabella giggled at something Giulio whispered to her. Valentina shot him a warning look, a reminder that the priest was still saying his blessings, but then Valentina smiled ruefully when she saw the laughter in her husband's eyes. Giovanni, the best man today, shifted forward in his seat next to Giulio and made a silly face at Isabella, who giggled even more.

Carly blinked again, fresh tears stinging the backs of her eyes. It was so wonderful to see Isabella being embraced by the Ghiraldinis, to see the wealth of love in their family.

She adjusted the straps of her gown, shifted in her seat, and trailed her eyes along the pastel tea roses and peonies that had been threaded into the long rows of Italian cypress trees flanking the lawn. She tried to ignore the yearning inside her for a family of her own.

Last night, after Valentina had dropped Isabella home and they had settled her, Max and she had had dinner together. It had been a confusing evening of a thousand different emotions—they had managed to maintain a degree of their previous amiable chatter but every now and again the fire between them would spill out and they would touch one another before springing away. When it had come to saying goodnight to one another, Max had kissed her with a gentleness that had nearly broken her apart and asked if she would spend the night with him.

She had been so tempted. Her knees had practically buckled with the desire to experience making love with him again. Never had it been so intense, so physically mind-blowing. Unfortunately it had also scared her. After, when she had lain in his arms in the boathouse, his hand stroking her hair, a deep storm of unexpected and unwanted emotion had risen within her. She had vaulted off the day bed and disappeared outside, a towel wrapped around herself, to collect her clothes. She had dressed on the jetty, not willing to face the likely consequences of going back into the boathouse—even more hot but damaging sex. Sleeping with Max had made her vulnerable. She had so desperately wanted it to be nothing more than fun but instead it had cracked open her heart. She had to protect herself better. Which was why she had said no to his invitation to spend last night with him. And why today she was working really hard at keeping everything light between them.

Isabella turned in her chair. She eyed Max seriously and then, with an angelic smile, her tiny teeth showing, she waved at him. Max waved back. Isabella's gaze then shifted to her. Carly waved at her. Isabella's smile died.

Carly inhaled a shaky breath. She tried not to take it

personally but her heart was on the floor. Isabella turned away and shuffled off her seat. Valentina fumbled to catch hold of her, casting a nervous glance towards the altar, but Isabella moved out of her reach, dropped to her knees and crawled under her chair. Popping up in front of Carly, the skirt of her pale pink flower-girl dress streaked with a knee-shaped grass stain, her headpiece of tiny rosebuds askew, she lifted her arms up, and gave Carly a heart-piercing smile.

Settling Isabella onto her lap, Carly buried her head for a moment into her curls. Her senses swam at her floral scent, at the weight of her body. Heat flooded her cheeks and those damn tears threatened again. But then, gathering herself, she drew back, rubbed the grass stain and adjusted Isabella's head piece. Only then did she look up to see Giulio and Valentina staring back at her. She exhaled in relief when they smiled and nodded as though they accepted and welcomed Isabella's fondness for her. But her relief was short-lived when she saw the deep disquiet marring Max's face.

Max clinked his shot glass against Giovanni's and then Tomaso's. *'Mille congratulazioni.'*

Tomaso nodded his acceptance of Max's congratulations and then all three of them swigged back their shot of ouzo.

Max coughed, while Tomaso gulped for air, before hitting his brother lightly on the arm with a closed fist. 'You are learning some bad habits in Athens, Giovanni,' Tomaso admonished his brother.

Giovanni's eyes flashed. 'You have a long night ahead of you. A little ouzo will give you energy.'

Max stepped away from the easy banter between the brothers, still thrown that they had insisted he join them in their private celebration of the wedding under the boughs of the huge eucalyptus tree that sat in the gardens over-looking the dance floor in front of the villa's courtyard. 'It's close to Isabella's bedtime. I should take her home,' Max said, shifting further away.

Giovanni held up the ouzo bottle in his hand. 'Have another drink with us.'

Before he could argue Giovanni poured another shot into the glasses. Tomaso raised his in toast. 'Here's to family.'

Max clinked his glass against theirs. Shook his head when Tomaso nearly choked on his drink again. He left his drink untouched.

His coughing fit over, Tomaso said, 'It's good to see you back in Villa Fiori, Max.' Tomaso cleared his throat, rolled his shoulders. 'We weren't sure if you would come.'

Max frowned. 'Isabella and I were always coming to your wedding. There was never any doubt about that.'

Tomaso and Giovanni looked unconvinced.

Then Giovanni's gaze shifted towards the dance floor. Couples were dancing beneath the gold chandeliers, streamers and globes of fresh flowers the florists had hung from invisible wires over the courtyard. And in the mid-dle of the dance floor, her head thrown back in laughter as she swung a giggling Isabella around and around, was Carly, one hand bunching up the length of her rose-pink gown to avoid tripping over it.

Her dress was perfect—its delicate colour highlighted the creamy perfection of her skin, the cut showcasing all her curves, her toned arms, the delicate strength of her col-larbone, her hair twisted into a tight bun. Max considered his shot glass, wondering if the ouzo would somehow douse the heat burning inside him. In their lovemaking Carly had been sensual and fearless. She'd given but also had taken what she needed from him. It had been hot and fiery love-making that had left him wanting more. Much more.

But Carly obviously thought differently.

He tossed the ouzo onto the ground. *Accidenti!* Her rejection last night stung like hell. And her cool indifference today wasn't much better. It was as if yesterday afternoon hadn't happened. At times today he wondered if he had actually dreamt it. Dreamt of that passion, that connection of skin against skin, gaze upon gaze. It wasn't as though she was avoiding him—the opposite, in fact, she had stuck by his side all day. Before the ceremony she had teasingly given him the thumbs up in approval of his tuxedo; smiled banally when he complimented her on her dress. It had only been during the wedding ceremony that he saw her drop her guard. He had seen her tears. That brief connection of arm against arm had exploded a whole pile of emotion in his heart. He had realised just how much he wanted her company, wanted her attention and awareness, how he wanted to be there for her.

Could they be friends?

On the dance floor Carly slowed her spinning.

Her hands wrapping around Carly's neck, Isabella planted a huge wet kiss on Carly's cheek. Max closed his eyes. He was allowing Isabella to grow too close to Carly.

'Carly *è stupendo*. Is there something between you—?'

Before Giovanni could say any more, Max interrupted, 'No, there isn't.'

Giovanni flashed him a smile and, walking away from them, did a little quickstep dance move and twirl on the lawn before calling back, 'I'm suddenly in the mood for dancing.'

Tomaso laughed. 'I reckon you might need to rescue Carly in a little while—the last thing you need is for your nanny to have a broken heart.'

Max was about to point out that Carly wasn't a nanny, but Tomaso waved in response to Bianca's beckoning to him from the dance floor—Giovanni having pointed her to where they were hiding out—and said with a chuckle, 'It looks like I can't avoid dancing any longer.'

Giovanni paid all his attention to Isabella at first, twirling her around, but then he edged in closer to Carly, his hip bumping against hers. Giovanni could dance. And he had a cheeky charm that women seemed to find irresistible.

Max squared his shoulders, stalked across the lawn and onto the dance floor. Isabella squealed in delight when she saw him. Max picked her up, tickled her on the belly. And held out his hand to Carly. He twirled her under his arm, moved her away from Giovanni.

Giovanni began to weave over, his hips gyrating much too suggestively. Max considered standing in Giovanni's way, perhaps stepping on his toes, but the arrival of Valentina and Giulio into their dancing group diverted all their attention.

Valentina shuffled her shoulders, her feet making small movements on the dance floor. Giulio grimaced and swayed his hips a fraction. A clearly bemused Tomaso and Bianca joined their ever-increasing circle. Giovanni clapped his hands in delight and then, grabbing his father's hand, pulled him into the centre of the group. Giulio attempted to copy Giovanni's moves, wriggling down towards the floor, his body loosening up with the beat of the music. Max laughed, taken aback but tickled by this more playful side of Giulio. In his arms Isabella chortled. Giulio smiled fondly at her delight and then gestured to Max for them to come and join him and Giovanni. Max shook his head. Giulio wiggled his way over to him. He held out his hand, gesturing with a nod to the centre of the group. Max hesitated. Giulio stopped dancing. Without looking, Max knew that everyone was waiting to see what was about to happen. The proud appeal in Giulio's eyes caught him right in the chest.

Max, shaking his head in disbelief, stepped forward.

A cheer went up from the rest of the family.

Isabella chuckled when he began to dance. Valentina after a while came and took Isabella from him. No doubt she was worried that she might get injured in the dance off that had sprouted up between him and Giovanni. Max tugged off his suit jacket, threw it in Carly's direction. She threw her head back in laughter when she caught it. And Max, already dizzy from his spinning and cavorting, swayed on his feet at how his heart splintered to see her infectious joy.

The wedding was still in full swing when it was time for them to take Isabella home. Kneeling down in the driveway, Carly removed Isabella's headpiece as Max said his goodbyes to Tomaso and Bianca, who had walked out with them. Giovanni then joined them and, smiling down at her, said, 'I never got to dance with you, Carly.' Raising an eyebrow in Max's direction, he added, 'I know when I'm beaten by a better man.'

Pulling an exhausted Isabella up into her arms, confused by what Giovanni meant, Carly was about to ask him, but Giulio and Valentina arriving to say goodbye stopped her. With tears in her eyes, Valentina leant in and hugged Isabella. Then Giulio joined in, his arm, like Valentina's, wrapping around Carly. Though she was thrown to be part of this unexpected group hug, Carly's heart danced with pleasure. Eventually Giulio pulled back and then eased a reluctant Valentina away, his arms wrapping around her shoulders protectively. His gaze shifted from Isabella to Carly. Quietly he said, 'Isabella is fond of you. It would be nice to see you again with Max and Isabella.'

Carly nodded, knowing she was blushing especially given the surprised expression of all the others who had heard Giulio. Her gaze moved over to Max. His expression was bewildered but then, with a quick nod, he led her and Isabella away to their awaiting car.

'Now, that's a wicked laugh if ever I heard one.'

An hour later Carly gasped and sat back in her chair, clasping a hand to her breastbone. 'Crikey, Max, don't creep up on me like that.'

Especially wearing a tuxedo, the bow tie undone, looking ever so sexily ruffled after a long day.

Placing the baby monitor on the terrace's coffee table, Max dropped down beside her. Carly edged into her side of the sofa. Max, a silent moonlit night, the bittersweet euphoria of having spent the day at a spectacular wedding filled with love and joy…they all spelt danger.

Max gestured to her phone. 'So what's so amusing?'

Carly swiped her phone screen before holding it out to Max. In the picture on her screen, Max and Giovanni were attempting to outdo themselves in a move that was akin to a Cossack dance.

Max groaned.

Carly flicked through some others photos. 'There are other photos I want to show you…'

'No, thanks.'

'These are gorgeous, honestly.' Carly frowned as she scrolled through the endless photos, wondering just how many photos she had managed to take today. 'Did you enjoy the day?'

Max ran his hand along his jawline as he considered her question. She squirmed in her seat to hear his skin pull against his bristle, imagining what it would feel like to have it pressed against her own skin…on her belly, on her breasts, between her legs.

Max's mouth tightened. Heat blasted in her chest. Had he guessed what she was thinking?

'Giovanni is interested in you…but I would advise you to stay clear of him.'

Carly dropped her phone. Stared at him. For a moment she felt a flash of vain pleasure—Giovanni was a good-looking guy after all, funny and a fantastic uncle to Isabella. But that soon dissipated to annoyance. Did Max actually think she would sleep with him one day and consider dating his brother-in-law the next? Anger bubbled in her stomach.

'I don't know, he's handsome, rich and available, there's a lot to be said for all three things,' she said in a breezy tone when in truth she wanted to fling her phone at him.

Max frowned but then a slow shrewd smile formed on his lips. 'I thought you said money doesn't matter to you.'

'It doesn't.' She threw her hands up into the air. 'For crying out loud, Max…we slept together yesterday.' She paused, trying to contain her anger. 'Do you actually think it meant so little to me that I would date *your* brother-in-law?'

Unperturbed by her anger, Max shifted forward in his seat. Placing a hand on the sofa between them, he leant in, those green eyes searching hers. 'What did it mean to you?'

Goosebumps jumped to attention along her body, domino style—up her arms, chasing around her neck, then down her spine. Did he really have to speak so low…as low and tenderly as he had whispered her name yesterday when his back had arched and his body at a precipice had stilled?

She tried to dredge up the laid-back front she had worked so hard to maintain all day, but it was nowhere to be found. She was too exhausted, she was too damned aware of Max, to keep up the pretence. 'It was very special.'

He nodded to her whisper, placed his hand lightly on her knee. Her heart sank in fear while her body did a hula-hula dance. She picked up her phone, needing a diversion before things got out of control. And given the sparks of desire flashing between them, one wrong move could prove fatal. She was *not* going to sleep with Max again. No way.

'Here! I found it! The photo I wanted to show you.'

Max reluctantly took the phone from her, his calculating gaze studying her first. He looked at the photo. Didn't say anything. Thrown, Carly asked, 'Isn't it the most adorable photo ever?'

Max stared at the photo, his throat closing over. He gripped the phone tighter, something twanging in his heart. Unbeknownst to him, Carly had taken a photo of him and Isabella when he had been talking to Valentina's sister and her family. His back was to the camera, his focus on the family, but Isabella, who was in full view of Carly, was staring up at him with love and adoration in her eyes.

He blinked, dazed by the rush of love for his daughter pounding through him.

He nodded blankly when Carly asked, 'Are you okay?'

Heat beat through his body. He yanked off his already open bow tie, which Isabella had undone when he had read her book to her earlier. He had pretended not to notice and when he had acted all confused when he pretended to spot it, Isabella had giggled in delight.

'She adores you.'

Max nodded. He bit the inside of his cheek, knowing it was crazy that he was struggling so much to talk, but what he was about to say came from the very depths of him, words that he had said before but without the intensity of emotion now coursing through him. 'I…and I love her.' He looked up and into Carly's cornflower gaze and heard himself say things he'd never thought he'd dare say to anyone. 'When Marta died… I was afraid to love Isabella.' He ran a hand through his hair. 'Losing Marta tore me apart. To lose Isabella would be incomprehensible.' He stopped, pain and shame sweeping over him.

'You wanted to protect yourself against further pain… that's understandable.'

'But not excusable. *Dio*, she was a three-month-old baby—what was I thinking?'

'You were in shock, in pain. You're not a robot, Max, you're human. These feelings happen.'

'I thought it would be best if she was independent, not reliant on me…in case anything ever happened to me.'

With a sigh Carly shifted in her seat. She laid her hand on top of his. 'You're a good dad, Max. Isabella has always been well cared for.'

The disquiet churning inside him stilled at her touch, at the sincerity of her tone. 'Will you send me a copy of this photo?'

'Of course.' She picked up her phone, swiped to some other photos. 'I'll make sure to send you the ones of you dancing too.'

He groaned. 'Those you can delete.'

Carly chuckled. 'No way! A hot Italian guy dancing… I can't wait to show them to my friends.'

He lunged for the phone. Carly shifted it out of his grasp, holding it high above her head. He leant into her. She fell against the back of the couch. He followed. His body was on hers, his mouth hovering over hers. 'Give me the phone, Carly.'

Her eyes twinkled, daring him. 'And what exactly are you going to do if I don't?'

He bit back the urge to growl. 'I'm going to kiss you and a whole lot more.'

Carly's eyes darkened. She breathed out a faint gasp. 'In that case I guess I won't be giving you the phone.'

Later that night, lying in Max's bed, her fingertips digging into his shoulders, her body taut with desire, Carly stared into Max's eyes, her heart splitting open at the desire, at the tenderness there, and in that moment, as his body arched and hers bowed up to meet him, she gave up all pretence of toughness and cynicism, all pretence that she was capable of protecting her heart against this incredible man.

She was in love with him.

CHAPTER TEN

THE FOLLOWING MORNING, Carly sank her nose into Isabella's cotton candy-striped pyjamas, inhaling lavender with an undertone of mashed bananas. Carly called out to Isabella, who had tucked Sunny into her bed and was attempting to read him *Sleepy Heads in Sleep World* even though she was holding the book upside down. 'Sweetheart, you have to learn to eat your bananas properly.'

In response, Isabella gave her a beam of a smile.

Carly ignored the painful tug on her heart and focused on packing Isabella's suitcase.

The job almost complete, the sound of familiar footsteps out in the corridor had her grabbing hold of the final few items from around the room and packing like a ninja suitcase packer. The sooner they got back to London, the better.

'I was wondering where the two of you had got to.'

Carly forced herself to smile breezily, to contort her face into what she hoped was a chilled-out expression. 'Isabella and I were playing with her toys.' She paused and gestured to all the toys strewn around the room. 'We got a little carried away in a name-and-find-it game. I'll tidy up once I have her case packed.'

She went and scooped up a bunch of Isabella's tiny socks from the top drawer of her wardrobe.

'You don't have to pack Isabella's suitcase,' Max said, coming closer.

She tried not to wince, wishing he would keep his distance from her. 'Luciana said that you had some urgent business to attend to. Why don't you go back to that?'

Max stilled. Carly grabbed Isabella's hairbrush and hairclips from her dressing table and packed them into the vanity bag that came with her suitcase.

'What's going on, Carly?'

Carly considered Max for a moment, seriously tempted to tell him that she was hacked off because she had woken this morning in *his* bed only to find that he had long vacated it, given how cool the sheets were on his side of the bed. She was hacked off she had slept with him last night. She was hacked off because she dreaded saying goodbye to Isabella. She was hacked off because last night, as Giulio and Valentina had hugged her and Isabella goodbye she had realised that she didn't want to say goodbye for ever to the Ghiraldini family. She was hacked off because last night, when Max had laid her down on his bed and with infinite care and tenderness brought her to climax time and time again, every defence in her had melted away. She was in love with him. So yes, she was majorly hacked off...and embarrassed.

But she wasn't going to let Max know any of that. Instead she said, 'I hate the thought of going back to work tomorrow. I have a meeting with my accountant. That's never fun.'

Max eyed her dubiously.

Carly kept his gaze, trying to remember everything she was hacked off about, but with his nearness, the inhaling of his freshly showered scent, she felt her anger, her defensiveness crumble so she pirouetted around and went and flung open Isabella's bedroom window, desperate for some fresh air.

'I've rearranged some meetings that I was due to attend later today in London. We can delay our flight until this evening. Let's take the boat out again, go for lunch in Argegno,' Max said.

Carly flipped the lid of the suitcase over and, zipping it

shut, dropped it down to the floor. 'I said I would meet a friend this afternoon.' Which was kind of the truth—she had told Agata, a friend from her college days, she would meet up with her some day this week. Given Max's suspicious look, he obviously wasn't buying it. But there was no way she was staying here a moment longer than she needed to.

She was holding onto her sanity with the thinnest of threads. She needed to get back to London, have some space and time to try to process just how much she had fallen in love with Max and Isabella.

And the worst part of it all was that in seeing Tomaso and Bianca's love for one another yesterday, the way the Ghiraldini family had each other's backs, she knew now more than ever that she wanted a family, love, a marriage of her own.

And what had she done? Only gone and fallen in love with a man who wanted none of that.

'Cancel your meeting with your friend.'

Carly startled at the soft plea in Max's words. He looked as though he really wanted to spend the day with her. Images of the three of them out on the lake, eating a lazy lunch in a waterside restaurant, had her wavering. But no. She *was* going to stay strong.

She shrugged, said, 'I don't want to,' before dropping to her knees to pick up the army of soft toys Isabella had scattered around the room.

She ignored Max when he said Luciana would take care of the tidying.

About to crawl behind the toy kitchen to rescue a dejected-looking toy pig, she came to a halt when Max's feet stepped in to block her way.

Sorely tempted to push him out of the way, she had enough sense to know that she would have little hope of budging him. This was the man who had effortlessly pinned her to the bed with his legs last night as his mouth wreaked havoc on her never-before-so-sensitive breasts. The pain had been delicious.

Now, she rocked back onto her haunches and glared up at him.

He didn't move an inch.

'I'd like to see you again in London.'

For a moment elation steamed through her. She was going to see him again! But then cold reality slammed into her. She nodded, smoothed her hands over her blue trousers. 'In a professional capacity, I assume.'

Glaring up at him, her cheeks flushed, a toy silver tiara on her head, Carly looked like an angry princess from one of Isabella's story books.

Max couldn't decide whether to crouch down and pull her into his arms or to back right off. This conversation wasn't going the way he had anticipated. This morning when he had woken at his usual time of five, for the first time in years he hadn't felt the need to jump right out of bed in a bid to ignore the loneliness that had been slowly eating him away.

Instead he had wanted to stay with Carly's body pushed against his. To make love with her again. But it was that thought, that…inevitability that had seen him reluctantly climb out of the bed and dive into the pool.

Last night, their lovemaking had been hot and wild at first, a crazy, lustful, head-spinning, time-stopping exploration of each other's bodies. But when he had carried her to his bedroom, Carly's giggles had faded, and when he had laid her down on his bed, everything had shifted between them. He had seen in her eyes the same tenderness, vulnerability, uncertainty grabbing his heart. They both knew that making love in the intimacy of his bedroom would change things. It would shift their relationship up a gear.

He had offered to take her back to her bedroom but she had said no, said that she wanted to spend the night with him.

Their lovemaking had been slow, tentative, achingly delicate…as though it had been the first time for them both.

He had made love to Carly with his heart jammed with emotion, his skin tingling with the connection, the consuming need burning between them.

When he had ploughed through the pool earlier this morning he had had to stop and pull himself out of the water, disorientated, breathless at just how close he felt to her, at the speed of what was happening between them. He needed to slow everything down, to back off from making love together for a while. Instead he wanted to get to know Carly fully without the emotional minefield of sex.

He knew it would be torture to see her and not act on the chemistry that detonated between them whenever they were in the same room. But they had both been hurt in the past, they needed to take things more slowly. He wanted to show Carly just how much he wanted her in his life but he didn't want to scare her away. So he had cleared his appointments for later today, intent on spending time with her. But Carly obviously had other ideas.

He backed up two steps, creating enough distance to ensure he couldn't touch her, and crouched down.

He picked up a purple plastic mirror and tossed it into the apple-green toy box Carly had been dragging behind her in her clean-up, trying not to let his nervousness and doubts show. 'I want to see you outside work—maybe we could go on a date?'

Carly sat back on her heels. 'Why?'

Taken aback by the coolness of her tone, the defensiveness in her eyes, Max wondered if he had read this all wrong. He certainly was out of practice with everything to do with dating. Panic rolled like waves in his stomach. He stood and went to the bedroom windows and breathed in some fresh air. From the lake he could hear a father on an outboard calling out instructions to the child who was alongside him sailing a dinghy and failing to catch the wind.

He turned, trying to ignore his male pride, trying to ignore the fear, the dread, the apprehension of inviting someone into his life. 'I enjoy your company. You're fun…even if your jokes aren't great.'

Given Carly's unimpressed scowl, he reckoned his attempt at humour had died.

Building bricks and trains and dolls were all gathered up and thrown into the toy box, which was then tidied away beside the bedroom's bookcase, before Carly stood and regarded him with her hands on her hips. 'So we'll meet as friends?'

'Yes.'

Her eyes narrowed, her lips pursed. 'I've enough friends, Max.'

He flinched at the coldness of her voice. He studied her for a moment, trying to figure out how to make all of this okay. 'We can be friends at first…then we can see how things work out.'

'What do you mean?'

'Let's date for a while, see how we get on. I want you in our life.'

Her nose flared and she tossed her head back. 'Why?'

Her tone was blunt, hacked off. He rolled his neck against the stiffness there. 'We're good together.'

Carly folded her arms, clearly unimpressed. He stumbled on. 'Maybe things can become more permanent between us after a while…it's too early to say if they will, of course. There's no point in rushing things, is there?'

Glancing back at Isabella, who was busy baking and cooking at the toy kitchen, Sunny sitting in the tiny sink, watching the proceedings, Carly stepped closer to him and whispered, 'Permanent?'

He hesitated for a moment… *Dio!* Why was she looking for so many answers? This was all getting out of control. He fought the urge to walk away, a primal fear gripping his heart, a fear of loving again and losing that person. But the need to keep Carly in their lives had him say, 'Maybe you'll move in with us.'

Carly shook her head. 'Look, Max, it was a good weekend. Let's not overcomplicate this.'

'Isabella will miss you.' Carly's furious expression had him rush on, gesturing to the villa, to the lake outside. 'I can give you a good life—we'll travel, come here to Lake Como.'

Carly stepped even closer, her blue eyes sparking. 'I don't want your money, your lifestyle. My job is in London. I don't have the time to be travelling or coming here with you.'

Thrown by her outright rejection, Max asked, 'So is this it? You don't want to meet me again?'

Carly bit her lip. 'Outside of you being my client, no. It's for the best.'

Max inhaled a breath before pointing towards the door. 'You go and pack. I'll finish up here.'

'I'm almost done and I've promised Isabella that I'll take her out to the swings once we're packed.'

Max went and picked up Isabella. If Carly did not want to be part of their lives, then he wasn't going to beg her…or prolong this goodbye. Anger, disbelief, hurt pride welled up inside him with a crushing intensity. 'I'll take care of Isabella. Go and pack. We'll leave for the airport immediately.'

* * *

Max's car passed a signpost for Regent's Park and London Zoo. For a moment Carly was about to turn around to Isabella and ask if she'd like to go there, to visit a real-life Sunny in the elephant enclosure. When she'd been writing *Sleepy Heads in Sleep World* she had often visited the zoo to observe the animals for inspiration. But she caught herself in time, the sensation of Max's gaze on her having her sitting ramrod straight in the passenger seat next to Max's driver, Thomas.

At the airport, she had been about to sit in the rear seat next to Isabella but Max had asked her to sit in the front seat instead. He had asked her in the same detached tone he had been using all day since their conversation in Isabella's bedroom. If you could call it a conversation. It had been more like a dance between two different viewpoints of reality—hers that their relationship had to end, Max's that they could just amble on, see where life would take them. Didn't he anticipate at all the hurt, the pain that would come as a result of his *laissez-faire* approach?

He was shielding Isabella from her. On the plane back to London, he had taken Isabella into the bedroom, saying he would try to get her to nap. But Carly had heard their voices and laughter. She had felt physically sick with the feeling of being excluded, an outsider once again. She had spent the journey alone, trying to focus on the sleeping plan for Isabella she had typed on her laptop and printed out using the plane's on-board printer.

Max had taken it from her when he and Isabella had come out for the landing, silently nodding when she had talked him through the key aspects of the plan. He'd been courteous, attentive but completely detached from her.

She squeezed the soft leather of the car seat, cursing the early afternoon traffic they were now snarled up in. She wanted to get home to her apartment. Sitting here, having

Max sitting behind her, hearing him and Isabella quietly chat to one another, was torture. She needed air, space to think. She needed to cry. Which annoyed her beyond belief. She had got herself into this mess. Once again, she had got a relationship all wrong—falling for Max was nothing but a rerun of her relationship with Robert.

She should have seen the signs with Robert, how he would never speak about his ex, but when her name was mentioned Carly saw the memories, the wistfulness in his eyes that took him away from her. It had been strange, an odd sensation, to be next to someone and know that in those moments, emotionally, they were with someone else.

Max was still in love with Marta. Why then did he want to see her again, even talk about things possibly becoming more permanent?

There were only two obvious conclusions. Because they were so good together in bed, or he was looking for a mother substitute for Isabella.

The car edged its way through the traffic lights close to Baker Street underground station.

When the car eventually pulled up outside her apartment block, Max told Thomas to remain in the car as he would see to Carly's luggage himself.

Carly ignored Max's look of displeasure when she stopped by Isabella's door and, opening it, leant in and gave her a cuddle. She wanted to say that she'd see her soon, she wanted to say that she loved her but instead she dragged in some air, inhaling her baby sweetness and playfully tickling Isabella on the belly, smiled brightly and said, 'Make sure to put Sunny to sleep early tonight. He'll be tired after his long trip on the aeroplane today.'

Isabella hugged Sunny closer to her. Nodded seriously. But as Carly pulled away her bottom lip dropped.

Emotion strangling her throat, Carly walked around the car to join Max at the top of the steps to her apartment.

She searched her bags for her keys, trying not to show how her hands were trembling. 'Call Nina during the week to arrange a follow-up appointment. If you have any questions in the meantime, feel free to call me.'

Max nodded, his jaw tight.

Carly wanted him to just go. To not prolong this goodbye. She found her keys and, lifting them up, attempted a smile. 'Found them. I can see myself in from here.'

'I'll carry your luggage in for you.'

No! The thought of Max coming into her apartment was too much. That was to be her sanctuary. She didn't want to have memories of him standing inside there saying goodbye every time she left or came home. She shook her head, 'I can take care of the luggage. You go. Isabella needs you.'

'How can I make this right?'

Her heart dropped, fresh tears flooding her eyes at his softly spoken question. She inhaled a shaky breath to see the confusion clouding his eyes. 'That first day outside my office, you stopped and looked like you were saying something...to someone.'

Wincing, Max dropped his head and then softly said, 'Marta.'

Max went to say something else but a cry from Isabella rang through the air. 'Car...ee. Car...ee.'

Carly stared towards the rear door that Max had left open when he had climbed out of the car. Isabella was calling her name. She wanted to run to her. Pick her up and hold her for ever. Emotion clumped in her throat.

She grabbed hold of her suitcase even though she was not sure her legs would carry her anywhere, took a weak step backwards. 'Go. Isabella needs you.'

CHAPTER ELEVEN

'WHO ARE YOU?'

Carly crouched down at the doorstep of the small terraced house to the little boy whose gaze was as curious as his question. 'I'm Carly and you must be Jacob.'

Jacob's amber eyes narrowed. 'Are you here to see my sister?' He shook his head before Carly could answer and said in an unimpressed tone, 'She's asleep. We have to be very quiet.' He paused to stare unhappily up at his mother, who had answered the door with him, and then in a poor attempt at a whisper added, 'Mummy says so.'

Carly swallowed down a smile at Jacob's disgruntled tone. 'I'm here to chat with your mum but I promise to be quiet. I'd like to chat with you too.'

Jacob's eyes brightened. 'Will you come and play with me?'

Carly clapped her hands softly and said, 'I'd love to.' Standing up, she said her hellos to Jacob's mum, Marsha, who had called her earlier in the week. Jacob, who was three, had in recent weeks being waking during the nights complaining of a monster in his bedroom wardrobe. Carly guessed that the arrival of his baby sister, Naomi, might have something to do with his waking.

An hour later, Carly stood on the doorstep saying her goodbyes. After playing with Jacob, which had involved her dressing up as a fire chief and pretending to drive the fire truck while wedged into his climbing frame in the garden, Carly had talked through a plan of action with Marsha, which included her spending some one-to-one time with Jacob, and for her to encourage visitors to spend time with him as well, thereby showing that he was just as important as ever in the household and not being displaced by his baby sister.

Crouching down, she high-fived Jacob. 'See you later, alligator.'

Jacob giggled and rushed in for a quick hug, almost sending Carly toppling backwards.

Carly and Marsha shared a smile and when Carly stood, Marsha, who was holding Naomi in her arms, let out a sigh. 'It was good to talk things through.' She paused and rolled her eyes. 'I was starting to stress myself out, which of course wasn't helping the situation, but now I feel more in control.'

Carly gave Marsha a quick hug and was about to leave when Jacob called up to her, 'You can cuddle Naomi too.'

Carly smiled down at Jacob. 'That's okay. I got so many cuddles from you today I think I'm full.'

Jacob giggled at how Carly patted her tummy but then shook his head seriously. 'No. You must…she's nice.'

Marsha's eyes shone with light tears. Taking Naomi into her arms, Carly crouched back down next to Jacob. 'When she's older, Naomi will be able to play with you.'

'Will she like my sandpit? I've a blue bucket she can use.'

'I bet she'll love your sandpit.'

'She can't have my special spade though.' Jacob leaned into her and whispered, 'That spade is magic—a pirate gave it to my daddy.'

'Wow!'

Jacob gave a nod, satisfied at Carly's amazement.

Standing, Carly gazed for a moment down at Naomi, her heart splitting open at her perfection.

Much too reluctantly she handed her back to Marsha and said, 'I'll call you next week to check how things are with you all. Have a nice weekend.'

As the door closed behind her Carly winced. It was Friday evening. The weekend stretched out in front of her. Friends had invited her out for drinks tonight but she had made up an excuse that she had paperwork to catch up on. Work she could handle right now, social conversation she couldn't.

She had waited all week to hear from Max. At the start of the week a knot of dread had sat in her stomach at the prospect of him calling or Nina telling her that he had made an appointment to see her. But as the week had dragged on the knot had disappeared to be replaced with a restlessness that willed him to call. She wanted to know how Isabella was doing. If she was sleeping okay. Had she learned new words? Was she still refusing to eat her yogurts? Was she still insistent on having *Sleepy Heads in Sleep World* read to her every night? Had she recovered from the light head cold she had developed in Lake Como?

She missed Isabella with her heart.

She missed Max with all her soul.

She missed his physical presence, his touch, how his eyes followed her as she moved around a room. She missed the passion, the disbelief in his eyes when they made love. She missed his wry sense of humour, his intelligence, his kindness. She missed seeing him hold Isabella. She missed seeing him blossom in expressing his love for his daughter that he had supressed for so long, believing he was doing right by her in making her independent and strong.

She missed the feeling of belonging, of family that had been there when they had breakfast together each morning, when they drove in the car. She missed his life-affirming kisses that infused her with hope and anticipation.

She walked past Hampstead underground station, deciding to walk home instead. She guessed the walk would take over ninety minutes, but it was preferable to facing the quietness of her apartment. She might stop off for a coffee on the way. Or browse some bookstores.

Her fingers itched with the urge to pull out her phone. To check if there were any missed calls. Maybe even call him.

She walked even faster. Past pavement-side cafés with laughing couples, couples holding hands, couples chatting seriously. Past fathers holding hands with their toddlers. Past mothers pushing strollers. Forcing herself to become breathless.

She was not going to rerun her relationship with Robert again.

She was not going to become involved with a man whose heart belonged to another.

Tomorrow she was meeting with her mum. Carly had called her earlier in the week. Seeing Max reach out to his in-laws, talking to him about her own relationships, she had realised that she wanted to try to connect with her mum again. Max was right. She wasn't a cynic. She was an optimist who wanted to believe in new beginnings. Maybe she and her mum could forge a new relationship, based on who they were now rather than on the past. Maybe with time, she could even forge one with her stepfamily.

There were some sights in life Max had never dreamt he would see. Giulio Ghiraldini sitting at the top of a red corkscrew slide, Isabella between his legs, was one of those sights.

'*Sbrigati, Giulio!* There's a queue forming behind you,' Valentina, standing on the soft play tiles beneath the slide, called up to Giulio.

Giulio raised both hands in a gesture that said Valentina should stop fussing, but then pushed off down the slide. Isabella's eyes and mouth popping open in wonder, Valentina clapped her hands in delight, while Max videoed the entire event on his phone. Tomaso and Giovanni would no doubt tease their father about it in the months ahead when Max shared it on the new online sharing group he had created for the family earlier in the week.

Giulio and Valentina had flown to London for the weekend. The day after he had returned from Tomaso's wedding, he had called them, suggesting that he and Isabella would video call them a few times each week.

The suggestion had been received with great enthusiasm and now he and Isabella called them before bath time most nights, Isabella insisting that she call her *nonna e nonno*, loving the funny faces her grandfather pulled unbeknownst to her *nonna*.

Leaving the playground, they walked towards the park's bamboo garden, Isabella tottering in the centre of the group, refusing to hold hands with anyone, determined to act all grown up. Carly had been right. By showering her with his attention and love, he had helped Isabella find a new confidence and desire to be independent. So many times over the past two weeks he had been tempted to call Carly to tell her of Isabella's progress. To hear her voice. To know how she was. But what was the point? She had made it clear she didn't want to see him again. Time and time again over the past couple of weeks he had asked himself why. Was she still in love with her ex?

He smiled down at his daughter as she weaved an unsteady but determined path on the concrete pavement. Carly had opened his heart fully to Isabella, allowed him to realise that he shouldn't fear loving her with all his being. His gaze shifted over to Giulio and Valentina. Carly had opened his heart to them too. She had shown him that it was not a weakness to ask for support. Isabella was blossoming in their company. And for him their support brought reassurance, a peace to know that there were others out there who cared for Isabella, who cared for him. Now, thanks to

Carly, he could fully see that allowing others into his life gave it more colour and meaning.

The other three carried on for a few steps before turning around. He waved them on, telling them he wanted to take a photograph of them walking with Isabella.

He took out his phone and snapped them, his throat tight at the sight of Isabella's yellow polka-dot dress blowing in the wind against her bare legs, her curls dancing with each step, Sunny tucked under her arm.

He stopped dead on the footpath.

Carly had thought him to be open, to be vulnerable. Not just with Isabella. But with his in-laws. She had given him the gift of tenderness, of being capable of stopping and understanding his own fears and need.

He had feared being hurt again, of losing someone. He had feared opening himself up to another person, showing his fragility.

But in all of that he had lost sight of Carly's fears and needs.

He cursed under his breath. Disbelieving just how thoughtless he had been. Carly feared trusting others. He had done nothing to prove to her that he would always be there for her, that he understood her. He had done nothing to make her feel secure, wanted, treasured. Instead he had reverted to his old ways of keeping others at a distance, of showing no vulnerability. He had tried to keep her in his life using logic when he should have spoken from his heart.

He hadn't told her he loved her.

He loved her.

Only now could he admit that to himself.

But in truth he had known he loved her the day he'd thought she was drowning. He would have given his life to save her.

But fear and the lifelong habit of distancing himself had stopped him admitting it to himself.

He opened up the gallery of photos on his phone, to the pictures they had taken of the three of them on the terrace of his villa before Giulio's sixtieth party.

They all looked goofy but incredibly happy in the photo. Even Isabella, who so often frowned at the sight of a camera, had a grin on her face as she tugged on Carly's neck.

Dio! They were meant to be together. But had he left it too late? Messed up too much?

CHAPTER TWELVE

As SHE TURNED the corner onto her street, Carly's footsteps faltered. Somebody was sitting on the steps outside her apartment block. She glanced around her. The street was empty. Lights and the shadow of flickering TV screens shone from some of the nearby houses. Would they hear her if she screamed?

The person on the steps stood. All six feet four of him.

Carly's heart missed a beat and then it raged in her chest.

Her footsteps clipped on the pavement. Within a few seconds she was standing in front of him.

'Max.' She tightened the belt of her jacket before clasping the strap of her handbag, eying him with hot anger.

'How are you?'

No! He was not doing this to her. Using those weapons of his soft green gaze and gentle tone on her. She was impervious to all of that now. 'What are you doing here?'

He blinked at her question before dropping down to join her on the pavement. Now that he was closer, out of the shadow of the steps and under a nearby street light, she could see the strain in his expression.

Her heart splintered.

Walk to him, Carly. Lay your head against his chest. Inhale his scent, his warmth that melts into your bones, wrap yourself in his strength.

Another, wiser voice popped into her head.

Don't you dare. You're enough of a mess as it is. Do you really want to make it worse?

'Can we go up to your apartment and talk?'

Carly shook her head.

'You were out?'

For a moment she toyed with the idea of pretending she'd been out on a date. She wanted to hurt him, just as she was hurting. Not a particularly noble sentiment, but there was nothing noble about her mood right now. 'Why are you here, Max? You scared me sitting there.'

'I'm sorry.'

Carly eyed him. Was he sorry for frightening her or was it a more general apology?

'How long have you been sitting here?' she asked.

He looked at his watch. 'About three hours.'

'Three hours! Are you crazy?'

'We need to talk and I knew you'd have to come out or go in eventually.'

'And if I didn't?'

'I'd have stayed here until you did.' And he would have—Carly could see it in the calm resolve of his gaze.

She waited for him to explain why he was here but instead he ran a hand tiredly against his neck, tilting his head. His jaw line was heavy with evening shadow, the lines at the corners of his eyes more pronounced than usual. He looked tired.

She gave a little gasp, raw panic coursing through her. 'Isabella—is everything okay?'

'She's fine.'

His voice held a tender certainty but Carly needed to know more. 'Who's minding her?'

'Giulio and Valentina.'

Carly paused, trying to make sense of his answer. 'Isabella is in Lake Como? Why are you here, then? Why aren't you with her?'

'Giulio and Valentina are here in London. They're staying with us.'

Thrown, Carly cleared her throat. 'Isabella must be delighted to have them stay.'

'As much as Giulio and Valentina are about spending time with her. They're spoiling her.'

Her head spun with how good it felt to hear the affection in his voice. She gritted her teeth. 'I hope they're keeping to her sleeping plan.'

'I'm insisting upon it.'

'Did you find a new nanny?'

'No. We've agreed that between the three of us we'll take care of Isabella for a while. Giulio and Valentina are staying in London for a few months. They're renting an apartment close to us and we'll all go to Lake Como for the month of August.'

Thrown by this news, missing Isabella even more than ever now that they were talking about her, Carly asked, 'How is she?'

'She's still waking at night, but usually only once. Bedtimes are easier, and she's still addicted to reading *Sleepy Heads in Sleep World.*'

Faced with his tender voice, her anger was slipping away from her. She needed to get away. She moved onto the steps. 'It's late.'

'She misses you.'

She somehow managed not to trip on the steps at his words and made it as far as the door before she turned and admitted, 'And I miss her.'

He moved onto the first step. 'Come and see us.'

Carly winced. Did he have no understanding of just how impossible all of this was for her? Her anger surged back and, walking towards him, she demanded, 'Why haven't you called? It's been two weeks. I'd have liked to have known sooner how she was.'

'I needed some space to think.'

'About *what*?'

He hesitated for a moment before answering, 'About us.' He shrugged and added, 'You could have called us, you know.'

There was disappointment, hurt in his voice that made her feel as if she had failed him somehow. 'I was going to call next week.'

He nodded at that but she could tell that he didn't believe her. 'There are things I need to say to you.'

Carly fumbled with her handbag, trying to locate her keys, knowing that talking would resolve nothing. 'Is there any point?'

'I've been sitting here for the past three hours so I sure hope there is.'

The hope, the solemnity etched in Max's face had her open the door and silently wait for him to follow her into the hallway, her heart pounding at the pride in his gaze as he passed her by.

Carly's apartment was on the second floor of a redbrick Georgian town house. The interior had been renovated in recent years but still retained the original ornate cornicing and fireplace in the living room. The walls were painted a soft green, an eastern-inspired rug on the varnished floorboards. The walls either side of the fireplace were covered in an array of paintings in various sizes and subjects.

He inspected them as Carly threw her handbag onto the grey linen sofa opposite the fireplace and removed her jacket.

'A family collection?' he asked, nodding to the pictures.

'No, just an addiction to car-boot sales and flea markets.'

Max smiled but inside his stomach was twisted into a hundred different nasty knots. He had been nervous outside on the street, but standing here, seeing Carly's home for the first time, his doubts were off the scale. She had a whole life without him—a job she thrived in, a beautiful home, a busy social life. What if she said no again? Was he doing the right thing? The right thing by Isabella? What if Carly said yes but six months, a year, two years down the line wanted out? Isabella would be three, four by then. How would she cope? How would he cope losing someone else he loved?

He loved Carly.

That thought galvanised him.

Carly had moved into her adjoining kitchen, filling the kettle, taking cups and glasses out of cupboards with a frenetic energy.

He held out his hand to her.

She stared at it as though it were a dangerous animal.

'Let's go and talk.'

For a moment it looked as if she was going to refuse, preferring to stay in the kitchen for the night boiling endless kettles of water instead of hearing what he wanted to say. But then with an impatient toss of her head she stalked back into the living room, where she sat on a primrose-yellow corded art deco chair and pointed him towards the sofa.

He sat as close as he could to her. Carly in response swung her knees away, while pushing herself into the furthest reaches of her chair.

Dio! He hadn't realised just how hard this was going to be. He rolled his shoulders, tried to release the tight tension in his throat that was making speech near impossible. His stomach was a bag of angry cats.

'When Marta died…' He paused as his voice cracked.

Carly inhaled deeply, her expression haunted. 'Max, please…'

'I want you to know everything about me. When Marta died I shut down. We had argued the night she died over Isabella not sleeping. She died when we were still angry with one another. I couldn't bear the guilt or the pain so I shut myself down to life, to the people around me. Even to my own daughter. And I was scared for Isabella, I wanted to protect her from life's unpredictability and cruelty by making her independent. But I was wrong. Being with you, all the lessons you have taught me in caring for Isabella— being open, being tender with her, the importance of reaching out to others—has taught me that isolating ourselves is not the answer. My mother wanted me to be fiercely independent but she was wrong.'

He took a deep breath to fight the lifelong certainty that to love others was to make you weak and vulnerable, a belief that he had tossed away when he met Marta only to later feel the full force of the devastation of losing her. Finally, he admitted, 'My mother was distraught when my father left us—she blamed her family for causing him to leave because they never liked him. She refused to ever speak to them again and closed us both off to the world. It was her way of coping with the pain of him leaving. I don't want to make her mistakes, to shut myself away from people who care. I want people in my life. I want you in my life.' He cleared his throat. 'I love you, Carly.'

Carly shot out of her seat. He was not going to do this to her. To tell her he loved her. To tell her lies just as Robert had.

She stood with her back to the fireplace and faced him down. 'You want a mother for Isabella.'

His expression shifted from dumbstruck to incredulous. He stood. '*Che cavolo!* Rubbish! Is that what you really think?'

He paced the room, his big body too large for her tiny living room, raking a hand through his hair. He yanked off the sports jacket he was wearing over faded jeans and flung it onto the back of the sofa. 'I… I…' He threw his hands up in disbelief. 'You don't trust me at all, do you?'

Carly shrugged, taken aback by the sadness in his voice, the disappointment in his eyes.

'Can't you see the risk I'm taking inviting you into our lives? Isabella has already lost her mother… I've lost someone I loved.' His voice cracked; he looked away in pain, in exasperation. '*Dio*, Carly, it would be so much easier not to love you, not to run the risk of you leaving us some day. Isabella says your name all the time. Last week she mistook a woman on the street for you. She tried to climb out of her stroller to get to you. She loves you, but I am *not* looking for a mother for her, that's not why I want you in our lives.'

'Is it because you're lonely?'

Her question was received with a disbelieving bark of laughter. 'Seriously? I've fallen in love with you because I'm lonely? I'm in love with you because you're intelligent, empathetic, beautiful. You bring out the best in me, you lighten my life. *Mi fai sognare*…you make me dream. I love you because we want the same things in life…we can have a good life together.'

She was unable to make sense of everything he was saying; memories of Robert's false promises had her saying tersely, 'Your lifestyle, your money isn't important to me.'

'That's not what I meant. I want to create a family with you. You, me and Isabella. Hopefully in the future there will be more *bambini* for us to love. You're the person I want by my side through life.'

Carly closed her eyes, but she couldn't stop the tear that slid down her cheek. She liked to think she was stoic by nature, a long way from being a drama queen, so she winced when she dropped to her knees, knowing just how over the top it was, but what she had to say literally chopped her off at her knees. She flinched, trying to find the right words, her insides one mass of tumbling emotion. She was aware of Max sitting back onto the sofa, his arms resting on his legs as he leant down to watch her. She stared at the tiny circular holes punched into the soft brown leather of his shoes.

His head inched down, trying to catch her gaze. 'Carly?'

She raised her head to be embraced by a look as tender as his quietly spoken question.

'What about Marta?'

His expression fell. 'What about her?'

'Are we doing the right thing by her?' Carly paused, her heart breaking in two. 'I don't want to dishonour her, Max. It's all so sad that she died so young. It feels so wrong to take her place.'

Max joined her on the floor. His eyes were awash with tears. 'This is why I love you, Carly. You are so incredibly kind and sensitive. You constantly think of others. Marta would have really liked you.'

Carly rubbed her hand over her eyes. They felt so tired and strained from holding back the tsunami of unshed tears clogging her head.

Max reached and gently wiped at the tears that had managed to break free. She hiccupped a little cry at his touch, the warmth of his fingertips like a warm blanket wrapping around her.

'I blamed myself for Marta's death but talking to you helped me see that I couldn't hold onto that guilt—it was serving no purpose other than to drive away those around me. That wasn't a way to honour Marta. It doesn't reflect the generous and outgoing person she was who embraced family and friends and would want me to do the same for Isabella. I've spoken to Giulio and Valentina about the night Marta died, how we had argued earlier that night. I needed them to know everything before I invited them to London.'

'How did they react?'

'Not well initially. They ended the call soon after. I

didn't hear from them for two days. But then Giulio called me. He said that all couples argue, especially when trying to cope with a newborn, that it's not the fairy tale of contentment the advertisers and movies would have us believe. He said that I had been a good husband to Marta, that he was proud to call me his son-in-law.' He stopped and once again brushed his thumb lightly against her cheek. His eyes shone brightly with tenderness, with gentle understanding, with love. 'They know that I'm here tonight.'

'They do?'

He smiled at her hiccupped question. 'I told them that I love you. They like you, Carly. They think you're good for me and Isabella.'

Startled, Carly sat back on her haunches. What must it have taken Max to tell his in-laws that he loved her. She stared into his eyes, a wonderful, glorious dawning slowly taking hold. He did love her. He really meant it.

'I loved Marta, but I love you now with all my heart. Marta will always be part of who I am, Isabella will be her legacy, but now I want to give you my heart…if you want it.'

A bubble of laughter erupted from Carly's throat. 'Of course I want your heart. That day when you arrived at my office, outside, you were upset. Something drew me to you. I wanted to know you better, to try to help. And then when we met, I just put what we had down to physical attraction. But it was deeper than that. It was an emotional connection that's hard to put into words.' Looking down, she frowned as she tried to find the right words, wanting him to know what was in her heart. 'It's like an incredible thrill yet a comfort, an ease in meeting the right person; but everything around us was so complicated. I thought I'd end up being hurt again so I tried resisting you so hard. It still feels unreal, and in truth it still scares me. Can we slow things down like you suggested in Italy?'

His hand ran against her arm, sending a thrilling warmth through her. 'Let's date for a while. I like the thought of walking you home at night, kissing you goodnight on the steps outside.'

She giggled at the mischief in his eyes. 'Will you come surfing with me?'

'Only if you promise to come and visit some of the buildings I've designed.'

Her smile widened. 'I'd love to see them. And I want to introduce you to all my friends.'

He pulled back a fraction from her, his expression sobering. 'Are you willing to become part of the Ghiraldini family?'

Carly edged away from him, the reality of entering into a relationship with Max starting to dawn on her. 'Does that mean you want to move back to Lake Como?'

His hand reached for hers. 'I'll go wherever you want to live.'

Did he really mean that? Did he see her needs as being equal to his? Was he willing to adapt to her way of life? 'So you'll stay here in London?'

He shrugged. 'If that's what you want.'

'And if I want to move to the Kent coast?'

He smiled. 'Then we'll go there and I'll design you the house of your dreams.'

Carly folded her arms, suddenly wanting to test him. 'I won't put up with you working crazy hours.'

His eyes glinted with self-satisfaction. 'Not a problem. I've been home by seven every night since we returned from Como.'

'And travel?'

'I've curtailed my business travel for now. But I do want to travel with you. I want to explore the world, live life to the full with you and Isabella at my side. And other children if they come along.'

Carly laughed at the excitement in his voice. 'But we're only dating for now.'

'You can't blame a guy for dreaming.'

Carly's heart flipped over and over again at the hope and love glittering in his green eyes. He loved her. She inhaled, trying to make sense of it all, needing him to understand the fears deep inside her, how much it hurt to be away from him. 'I've been miserable for the past two weeks. And as the days went by, I got more and more furious when you didn't call. But my anger really wasn't about you not calling, it was because I was so scared I'd never see you again. I pushed you away in Como because I couldn't face being second best in your life.'

His expression grew incredulous. 'Never! You will *never* be that. You'll always be the centre of my life.'

Carly smiled at his certainty, at the love, at the astonishing joy and security swelling inside her. 'In telling the Ghiraldinis, by everything you have said tonight, I know that I can trust you.' She paused as tears welled in her eyes again. 'I've missed you.' Her voice cracked but she continued on. 'I can be myself with you. You're supportive, you listen to me. You're never dismissive. You get me.' She paused and softly whispered, her heart aching with love, *'Ti amo.'*

'Veramente?'

'Sì!'

'Quanto?'

'Mucho.'

He threw his head back at that, his deep laughter reverberating around the room. 'That's Spanish. I think you mean *molto*…at least, I hope you are trying to say that you love me a lot.'

Carly's answer to that was to lean into him, her eyes swallowing up the happiness in his, her mouth landing on his smiling lips. He gave a moan and deepened their kiss. It was a kiss full of love and tenderness and laughter and wonder.

It was a kiss that ended with them both lying on the living-room floor, wrapped in each other's arms, smiling into each other's eyes in happiness.

'Knock! Knock!'

Max shook his head ruefully. 'Who's there?'

'Olive,' Carly replied, laughter bubbling in her throat.

'Olive who?'

'Olive you and I don't care who knows it!'

Max groaned but within seconds his mouth was on hers again. And they kissed and chatted late into the night, fighting the urge to move into Carly's bedroom, preferring instead to wait, to spend time opening their hearts ever more to one another.

EPILOGUE

THE FOLLOWING YEAR, on a hot August day, Carly walked through the rose gardens of Villa Fiori, the heavy floral scent and view of Lake Como bright and dazzling in the fierce heat, making her head spin with even more disbelieving happiness.

Her smile grew even wider and with a laugh she picked up the long skirt of her bridal gown and began to run towards the villa's private chapel. Which wasn't easy to do in four-inch heels and thirty-degree heat.

Waiting at the door of the chapel, dressed in a tuxedo, his wide smile glorious, Max lifted Isabella up and pointed towards Carly.

'Car-lee! Car-lee!' Isabella shouted, waving her bouquet of roses she had personally selected from the rose garden before breakfast this morning, aided by a local florist.

Inside the chapel, heads turned at Isabella's call. The chapel could seat thirty. The perfect number for their wedding. The Ghiraldinis and Vittoria and her family, along with some other of Max's friends from London sat on the right-hand side of the aisle. On the left-hand side were Carly's friends and family. Her dad had even travelled from New Zealand for the occasion. Carly had been torn about whether to ask him to walk her down the aisle, but in the end had decided she wanted Max, Isabella and herself to walk together, to signify that they were about to become a family.

Her relationship with her mother and stepfamily was growing stronger. Aided by the confidence Max's love and encouragement had given her, she had spoken frankly with her mum and later with Alan about the past. It had healed some wounds and allowed them to focus on the future. And her stepsisters were seeing beyond the child who had arrived into their lives at a time when they too were struggling with all the changes in their home.

She slowed as she neared the chapel.

Suddenly she felt shy.

Max lowered Isabella, who ran and hugged Carly fiercely around her knees before running into the shadowed light of the chapel in response to her uncle Giovanni's teasing call.

Max took Carly's hand and drew her away from the chapel door and from the view of everyone inside.

'*Come sei bella.*'

Carly shivered at the intensity of his gaze. 'And you look very handsome.'

His fingers tracing against her cheek, he lowered his head and whispered against her ear, 'Thank you for agreeing to be my wife.'

Her head swam at the sensual tone of his voice, at the love swirling in her heart. 'There's something you need to know.'

He reared back, worry darkening his gaze. 'What?'

She smiled. And smiled even more. Eventually she managed to say, 'I'm pregnant.'

'*Fai sul serio?*'

'Yes, seriously.'

He shook his head and smiled, his eyes alight with joy. But then his smile disappeared with a shake of his head. 'You shouldn't be running!'

'I couldn't help it, not when you were waiting for me.'

His frown shifted into a tender gaze. '*Il mio cuore è solo tua*—my heart is yours.'

Carly laid her hand on his cheek, as his hand touched against her stomach. Her heart fluttered out of her chest into the wonder and beauty of the day and she said, '*E tu mi hai rubato il cuore*…and you have stolen my heart.'

* * * * *

A NEW LEASH
ON LOVE

MELISSA SENATE

Dedicated with appreciation to animal shelters
and rescue organizations worldwide.
Thank you for all you do.

Chapter One

The gray-muzzled, three-legged Lab mix gnawing on a chew toy in his kennel at the Furever Paws Animal Rescue sure reminded Matt Fielding of himself. The dog was big, and so was Matt, at six foot one, with muscles honed by the United States Army. Matt wasn't missing a leg, but he'd come scarily close, an IED injuring him to the point that he'd been medically retired three months ago, spending that time—until yesterday—in base rehab. He had only a slight limp now, but kneeling down in front of the old dog's kennel had taken a good fifteen seconds.

I'd take you home in a heartbeat, Hank, he thought, his gaze on the dog's chart. The ten-year-old was an "owner surrender." Among the sadder words, for sure. His heart went out to the old guy stuck in this limbo between homes—like Matt was. But his sister would kill him if he walked through the door of her pristine house with a huge senior dog. And getting on her bad side right now wasn't a good idea.

The former army corporal had his order—and it was to find his sister's eight-year-old daughter, Matt's adored niece, Ellie, a suitable puppy. Suitable, of course, was a relative term. Old Hank might have spoken to Matt's soul, but he wasn't here to find himself a dog. Pets required commitment and a solid home, not a guy who had no idea where he'd be a week or two from now. Thirty-six and his life up in the air. If anyone had told Matt, so focused from the time he joined the army at eighteen, that one day he'd be at a loss for what came next, he wouldn't have believed it. Until three months ago, he *was* the US Army. Now, he was a civilian. With a slight limp.

It's barely noticeable and is symbolic of your service, so don't let it get you down, his sister had said yesterday when he'd arrived back in his hometown of Spring Forest, North Carolina, for the first time in five years. Little Ellie had saluted him, and he'd swept her up in a hug. But living in his sister's guest room, despite his adorable niece telling him knock-knock jokes that made no sense but still made him laugh, wasn't ideal. He needed to figure out what came next.

Right now, though, he needed to focus on his mission. *One thing at a time, one moment at a time,* his doc and the nurses at the rehab had said over and over.

So, back to suitable pups.

"Hank is one of my favorites," a woman said, and Matt almost jumped.

He knew that voice. He turned to the left and looked up, and standing not ten feet away was Claire Asher.

Claire.

From the look on her beautiful face, it was obvious she hadn't realized it was him. For a moment he couldn't find his voice. All he could do was take in the sight of her, his chest tight and his throat closed. He'd spent so many nights over the past eighteen years thinking about her, wondering how she was, where she was, if she was happy, his memories getting him through some iffy times. And now she stood almost within reach, pale brown eyes wide, mouth dropped open.

She had a leash in her hand and a big cinnamon-colored dog in a purple polka-dotted harness beside her. *A boxer, maybe?* Matt wondered, finding it easier to focus on the dog than the woman—who was staring at him with the same shock that had to be on his face.

"Matt?" she said, wonder in her voice.

The dog next to her tilted her head, his dark-brown ears flopping to the right.

He nodded and stood up, which took the same fifteen seconds getting down had. "I'm here to find a dog for my niece." Going through his mind was, *You look amazing. How are you? I've thought about you constantly. What are you doing here? I've missed you.* Thank God none of that had come rushing out of his mouth.

"Ellie," she said, surprising him. "I've run into your sister a few times over the years."

He nodded, his gaze going to her left hand. No ring. Hadn't he heard she'd gotten married a while back?

"You look great, Claire." She really did. Tall and as slender as she'd been back in high school, she was the

Claire Asher he remembered—would never forget. Her silky, wavy, light blond hair was shoulder-length instead of halfway down her back, and the faintest of crinkles at the corners of those green eyes spoke of the passage of years. The last time he'd seen Claire she was seventeen. Now, she was thirty-five.

"Are you on leave?" she asked.

He shook his head. "I'm a civilian now. Just got back in town yesterday. I'm staying with my sister for a bit. In fact, my sister is why I'm here. She and her husband promised Ellie a puppy for her birthday next month, so I told Laura I'd scout it out. I heard great things about Furever Paws just from asking about pet shelters at the coffee shop."

Claire beamed. "It's a very special place. I volunteer here." She gave the dog beside her a pat. "This is Dempsey. I'm fostering her until she finds a forever home."

"A *furever* home," he said, pointing at the rectangular wooden sign on the wall with the message in silver script: *Where furbabies find their furever homes.*

She smiled—that beautiful Claire Asher smile that used to drive him wild.

"If only you'd come in yesterday or this morning," she said. "Every Saturday and Sunday we hold adoption events here at the shelter. Four puppies found forever— *furever*—homes, plus five adult dogs and five cats."

"So these dogs in the kennels weren't chosen?" he asked, eyeing Hank, who was still chewing on his toy bone.

"Not this weekend. But we get a crowd every Saturday and Sunday, and sometimes it takes a while to find an ideal match. That's the most important part of the process—that the match be just right, for the pet and the adoptive family."

He nodded. "Is there a match for an eight-year-old girl whose requirements are 'super cute, snuggly and won't destroy a prized stuffed animal collection'?"

Claire laughed. "Follow me. I think I know just the pup." She led him down the row of kennels to the end. A puppy was spinning circles in the kennel, chasing her tail and letting out loud yips.

"My ears," Matt said with a smile. The puppy sure ticked off the "adorable" requirement. A springer spaniel mix, according to the chart, five months old, she was chestnut-brown and white with long, ruffled, floppy ears. Ellie would go nuts over her.

"Yeah, that's why she's still here. She yipped for twenty minutes straight at both adoption events. Including every time someone came near her kennel. She's only been here a few days, though. Another volunteer and I have been working with her a bit. She just needs some training. She's very sweet."

And loud, Matt thought. *And...active.* "Does she ever actually catch her tail and stop spinning?"

Claire laughed again. "Yes. Peanut butter treats get her to do anything."

"Would she be right for Ellie?" he asked. "My sister likes calm and orderly. I think she wants an old dog in a puppy's body."

"Well, it's important to match temperaments, and puppies can be trained, but puppies are puppies—little kids. They make noise, they're super active, they eat shoes."

"Ellie never ate a shoe, far as I know."

She laughed and touched his arm, the most casual gesture, but the feel of her fingers on his skin sent a lightning bolt through him. Standing here with her, her hand on him, it was as if they'd never broken up. Claire and Matt, high school sweethearts, married with four kids, four dogs, four cats—that's how many Claire had said she wanted of each. Plus a parrot and lovebirds. And a box turtle. He could go on.

Sometimes, over the years, late at night, Matt would berate himself for breaking up with Claire after graduation. He'd told her he needed to be focused on being the best soldier he could be, leaving it at that, and the pain on Claire's face had almost made him tell her the truth. That he wasn't and had never been and never would be good enough for her, that he'd hold her back, keep studious, bookish, intelligent Claire from fulfilling her big dreams of leaving Spring Forest for the big city. Matt wasn't a big city guy, and he'd planned to be career-army. Now, he didn't know what he was. Too many rough tours of duty, first as a soldier, then as a mechanic on dangerous missions, had left him…broken.

And here in Spring Forest, he didn't recognize himself or belong.

Focus on the mission, not yourself, he ordered himself. "I think my sister wants a temperament like Dempsey's," Matt said, gesturing at Claire's foster dog. The pooch was sitting, hadn't made a peep and didn't react in the slightest to the commotion around her.

"Dempsey is the best," Claire said. "A couple months ago, she was found chained outside an abandoned house. I don't think she ever had a home before I took her in, so

I've worked hard at acclimating her to the good life—which means passing muster on housetraining, manners, obedience, the whole thing. Now she's ready for a home, but she keeps getting passed over."

She knelt down beside the boxer and gave her a double scratch on the sides of her neck, then a kiss on her brown snout. Claire shook her head and stood up, her gaze on the dog.

He might not know Claire anymore, but a stranger could tell how much she loved that dog.

"Can't you adopt her?" he asked.

"I always want to adopt every dog I foster, but that's not my calling here," she explained. "Fostering is about preparing dogs for adoption so they can find homes. If I adopted every dog I fostered, I'd have over twenty at this point. Plus, every time a dog I work with finds a home, I can foster a new pooch."

"Must be hard to let them go," he said. "Don't you get attached?"

"Definitely," she said. "But because we do such a good job of matching furbabies and adoptive parents, I know they're going to a great home. I do worry about how attached I am to Dempsey, though. I can't explain it, but we definitely have a special bond." She gave the boxer mix another scratch on the head, and the dog looked up at her with such trust in her eyes, even Matt's battered heart was touched. "Oftentimes, that bond is there right away."

"I had no idea about any of this," he said. "There's more involved in choosing a dog than I realized. Can you help me find the right puppy for Ellie?"

"Of course," she said. "There are a few other puppies here that Ellie might like, but they all need some training. Maybe you can bring Ellie back with you and we can see who she bonds with. Furever Paws is in the process of finding a new director, so I'm helping with just about everything, from meet and greets to training to fostering to cleaning out kennels."

He glanced around the kennel area of the shelter, which had a warm, welcoming vibe to it. "It's great of you to give your time," he said. "When should I bring my niece in tomorrow?"

"I'm done teaching at the middle school at three, so I usually arrive at three thirty."

So she *had* become a teacher. That had always been her dream. But back in high school she'd wanted to leave Spring Forest and see the world, teaching her way through it. Maybe she had, for all he knew. "Works for Ellie too," he said. "See you tomorrow, then."

For a second they just looked at each other, neither making a move to leave. He wished he could pull her into his arms and hug her, hold her tight, tell her how good it was to see her, to hear her voice, to talk to her. He'd missed her so much and hadn't even known it. Which was probably a good thing. He had nothing to offer her.

As he gave Dempsey a pat and turned to walk away, he couldn't quite figure out how he could be so relieved to be leaving and so looking forward to coming back.

He paused in front of Hank's kennel. *Life is complicated, huh, boy?*

Hank tilted his head, and Matt took that as a nod.

To catch her breath and decompress, Claire took Dempsey into the fenced yard, which was thankfully empty of other volunteers. She let Dempsey off leash and for a few moments watched the dog run around the grass, sniffing and wagging her tail.

Matt Fielding. Everyone always said you never forgot your first love, and that had been very true for Claire. She'd truly believed he would be the man she'd marry and spend the rest of her life with. And then boom— a few days after a magical prom night, he'd broken up with her.

Her first boyfriend in college had proposed, and maybe the promised security had had something to do with why she'd said yes when she hadn't loved him the way she'd loved Matt. To this day, she didn't know if that had contributed to her divorce, but five years into her marriage, she'd found out that her ex-husband was cheating and in love with someone else. Now, she was living in the house they'd built out in the Kingdom Creek development, without the husband or the kids they'd talked about or the dogs they were going to adopt.

The craziest thing was that, just last week, her sister had said that Claire's problem was that she'd never gotten over Matt, and to do so she'd need to find a guy who looked like him. Tall and muscular, with those blue eyes, Matt was so good-looking and so…hot that few men in town even came close to resembling him. But apparently her sister had found someone who fit the bill, and had arranged a double date for tonight.

Half of her wanted to cancel. The other half thought she'd better protect herself against Matt's being back by going out on this date, even if her heart wouldn't be in it. Claire wanted a relationship—she wanted love and to find the man she'd spend forever with. She wanted a child—children, hopefully—and at thirty-five, she wasn't exactly a spring chicken.

"How did everything get so topsy-turvy, Demps?" she asked the dog, who'd come over with a half-eaten tennis ball. "I know you know all about that," she added, throwing the ball. Dempsey, in all her fast, muscular glory, chased after it, leaping through the air like a deer.

There was nothing like watching dogs at play to make Claire feel better and forget about her love life— the old, the nonexistent and the upcoming. She smiled as Dempsey dropped the ball at her feet. She threw it a few more times, then left the dog in the yard to play while she went to help clean the kennels that were now empty due to the lucky pups that had been adopted today.

As she reentered the shelter, she saw Birdie and Bunny Whitaker in their waterproof aprons, hard at work with the disinfectant and hose. Claire adored the sixty-something sisters—no-nonsense Birdie and dreamer Bunny—who lived together in the lovely farmhouse on Whitaker Acres, the same property the shelter was on. Opening Furever Paws had been a longtime dream of the Whitaker sisters ever since people had begun abandoning animals on Whitaker land, a pocket of rural country in what had become urban sprawl. At first they'd started an animal refuge, but when it became too much for them to handle financially, they filed for nonprofit status and started the Furever Paws Animal Rescue almost twenty years ago. Aside from the shelter with dogs and cats, the sisters kept goats, pigs, geese and even a pair of llamas on the property. They opened up Whitaker Acres to the public a few times a year so that visitors could enjoy the land and animals. Kids loved the place.

As Claire cleaned Snowball's kennel—the white shepherd-Lab mix had been adopted this morning and immediately renamed Hermione—she was glad the shelter could take in more strays and drop-offs. Furever Paws had room for about a dozen each of dogs and cats, and twice that many were cared for in foster homes, like Dempsey.

"I'll miss that adorable Snowball," Birdie said, hosing down the kennel across the way. "For twenty years I've been telling myself not to get attached to our animals." She shook her head. "Old fool." Tall and strong, her short silver hair gleaming in the afternoon sunlight, Birdie grabbed the mop, dunked it in the cleaning solution and went at the floor of the kennel until it met her satisfaction.

"I already miss Annie Jo," Bunny said, taking out the bed, blanket and toys in the next kennel and stuffing them in the huge laundry bin. Bunny looked a lot like Birdie but was shorter and plumper, her silver curls soft against her sweet face. "I love what her family renamed her—Peaches. Back in the day, a beau called me that," she added, wiggling her hips.

Claire smiled. The shelter always named the strays and those left on the doorstep. Every now and then, adopters kept the shelter names—most recently a cat named Princess Leia, who'd been there for months. Birdie and Bunny loved naming the incoming animals, and whenever they couldn't come up with a name, they held a meeting with the staff—the full-time employees, such as the shelter director, foster director and vet technician—and the volunteers, like Claire.

"Who was that very handsome man here a little while ago?" Bunny asked with a sly smile as she started sweeping out the kennel, reaching over for a stray piece of kibble that Annie Jo—Peaches—had missed. "My, he was nice to look at."

"I'm surprised you didn't rush over to ask how you could help him," Birdie said to her starry-eyed sister, wringing out the mop in the big bucket.

"Well, I *would* have," Bunny said, "but I saw Claire come back in with Dempsey and decided to leave him for her. Trust me, if I were even *ten* years younger…"

Claire laughed as Birdie shook her head again, her trademark move. Neither Whitaker sister had ever married, though Claire did know that Bunny had been engaged in her early twenties until her fiancé had tragically died. Birdie never talked about her love life, and though Claire had tried a time or two to get Bunny to spill about Birdie's romantic life, the sisters were clearly loyal to each other's secrets. As they should be.

But no matter how much or how little experience the Whitaker sisters had in the romance department, they were both wise—Birdie in common sense and Bunny in keeping an open mind and heart. Talking to the two always set Claire straight, or at least made her feel better.

Which was why she was going to be honest right now.

"That was the guy who broke my heart into a million pieces after high school graduation," she said. "Matt Fielding. I cried for six months straight."

"And then married the first guy who asked you out," Birdie said with an *uh-huh* look on her face.

"Yup," Claire said, spraying disinfectant on the bars of the last kennel and wiping them down with a clean rag. "But there's hope for me. Guess who has a blind date tonight? My sister and her husband set me up."

"Ooh," Bunny said, her blue eyes twinkling. "How exciting. To me, blind dates are synonymous with 'you never know.' Could be the man of your dreams."

Birdie wrinkled up her face. "Blind dates are usually the pits." She glanced at Claire, instantly contrite, then threw her arms up in the air. "Oh, come on. They are."

Claire laughed. "Well, if the date takes my mind off the fact that my first love is back in town? Mission accomplished."

"Oh boy," Birdie said, pausing the mop. "Someone is still very hung up on her first love."

"Oh dear," Bunny agreed.

And before Claire could say that *of course* she was— *you did see him, after all*—that cute little springer spaniel she'd shown Matt started howling up a storm.

"Someone wants her dinner *now*," Bunny said with a laugh.

"I'm on feeding duty for the dogs," Claire said, putting the disinfectant back on the supplies shelf and the rag in Bunny's laundry basket. "If I don't see you two before I leave for the day, congrats on a great Sunday. Five adult dogs adopted plus the puppies and cats."

"It was a good day," Bunny said. "Good luck on that date tonight."

Claire smiled. "Who knows? Maybe he *will* be the man of my dreams."

She was putting on a brave front for the sisters—not that she needed to, since she could always be honest with them. But sometimes Claire reverted to that old need to save face, to not seem like she cared quite so much that she was single, when she wanted to be partnered, to find that special someone to share her life with, to build a life with. She loved Dempsey to pieces, but most nights, unless she had book club or a social event like someone else's engagement party or birthday, it was her and the boxer mix snuggled on the sofa in her living room, watching *Dancing with the Stars* or a Netflix movie, a rawhide chew for Dempsey and a single-serve bag of microwave popcorn for her.

There was room on that couch for a man.

But in any case, Matt Fielding was not the man of her dreams, whether she was "hung up or him" or not. Seventeen-year-old Claire had been madly in love. Now, she was a thirty-five-year-old divorced woman staring down her biological clock. "Man of her dreams" was silly nonsense. Hadn't the supposed man of her dreams dumped her almost two decades ago as if she'd meant nothing? Ha, like that was part of the dream?

Matt Fielding was not the man of her dreams.

If she said it enough, she might believe it.

And if there was no such thing, then what *was* she looking for in a partner?

She'd never put much stock in checklists, since she could rattle off a list of adjectives, like *kind*, and non-negotiables, like *doesn't rip apart his exes or his mother on the date*, but everything came down to chemistry. How you felt with someone. How someone made you feel. If your head and heart were engaged. She'd never experienced chemistry the way she had with Matt Fielding. But her motto ever since she'd started volunteering for Furever Paws was: Everything is possible. The most timid dog, the hissiest cat, could become someone's dearest treasure. *Everything is possible.* Including Claire finding love again. At thirty-five.

She peeled off her waterproof gloves and tossed them in the used-gloves bin, then headed toward the door to start filling bowls with kibble and sneaking in medicines where needed.

"Oh, Claire," Birdie said. "Some advice. In the first five minutes, ask your date if he likes dogs. If he says no, you'll know he's not for you."

Bunny tilted her head. "Now, Birdie. Not everyone loves animals like we do."

Apparently, the entire Whitaker family loved animals to the point that all their nicknames were inspired by animals. Birdie's real name was Bernadette. Bunny's was Gwendolyn. There was a Moose—Doug—who'd sadly died long ago. And a Gator, aka Greg, who advised the sisters on financial matters.

"The man of Claire's dreams will love dogs," Birdie said. "That's nonnegotiable. If her blind date says dogs slobber and bark and are a pain in the neck, she can tune him out the rest of the night."

Claire smiled. As usual, Birdie Whitaker was right.

Chapter Two

Matt held his niece's hand as they entered the Main Street Grille later that night, the smell of burgers and fish and chips reminding him how hungry he was. His sister, Laura, and her husband, Kurt, had insisted on taking him out to dinner to celebrate his homecoming.

"His home*staying*!" Ellie had said, squeezing him into one of her famous hugs.

He adored the eight-year-old. He barely knew her—had rarely seen her since she'd been born because of his tours—but the moment he'd arrived yesterday, she'd latched on to him like he was the fun, exciting uncle she'd missed out on, and of course, he couldn't let her down. He'd played soccer with her. He'd read her two bedtime stories last night, then she'd read him one, and he'd almost fallen asleep right there in her pink-and-purple room. This morning, he'd played Hiker Barbie with her in the backyard, his Barbie falling into a ravine, and her Barbie saving her with her search-and-rescue skills and the help of Barbie's golden retriever, Tanner. She'd spent a good hour talking to Matt about dogs, after she'd instructed Tanner to grab his Barbie's jeans cuff and pull her up to safety. The girl was dog-crazy. And he was Ellie-crazy. He was determined to help her find just the right pooch to love.

With Claire Asher's help. Amazing.

"We love this restaurant," Laura said as the hostess led them through the dimly lit space to a table for four near a window. "During the day, it's more of a diner, but at night it transforms into a pub. Apparently, it's quite the nostalgic place to get engaged."

Matt glanced around the restaurant. There were quite a few obvious dates.

And, oh hell, was that *Claire*?

On an obvious date.

He turned away so that his staring wouldn't draw her attention. Then, as he sat down, he took another glance. Dammit. Yes, it was. Four tables away, diagonally. She was sitting with her own sister, Della, and two men were across from them. The one across from Claire looked slick. He had gelled hair and trendy eyeglasses and was holding court, making Claire laugh.

Crud. He used to make Claire Asher laugh.

At least she's happy, he told himself.

"What are you having, Uncle Matt?" Ellie asked. "I'm getting the mac and cheese. No, the cowabunga burger. No, the mac and cheese. Or should I have the spaghetti and meatballs?"

He focused his attention on his niece. The poor thing had an incredibly crooked strawberry-blond braid with weird tufts sticking out. Ellie had asked him to do the honors for tonight's "special dinner," and Laura had given the tutorial as he went. When he was done, his sister had had to leave the room to keep herself from bursting into laughter. But Ellie, checking out his handiwork with a hand mirror and her back to the hall mirror, declared her braid *just perfect!*

"Well, I know your favorite is mac and cheese," he said, "and since this is a special night, I think you should get your favorite." Matt forced himself to look at the menu and not Claire.

But she looked so damned pretty. The candle on the table just slightly illuminated her. She'd dolled up a bit since her shift at the shelter. Her pink-red lips were glossy, and her light blond hair was sleek to her shoulders. She wore an off-white V-neck sweater, and a delicate gold chain around her neck.

"That's right," his sister said, smiling at Ellie. "This is a special night—celebrating Uncle Matt's long-awaited homecoming."

"Homestaying!" Ellie said with a grin.

That got his attention. Because *was* this something to celebrate? Thirty-six and living in his sister's guest room? No clue where he was headed, what he'd do. Visiting his family while he figured things out made sense, he reminded himself. He had ideas, of course. And skills. But he felt wrong in his skin, suddenly adrift in this different life.

You're an American hero and don't you forget it, his sister had said when he'd mentioned that earlier. *You'll adapt and build a new life—hopefully here in town.*

With Claire Asher to run into everywhere he went? No, sir. He was two for two on his first full day in Spring Forest. He couldn't do that to himself on a daily basis. But until he decided where to go and what to do, Spring Forest, it was.

He took one more look at Claire out the side of his menu. *Oh please.* Her date was offering her a bite of something. As Claire smiled and leaned forward to accept the fork—with her hand, thank God, and not with those luscious lips—Matt felt his gut tighten and his appetite disappear.

He'd help Ellie find her dog. Which meant seeing Claire one more time tomorrow. And then maybe he'd leave town. There was no way he could figure out what the hell he was going to do with his life if he was going to constantly run into her—and be unable to stop thinking about her.

Dammit.

Now she was laughing at something Slick had said. Great. Tonight was a *real* celebration.

Claire's date liked dogs. Loved them, in fact. He—Andrew, thirty-five, divorced, two children of whom he shared joint custody—even had a dog, a yellow Lab named Sully.

And Andrew was very attractive. Her sister hadn't been kidding about him looking like Matt, to a degree. They had the same coloring, the dark hair—though Matt's was more military-short—the blue eyes, the strong nose and square jawline, both men managing to look both refined and rugged at the same time. Andrew was in a suit and tie, but Claire had seen Matt Fielding in a suit only once—on prom night, the black tuxedo he'd paired with a skinny white silk tie and black Converse high-tops. That night, she'd thought there was nothing sexier on the planet than her boyfriend.

Her date for tonight was charming and kind and attentive, asking all kinds of questions about her job as a teacher. He showed her photos of his kids and beamed with pride about them, which Claire found sweet and touching. Over the past few years, when she'd started worrying that she wouldn't find Mr. Right-Part-Two, she'd thought about marrying a man with kids and becoming a great stepmother. And there was adoption, of course. Her single friend Sally had adopted a little girl from foster care, and though there were challenges, she'd never seen her friend so happy, so fulfilled.

Another of Claire's mottoes over the past few years had been: If you want to find your life partner, if you want to have a child, however that child may come into your life, you have to keep your mind and heart open.

And now here was seemingly perfect Andrew. Even clear-eyed, hard-nosed Birdie Whitaker would be impressed by him and the prospects of a second date. She could just hear romantic Bunny running down how things would go: *And then a* third *date at that revolving restaurant on the zillionth floor in the fancy hotel in Raleigh. Then amazing sex in your suite for the night. Then exclusivity. Then a proposal on your six-month-iversary. You'll be married to a wonderful man and have stepchildren to dote on and love by summer—you could be a June bride if you're only engaged four months!* Oh God, sometimes Claire thought it would be wonderful to be Bunny.

Problem was, though, that despite how wonderful Andrew seemed, Claire felt zero chemistry. Zero pull. The thought of getting to know him better didn't really interest her. The idea of kissing him left her cold.

No fair! And she knew exactly why this man who loved dogs, who'd even showed her a slew of photos of handsome Sully on his phone, wasn't having any effect on any part of her at all.

Because for the past few hours, as she'd been getting ready for the date, Matt had been on her mind. How could he not be? She hadn't seen him in almost twenty years and then, whammo, there he was today, at her sanctuary, the place where she always felt at home, at peace. Matt Fielding suddenly kneeling in front of a dog's kennel at Furever Paws. Unbelievable.

She'd started out the evening thinking she would not let being all verklempt at seeing her first love derail this date. And so she'd put a little more effort than she otherwise might have into her hair and makeup and outfit, as if trying to force herself to give the date a real shot instead of knowing her heart just wouldn't be in it.

And now, as Andrew signaled their waiter for their check, which he insisted on paying for the table, all she wanted was to be back home, sipping this excellent chardonnay in a hot bath to soothe her muscles after the long day at the shelter. And to deal with being flooded by memories of Matt. The first time they'd met. Kissed. When he'd opened up about his older brother, who hadn't come home from Afghanistan. His parents' pride and worry that Matt had enlisted in his brother's honor. That they may lose another son. Matt had promised his mother he'd email every night to say good-night, to let her know he was okay. And he had for years; his sister, Laura, had shared that with her when they'd run into each other a few years back.

Matt had ended up outliving his parents, and when Laura had let Claire know when they'd run into each other another time, she'd said that Matt got through it only because he wouldn't have to worry about shattering their hearts a second time, after all.

All these memories had come rushing back while she'd been applying mascara and stepping into a gentle spray of Chanel N° 19. Her date with Andrew Haverman, attorney-at-law, never stood a chance.

Claire shook her head at herself.

"So, I hope we can go for a drink," Andrew said as he signed the credit card slip. He slid a hopeful, very-interested smile at Claire.

Claire's sister stood up, prompting her husband to do the same. "We have to get up pretty early tomorrow. You two go, though," she added with her own hopeful smile, glancing from Claire to Andrew and back to Claire.

Don't you dare mess this up! Claire could hear Della shouting telepathically to her. *Get Matt Fielding out of your head this instant! I know you! GET. HIM. OUT! Andrew has a dog named Sully!*

Despite the dog, despite everything, she couldn't get Matt out of her head. As her date was pocketing his shiny gold credit card and receipt, she glanced around the restaurant, trying to think of an excuse. She didn't want to go for a drink, extend the date. She didn't want to see this man again, despite, despite, despite. Avoiding her sister's narrowed stare, Claire kept looking around the restaurant, sending a smile to a former student at a table with her parents, another smile to a couple who'd adopted two kittens from Furever Paws a few weeks ago—and then her smile froze.

Claire felt her eyes widen as her gaze was caught on a very crooked strawberry-blond braid halfway down a little girl's back. She'd seen a similarly hued braid—though a very tidy one—on Matt's niece when she'd run into his sister and the girl a couple of months ago in the supermarket.

Oh God. Don't let me look next to her and see Matt.

But there he was. Now staring at her. Glaring at her, actually.

Whoa there, guy.

But suddenly her date was standing up too, and so she had to. Her group would walk right past Matt's table. There was no way she couldn't say hello, if not to Matt, then to his sister.

Awk-ward.

"You've *got* to be kidding me," Claire's sister hiss-whispered in her ear as they headed toward the door—toward Matt's table. "No wonder you've been so distracted!"

"Actually, I just noticed him a few seconds ago," Claire admitted. If she'd known he was there this whole time, she would have excused herself to the restroom to hyperventilate.

"Claire!" Matt's sister said with a surprised smile as they were about to pass.

Oh hell. Claire paused as her group moved on to the waiting area, collecting their coats from the racks. Her sister was furiously gesturing her over by tipping her head to the side, her mouth in a comical grimace.

"I hear I owe you a big thank-you, Claire!" Laura was saying. She sat across from Matt and next to her husband. "Matt mentioned he ran into you at Furever Paws and that you're going to help Ellie choose a puppy tomorrow."

Claire glanced at Matt, who was now sitting with a total lack of expression on his handsome face. Better than the glare? Not really.

"I'm so excited, I'm going to explode," Ellie said, her hazel eyes shining. "Thank you for helping me! I can't wait to see the puppies!"

Aww. Ellie was adorable and sweet. "My pleasure," Claire said.

"Just remember the rules, Matt and Ellie," Laura said, raising an eyebrow between the two. "House-trained is a must. And the puppy must know basic commands before he walks into our home. Oh—and no bigger than medium-sized when fully grown."

Uh-oh, Claire thought. She'd have her work cut out for her there. Did any of the puppies fit the bill? Certainly not the springer spaniel, who'd peed right on Claire's foot this morning while she'd been fluffing her blanket. Though she *was* expected to be medium-sized. And the three other contenders were housetrained, but two would be huge, and a consistent "sit" was still beyond all of them, in spite of lots of training with high-value treats.

"Your date is waiting for you," Matt practically growled, gesturing toward the door.

Her sister was still furiously head-gesturing for Claire to get the hell away from Matt Fielding and join the present and possible future—not be stuck in the past.

Awk-ward, she thought again as she smiled at everyone and dashed toward her group.

But as her date held the door open for her, she dared a glance back at Matt.

And he was looking right at her, his expression more readable now. He was angry-jealous!

He'd dumped her, remember? To live his own life on his terms.

"So, that nightcap?" her date asked, helping her into her coat.

Do not look over at Matt, she ordered herself, aware that he had to be watching right then.

"To be honest, I just saw a ghost," she said, surprising herself with her candor. "I think I'd like to just call it a night."

Her sister rolled her eyes and shook her head so imperceptibly that likely only Claire caught it.

Her date looked confused.

"An ex," her brother-in-law explained to Andrew.

"Ah. I get it," Andrew said. "Happened to me just last night while on another blind date, and crazy as it was, I ended up with the ex for the rest of the night." A salacious expression lit his face. "One-time thing," he rushed to say, seeming to realize he'd said too much.

At least Claire wouldn't have to feel too bad about ditching him.

As they headed to her sister's SUV, she could still see Matt's face so clearly in her mind. How could she not be over him? How? Eighteen years later?

He was coming to the shelter tomorrow. She'd see him again. He had a purpose and so did she, and then he'd leave and that would be that.

Yeah, right.

Corporal McCabbers was telling Matt about his girlfriend back home; Penny was her name, with long red hair and green eyes. He and McCabbers sat in the back of the vehicle, headed for a broken-down US Army truck that they had to get running pronto.

Ten more days and I'm home, McCabbers was saying, and Matt envied his buddy's ability to lose himself in his memories and hopes for the future—because his woman was still his woman. Matt had a string of hookups and failed off-base, short-term relationships. There'd been women over the years, but Claire Asher's face was always the one he saw in his dreams, his fantasies.

And home? There'd been no home for almost two decades. Home was wherever Matt was.

"There's the truck," he heard the driver call.

He and McCabbers waited for their vehicle to stop, for the all-clear from the driver to duck out toward the truck under cover of night.

No sooner had their boots hit the dry, dusty ground

than a burst of flame erupted before Matt's eyes, the explosion throwing him back hard.

The pain in his left leg was unlike anything he'd felt before. "Fielding!" he heard McCabbers shouting. "Fielding!" And then he'd felt nothing at all.

Matt bolted up, a trickle of sweat running down his chest, his breath ragged and coming hard. He glanced around, and then closed his eyes.

He was home. His sister's house.

Letting out a breath, he dropped back down on the soft sheets and pulled the comforter up to his chest.

He didn't have the nightmares as often as he used to. In rehab, where he'd woken up after being unconscious for two days, he'd had the dreams every time he'd fallen asleep. But as his wounds healed and his leg strengthened, the nightmares had lessened. The memories remained though.

He could still picture dragging himself over to McCabbers and tying his shirt around the wound in his buddy's leg, which had looked a hell of a lot worse than Matt's own. The driver of their vehicle had been able to get back to them, dragging him and McCabbers into the truck and booking it out of there, saving their lives. McCabbers had gone on to marry his girlfriend six months later in Las Vegas, on one crutch but otherwise alive and well.

Matt had a hell of a lot to be grateful for. And Claire Asher deserved to be happy. Wasn't that why he'd broken up with her all those years ago? So she could have a better life than the one he'd be able to share with her?

Still, he couldn't stop speculating about how Claire's

evening had progressed. If it had progressed. If she'd invited Slick home. If he was still there.

None of your business, he reminded himself. Help your niece find the perfect puppy, then pack up and find a place where you belong.

Chapter Three

"That very good-looking man and a little girl are out front," Bunny whispered with a smile as Claire came in the back door of Furever Paws on Monday afternoon. Claire returned Sunshine to her kennel and secured the door, noting the time of the walk on the big whiteboard on the wall. The year-old rottie mix had been at the kennel for two days, and was slowly warming up to walking on a leash. "Says he's here to see Claire Asher about adopting a puppy." Bunny smiled slyly.

Claire shook her head at Bunny's expression. "Well, he is."

"I can't wait to hear about your date," Bunny said, her blue eyes twinkling. "Find me later and tell me everything."

Do I want to be reminded of any of it? No. "There's

nothing really to tell. No chemistry, even if he was great on paper."

Bunny nodded. "I get it. A blind date, no matter if he's Pierce Brosnan, can't compete with a first love on the brain."

Especially when that first love is in the same restaurant.

Claire glanced at the clock. It was exactly three thirty. She'd practically raced here after finishing up at school, grateful that her last period of the day was monitoring a study hall. She'd wanted to get to the shelter with some time to spare before Matt arrived so that she wouldn't be flustered. So, she'd taken Sunshine out, grounded herself on her turf and was ready by the time she got back inside.

Claire left the dog kennels and headed to the main lobby. She almost sucked in her breath at the sight of Matt, looking as good as Bunny had noted. He wore a navy-blue Henley, a black leather jacket and dark jeans.

She gave him a fast smile, then turned her focus on Ellie, who was practically jumping in place.

"Hi, Miss Claire!" Ellie said with a huge grin on her adorable face. "I can't wait to see the puppies! Can you believe my mom finally said okay to me having a dog? I've been waiting years!"

"Well, you *are* only eight," Matt pointed out, giving her still-crooked braid a playful pull.

"I've wanted a dog since I was two," Ellie said. "But I had to show my mom I could take care of a dog. And I can! And I will!"

Her handsome uncle smiled. "I know it."

"Well, to the kennels, then," Claire said, leading the way. This was good. They were both ignoring running into each other last night. "We have four puppies and three dogs between a year and a half and two—they've got a lot of puppy in them too. Let's start with the puppies and see who you like."

She glanced at Matt, who was quiet.

"Just one rule," Claire added to the girl. "No putting your fingers in the kennels. Some dogs might nip because they're a little nervous or need more training time."

At Ellie's serious nod, Claire stopped in front of a six-month-old shepherd mix, Tabitha, whose amber eyes darted over at them. She stood and barked up a storm, sending the other dogs into a commotion, and ambled over to the bars of the kennel. She sniffed the air for a treat and when one wasn't forthcoming, she padded back over to her bed and began chewing on her rope toy. Tabitha had an ear infection that required medication for the next week, and the irritation might have been making her act out a bit.

"She's really cute," Ellie said with a bit of a frown. She knelt down in front of the cage. "Hi, puppy. I'm Ellie."

The puppy barked like crazy again and came over and sniffed the air again, then went back to her bed.

Ellie tilted her head and bit her lip. Claire could immediately tell the girl didn't feel a connection with Tabitha.

"And next we have a five-month-old springer spaniel puppy," Claire said, moving to the spinning pooch in the next kennel. In true form, Belle began spinning in circles, trying to chase her tail.

Ellie gasped. She dropped down on her knees in front of the kennel, watching the puppy with delight on her face. "Hi, there! Hi, puppy!"

The puppy stopped spinning and came closer to Ellie.

"Remember, sweetheart, don't put your fingers in the kennel," Matt said, and Claire nodded at him.

Belle barked, excitedly wagging her tail, jumping up at the kennel door and trying to sniff Ellie. She sat down and barked at Ellie, then made a play bow.

"She wants to play with me!" Ellie said. "You are so adorable!" she added. "You're exactly what I dreamed about!"

Belle began barking like crazy and spinning around, desperately trying to catch her tail in her mouth.

Claire widened her eyes and looked at Matt, who was grimacing.

Ellie laughed, her entire face lit up with happiness. "I see your name is Belle, and I know that means beautiful, and you are, but I think you look more like a Sparkle. That's what I'd name you, Sparkle." She bolted up. "This is the one! This is my puppy!"

Claire couldn't remember the last time she saw someone so excited, and she saw excited kids a lot during the course of adoptions.

"Yup, you're the one, Sparkle!" Ellie said, dropping down to her knees again and smiling at the puppy.

Who squatted and peed right on the floor, the mess seeping into the corridor to the point that they all jumped back.

"Oops," Ellie said. Then she seemed to remember what her mom said about housetraining, and worry slid into her expression. Her shoulders slumped, and her face scrunched up for a moment. Claire could tell the girl was trying not to cry.

"Well, Sparkle is definitely not housetrained," Matt said gently, a hand on his niece's shoulder. "And she sure is noisy and busy. Why don't we—"

"I'll clean it up!" Ellie added, looking from her uncle to Claire, and back at the puppy, and then back at Claire. "Are there paper towels or something?"

Claire smiled and got the roll of heavy-duty brown paper towels. "I'll take care of it, honey." She quickly mopped up the mess.

"Your mom made her requirements very clear, sweets," Matt said. "So even though Sparkle is cute, she's a long way from being trained and she seems kind of hyper."

Ellie's little shoulders slumped again, and she sucked in a breath.

Aww. This was always a difficult thing, when someone fell for an animal that wasn't the right fit for the home. "Ellie," Claire said, "two kennels down is an adorable chiweenie named Tucker who's housetrained and knows basic commands. A chiweenie is a cross between a Chihuahua and a dachshund. He'll be small even when fully grown, so he's a great size for a kid."

Ellie followed Claire to Tucker's kennel, her head hung low. "I've never heard of a chiweenie before." But there was no excitement in her voice.

"Meet Tucker," Claire said, gesturing at the little

dog, who was as calm as could be. He lay on his bed, gnawing on a rope toy. He was very cute, with floppy, cinnamon-colored ears and a long snout, and tended to look like he was smiling.

Ellie gave him something of a smile. "Hi, Tucker. You seem nice."

Tucker didn't even glance up.

"He can be slow to warm up to people," Claire explained.

But Ellie raced back to Sparkle's kennel and knelt in front of it. "I wish I could take you home, Sparkle." She sat there and watched the dog chasing her tail.

Claire looked at Matt, whose expression matched his niece's. This couldn't be easy, and she probably should have thought to warn him that something like this could happen. She'd been a little too shocked yesterday when she'd seen him at the shelter to even form an extra thought. And last night at the restaurant, all rational thought had *poofed* from her head.

"Well, let's look at the other pups," Matt said, reaching his hand toward Ellie. He glanced at Claire. "I'll bet there's another puppy that Ellie will fall in love with."

"Definitely," Claire said. "Because guess who's next, Ellie? A super sweet year-old shepherd mix named Dumpling. I'll bet you'll like him. He's super snuggly." He was inconsistent on commands, but he did know *stay*. He was slated to be on the large side of medium, which might be stretching it. Sometimes it was impossible to really know how big a dog would get.

"I guess I can meet him." But Ellie didn't get up from where she sat in front of Belle's cage. And even from here, Claire could see the glistening of Ellie's eyes. The girl was trying hard not to cry.

"Honey, maybe we could come back next weekend for the adoption event," Matt said. "These puppies will have had an extra week of training, and you might just fall in love with a dog you barely noticed this time."

"Okay, Uncle Matt," Ellie said, but she still didn't stand up. "It's okay, Sparkle. You'll find someone to love you, and you'll be best friends. That's what my mom tells me when I'm sad about not having a best friend."

Claire held her breath and glanced at Matt, whose broad shoulders slumped.

"As long as I'm nice and friendly, I'm doing my best," Ellie said to the puppy. "Then one day I'll make a best friend. It can happen anytime, Mommy said."

Claire swallowed.

Ellie let out a little sigh. "You'd be a great best friend, Sparkle. But maybe another girl will come here today, and you'll get to go home with her. Just be nice and friendly, okay, Sparkle?"

Oh God.

Ellie stood, tears shimmering in her eyes. "Bye, Sparkle. I love you."

Claire looked at Matt. He looked like he might cry too. And she'd seen him cry. Just once, a long, long time ago when he lost his brother.

Matt cleared his throat. "Tucker might be just right for you, once he gets to know you," he said, kneeling down to be eye level with his niece. "Then you get to say *chiweenie* a lot. 'I'm taking my chiweenie out. Chiweenie, where are you?'"

"I guess," Ellie said. She started to follow Matt toward Tucker's kennel next door. "Uncle Matt?" she asked, stopping. "I know Sparkle isn't housetrained like Mommy wants, but I could housetrain her. I've read all about how."

Matt seemed to consider that. "Well, let me send your mom a picture of her." He took out his cell phone and snapped a photo. "Ooh, that's a good one. I'll let her know Sparkle doesn't exactly meet the requirements, but that we're both willing to work extra hard training her." He texted something and then waited.

Claire was hoping Laura would be unable to resist the puppy's adorableness.

His phone pinged. "'Not housetrained?'" he read aloud. "'Doesn't know a single command? I'm sorry, Matt. No.'" He turned to Ellie. "Sweetie, you'll be at school from the time you leave at seven thirty until you get home at three," Matt said gently. "That's all day. That would put everything to do with caring for Sparkle on your mom's shoulders."

"Yeah," Ellie whispered, and her face scrunched up again. Claire knew the girl was willing herself not to cry.

"Could we put a hold on Belle—Sparkle?" Matt asked. "Just until we can talk to my sister face-to-face? Maybe she'll compromise on a requirement."

"But not both," Ellie said, her face crumpling again. "Sparkle isn't housetrained. She doesn't know any commands."

Claire's heart was so heavy, her knees might not hold

her up much longer. "I'll put a hold until tomorrow," she assured him.

Ellie looked both hopeful and not. "Thanks for showing me the puppies, Miss Claire. Bye, Sparkle. I love you."

The little brown-and-white pup gave a little bark and then continued chasing her tail.

"She said bye back!" Ellie said, a smile breaking through.

Matt smiled and took his niece's hand. "Why did I think this would be a snap?" he whispered to Claire.

"Few things ever are," Claire said.

He held her gaze for a moment. "I'll be in touch as soon as I can."

So much for keeping her distance, cutting contact, moving on. Claire bit her lip and nodded, watching the pair walk away, Matt's arm around the little girl's dejected shoulders.

Oh, am I in trouble, she thought.

"No and no," Laura whispered after Matt made another pitch to his sister for Sparkle. They stood at the kitchen island, Matt badly chopping peppers for a salad while Laura checked the chicken roasting in the oven. The house sure smelled good. "But look at this face," he said, picking up his phone and showing her the adorable pup again.

"You're getting pepper bits on your phone," Laura said, refusing to look at the photo. "And could you cut those a little thinner?"

"Uh-oh, you're mad at me."

"Of course I am!" she said. "I explicitly said the dog had to be housetrained and know basic commands. This Sparkle is neither! And now I'm the bad guy."

"I know, and I'm sorry. But she's incredibly cute," Matt said. "And Ellie fell for her hard."

Laura sighed and put on oven mitts to take out the baked potatoes. "I just had all the area rugs cleaned, and the bedroom carpets are brand-new. I work part-time, I volunteer at Ellie's school. I can't housetrain a puppy, Matt."

Wait a minute.

Yes.

Of course!

Why hadn't this occurred to him before? "*I'll* train the puppy," he said. "I'll read a book, watch some videos. I'm sure I'll figure it out."

Laura looked at him. "Matt, honey, I appreciate that, but no. I don't want accidents in the house for weeks on end. I don't want a dog that doesn't stop or stay when I need it to. Sorry, Matt, but I'm putting my foot down."

She had every right. "Ah hell, I really screwed this up," he said. "I shouldn't have taken Ellie to see puppies she wouldn't be able to adopt."

His sister put a hand on his arm. "I'm sure that just the right puppy will come along."

"I guess," he said, hating that he'd have to disappoint his niece—and Claire.

"Thanks for helping with the salad," she said, eyeing the bowl of misshapen lettuce and oddly shaped peppers and cucumbers. She laughed, then shrugged. "I'll call it Uncle Salad."

"I'd better go call Claire and let her know to release the hold on Sparkle," he said.

Laura nodded. "I am sorry it didn't work out with this particular dog. And I do appreciate you doing the heavy lifting with the search. It's not easy being the yes or no woman."

He smiled. "I know."

"Dinner in ten minutes," she said, which meant he'd better go tell Claire now, and then Ellie.

His sister had always been no-nonsense, though when you had kids you probably had to be, or you'd end up with four untrained puppies peeing on the area rugs.

He nodded and headed up to the guest room and closed the door. Phone in hand, he sat on the bed and fished out the card Claire had given him, the shelter's information on one side, her cell phone on the back.

He punched in her number. The sound of her voice saying *hello?* sent a little tremor through him. He'd probably never get used to just calling her up, hearing her voice, running into her.

"Hi, Claire, it's Matt. You can let the hold go, unfortunately."

"I'm sorry. Is Ellie okay?"

"No. My sister's mad at me for making her the bad guy, so my brother-in-law is probably getting an earful right now and will be pissed at me too."

"Oh no," Claire said.

"I even offered to train Sparkle myself, but my sister won't go for it. I get it, but I wish this could have worked out."

"You'd be willing to train the puppy?" Claire asked.

"Sure. I mean, I know I don't have experience, but I'd do my research. It's not like I'm focused on anything else right now."

She was silent for a second, then said, "Matt, I have a crazy idea."

"I'm all ears."

"I live in the Kingdom Creek development—a house with a big fenced yard. There's a small one-bedroom apartment over the garage. Maybe you could move in temporarily to foster and train Sparkle, and when she's ready, she can be adopted by Ellie. Your niece can even help you train her."

Huh. Win-win for everyone, especially him in the short-term. He'd have his own place, even if it was connected to Claire's house. He'd have some space to figure out his future. And Claire had used the word *temporarily*, so she was making it clear he'd go when the puppy was trained.

Best of all, he had an immediate mission: to train a cute puppy for his beloved niece.

"I'll move in tomorrow," he said.

There was silence for a moment, then she rattled off the address and some information about the place. The apartment came with basic furnishings, so he'd just have to move his big duffel bag.

"Thanks, Claire," he said. "I know I'm probably not your first choice of tenant."

"At least I know you. Or did," she said. "The last couple I rented to was a disaster."

Or did. The words hit him like a left hook in the gut. "See you tomorrow," he said, needing to get off the phone, to break the connection with her.

But despite her saying goodbye and the click in his ear, an image of Claire Asher in a long, pale pink dress came storming into his mind. Prom night, so many years ago. They'd long planned to lose their virginity to each other that night as a tribute to their past and a promise for their future, but as the night went on, Matt knew he wouldn't touch her. She'd known he was going to enlist, like his brother had before him, but she kept talking about when he came home, saying that she'd wait for him, reminding him she'd be semi-local in Chapel Hill for college but that she could transfer depending on where he got stationed. But on prom night, with Claire looking like a movie star in that beautiful pink gown, the whole world open to her, all Matt could think about was smart, interesting Claire putting her life on hold when she deserved so much more.

Except she'd stayed in Spring Forest. Had gone to the local college. Married a hometown guy. Why? Why hadn't she used the opportunity of being free to spread those glittering wings of hers? He didn't understand it.

He supposed he'd have a lot of chances to ask her now that he'd be living in her house.

Chapter Four

"**Y**ou *what*?" Claire's sister, Della, said as she handed Claire her sesame chicken from the Taste of China delivery bag. Della had come over to catch up on the blind date, running into Matt at the restaurant, and what-is-this-about-helping-him-and-his-niece-pick-out-a-puppy? By the time Claire got to the part about Matt moving into the "in-law apartment" to train the dog, Della was shaking her head with older sister wisdom. "You're going to be living together!"

"Hardly," Claire said, opening up the container of sesame chicken. Nothing, not even her nerves, could spoil her appetite for this deliciousness. "The apartment is completely separate with its own entrance. I'll rarely see him." She pulled apart her chopsticks and dug in.

Della narrowed her gaze and picked up a succulent

bite of beef in garlic sauce and a broccoli spear. "Except the entrance is up those deck stairs." She pointed with her chopsticks toward the sliding glass door to the back-yard, where Dempsey lay in her memory foam dog bed. "You'll see him every time you're sitting here. And con-sidering we're in your living room and your kitchen is directly in front of us, you'll be seeing him constantly."

"He *is* nice to look at," Claire said. "So that's a plus."

Della put down her chopsticks. "Honey. There isn't even a word for how badly he hurt you. You can't go through that again. *I* can't!"

Yup, Claire remembered. All her plans for herself had gone up in smoke. Maybe another girl would have rallied and gone off to the University of North Carolina in Chapel Hill, as planned. Planned—ha! Back then "the plan" had been for Matt to be in basic training, then stationed somewhere stateside or overseas, and they'd see each other when he could come home for precious and rare breaks. She'd graduate, he'd come home for good and then they'd plan what was next. Except in-stead, he'd broken up with her with barely an explana-tion, and she'd been so heartbroken and confused that the pain had messed with her head. She'd been unable to think straight, to think of anything except how her life had been derailed.

Her poor sister had tried to get her to see that it was also an opportunity, to go to school and start her new life far away. But Claire hadn't been able to pull herself up and out of her heartache. She hadn't gone away to school, hadn't gone to college at all that first semester. Instead, she'd cried constantly, unwilling to get out of bed, unwilling to imagine a future without the guy she loved—without Matt Fielding.

Her sister had come over every day, bringing her food she ate one bite of, brushing her hair, making her bed around her, and finally, after three weeks, dragging her out of bed for a sisters trip to the Bahamas, whether she wanted to go or not. Della had packed her suitcase and forced her on the plane. The white sand and turquoise water, the fruity drinks and warm, breezy air had helped restore her.

Back home, she'd finally enrolled in the local college, married her second boyfriend, a man she hadn't realized was all wrong for her. Luckily, by then, her passion for becoming a teacher, particularly of middle school kids in the throes of figuring out who they were, had gripped her. Claire had run with it, getting her master's and advising extracurricular groups. She loved teaching. By the time her marriage had fallen apart, Claire had had her own busy life, which included volunteering at Furever Paws. Or at least that was what she'd told herself to explain why her husband's betrayal hadn't steamrollered her the way it should have.

I don't believe you ever really loved me, her husband had said when he told her he'd fallen for someone else, really fallen, and that he was leaving Claire. But he was wrong; she had loved him, very much. *I think you rebounded with me after your high school sweetheart destroyed you.*

Destroyed. Heavy word. One her sister would apply, as well. But Claire hadn't been destroyed. People had to be resilient, had to move on. Still, no sense not being careful with yourself to avoid having your heart smashed to smithereens in the future.

Claire smiled and squeezed her sister's hand. "Eat up. And stop worrying. Matt Fielding and I aren't getting back together. I'm just bringing together a little girl and a puppy."

"Except Matt and said puppy are moving in upstairs."

Claire put down her bite of sesame chicken. She could lie to herself all she wanted, but she'd never been able to lie to Della, who saw through her. "Every time I see him, my heart races and my stomach flip-flops, and these little chills slide up my spine."

"Yeah, that's called not having gotten over your first boyfriend. Who broke your heart. Who's moving upstairs. Who you said has no plans—to stay or go."

Claire sobered up fast. She had to be careful about Matt.

"I'm just saying, Claire. You want what you want—a husband and child. A family. You've been saying yes to men who ask you out in the supermarket. You've been saying yes to blind dates—although, you derailed a perfectly good one, even though I suppose you might have dodged a bullet with that one too. You know what you want. So don't get sucked in by a handsome face and memories, Claire. He hurt you terribly."

It didn't mean he'd hurt her again, though. Necessarily. Eighteen years was a long time. Maybe this was meant to be their second chance. He'd been put in her path. And now he was moving into her rental apartment. *Oh God.* Their second chance? Now she was concocting a fantasy about him? Why did he have such a hold on her after all this time?

What she needed to do was to focus on what she wanted out of life: the right partner and a child. That meant really getting out there, and so that was what she would do. She'd kissed her share of frogs since her divorce, but there was bound to be a "prince" out there somewhere. She'd focus on finding him, and then the hold Matt had on her heart, mind and soul would be released.

Right? Yes, right.

"I'll be careful," she promised her sister. "And by the way, I'm open to more blind dates."

"That's my girl," her sister said, stealing a hunk of sesame chicken from her container.

Maybe she'd even join a dating service to speed things up, vet the men via email "chats" before they even met.

"But no matter what, I'm here if you need me," her sister said. Knowingly.

Claire bit her lip. Even her wise sibling knew how strong the Matt Fielding hold was.

Cripes.

"Guess what, Ellie-Belly?" Matt said, sitting down on the round braided rug in his niece's bedroom. *Not bad*, he told himself as he realized he got down on his bad leg in record time and without wincing.

Ellie was playing "dog tea," serving her huge stuffed dogs who were sitting around the rug in a semicircle. Half had fallen over, but she'd prop them back up when it was their time for tea.

"What?" she asked, pouring for the white poodle beside her.

"What do you think about me moving to my own place nearby and fostering Sparkle and training her so that you could adopt her in about a month's time?"

Ellie gasped so loud that his sister came running up the stairs.

"Everything okay?" Laura asked, looking from her daughter to her brother.

Ellie flew into Matt's arms. "Uncle Matt just told me he's going to train Sparkle for me so we can adopt her!"

Laura smiled. "He told me all about it. I'll miss having you around, though, Matt. You just got here."

"I'll be five minutes away," he said. "And, Ellie, you're welcome to come over whenever your mom says it's okay. You can help me train Sparkle."

"This is the best day of my life so far," Ellie said, throwing her arms around Matt for another hug. "Thank you."

"Anything for my favorite niece," Matt said.

"Aren't I your only niece?" Ellie asked.

"What about Sparkle? Isn't she my other niece?"

"I guess she is!" Ellie said. "But don't tell her I'm your favorite. She'll get jealous."

"I won't."

He glanced at Laura, who was smiling. He looked at Ellie, who was also smiling. Even the stuffed dogs were smiling.

But he wondered if Claire was even remotely happy about the situation. She saw a win-win for everyone and had made the offer. But he couldn't imagine she'd be happy having him on her property.

"Matt, could you help me with something downstairs?" his sister asked, gesturing her head toward the door.

He already knew what this was about. When he'd told his sister about Claire's offer, she'd said it sounded like big-time trouble—for Claire. He'd brushed Laura off and finally gotten her okay for Ellie's sake, and then sprinted upstairs to avoid Laura's questions.

Downstairs, she pulled him into the laundry room and shut the door. "Look, it's been almost two decades since you and Claire broke up. So maybe there's no unfinished business. But I'm telling you right now, brother, do not play with that woman's head. Don't start something you can't finish."

"Who says I'm starting anything?"

"Hmm, moving into your first love's house? She's divorced. You're single. Trust me, something is going to happen."

"And?" he asked. Why did he feel so defensive? Because deep down he wanted something to happen? "What if something does?"

"Men." She shook her head slowly. "You're figuring out what to do with your life. Claire Asher is living hers. She's clearly dating. You hurt her once, Matt. All I'm saying is, if you're not sure about her, don't even go there. Leave her be."

"I'm not sure about *anything*," he said.

"Which is why she deserves better than a three-week stand, or however long it takes you to train Sparkle."

He sighed inwardly because his sister was right. As usual.

* * *

The next afternoon, Claire waited for Matt in the gift shop area of the lobby, putting together a box of necessities for Sparkle. She'd included a cute purple collar with white stars, a silver, bone-shaped temporary name tag with Sparkle's name and Matt's cell phone number engraved on it, two different types of leashes, a water bowl, a food bowl, the kibble Sparkle had been eating, a few toys and a packet of information on training and caring for a puppy. Since Matt would be officially fostering the pup, the shelter would take care of Sparkle's vet appointments, and right now the dog was up-to-date on all shots. In about six weeks or so, Sparkle would be ready to be spayed, but right now, all Matt had to focus on was training the pup to live with his sister's family.

When Matt walked in, Claire gave up on pretending she wasn't hopelessly attracted to the man. First love aside, Matt was fostering Sparkle so that his little niece could have the dog she'd fallen in love with. That was pure kindness, especially since Matt had never had a dog nor grown up with one.

"Everything you need for Sparkle is in here," she said quickly, willing herself not to stare at him. "Let's leave this for now, and we'll pick it up when we bring Sparkle through."

"Me, a dog trainer," he said with a smile. "Who knew?"

"What you're doing for your niece is really wonderful," she said as they headed to the kennels.

"I'm just glad I can."

As they entered the kennel area, Matt made a beeline for Hank. "Poor guy," he said. Hank looked at him, staring woefully. The dog got up and walked to the edge of the kennel, and Matt slowly knelt down to say hi. "Hey, guy." Couldn't be so great to be cooped up in there. "Maybe I can take Hank for a walk before we get Sparkle," he said to Claire. "I feel for him."

She smiled. "He'd love it." She picked up a leash from the rack and told Hank to sit, which he did, then she entered the kennel and closed it behind her. She put the leash on, then led him out and latched the kennel again. "There's a path out that side door you can take. It's a quarter-mile loop. I'll go finalize Sparkle's papers, and then we'll be good to go by the time you come back with Hank."

Again, he knelt down beside the senior dog, and she noticed it took him a beat longer than expected. Injury, she figured.

He gave Hank a scratch, then stood up as slowly. "How is this dog still at Furever Paws? He seems like such a good dog—he's calm, he's an old soul and he's awesome looking."

All true, she thought, her heart squeezing for the man and the dog. "I know. But older dogs, especially big ones, tend to languish. We make sure he gets lots of love and TLC."

He nodded and looked at Hank. "See you in a few," he said to Claire.

As she watched him walk away with Hank, she knew she was sunk.

Twenty minutes later, the paperwork was complete and Matt was back, Hank looking quite happy.

"You can do as I did just before," Claire told him, "Lead him in on leash, latch the kennel behind you, unleash him, ask him to sit, then come out and relatch."

"Got it." He did as instructed, standing in front of the kennel as though he was having a hard time walking away.

"And how about a biscuit for being such a great dog?" Claire asked, handing Matt the bone-shaped treat.

Matt slipped it through the kennel bars, and Hank slowly ambled over and picked it up with his mouth, then took it to his bed and began nibbling.

"See you next time, big guy," Matt said.

A few kennels down, Claire had Matt do the same with Sparkle, grabbing her favorite pink-and-purple-striped blankie to put in the box of her things.

"Wow, you are crazy cute," Matt said, kneeling down again and giving Sparkle a pat. "No wonder Ellie went nuts over you."

Sparkle barked up a storm, jumping up on Matt's leg.

"No jump," Claire said firmly. Sparkle remained where she was. "No jump," she repeated, gently moving the dog off Matt. "She'll get the hang of it."

"We'll learn together," he told the puppy. "We're both beginners."

I can help you, she wanted to say. *I'll share everything I know.* But then she'd be with him more than would be healthy for her heart and peace of mind.

In the lobby, Claire grabbed the box of Sparkle's things. She took a final look through, making sure she hadn't forgotten anything.

"What do I owe you for that?" Matt asked, taking out his wallet.

"Oh, since you're fostering, it's on us," she said.

"As a donation then," he said.

That was nice. She named a figure and he walked up to the counter, where Birdie happened to be sitting, training a volunteer on front desk coverage. She could tell Birdie liked Matt's generosity.

"You're doing a wonderful thing by fostering this pup and training her for your niece," Birdie said, giving Matt a serious once-over with her assessing blue eyes. "If you need anything or have any questions, call the shelter anytime. And of course, you'll have one of our best resources steps away," she added, nodding at Claire.

Matt glanced at Claire and smiled, then turned back to Birdie. "Thanks. I appreciate that. And I'm sure I will have many, many questions."

The bell jangled over the front door to Furever Paws, and a thirtyish blonde woman wearing sunglasses and high heels walked in.

"I'd like to adopt a dog," the woman said, despite the fact that Birdie was in midsentence with her trainee. "Small, under twenty pounds. A female. She can't bark. And I don't like dogs with bug eyes." She glanced at Sparkle. "Oh, this one's cute. Did you just adopt her?"

"Yes," Matt said, picking up Sparkle and holding her against his chest, one arm seemingly protecting the puppy from the woman's long pink nails. "She's taken."

Claire stared at the woman. *Bug eyes? I don't like dogs that bark? Exqueeze me?* "Cute indeed but she's a big barker."

The blonde shivered and pushed her big white sunglasses on top of her head. "Oh. Well, I said I wanted a nonbarking dog. I can't stand yippers."

Birdie cleared her throat, her blue eyes steely. "Dogs bark. It's what they do."

Sparkle let out a series of yips to prove Birdie's point.

"My ears," the blonde said, covering them with her hands.

Could she *be* more dramatic?

"We have some beautiful short-haired cats," Claire said to the woman. "Mirabelle is particularly stunning. Cats, of course, don't bark. And they're under twenty pounds."

The woman raised an eyebrow. "Mirabelle? I do like that name. Cats are very queenly. Yes, I'd like to see her."

Birdie smiled and stood. "I'll show you the way."

The woman followed, her heels clicking on the floor.

"Why come in saying you want a dog if you can't handle barking?" Matt asked as they headed for their cars.

"Some folks like the idea of a dog, but the reality is quite different than their fantasy," Claire explained. "And others ignore what they don't want in a pet because they can't resist how the animal looks." She shook her head. "Last week, someone brought back a dog because she didn't like the way it followed her from room to room."

"You're kidding."

She shook her head. "I wish I were. I truly do."

"I guess some people don't know what they're letting themselves in for," Matt said. "Like me."

Claire laughed. "But you're doing this for a good

cause." She reached her car and put the box in the back-seat. "We'll be at the house in no time—Kingdom Creek is just minutes away. I think you'll like the privacy of the development."

"Kingdom Creek. Sounds fancy."

She shrugged. "It was the house I lived in with my husband. Was supposed to be *our* forever home. For a family and two rescue dogs and four cats. Maybe some birds and rabbits too. Now it's just me. And Dempsey, of course. Thank God for Dempsey."

Oh God. Had she said all that? *Our forever home?* What was wrong with her? *Just stop talking, Claire.*

"How long have you been divorced?" he asked, presumably setting Sparkle down in case she had to do her business. The puppy immediately set to sniffing around her, and Claire focused on that instead of meeting Matt's eyes.

"Three years. He started cheating on me the year prior to our breakup. But he married his affair so he thinks that makes it okay."

She felt her cheeks flush with heat. Hadn't she just told herself to stop talking? The man was making her nervous. That had to be it.

"Cheating is never okay," Matt said, holding her gaze for a second. "I'm sorry you went through all that."

"What's that saying? What doesn't kill you makes you stronger?" *I got through you, Matt Fielding—of course I got through my divorce.*

"Don't I know it," he said with a kind of wistful nod.

"Guess we've both been through a thing or two."

He nodded again. "We both had been through a thing or two when we were a couple, Claire. I'd lost my brother. You'd lost your dad. It's always friggen something."

"Yeah," she said. "It is. Thank God for cuddly dogs, huh?"

He smiled and scooped Sparkle up, giving her a nuzzle. "I'll be right behind you." He nodded at the car next to hers.

A lone duffel was in the backseat. Was that everything he had? She supposed he couldn't accumulate a life's worth of possessions while on multiple tours of duty.

Fifteen minutes. And then Matt Fielding would be moving into her house, their bedrooms separated only by drywall. It had to be the worst—and best—idea she ever had.

"And this is the bedroom," Claire said as Matt followed her into the large room of the second-floor apartment.

He liked the place. The apartment was a decent size, the living room spacious, with French doors leading to the small deck and stairs down to the backyard. That was his entrance, so he wouldn't necessarily run into Claire unless she happened to be out with Dempsey in this part of the yard. The bathroom had a big tub and spa-type shower, which was a plus when you were six foot one. He barely noticed the kitchen since he didn't cook much, other than basic spaghetti with jarred marinara sauce and never-toasted-right toast. But he did notice the windows—lots of them. Matt could breathe here, relax here. Considering that the proximity of Claire Asher made those things difficult from the get-go, it was a real testament to how comfortable he felt in the apartment.

He put his duffel bag on the queen-size bed. He and Claire had created a lot of memories in their two years as a teenage couple, but "the bedroom" hadn't been a part of them. He'd barely touched her, though he'd been dying to. Hands skimming over her shirts and sweaters, sometimes slipping underneath. That was as far as they'd gone in those days. They'd been lip-locked constantly, and he'd fantasized every night about sex and particularly sex with Claire Asher. Now, standing inches from a bed, her light perfume enveloping him, awareness of her driving him mad, he wanted to lie down and take her with him.

Instead, he leaned down to give Sparkle a pat for being a good dog and not barking or peeing on the rug, as she'd done on the tour of the kitchen. Claire hadn't blinked. She'd grabbed paper towels, followed up with a Swiffer and that had been that. "It's a nice place. Don't you agree, Sparkle? A good training center for you."

Sparkle barked twice, looking up at him. The bedroom carpet was soft, which had to be a plus for a little dog.

"I'll take that as a yes," Claire said with a smile. "Okay, back to the kitchen. I have a whole folder of info for you."

"Info?" he repeated, following her down the hall.

"For your new life as a foster dad who'll be training a five-month-old puppy."

As she turned to head out of the bedroom, he reached for her hand, and she whirled around.

"I'm not even sure if I said thank you. For this," he

added, gesturing at the room. "You saved the day for my family. Now I have an excited niece, a not-pissed-off sister and a not-pissed-off brother-in-law."

She laughed. "Well, the apartment was empty and the situation presented itself, so..."

"So, here we are."

"Here we are," she repeated, then cleared her throat and turned to go again. This *had* to be kind of uncomfortable for her. It sure as hell was for him. But in equally good and bad ways.

Back in the small white kitchen, Claire picked up a folder and opened it. "Okay, straight to business. This contains everything you need to know about training lessons and basic puppy care."

The little brown-and-white dog began turning in circles, trying to catch her tail, which was her trademark move. "Hey, Sparkle," Matt said.

The dog ignored him.

"Sparkle," Matt said again.

Ignored by a twelve-pound spinning pooch.

"Page two," Claire said, pointing at the folder. She turned to the bags she'd brought from the shelter, and took out a pack of small training treats.

She held a treat in her hand, her fist closed over it, and waved it near the dog. "Sparkle."

The dog stopped and looked at her hand.

"Yup, she definitely smells the treat. She can't see it, but she can smell it." The dog sniffed around. "Sparkle!" Claire said again.

The dog looked at her.

"Good dog!" Claire said, and gave her the treat. "We're teaching Sparkle her name. Every time you say her name and she looks at you—actually makes eye contact—give her a tiny treat. After she associates the word Sparkle with a treat, she'll realize she gets a treat every time she acknowledges it. Then we'll move on to calling her from another room."

"Huh. I guess I always wondered how dogs learned their names."

"I do expect you to do your homework," she said, pointing at the folder.

"Yes, Teacher. I absolutely will."

She smiled, and it lit up her entire face. "Now for a housetraining lesson. The plan will be to take Sparkle out first thing in the morning, then every hour, immediately after she eats, after she wakes from a nap and before bed. She'll get used to the idea that doing her business is meant for outside, not inside."

"Did you say every hour?"

Claire laughed. "It'll take a few days, but then you can stop that and move to after meals and naps."

"Well, Sparkle," he said, and before he could continue, the little spinning creature looked right at him! "Hey, she looked at me!" He reached into the bag for a treat and gave it to her. Sparkle sure did like these treats.

"Perfect. It really happens fast. In a couple of days, she'll know it's her name, and we can work on more commands like *come* and *stay*."

"You're a good dog," he said to Sparkle. The puppy turned and looked at him, which earned her another treat.

Claire smiled. "So she's had a few treats, and she last went potty on the kitchen floor. We don't want her to associate eliminating with the kitchen, so let's take her out. If she pees or poops, she gets a treat."

"Will she gain a hundred pounds?" he asked.

Claire smiled. "These treats are tiny and temporary. Plus, Sparkle is so busy and will get so much exercise running around the fenced yard that she can have all the treats she deserves."

"Key word is deserves, I figure," he said.

"Absolutely. No treats for just being adorable."

He laughed. "I'm getting the hang of this."

She handed him the leash. "Let's take her outside."

He followed her through the French doors to the small deck, and then down the stairs to the fenced yard.

Sparkle did her business, which got her a "good dog" and a treat. This dog training business was going all right so far.

"Well, I have two classes of essays to grade," she said. "But text or call if you need me."

Wait. You're leaving? Suddenly Matt felt a little out of his element at the idea of being all alone with the puppy. Sparkle was sturdy enough, he supposed, but there was something fragile about her too. She was a baby. Maybe that was it. "What should I do with her?" he asked.

Claire laughed. "Well, you could play with her out here, just watch her explore the yard and sniff around. Then you can take her upstairs and let her get acclimated to the apartment, show her where her crate and bed are, her food bowls, that kind of thing."

"And then what?"

She tilted her head, looking at him as if he'd gone a little crazy. "And then you just be."

"Be?"

"You go about your life. Unpack. Make yourself a cup of coffee. Take a shower. Watch TV. She'll do her thing. You'll be sitting on the couch and might find her trying to jump up to curl up next to you."

"Is she allowed on the couch?" he asked.

"This is a very dog-centric house," she said. "So, yes."

Sparkle came back over and sniffed his shoe, then looked up at him expectantly. He had a feeling she wanted another treat.

"I guess I'll let her explore out here a bit more, and then take her up. I can do my homework while she explores her new digs. I have to read up on the crate training thing."

"Well, I'm here if you need me," she said, kneeling down to pet Sparkle. Then she stood back up and entered the house through the sliding glass door beyond her patio. Right under his deck.

The minute she was gone, he missed her.

"It's just you and me, Sparkle," he said. He threw one of the little balls he'd stuffed in his other pocket—the one that wasn't chock-full of treats—and Sparkle went flying after it. He laughed. "Fetch!" he called. She did not fetch. In fact, she ignored the ball in favor of a leaf being tossed around in the breeze. He laughed and watched the pup explore the yard, sniffing at every blade of grass, and, ten minutes later, he realized he felt something he hadn't in a long time.

Almost relaxed.

Chapter Five

The force of the explosion propelled him backward and he slammed against a tree, his leg twisted at a strange angle, warm, sticky blood running down his temple. McCubbers. He had to check on McCubbers... He could hear whimpering. Fear. Pain. The sound— that whimpering—was inside his head, all around him. McCubbers, I'm trying to get to you...

Matt bolted upright, his breath ragged. Again, the soft bedding confused him until he realized he wasn't in Afghanistan; he was in his new apartment at Claire's house. He took in the pale gray walls, slightly illuminated by the moon, and the dresser with the square mirror over it. He closed his eyes and took a deep, calming breath.

Damn nightmare. Always the same one.

Except he could still hear the whimpering.

McCubbers definitely never made a high-pitched sound like that. Where the hell was it coming from? He glanced around for the source of the sound.

His gaze landed on the kennel across from his bed. Sparkle stood by the door, whining and whimpering.

"Hey, there," he said, getting out of bed. "Someone has to go outside?" He glanced at the time on his phone. Only 3:13 a.m. Such was the life of a puppy trainer. He slid his feet into his sneakers, put on his leather jacket, then unlatched the kennel and took Sparkle outside and down the deck stairs, trying to be quiet so as not to wake Claire. He had no idea where her bedroom was in relation to his deck or this part of the yard.

He led Sparkle to the grass on the far side of the yard. "Go potty," he whispered to the pup, per what he'd read in the pile of training articles Claire had given him. Apparently, it was a good idea for a dog to have a "spot," so they'd do their business quickly—a good thing in the middle of the night and when it was freezing. Right now, it was both. He still had two treats in his pocket, and gave one to Sparkle with a "good dog."

Back upstairs, he took off his jacket and sneakers, gave the little dog a pat, then put her back in the kennel and got into bed. Man, these sheets were soft. And the down comforter and pillows were already lulling him to sleep.

Whimper. Whine. Whiiiine. Whimper.

He peeled open an eye. "How am I supposed to sleep with that racket?" he asked Sparkle.

More whimpering. More whining.

"I'm not supposed to reward that," he said, getting out of bed again. "Tell you what. If you stop making those annoying sounds, I'll let you out for a little while. You can understand a bargain, right, Sparkle?"

And don't tell my sister, he added silently as he walked to the kennel. Sparkle immediately piped down. She looked positively thrilled when Matt opened the door. He scooped her up and brought up to his bed, the little brown-and-white mutt curling up beside him. She leaned over and licked his arm, then got up, turned around in a circle three times and settled back down with a sigh.

Dogs sighed? Who knew?

Her little eyes closed.

"Hey, wait a minute, sneaky. You can't get comfortable. You have to sleep in your kennel."

Sparkle started snoring, another thing he didn't know dogs did. The sturdy little weight of her felt kind of comforting next to him, and honestly, Matt was too tired to put her back in the kennel. He'd confess to Claire in the morning and see how bad an infraction it was.

"I'm already in the doghouse with Claire just by virtue of being me," he whispered to Sparkle, who opened her eyes as if she really was listening. "So best behavior tomorrow, got it?"

Sparkle got up and came closer, licked his face and burrowed her way under the comforter, stretching out on her side against his rib cage. He smiled and shook his head, giving her exposed belly a gentle rub.

"Who's training who here?" he whispered as the dog's eyes closed.

* * *

As Claire was bringing Dempsey outside the next morning at 6:00 a.m., she saw Matt in the yard, tossing a ball for Sparkle. The puppy did not fetch. She tilted her head and went running in the opposite direction.

Claire laughed and reached into her pockets for her fleece gloves. It was pretty chilly this morning. "Well, we can work on fetch once she's got the basics down."

Matt whirled around as though surprised to see her. "I thought fetch was hardwired into dogs," he said with that killer smile.

How could he look this good at six in the morning, with hardly any sleep? At around 3:00 a.m., she'd heard him open the door to his deck and go outside. She'd forced herself to stay in bed and not tiptoe over to watch him. Of course, she'd lain awake for more than an hour, remembering, wondering, thinking. She must have kissed Matt Fielding three thousand times in the two years they'd been a couple. Being in his arms or holding his hand or having his arm slung around her shoulders had always felt so good, so comforting, so right.

He'd told her that he was a virgin too and that he wanted his first time to be with her, but he wouldn't pressure her—he wanted her to tell him when she was ready. She'd felt ready but afraid in a way she couldn't explain to herself, let alone him, so she'd started telling him she'd be ready on prom night. Far enough away that she could mentally and emotionally prepare herself. For what, she didn't know. Sex, particularly with the love of her life, had seemed huge, monumental—the biggest deal in the world.

And then instead of sneaking off to a motel at midnight after the prom in their high school gym, where she and Matt had slow danced and kissed through most of the songs, he'd broken up with her. In his car, in the high school parking lot. He'd said he was sorry, but it had to be over between them, it was for the best; she'd see. She'd been so speechless she couldn't even form words in her head beyond *What?* And then she'd gone running from his car, her high-heeled sandals in her hand, and because she lived three houses from the school, he'd let her go.

All that next day she'd forced herself not to call him, storm his house, demand to know what the hell he was doing to them. She'd lasted two hours. She'd pounded on the Fieldings' door, but his mother had told Claire that Matt wasn't home, that he'd started his own pre-boot-camp regimen and was probably at the high school field. She'd wanted to rush over there but hadn't, hoping, praying he'd come for her once some time, meaning hours, had passed. He hadn't. So she'd gone to his house again, his mother casting compassionate glances at her as Matt reiterated everything he'd said the night before. It was for the best, he was leaving in the morning, separate paths, separate ways. He'd been so resolute, no tears in his eyes, when Claire had been gushing tears and choking on her sobs to the point that his mother had come into the kitchen with tissues and then hurried out to give them privacy again.

That was the last time she'd seen Matt Fielding until the other day at Furever Paws.

Her sister had said it was a good thing she hadn't lost

her virginity to Matt, but Claire had always wished she had. That way, she could have hated him for using her for sex, *then* dumping her. Instead, he'd kept his hands to himself. Ugh, the whole thing was so complicated. Good guy one way. Jerk another.

But still so freaking gorgeous. And sexy. All that sunlit thick, brown hair. The intense blue eyes framed by long, dark lashes. His shoulders in that black leather jacket. His long, muscular legs in those worn jeans. Matt was pure hotness. Always had been, but now the tall, lanky guy he'd been had been replaced with a man.

Stop staring, she ordered herself.

Oh gosh—what had he said? Something about fetch being hardwired into dogs. "Well, the springer spaniel side of Sparkle has the retrieving thing to a science, but whatever she's mixed with might not."

"Ah, makes sense. I still have a lot to learn," he said. "How bad is it that I let Sparkle sleep on my bed last night?"

He'd always been a softie. Except when it came to not dumping her, that was. "It can be irresistible to let a dog—especially a puppy—sleep with you. It's really up to you, well, your sister and what her future plans are. If she's going to let Sparkle sleep with Ellie, then it's fine. Otherwise, it's better to get her used to sleeping in the kennel for consistency."

"Got it. I'll have to ask Laura. She can be a real marshmallow about some things. I can see her letting Sparkle sleep with Ellie. I know that's what Ellie will want, for sure."

Claire was about to respond when raised voices coming from the house next door stopped her.

"I'm not breaking up with her, and you can't make me!" a boy's voice hiss-whispered from the next yard.

"She's all wrong for you!" a woman's voice said. "She's trouble and she'll bring you down. Suddenly you're thinking of *not* going to college? Over my dead body!"

"Whatever!" the boy shouted. Then a door slammed.

Claire glanced at Matt and whispered, "Seventeen-year-old Justin next door. For the past few months I've never seen him without a long-haired blonde."

"Blondes are trouble for sure," he said, reaching out to move a strand of hair the wind had blown across her cheek.

Claire froze, his touch so unexpected and so undeniably welcome that she couldn't speak.

"Sorry. Overstepped," he said, moving backward a bit. "I—" He clamped down on whatever he'd been about to say.

"If anyone's trouble, it's first loves living on your property, making you remember the good ole days." *Oh God.* Had she really just said that? *Sure, Claire, open up that can o' worms. Are you crazy?*

"Tell me about it," he said. "I was up half the night remembering."

"What were you remembering?" she asked. Because she couldn't resist. And she had to know.

"How crazy about you I was," he said.

"I thought you were. In fact, I thought you were as

crazy about me as I was for you. But you dumped me. Remember that?"

Oh God, again. Had she actually said *that*? What was the point of having this discussion almost two decades later? *Lame, Claire.*

But then again, they'd never had this discussion. He'd broken her heart and then he was gone. Until a few days ago. So why not have it out, right here, right now? Being around Matt made her feel like that seventeen-year-old girl—in love, the whole world in front of her, everything possible. Until it wasn't.

He turned away, his attention on Sparkle for a moment as the little dog sniffed a tree trunk a few feet away. "I 'dumped' you because I was trouble."

"Oh, right. The imminent soldier, about to go off to serve his country, enlisting in his fallen brother's memory. Oh yeah, you were big trouble."

"I mean that I would have held you back," he said, his gaze on her. "You wanted so much back then. You had so many dreams and plans. And I didn't have any of that in me."

"Funny how I managed to be so in love with you," she said, shaking her head.

"I honestly don't know why you were. I had nothing to offer to you. I have less to offer you now. If I wanted to, I mean. If you wanted to—Oh, earth, swallow me up," he said, shaking his head. "Forget everything I just said. I'm just saying I would have held you back."

"Why would you make that decision for me?" she asked.

"Because I loved you that much, Claire. That's why."

He looked at her, then at the ground, as if coming to some kind of decision. "I have some calls to make. Sparkle, come on, girl."

The dog glanced at him. He pulled a treat from the pocket of his leather jacket and the dog came running over. "Good, Sparkle," he said, holding out his palm. She grabbed the treat and followed him as he started for the stairs.

Because I loved you that much... Claire was so choked up she couldn't speak. And what would she say anyway? All of that was so far in the past.

I have even less to offer you now.

If that was how he felt, then he surely wasn't going to be her husband and the father of her children.

Do. Not. Get. Sucked. Into. The. Past. This man just told you he's not going to be what you want or need. Believe him. Don't be a fool.

But people could change their minds. People's minds could be changed.

Now she was arguing with herself?

There was only one way to nip this in the ole bud— take charge of herself before Matt Fielding got under her skin.

"Hey, Matt," she called up to where he was on the deck landing.

He stopped and looked down at her—clearly bracing himself for what she was going to say. Because regardless of how much time had passed between then and now, she knew him. For a moment, she let herself take him in, the way the morning sunlight hit his hair.

"You're doing great with Sparkle," she said.

She could actually see his shoulders relax.

"Thanks," he said. "My teacher prepared some great material, and I read the homework assignments."

She smiled up at him and nodded. He went inside, closing the sliding glass door behind him.

Yup, that's right, Asher. Keep it focused on the dog. Lighthearted. All about the dog. Because you're getting Matt Fielding out of your system right now. That was the only way she'd survive sharing her home, her yard, her love of dogs with him. She had to create barriers and distance.

She had to find the man she was looking for. The man she'd share her life with. A husband. A father for the child she wanted. Matthew Fielding was not that man.

She went back inside and fired up her laptop, typing *dating sites* into the search engine. There were so many, some easy to nix because of their ridiculous names, like Hotties4U.com. Her gaze stopped on SecondChance-Sweethearts.com. Now that was more Claire's style. And this was all about a second chance at love, right?

She clicked onto the Create A Profile page. Hmm, she needed a user name. She typed in *AlwaysLearning.* "What are the three qualities that best describe you in a nutshell?" How was she supposed to answer that? She grabbed her phone and texted her sister with the question.

Della responded right away. Are you taking a Cosmo quiz or filling out a dating profile? Hoping for the latter!

Latter. Help!

Kind. Responsible. Seeking. Sounds a little dry but hey, you want to weed out the sex fiends and idiots.

That's definitely true. Seeking? Seeking what?

That's for him to find out. Many hims!

Ah. Her sister was good at these things.

She wrote her paragraph about her interests, blah, blah, blah, how much she loved teaching, about helping young people light up about books and express themselves, that she loved old movies and superhero flicks, that she could eat pasta every night for the rest of her life and never get bored, that she was looking for a man who was ready to start a family. She deleted that last part, then re-added it. That *was* what she was looking for. A life partner. A husband. A father for her children. So it made no sense *not* to put it out there.

She uploaded a recent photo, one Della had taken at her husband's birthday dinner party two months ago. Not too close up, not too far away, head to toe.

She paid up her $14.95 for a one-month membership and hit Submit before she could chicken out.

Take that, Matt Fielding.

Not five minutes later, as Claire was about to check her SecondChanceSweethearts account to see if she had any messages from hordes of men "wanting to know her better," the doorbell rang. Dempsey shot up with a bark and hurried to the door, staring at it.

She finished filling up her mug with toffee-flavored coffee and set it down, then walked over to the door. "Hey, Dempsey, maybe the perfect man is at the door, sent by SecondChanceSweehearts." Now, granted, she always talked to Dempsey regardless of the boxer mix's ability to respond. But she still might be losing her mind if she expected her Mr. Right to be at the door.

Actually, it was Matt Fielding at the door.

"I thought I should formally ring the doorbell rather than just go down the deck steps to your side door," he explained.

The side door was completely private, opening to the fenced-in yard, with evergreens completely blocking the view to the next house. She rarely closed the curtains since no one could see her sitting in her living room, watching a romantic comedy with Dempsey and a big bowl of popcorn. But now, anytime Matt came down those steps, he would see her.

"Everything okay?" she asked.

He nodded, then gave Dempsey, who stood beside her, a scratch on the head. "Just thought you should know the stair railing on the left side heading upstairs is loose. I could easily take care of it. I'm a trained mechanic, so I'm generally pretty handy if anything needs to be fixed. You refused to take any rent while I'm living here, so I insist on offering my services in trade."

She thought of Matt in her living room, kitchen, bedroom…a tool belt slung low on his hips, fixing all manner of things as she watched his muscles ripple and his very sexy rear fill out the faded old jeans he wore. "A cabinet in the kitchen has a loose hinge, and I never get around to finding the power drill," she said. "And I've been wanting to bolt the bookcase in the living room to the wall. You're going to be sorry you asked. I can probably come up with a list of ten things I've been meaning to call someone about."

Wait a minute, dummy! Was she really finding stuff for Matt to do inside her home? What the heck was wrong with her?

You want to be around him. And not just to stare at him when you think he doesn't notice.

"I can take care of all that," he said. "I assume you're working today—I can come back at three thirty if that's good for you."

Tell him it's not. Tell him you'll fix all the stuff yourself, or that you forgot you already hired a handyman. Tell him anything, but don't let him inside your home! "That works," she heard herself say. "I'm not due at Furever Paws till five today to help close up for the night."

"See you then," he said with a nod to Dempsey, and then disappeared down the stairs.

Fool, she chastised herself as she closed the door. *Your knees can barely hold you up when you look at Matt. Now, he's going to be in your kitchen and living room on a regular basis.*

She had no doubt she'd find some reason to get him in her bedroom. That was how ridiculously attracted to him she was. Had it just been too long since she'd been with a man? Did *since her divorce* count as too long?

Way too long, her sister had said, which was why she'd begun setting Claire up with anyone who was single.

Ding!

Claire went to her laptop on the desk in the living

room. She had four messages from the dating website. *That was fast.*

And necessary. Because if Matt was going to be Mr. Fix It in her home, she'd need more than a distraction from him. She'd need to know she was taking steps to protect herself from getting wrapped up in the past, in hoping for something that couldn't be.

HOT4U, whose profile photos were all shirtless, loved "quiet nights at home with his special lady." *Yeah, no doubt. Next!* Except the next two weren't much better. Online dating might not be the way to go. Hadn't her friend and fellow teacher Sandy mentioned that she had a single cousin who might be "just right for you"? She should forget online dating and focus on fix-ups from trustworthy people.

Claire took a fast look at the fourth message. Hmm. BigReader had one photo, a side view of an attractive, dark-haired man on a boat of some kind. He was thirty-seven, an accountant, loved historical biographies, and here was the big one: he loved dogs.

Claire hit reply.

Within twenty minutes, she had a date for dinner tomorrow night.

Matt spent the day working with Sparkle and showing the little pup around town. He'd run into some old friends and now had plans for barbecue—"feel free to bring a date"—and beers at the dive bar on the outskirts of town.

"Didn't take you for the kind of guy who'd have some fluffy puppy with a purple collar," his old rival on the baseball team had said. Before he could say a word, a buddy had added, "Matt has a thigh-to-shin gash in his leg from his service to our country, so shut up." The rival had stuck his hand out and Matt shook it, and just like that, he was one of the guys again. But did he really want to make friends, build any kind of life here when he'd run into Claire all the time? No. He'd train the puppy for Ellie, fix all the broken things in Claire's house and then ride into the unknown. At least that was a plan, even if there was no actual plan.

He'd have to leave town. He'd thought about Claire all day—from old memories to how she'd looked this morning. Claire owned a house. She had an important career. She was passionate about her volunteer work. She had everything. And Matt? At this point, all he had was a duffel bag of clothes and a twelve-pound puppy that he'd be handing over once she was trained. *So leave your fantasies about her in your head*, he reminded himself as, tool belt on and power drill in hand, he rang her doorbell at three thirty. *Don't think about kissing her, even though you want to. Don't imagine her naked, even though you can't help it. Don't picture the two of you in bed, despite being unable to shake the image.*

She opened the door, and he immediately thought about kissing her—dropping the power drill on the floor and telling her he'd been able to think of little else but her since he'd run into her at the shelter his first full day home. But Dempsey was standing guard next to her, as always, peering up at him with those soulful eyes, reminding him of his promise to himself—and secretly, to her. Not to get involved. Claire Asher had always deserved better than him, better than what he could offer.

She wore a blue velvet jacket and a black-and-white skirt. Her teacher clothes. She smelled fantastic, like spicy flowers. Her hair was in a low bun and man, did he want to feel those silky blond tresses running through his fingers.

"I just got home," she said, opening the door wider and gesturing for him to enter. "I'll go change and meet you back in the living room. You can check out the bookcase that I want anchored. I keep being afraid that a dog Dempsey's size could pull it down if she jumped up. Hasn't happened yet, but it worries me."

"I'll take care of it," he said. He went to kneel down, and for some reason today—maybe the threat of rain in the air—he winced and it took double the usual time to get down. But he was halfway there and it would hurt worse to stand back up, so he balanced himself on the edge of the couch and eased into the kneel. *Don't say anything. Don't ask*, he sent telepathically to Claire as she gave Dempsey a rigorous pat on her soft but bristly fur. Sparkle was like a down pillow compared to Dempsey.

"War injury?" she asked.

Crud. He hated when attention was called to it, even though the ole bad leg had given him a pass for carting around such a too-cute puppy in a striped purple collar this morning.

He nodded, focusing on Dempsey. "IED."

Now it was her turn to wince. "Does it hurt much?"

Crud again. He didn't want that look in her eyes.

Concern. Worry. Claire was a runner, or at least she had been, and back when they were a couple she was even faster than him. Now, he wasn't even sure he could walk a half mile, let alone run a 5K.

"Sometimes," he admitted.

"Sorry," she said.

He pulled himself up, wincing again, and he saw her reach her arm out as if to steady him if he needed it. This was exactly what he wanted to avoid. Feeling like half a man. He mentally shook his head away from those "poor me" bullcrap thoughts; he was lucky as hell and he knew it. Two in his unit had come back with much worse injuries.

"I'll go check out the bookcase," he said, heading over to it without looking at her.

He could feel her lingering in the room, and knew she was wondering if she should say something, do something. How could he know her so well after all this time? Maybe when it came to the important people in your life, those who got under your skin, those who helped make you who you were, that feeling of "knowing them" never went away.

Great.

The bookcase. *Focus on the damned bookcase*, he told himself. He heard the soft click of Dempsey's nails on the hardwood floor, which meant Claire was leaving the room and Dempsey was following. *Good.*

The bookcase was waist-high and full of interesting things, like the stained-glass jewelry box he knew she'd inherited from her great-grandmother when she was sixteen, a lopsided vase she'd made in pottery class back in high school, a lot of books and family photos. On the top of the bookshelf was an open photo album. *Whoa.* The page was full of photos of him and Claire as a couple and some of him solo. He put down the power drill and picked up the album.

Had he really ever been that young? From seventeen to a hundred.

He turned to the first page and looked at each photo, smiling at Claire as a toddler with birthday cake all over her face, Claire as a little girl on a two-wheeler, her beloved father holding on to the back of the seat, Claire as a sixteen-year-old, with a tall, skinny boy standing a respectful distance away for the photo. *God, look at me*, he thought, *madly in love, afraid to show it, barely able to believe she liked me back.*

"Oh, um, I—" Claire said.

He turned around, still holding the album. Claire's cheeks were red, as though she were embarrassed at having been caught reminiscing. Which was exactly what he was doing now. She'd changed into jeans and a yellow sweater, and reminded him of the girl he'd known, who used to drive him wild just by existing.

"I can't believe I was ever that young," he said, his gaze back on the photograph of the two of them. "Or that the most beautiful girl in the world was mine." Okay, that had come out of his mouth without his say-so. But he sure had been thinking it. Back then and now. He stared down at the book and flipped the page. He and Claire dancing at prom. Kissing.

She walked over to him and glanced at the page. She pointed at the top left photo, of the two of them arm in arm for the "professional" couple shot the principal had taken of all the attendees. "I sure had no idea then what was going to happen by the end of the night. I thought my boyfriend and I would be sneaking off to a motel. Instead, I was sobbing in my room with a pillow over my head."

Punch to the gut. He hated how much he'd hurt her back then. "If you had any idea how much I wanted you that night, Claire," he said, putting the album down. He took her hands, and she looked up at him. "I was madly in love with you."

"I don't want to talk about the past," she said. "What I want is for you to kiss me."

Me too, he thought, everything else fading away. Like reason and the real world. He stepped closer and put his hands on her beautiful face, then leaned in to kiss her, gently and sweetly in case she changed her mind midway.

But that didn't seem to happen because she deepened the kiss, snaking her hands through his hair. She kiss-walked him backward to the couch and straddled him, trailing kisses along his neck. He was going to explode.

And then she began unbuttoning his shirt, her hands cool on his hot skin. Five seconds later, he had her sweater off, one hand slipping down under the waistband of her soft, sexy jeans.

"Help me get you out of my system," she whispered in his ear. "This is what I need."

He pulled back, her words a splash of cold water on his head. "What?"

"You and me," she said. "It's not going to happen—in

the long run, right? Just like last time. So let me get you out of my system once and for all." She ran her hands inside his shirt, over his chest.

It felt so good. But he didn't believe her. So he pulled away and stood up.

"You think sex will get me out of your system?" He shook his head. "I already think about you all damned day, Claire. Sex will make me unable to do anything else. Sparkle will be peeing all over the apartment."

"So once again you're not going to sleep with me for my own good?" She walked away and stopped by the sliding glass door, then turned to glare at him. "How about you let me make my own decisions for *myself*."

"I won't sleep with you when I know I'm leaving soon," he said. "If that's 'like last time,' then so be it. I'm wrong for you. Just like eighteen years ago."

"I think I hear Sparkle whimpering," she said through gritted teeth, crossing her arms over her chest.

"No, you don't," he said. He'd become attuned to every little noise the puppy made over the past couple of days. If Sparkle had made a single peep, he'd have heard it. Claire wanted him gone, but shouldn't they talk about this? Shouldn't they get it straight and right between them? She had to understand where he was coming from.

She lifted her chin. "I have to grade essays. So this isn't a good day for you to work in the house, after all."

This wasn't what he wanted either. This bad kind of tension between them. He hated the thought of leaving this way.

"Claire, if you only knew—"

She held up a hand. "Matt, you've said it all. You find me attractive, but can't—on all levels. Have I got that right?"

Oh hell.

Her phone rang and so he headed to the door. *Don't say you're sorry or she'll conk you over the head*, he told himself.

So, he didn't, but he wanted to. He *was* sorry. And wished things could be different. Wished *he* were different.

Chapter Six

Ridiculous. This morning, Claire had been sure the way to get Matt Fielding out of her system was to spend $14.95 on an online dating service. Suddenly, just several hours later, the way to get over him was to ravish his body in her bed? To finally have sex with him? Was she insane?

Thank God he'd put the kibosh on that. Right? She went back and forth, depending on the minute. Yes, it was a good thing. She'd be a mess if she finally slept with the man she couldn't get over after eighteen years. And she couldn't afford to be an emotional mess. She had hormonal, pimply faced, identity-seeking preteens depending on her to be the calm, rational one. She had a foster dog who needed to be fed, exercised and played with. And she needed to be present for the dogs at Furever Paws, not be all teary-eyed and unfocused.

So, yes, score one for Matt. But then she'd think that maybe sex with him really would do the job, that the mystery of him, of "it," would *poof!*—disappear. She'd know what sex with him was like, and she'd move on. Wasn't that a possibility?

Luckily, Claire really didn't have time to vacillate endlessly about sleeping with Matt or not. She was due at Furever Paws at five, and then she was meeting Big-Reader, aka Connor Hearon, at the Main Street Grille at seven for dinner. He'd said during their two message exchanges that it was unusual to make dinner plans before spending much time emailing back and forth and chatting on the phone, but he had "a feeling about her." Claire, unfortunately, had lost all feeling and interest in meeting Connor, but she was not going to let Matt derail another date with a potential beau who could be what she needed and wanted right now. To be safe, she'd texted her friend and fellow Furever Paws volunteer, Amanda Sylvester, manager and co-owner of the Main Street Grille, to let her know she was meeting an online date there at seven and to keep an eye out for anything strange. Not that Claire knew what that would constitute. It just seemed a good precaution. Then she texted her sister BigReader's details as a "just in case" too.

You're my hero, her sister texted. Very happy you're putting yourself out there. This time next year, rock-a-bye baby… :)

Getting a little ahead of yourself, there, sister dear,

Claire thought. But at least Della had made her smile. Because was putting herself out there supposed to feel this…unexciting? Once again, she blamed Matt Fielding.

That really was handy, sticking him with the blame for everything.

Matt wanted to pick up another pack of training treats for Sparkle, so he drove out to Furever Paws. He could probably find the same treats at the supermarket, but he liked the idea of spending his money at the shelter. And he'd run out of places to go to avoid going home—he still felt funny thinking of the apartment at Claire's as home, but it was for now. Since their argument, he'd vacuumed all the dog hair and errant treats around the apartment, gone grocery shopping, returned his "not him" rental car and bought himself a used black Mustang from a car dealer he'd heard good things about. Then he'd spent a couple of hours in the park with Sparkle and worn the puppy out. They'd practiced commands—*come* and *stay*—and Sparkle was getting the hang of it. A woman had come over, oohing and aahing over Sparkle's cuteness, and because it was such a small world, she turned out to be his niece Ellie's third-grade teacher. Mrs. Panetta, whom he'd heard Ellie rave about, gave Sparkle an A+ for cuteness and her *stay* command.

When he'd left the pup at home ten minutes ago, she was fast asleep in the kennel, curled up with her bounty of toys in her little bed.

Matt pulled into a spot in the small gravel parking lot

at Furever Paws. Huge oak trees surrounded the sturdy, dark-gray, one-story building. He walked up the porch steps, the logo—a large image of a cat and dog silhouetted inside a heart—painted on the front greeting him. He pulled open the glass door and walked into the small lobby. He remembered tall, gray-haired Birdie, one of the owners, from the last time he was here.

"Afternoon, ma'am," he said. "I'm Ma—"

Birdie turned her sharp blue eyes from the computer screen to him. "You left here a few days ago with one of our not-ready-for-prime-time pups," she said, her stern expression softening into a smile. "I know exactly who you are. It's nice to see you again, Matt. And call me Birdie. I'm not the ma'am type. *Pleeeze.*"

He laughed. "Well, Birdie, I'm here to pick up some more training treats for Sparkle. We're going to work on the *lie down* command tomorrow."

"Our gift shop has plenty," she said, gesturing to the wall along the side of the lobby. Claire had mentioned that the supplies were mostly donated; sales benefited the shelter, and he was glad to help.

He heard barking coming from down a long hallway behind the lobby. He could see a couple of doors marked Staff Only, and one at the far end that said Veterinary Clinic. There were two additional rooms, one marked Cats and one marked Dogs. From his vantage point, he could see through the large glass window of the Dogs room; a couple was sitting down and petting Tucker, the little chiweenie who seemed a lot more interested in them than he'd been in Matt and Ellie the other day.

The woman in the room tried to pick up Tucker and

got barked at; Matt could hear the loud barks from where he stood. Then another woman moved into view—and Matt would know that blond hair anywhere. Claire. How had he forgotten that she'd said she'd be volunteering at five? "He will not do at all!" the woman snapped as she opened the door and huffed out, followed by her husband and an exasperated Claire, with little Tucker on a leash.

Maybe he's nervous and doesn't want to be picked up by a total stranger who's hovering over him, he wanted to shout. *Jeez*.

"Perhaps you could come to our adoption event his weekend," Claire was saying. "Many of our adoptable dogs are with foster parents, but they'll all be here this Saturday and Sunday."

"Well, if they're less ferocious than him," the man said.

Matt almost burst out laughing. Tucker was what— thirteen pounds soaking wet?

"Tucker isn't ferocious," Claire said, and Matt was impressed by the warmth in her voice. "Just a combination of timid and stressed."

"Well, you did tell us he could be skittish and barky," the woman said, her tone calmer. "My fault for insisting on meeting him just because he sounded cute."

Huh. Now Matt could see why Claire's way—being civil and kind and gently explaining—was smarter than his, which would have been to tell the woman she didn't seem like a dog person.

And he was starting to become one himself. So he sort of knew.

"Tucker could use a dedicated foster parent, but right now, all our foster homes are full," Claire added.

The woman eyed Tucker with disdain. Humph.

"He's not the one," the man with her said. "We're looking for 'just right.' A dog with a certain personality."

Matt sighed. From everything he'd read, even the most "just right" rescue dog wouldn't show his true personality till he or she was settled and comfortable in a new home. Basic temperament, sure. But personality would take time to emerge.

"Well, we'll be back Saturday," the woman said, and the couple headed for the door.

He watched Birdie send Claire a look that told him this kind of thing was common. Expectations and reality meeting and clashing.

Finally, Claire turned and noticed Matt, and he saw her stiffen. "Oh, hi. I didn't realize you were here. Everything okay with Sparkle?"

He nodded. "I could use more training treats," he said, holding up the four pouches he'd picked up from the wall display.

She nodded. "I'd better get Tucker back to his kennel."

"Can I follow you? I'd like to say hi to ole Hank, maybe walk him if that's all right?"

Birdie smiled. "He'd love that."

Did Claire just shoot Birdie a look? One that said, *Oh thanks, I wanted to flee his presence*? Yeah, he was pretty sure of it.

He followed Claire down the hallway. She pushed through the door to the Dogs room, Tucker following on his little legs. The dog seemed instantly calmer. He must have gotten used to this area, to the twelve or so big kennels with gated access to the outside—a small fenced area with grass and gravel. This had become home for the pint-size mutt. Matt sure hoped it wouldn't be for too much longer.

Claire put Tucker back in his kennel, and he immediately went to his bed and settled down with his chew toy. Then she joined Matt at Hank's kennel. The big brown dog with the pointy ears was sitting at the front as if he knew Matt was here to take him out for a stroll.

"Hey, ole guy," Matt said, kneeling down, easier this time than yesterday. "How are ya?" He glanced up at Claire. "Can I slip him one of these?" he asked, pulling a treat from the pocket of his leather jacket.

She smiled. "He'd love it." She looked at Hank, her expression clouding up a bit. "A man came in to look at the dogs soon after I started my shift. The guy liked Hank's soulful eyes on his first walk-through of the area, so I brought Hank into the meeting room, hopeful he'd found a match. But he decided he couldn't deal with a three-legged dog. He also didn't like the way Hank's ears didn't flop." She shook her head. "I love Hank's ears."

Matt did too. Seriously, those huge pointy ears almost made Hank look like he could fly by batting them. "Passed up again, huh, guy?" he said, his heart going out to the beautiful dog. "How long has he been here?"

"Almost a month."

"Cooped up here a month? And no one wants him because he's missing a leg and doesn't have floppy ears?" He shook his head. Hell, Hank didn't wince or take fifteen seconds to get up and down the way Matt did with two legs. Hank *ruled*. Hank was the best. Hank was... his? "You know what, Hank? If it's all right with you, I'd like to take you home."

Claire gasped. "Really? That would be amazing!"

Ten seconds ago, he'd had no idea that he wanted to adopt Hank, but he must have wanted to all along. The idea of it was so *right*. He was meant to bring this dog home. Matt wasn't sure of much these days, but he knew that. "Hank's so calm I'm sure he'd be gentle with Sparkle, right?"

"Oh, yes. Those two have played together in the yard a few times since Sparkle first came in. They're great together."

Man, it was nice to see that smile again, such pure joy on Claire's face. Earlier, he'd been responsible for taking it off. Now, he'd put it back.

"Well, if I'm approved to adopt Hank, I'd like to give him a forever home."

"You mean a *fur*ever home," she said with a grin. She wrapped her arms around him and squeezed, then stepped back, her smile fading. "Sorry about that. Just a little excited for one of my favorites. Oh, Matt, I just know you two are a pair."

He held her gaze, her green eyes sparkling. He loved making her so happy. Even if it was about a dog and not the two of them.

And just like that, Matt left with Sparkle's training treats and a whole bunch of other stuff for his new dog, Hank, including a spiffy navy-blue collar and leash, a huge memory foam dog bed, a soft quilt and the toys that Claire said he seemed to like best. A small fortune later, but worth every penny, Matt and Claire had everything in his car, including Hank, who rode shotgun in the front seat. Matt put the passenger-seat window all the way down so Hank could put his face out if he wanted, even in the February chill.

"Your days in a kennel are over, buddy," Matt said, giving Hank a rub along his soft back.

Hank glanced at him in appreciation, Matt could tell, and stuck his snout out the window. The ole guy was smiling. No doubt.

"I could cry, I'm so happy for him," Claire said as she stood in front of the driver's window. "And not only does Hank get a great home, I get to see him all the time!"

Matt gave her a more rueful smile than he'd intended. Seeing each other all the time probably wasn't a good idea. Living in Claire's house probably wasn't a good idea. Hadn't his smart sister said exactly that?

Right now, he was going to focus on getting his new dog settled. He'd think about what the hell he was going to do about Claire Asher later. Much later. Because as much as he knew living on her property was a problem, he didn't want to leave.

BigReader, aka Connor Hearon, was as attractive as his photo had indicated. Tall and lanky, with a mop of light brown hair and warm brown eyes, he gave her hope that she could find another man besides Matt Fielding attractive and interesting. Of course, Matt was on her mind. Taking over her mind, actually. When Connor mentioned he was reading a certain biography, Claire's first thought was that Matt would love the book about a climb up Mt. Everest, since he'd loved reading adventure memoirs as a teenager. When Connor ordered the Main Street Grille's special pasta entrée, Claire thought about how Matt would have gone for that too.

What. Was. Wrong. With. Her?

She knew what. Matt Fielding had adopted Hank. A three-legged senior dog that no one else had wanted. Who'd been languishing at Furever Paws for a month. And he'd adopted him despite already fostering and training a puppy for his niece. So, no matter what Matt said, his actions spoke louder to her soul than his words did to her brain. Did that even make any sense? It did to her heart, unfortunately.

He told you! He's leaving town! He's got some crazy notion stuck in his head that he's not good enough for you, that he has nothing to offer you. That all he has in this world is a duffel bag. And now a dog.

She let herself remember him telling her all that. She *made* herself remember how he'd stopped them from ending up in bed—twice.

And then she forced herself to pay more attention to Connor and push Matt from her consciousness. She focused on the outdoorsman crinkles on the sides of those kind, intelligent eyes.

You know who else has a dog? This guy. BigReader. A man whose profile had stated that he wanted a long-term relationship leading to marriage and children.

"So you're divorced?" Connor asked, twirling his fork in his pasta.

"It's been three years," she said, then bit into her black bean burger. "But I just entered the dating world about six months ago. Ready to get back out there and all."

He nodded. "I've been out there for the past six months too. Eye-opening, huh?"

She smiled. "Well, this is actually my first attempt at online dating. I've been saying yes to fix-ups, but I thought I'd start engineering my own future."

"Fix-ups have gone more my way," he said. "I've noticed a lot of women fib about this or that. Like weight." He puffed out his cheeks.

Uh, really? Did he just say that? *Do* that? "Well, I've heard men post ten-year-old photos of themselves when they had more hair."

BigReader had a head full of hair, so it wasn't as though she was insulting him. Their conversation had taken a bit of a sharp turn, so she wanted to direct it back to kinder, gentler territory.

He seemed to realize that he was being a jerk. "Sorry. I don't mean you. You could probably stand to gain a good five pounds," he added, eyeing her breasts.

Get. Me. Out. Of. Here.

"Oh God, I'm really blowing this, aren't I?" He chuckled, because apparently that was hilarious. "I guess I'm just a little gun-shy about relationships. My last girlfriend was two-timing me. And the girlfriend before that was in it because she thought I made a pot of money." He snorted.

Jeez, couldn't he talk about movies or waterways he'd boated down?

She'd finish her dinner and make an excuse to leave immediately. "Well, at least you have that gorgeous dog, right?" she said, swiping a fry through ketchup. She recalled his profile pic with the majestic golden retriever sitting beside him on the boat. "It's amazing how much joy dogs bring to people's lives. When you're feeling down or you're under the weather, a warm nose and furry body next to you can be so comforting."

He snorted again—this time with a bitter edge. "I lost the dog in the divorce. More like I had no problem letting the ex have Banjo so I could demand what I really wanted. Worked like a charm."

Jerk.

He slurped his pasta, and there was no way she could sit there another second. Just when she was thinking of how she could end this date before he even finished his meal, her friend Amanda came over to the table. "How is everything?"

Claire knew Amanda pretty well since they'd spent many hours together at Furever Paws, and she could see the slight raise of her eyebrow—the question was more directed at how Claire thought the *date* was going.

BigReader held up a finger and made a show of finishing chewing. "The pasta's great, but, honestly? I didn't love the dressing on my salad. I like my Italian a little more…something."

"I'm sorry to hear that," Amanda said, her blue eyes on Connor. "I hope a complimentary dessert will make you forget all about that salad dressing. We have some great offerings tonight—"

"Gotta watch my figure for the online dating thing," he said on a laugh.

Amanda offered Claire a rueful smile, clearly able to see for herself how this date was going, then headed to another table.

"So," Connor said. "Back to your place for a nightcap?"

"I don't think we're a match," Claire replied honestly.

He shrugged again. "No worries. It's a numbers game. You gotta be in it to win it, right?"

Claire just wanted to be out of there. "Being in it isn't easy. It's hard sitting across from someone you have little in common with and didn't know yesterday when there are so many expectations."

"Well, there's your problem, Claire. Expectations. If you're attracted, great. A little making out, even sex. If you're not attracted, buh-bye. Next."

"Well, I guess it's *next* then."

"With that attitude, you'll be single for the rest of your life." He got up and put a twenty-dollar bill on the table, which would barely cover his entrée, his two beers and his share of the tip. "Good luck out there. You'll need it."

"You too," she said, shaking her head, as BigReader made his exit.

"Good riddance to bad date-ish," Amanda said, sliding a slice of chocolate cake in front of Claire. "Compliments of the Main Street Grille for putting up with that guy for an hour."

Claire laughed. And dug in. But now what? How many of these dates was she supposed to go on? If it really *was* a numbers game, she didn't have the energy to date that many frogs to find someone close to a prince. Maybe she should stop forcing it. Let it happen naturally, organically. She had met a few single men while volunteering at Furever Paws, but sharing a love of dogs didn't necessarily mean they'd have much else in common. There was always the upcoming regional teachers conference, which might be a source of potential Mr. Rights. The local parks were full of them too. Joggers. Dog walkers. Bench readers. So she wasn't completely a hopeless case. Except maybe when it came to one man.

The man who refused to be Mr. Right was probably in her own backyard right now with his two pooches. She wanted to be home more than anything else in the world. But since her plan to distract herself from Matt's magnetic pull was a big bust, how was she going to protect her heart against him?

Matt had already taken a thousand pictures of Sparkle being cute, texting them to his sister to share with his niece, but now he had the photo of all photos. Hank, his big body curled up in his memory foam bed, the little brown-and-white puppy nestled alongside his belly.

Laura sent back an aww! and said Ellie was dying to come over to meet Hank and work with Sparkle—how about tomorrow?—so he set that up. After a month in the shelter, Hank deserved getting special fuss treatment from an eight-year-old dog enthusiast.

He glanced at the time on his phone—eight forty-five. "Come on, lazybones," he said to the pooches. "Let's go outside, and then you can curl right back up."

All he had to do to communicate his intentions was pick up a leash. Hank ambled over, Sparkle trotting beside him and giving his one front leg a sniff. Matt put on his leather jacket, eager for the days when he wouldn't have to shiver outside at night, and brought the dogs out. Hands in his pockets, he stood at the far end of the yard, away from Claire's patio. The lights were off inside, and he wondered where she was. *Date?*

Don't think about it, he told himself. The dogs did their business, so he threw a ball for them, Hank flying after it, Sparkle on his heels. Wow, Hank could run well on three legs. He was so much bigger and faster than Sparkle that he got the ball before her every time.

He heard a car pull into the driveway on the other side of the house. Claire. He listened for the front door opening and closing, then saw lights flick on inside. The sliding glass door to the yard opened, and she came out with Dempsey. He couldn't help noticing she was dressed up. And wearing makeup, similar to how she'd looked when he'd run into her on her date with Slick. Both "dog shelter Claire," with a fresh-scrubbed face, ponytail and old jeans, and "date Claire" were stunning.

"Date?" he asked before he could tell his brain not to spit it out.

"Actually, yes." She threw a ball for Dempsey, who was too busy sniffing—and being sniffed by—Hank. The three dogs were moving in a comical circle of sniffing noses, bellies and butts, then stopping to stare off at some unseen critter before resuming their nose work.

"Find Mr. Right?" he asked, his chest tightening.

Why the hell was he even going there? He didn't want to have this conversation.

"He used the dog as a pawn in his divorce to get what he wanted from his ex. She could have the dog, which he said he didn't want anyway, so he could get *x, y, z*. God, I hate people."

"*Some* people," he said. "You have the right to hate me, Claire. But I hope you don't. You—" *Shut up*, he told himself, clamping his lips shut. He threw a ball for the dogs, and this time they all went for it, Dempsey winning.

"I what?" she asked with something of a wince. He hated that he made her brace herself.

"You once made me want to be a better person," he said. "Yeah, I enlisted in tribute to my brother and to serve my country, but I also knew the army would give me direction—turn me into a good man."

She shoved her hands in her pockets, and suddenly he was aware again of how cold it was. "You were a perfectly good young man in high school," she said.

He shook his head. "I wasn't. You had a thing for me, so you didn't really care that I was barely scraping by in my classes or got into fights with bullies who liked to pick on those who wouldn't or couldn't fight back. I might have been sticking up for kids, but I got sent to the principal and suspended to the point that one more suspension would have gotten me expelled."

"Not everyone is academically oriented," she said. "And how terrible that you stood up for the underdogs. What a terrible person you were, Matthew Fielding."

A rush of dread filled his lungs. She didn't get it. "I had nothing back then and I have nothing now, Claire."

"Then why do I like you so much?" she asked. "Then *and* now? Huh? Answer that."

"Because you're romanticizing old times. Because I seem like some kind of hero for taking in that spinning pup and calming her down, and for adopting Hank, who's the coolest dog in the world. No medal deserved there."

"You're consistent," she said. "I'll give you that."

"The truth is the truth. I am exactly who I appear to be."

"I know," she said, shaking her head, but there was a hint of a smile on her pretty face. "So, it pays to know the owner of the Main Street Grille. Amanda, who also volunteers at Furever Paws, gave me an extra slice of chocolate layer cake in a doggie bag for my 'awesome new tenant who adopted Hank.' That's you."

"But it's a doggie bag, so shouldn't these guys have it?"

She did smile this time. "You know full well that chocolate is toxic for dogs, so it's all ours. I'll give them each a peanut butter treat for welcoming Hank so nicely."

He guessed that meant he was going inside her house, having that slice of cake, continuing this too-personal conversation. He could—and would—turn it back to dogs.

She called the dogs to follow her, and they all trooped inside, Matt glad to get Claire out of the cold. In the kitchen, Claire gave them all treats, and then Dempsey showed Hank around the house, Sparkle at their heels.

All three dogs ended up sitting in front of the door to the deck, staring out at night critters no one could detect.

"This cake is really something," Claire said, setting the slice on a plate and placing it on the kitchen table. She took two beers out of the refrigerator and slid one beside the cake.

Matt took a bite. Mmm, chocolate heaven. "This was thoughtful of you."

She took a sip of beer. "Well, you did a very thoughtful thing."

He raised an eyebrow. "Ah, you mean adopting Hank."

"It's a big deal," she said. "We were really worried he'd never find a home, and then, whammo, the perfect owner and home presents itself."

"I'm hardly perfect. And I don't have a home, Claire. Again, again, again, you make me out to be something I'm not."

"Or you just don't see yourself the way I do. The way a lot of people do."

"Were you always this bossy and stubborn?" he asked, then took another forkful of cake. "Oh, wait, you were." He smiled.

She smiled back at him. "So enough about us, tell me about you. How did your first few hours with Hank go?"

"Great. He's so calm. And even though Sparkle has mellowed a lot from when I took her in, I think Hank is even more of a calming influence on her. Nothing throws him. A slammed door, a pot lid dropping. He's unflappable. And did you see the way he can chase a ball? He's amazing."

She scooched her chair close and kissed him on the cheek, then threw her arms around him.

And, oh hell, it felt so good that he wrapped his arms around her and tilted up her chin. "I want to kiss you more than anything right now." He wasn't going to deny himself this. The pull was too strong. The need too great.

"Be my guest," she said, puckering up.

He laughed. "How am I supposed to kiss you when I'm laughing?"

"Like this," she said, covering his lips with hers, the softness making him melt into a puddle on the chair. Everything about her was soft and smelled like spicy flowers. He couldn't get close enough.

"Want the rest of the cake?" he asked.

"No. I just want more of you," she said.

"Good." He scooped her up, his leg only slightly bothering him, and followed her directions to her bedroom, laying her down on the bed.

In seconds, her dress was over her head and in a heap on the floor, along with his shirt and pants. She kissed a trail along his neck and collarbone, her hands all over his chest and pushing down at the waistband of his boxer briefs.

"You're sure?" he whispered. "Despite everything?"

"I'm sure," she whispered back. She pulled open the drawer of her bedside table and took out a box of condoms. "These might be a few years old."

He found the expiration date. "These are actually good until *tomorrow*."

Surprise lit her green eyes. "Meant to be, then."

He didn't know about that.

But he couldn't resist Claire. Not tonight. Not for another moment. Being with her felt so good, made him
feel good about himself, even if afterward...

She said she was sure. She wanted to be taken at her
word, had told him to stop making decisions for her, so
maybe he really could let himself have this. Tonight.
With Claire. Hell, maybe she was right, and it would
get him out of her system and she could move on. And
he would leave Spring Forest, headed for who knew
where, Hank beside him, to start fresh.

Her hands were all over his back, in his hair, and then
the boxer briefs were being pushed down. He undid her
lacy black bra, inhaling that light perfume in her lush
cleavage, and then her hands moved lower, and he lost
all ability to think. Finally, eighteen years after meeting Claire, Matt made love to the only woman he'd
ever loved.

Chapter Seven

He was gone before she woke up, and as a teacher, Claire woke up at the crack of dawn.

Which meant he'd sneaked away in the middle of the night, unable to deal with the aftermath.

Ah, there was a note on her bedside table, sticking out under her phone.

C—Have early plans, didn't want to wake you.
Took the dogs out, Dempsey too. See you later.
—M

Who had plans at 6:00 a.m.? No one, that's who. Plans to get away, maybe.

That was fine. Listen when someone tells you who they are and how they're going to hurt you. Wasn't that one of her many mottoes? Matt Fielding had made his intentions clear. And so she couldn't fault him for not spooning her all night and then waking her up with kisses along her shoulder, whispering sweet everythings in her ear. There was no everything. There was no anything!

That's fine, she repeated, getting out bed, grateful, at least, that she didn't have to open the deck door to let Dempsey out in the winter chill. A dog walker came every weekday at noon to let Dempsey out and throw a ball for her, and Claire had thought about asking Matt if he'd do that when he took out Sparkle and Hank at midday, but it was probably better that he didn't have a key to her house.

Sigh. At least the sex was amazing, she thought as she went into the bathroom and turned on the shower. *Amazing.* Being with Matt was everything she'd always imagined and more.

But he was leaving town after he finished training Sparkle.

Just keep your heart out of it, and you'll be okay. He'd done the shelter two big favors by fostering one dog and adopting another. He'd done her body a big favor by making her feel like liquid. Granted, she was all hunched and tense now, but it was worth it.

Her head set on straight, Claire got ready for work, with her heart only slightly sunk. By the time she arrived at the middle school, her mind was on her students—a welcome distraction, as they demanded so much from her in so many ways. They were reading the novel *Wonder*, which had every one of them fully engaged, and the day was spent on projects related to the book's themes of inclusion, acceptance and the power of friendship.

After the dismissal bell rang for the end of the school day, Claire graded quizzes and killed some time tidying her up her desk to avoid going home before Divorce Club—which was the pet name for the "book" club she belonged to. Two teachers at the middle school had started it, but when they discovered that all four members were divorced, talk had quickly turned from the book they were supposed to read to their lives and marriage and divorce. They met at a different member's house every two weeks. The meeting didn't start till four thirty, but Claire didn't want to go home and run into Matt. She just wasn't ready to see him or listen to his excuses or however he'd awkwardly explain his disappearing act.

Ah. Finally time. Claire drove over to Danielle Peterwell's house, which was near the area where Claire had grown up. She took a detour of a few blocks to drive past the house she'd lived in with her parents and Della and various dogs over the years. Nostalgia gripped her, and she sat there in her car for a few minutes, until a woman came out of the house with a baby in a carrier and a little boy. The boy scampered across the lawn for a few seconds—like Sparkle, Claire thought with a half smile—then she watched the woman put the carrier into the car and help buckle the boy into his seat.

Huh. Maybe the universe was trying to tell her something by having her stop here. Being all hung up on Matt wasn't going to get her that baby and little boy and a partner to share her life with.

She lifted her chin and drove over to Danielle's, determined to keep her head on straight—and on what she wanted most of all: a family.

At Divorce Club, the members all said their hellos and attacked the very nice spread the hostess had set out: miniquiches, fruit and a light sangria.

"Now last time, I'm pretty sure Claire had a blind date set up by her sister?" Jen Garcia said. "Do tell," she added, taking a sip of sangria.

She'd almost forgotten all about that guy—Andrew something. The lawyer her sister had fixed her up with. Two dates ago. "It actually started out pretty well, but he basically told me at the end of the date that he'd hooked up with his ex the night before."

"He randomly told his blind date that?" Lara Willkowski asked. "Idiot."

"Well, I kind of saw an old boyfriend at the restaurant," Claire admitted, "and when the date asked if I wanted to go for a drink after dinner, I told the truth about being sort of distracted."

"Date fail," Danielle said with a grin.

"Hey, wait," Lara said. "Was the old boyfriend Matt Fielding? From high school?"

Claire nodded and slugged some sangria.

Lara plucked a miniquiche from the tray. "I thought I recognized him. I saw him in the park the other day with an adorable little puppy."

"He's fostering the pup for his sister while he trains her. Sparkle's a gift for his young niece."

"Wow, *that's* nice of him," Danielle said pointedly. The group knew how passionate Claire was about

Furever Paws. "And yesterday he adopted a ten-year-old, three-legged dog named Hank," Claire said. "I'm sunk."

She wasn't going to mention last night. She basically had to forget it herself.

"And…?" Jen prompted.

Claire shrugged. "We're kind of on different paths."

Luckily, Danielle started talking about how she and the first guy she dated after her divorce were on different paths too, to the point that he moved to Nepal to climb very tall mountains. Which led to a conversation change to outdoorsy men who liked to hike when Danielle just wanted to go out to lunch or dinner and wear cute shoes. Jen, who loved to hike, had had a date with a couch potato the other night, and they were both willing to give it another try.

But there was nothing to *try* when it came to Matt. Claire just had to accept that they were in two very different places in their lives and looking for different things. She had to let him go.

Even after that glorious sex. Even after feeling so close to him that while he was making love to her, she kept thinking: *this is what homecoming feels like.*

Keep it together, Claire, she ordered herself. *Don't get all emotional right now.* The Divorce Club crew was great and would rally around her, but she didn't want the focus to be on herself.

She thought about what her late mother had told her when she was struggling in the aftermath of her divorce. *You sit with how you feel, and you accept that you're heartbroken. You don't have to pretend to feel fine. Just let yourself feel what you feel and grieve. It's all part of the process.*

Now, she'd take that good advice again and let herself sit with her feelings about Matt, though her emotions were all over the place, her thoughts about the situation ping-ponging as if Dempsey and Hank had the rackets. She'd always loved Matt and always would.

And unfortunately, last night, she'd fallen deeper.

"So do you think there's a chance you and Matt could pick up where you left off?" Danielle asked as she set out the dessert tray; four slices of cherry cheesecake. Claire was going to eat every ounce of that cake, despite the chocolate cake she'd had last night. In fact, she would probably let herself have all the decadent desserts she wanted this entire week.

"Only in my fantasies," Claire said.

"You never know," Jen said, forking a piece of cheesecake. "That's become my new motto."

But Claire *did* know. Unless she wanted to break her own heart this time, she'd keep her emotional distance from Matt Fielding.

Using a high-backed chair for support, Matt did the exercises his new physical therapist had had him do this morning. Zeke Harper, an old buddy from town, whom he'd run into at the park a few weeks ago while teaching Sparkle the *come* command, had recommended him. Zeke knew the guy from volunteering at a veterans' center, and had mentioned that Matt still had some stiffness from his IED injury. The guy had offered to work with Matt free of charge, but could only fit him in at 7:00 a.m. The workout had hurt but had felt good. Just like now.

When he'd woken up in Claire's bed this morning, he'd almost been amazed it hadn't been a dream. He'd lain there, also aware that for the first time in months, he hadn't had a nightmare about the day he'd been injured, the day that had sent him home. He'd opened his eyes to find Hank sitting at the edge of the bed, staring at him with those soulful, amber-colored eyes. Sparkle and Dempsey, meanwhile, were curled in Dempsey's dog bed on the other side of the bedroom.

And then there was Claire. His beautiful Claire, whose face and voice and memory had seen him through the worst of his recuperation, like an angel. He'd never expected to run into her in Spring Forest; he'd never imagined in a million years she'd still be in their old hometown. And then he woke up in her bed, naked, next to a naked Claire.

He shouldn't have touched her, but maybe she was right about them getting each other out of their systems.

Not that that was working yet. He'd thought of little else all day but how good last night was, how comfortable and natural and right. He had to keep reminding himself to keep things on a physical level, to keep emotions out of it.

Because he was leaving. Probably sometime in mid- to late March, a few weeks, six at most, he figured. Sparkle was coming along so well in her training that she'd be good to go very soon. Ellie had come over after school today as planned, and Matt had taught her what he knew. If Ellie thought he walked on water before, now she looked at him with wonder and called him the Dog Prince.

That had made him laugh. Matt Fielding, anyone's prince. Even a dog's.

"Right, Hank?" he asked, giving the old guy a belly rub. Hank immediately stretched out his long body so that Matt wouldn't stop. "Maybe I am the Dog Prince. Or do I have that backward?" he asked, giving Hank a vigorous rub. "You're the best, dude," he said.

Hank just stared at him, but Matt knew the dog could understand him.

A car pulled into the driveway, which told him Claire was home. He owed her an explanation for leaving the way he did that morning. After the night they'd shared. Despite the note, he had to say *something*.

He heard her deck door open, so he went down the stairs to the yard. The weather had turned colder, just above freezing, and she stood there, her arms wrapped around her coat.

"Hey," he said as she reached the bottom landing. He should have put on gloves. He shoved his hands in the pockets of his leather jacket.

She glanced over at him. "Hi." She threw a ball for Dempsey, who went flying after it.

"I just wanted to explain why I left so early," he said, looking everywhere but at her.

"No need. You've made yourself clear, Matt. You don't owe me explanations. And I don't regret last night. Not a single second of it. And that includes you leaving at the crack of dawn. Last night was a long time coming."

He tilted his head. "Yes, it was."

"Well, it's freezing out here, so I'm going to get Dempsey back inside."

He nodded, wishing he could go with her, wishing for a repeat of last night, wishing again that things were different, that he had a future to offer her.

As she opened the sliding glass door and Dempsey scooted through, he said, "Claire?"

She turned.

"Did it work? Did you get me out of your system?"

She looked at him for a moment. "No."

Neither did I, he thought as she disappeared inside. *Neither did I.*

Claire avoided Matt the following week, which was difficult since she always waited until he came back in with his dogs early in the morning before taking Dempsey out. She wished things weren't so strained between them. She missed Sparkle and Hank. And Matt's niece, Ellie, had been over twice after school when Claire had gotten home. She'd wanted more than anything to join them in the yard to watch Matt teach Ellie training tips. But she'd stayed inside.

Ugh. This wasn't what she wanted. But in a month, he'd leave in that black Mustang and she'd be here, living the same old life, just like the one she'd had before he'd come back. Except she honestly didn't think she could do that. His return had changed something in the air, changed *her*, and when he was gone, there was no way in hell she was going on bad date after bad date to find her life partner and the father of the child she wanted so badly.

"I should just devote my life to dogs," she said to

Dempsey, running her hand over the fur on the dog's back and sides. She got a lick on the hand for that. As usual, Dempsey seemed to know when she needed comfort and curled up beside her on the couch, her head on Claire's thigh. "Dogs are not confusing like certain tall, dark and very good-looking humans."

On Saturday morning, Claire woke up early to head over to Furever Paws for the weekend adoption event. She would be walking Dempsey around the shelter with an Adopt Me! banner draped over her back. These events brought a lot of visitors to the property, so the staff and volunteers typically walked a few dogs around that they wanted to highlight. The other dogs were kept in their kennels, because the large number of people, with their strange smells and grabbing hands, could be stressful for them.

"Hi, Claire," Bunny said, putting the banner over Cutie Pie, the shepherd mix she'd been fostering.

Claire smiled at Bunny. "Everything set for the event?"

Bunny nodded, surveying Cutie Pie and grabbing a red bandanna from the display wall. She tied it around the dog's neck. "There. Now you're ready for your close-up." She straightened and glanced around, then leaned close to Claire. "Isn't Matt with you?"

Claire raised an eyebrow. "Matt is most definitely not with me. Why would he be?"

Bunny headed over to the desk where two volunteers were stacking adoption applications, foster applications, and information packets. "He called last night and asked if we could use some extra help for the adoption event. I said of course."

Why was Matt so damn helpful except when it came to their relationship?

"We got some very promising applications online for four dogs and six cats," Birdie said as she came in from the back hallway. "I've approved three for the dogs and four for the cats. One of the rejected cat applicants thought her already thirteen black cats might like another now that they're bored of each other." She rolled her eyes. "And the other one has a dog who hates cats but would surely learn to love pretty, long-haired Glenda."

Claire shook her head. "Well, good for the ones who passed muster." She knew the dog adoption applications would require a home visit, but if everything checked out, those dogs would be going to their forever homes. "I guess Dempsey wasn't among them?"

"Sorry," Birdie said. "I don't know why she keeps being passed up." She bent down and petted Dempsey. "You're a beautiful, sweet dog and someone is going to snatch you up soon. Mark my words."

There was a knock at the door. The shelter wasn't open yet, so it had to be a volunteer without a key. Matt.

Yup, there he was. Looking gorgeous in his black leather jacket, jeans and work boots. He greeted Birdie and Bunny and nodded at Claire. She nodded back.

"How can I help?" he asked.

Birdie set him to work hanging Adoption Event banners on the upper walls. As more volunteers and foster parents came in with their dogs, Claire lost track of Matt. Then she spotted him standing near the door with Birdie, who'd handed him a stack of information packets so that he could greet each potential adopter with all the info they needed on the available dogs and cats.

The morning passed in a whirlwind of activity. So many people came through the doors. Seven cats found new homes, and the four preapproved applicants for the dogs had all confirmed they wanted the dogs they'd fallen for online now that they'd met them in person. Two volunteers would do home checks today, and then the adoptions would be made official.

"I keep seeing Dempsey's profile on your website and clicking on it," a woman said to Claire, bending to pet Dempsey, who sat beside her. "I just love her coloring. Like my hair," she added on a laugh.

"Like cinnamon," Claire agreed, though she didn't think it was much of a reason to be drawn to a dog. Or maybe it was. People fell in love for all kinds of reasons.

"She's awfully big, though," the woman added, giving Dempsey a pat. "Aren't you, you big thing," she singsonged in baby talk.

Dempsey eyed the woman as if she were above baby talk, but Claire knew Dempsey loved it. When it came to shelter animals, baby talk was a very welcome thing.

After answering the woman's many questions, Claire asked if she'd like to fill out an application.

"I don't know," the woman said. "I was thinking of a much smaller dog. A cuter dog, you know? Not that Dempsey isn't cute. She's just so…boxer-y."

Sigh. "Well, she is a boxer mix."

This woman sounded all wrong for Dempsey. Like she'd maybe take her and then return her two weeks later. "You know what? Dempsey is beautiful, and I always seem to come back to her. So, maybe I can take her for a walk outside and see how it goes?"

Claire set her up with a leash and led the woman to

the fenced yard. She stood by the door while the woman walked Dempsey. At least the prospective adopter was affectionate, giving Dempsey lots of TLC.

"I'd like to put in an application," the woman said when she returned.

Claire expected to be elated, but instead her heart felt like it weighed two thousand pounds. Granted, Dempsey's potential new mom was a bit wishy-washy, but adopting a dog was a big decision. Better to talk it out than be impulsive.

"Great," Claire said, handing the woman an application. "Why don't you take a seat here and fill it out." She gestured at the rectangular table that Matt had set up in the lobby with chairs and a canister of pens. "Then I'll go over it and pass it to one of the owners for final approval."

"Could that happen today? I was planning to binge-watch season two of my favorite show on Netflix, and I'd hate to have to be interrupted to walk her, especially in the cold."

Oh brother. *You can watch your shows anytime. Bringing home a new dog is a special occasion.* Claire frowned and rubbed Dempsey's side. "Well, we'll see," was all she would and could say.

As the woman got busy filling out the application, Claire put Dempsey into one of the kennels with a chew toy. "I'll be back for you, I promise." A strange feeling was lodged in her stomach, something she couldn't quite identify.

"Crazy day," a familiar voice said.

Matt. She locked Dempsey's kennel and stood up.

"Someone put in an application for Dempsey. I can't believe it. She might have a permanent home."

"Looking good?" he asked.

Claire shrugged. "Hard to tell. People sometimes say nutty things when they're in unfamiliar territory. She'd be a first-time dog owner. I guess I need to give her the benefit of the doubt until I read through her application."

"Miss?" called a high-pitched voice. "Miss?"

Claire glanced out the window and down the hallway, toward the voice. The woman who wanted to adopt Dempsey was standing and waving at her. "Guess her application is ready."

Matt gave her a gentle smile. "I'm not quite sure if you want Dempsey to be adopted or not."

"Of course I want her to be adopted," she snapped. "I've fostered twenty-one dogs since I started volunteering here. Giving them up to the right home is the point." Her voice was sharper than she'd intended, and she let out a breath. "Sorry. Didn't mean to take your head off. Dempsey is special. I just want her to be in the right home."

"Understood," he said, putting a hand on her shoulder, and it felt so good, so comforting that she wanted him to pull her against him and hold her tight.

She'd always known she'd have to say goodbye to Dempsey someday. Same with Matt. The two in the same time frame? That, she wasn't so sure she could bear.

But she sucked in a breath and left the Dogs room to go read over the application belonging to Dempsey's potential adopter, her legs like lead.

Chapter Eight

Claire held Gwyneth Cardle's application for Dempsey and read each line carefully. The woman lived in a single-family home, but there was no fenced yard.

"Since you don't have a fenced yard, are you prepared to walk Dempsey at least three times a day, for taking care of business and exercise?"

"Three times?" Gwyneth said, her eyes popping. "I'm figuring on walking her right before I leave for work at eight thirtyish, and then when I get home at five thirty."

Claire stared at her. "You realize that's nine hours."

"She's a big dog, though. I read that big dogs can hold it longer."

Claire marked an *X* next to Residence Information.

"So, Dempsey will be alone for nine hours each

weekday?" Claire asked. "No contact with people or dogs and no potty break or exercise?"

"I work," the woman snapped. "So sue me."

"You could hire a dog walker to come at noon," Claire said. "I work and that's what I do."

"Not everyone can afford that," Gwyneth muttered. "She'll have to hold it in."

Claire marked an *X* next to Understands Dogs' Needs and went over the rest of her application, which was as dismal. Under the area that asked what provisions she would make for the dog if she went on vacation, Gwyneth had written: "I really don't know."

Next.

If there would be a next. *Looks like you're mine a bit longer, Dempsey*, she thought, a feeling she recognized all too well as relief washing over her.

"Thanks so much for filling out the application and for your interest in Dempsey," she said to Gwyneth. "I'll pass the application to one of the shelter owners, and we'll be in touch by the end of the day."

"Could you not call before five?" she asked, putting on her jacket. "I'm planning on watching five episodes of my show today, so…"

Claire mentally rolled her eyes. "Well, one of the Whitaker sisters will contact you via email. So, no worries."

As Claire watched the woman walk away and stick her finger in an adoptable kitten's kennel in the lobby, despite the big sign that read: Please Do Not Put Fingers in Kennels, she thought about how satisfying it would be to stamp the application with Not Recommended.

On her way to the desk to do just that, Claire's phone pinged with a text. Jasmine, one of her teacher friends from the middle school.

Help! Babysitter canceled and tonight's my brother-in-law's wedding. Can you take Tyler? Six to midnightish.

Ooh. Tyler was a precious, adorable, baby-shampoo-scented seven-month-old with huge brown eyes and a gummy smile.

She texted back, Of course! I'll come pick him up so you don't get baby spit-up on the gorgeous dress I'm sure you're wearing.

Thank you!!! I owe you BIG.

Clare smiled. *Au contraire.* She loved babysitting, especially babies.

And what better way to try to get Matt out of her system than to focus on what she wanted for herself: a child.

That night, as Matt took Sparkle and Hank into the yard, he could have sworn he saw Claire walking back and forth in her living room with a baby in her arms. Seeing things?

Nope. Because there she was again. Walking and patting the baby on the back.

He swallowed. How many nights had he thought about "what might have been?" if he and Claire had married. Had children. Sometimes he'd think of them with a baby, sometimes with six kids. And then the images would fade because *come on*. Matt Fielding, someone's father? A thirty-six-year-old man with a duffel bag and a three-legged dog to his name?

He could see Dempsey staring forlornly out the glass door, hoping to be let out to play with her friends. But Claire clearly had her hands full and looked a bit exasperated.

As she looked out and spotted him, he quickly held up a hand and came over to the door. She slid it open just a bit since she obviously didn't want to let the cold air inside to chill the baby.

"I'll take Dempsey if it's easier on you," he said.

"Oh, thank God," she sputtered. "I love Tyler to pieces, but he's been crying for half an hour. He was fine when I picked him up from my colleague's house."

"So you're babysitting for the night?" he asked.

She nodded, rocking the baby in her arms. "It's okay, little guy," she cooed to the baby. "Everything is okay."

A bell dinged, and Claire glanced toward the left. "Oh crud. That's my oven timer. Could you hold Tyler for just a minute while I get the cookies out of the oven?"

What? She wanted him to hold the baby? The squawking, red-faced baby?

"Matt?" she asked. "I don't want to just put him down in his bouncer while he's so miserable."

"Okay," he said, stepping inside the living room and closing the sliding glass door behind him. He held out his arms, clueless as to how to take a baby, let alone hold one. She handed the baby over, and maybe it was the change of scenery of his face versus Claire's, but the baby stopped crying. Matt took him under the arms and cradled him against his chest, finding that holding the tot was just sort of instinctive. "Name's Matt," he said to the baby.

Claire burst out laughing from the kitchen. She poked her head out of the kitchen doorway. "Oh God, I needed that. Thank you." She poked her head back in and continued laughing.

"Something funny about what I said?" he asked, eyes narrowed toward the kitchen, from where the smell of warm cookies emanated.

She came back inside the living room, grinning. "Yes, actually. 'Name's Matt,'" she said, making her voice deeper. She chuckled and reached out to caress the baby's face.

"Well, shouldn't I introduce myself?"

"You don't spend much time around babies, do you?" she asked.

"Nope. But look at me now? Baby whisperer." He rocked the baby a bit as he had seen Claire do earlier. Tyler laughed.

Matt's mouth dropped open. "He laughed! Babies laugh?"

"They sure do. And he sure seems to like you. You *are* the baby whisperer."

"Whodathunk," he said, moving to the couch to sit down. Tyler immediately grabbed his chin.

"The dogs are all right on their own?" he asked.

Claire went to the glass door and peered out. "Hank appears to be overseeing the other two as he gnaws on a rope toy. Sparkle is sniffing under the tree, and Dempsey is digging in the spot I made for her to do just that."

"So, since you're babysitting and not bringing Dempsey to her new home, I assume that woman's application didn't work out."

"She thought leaving a dog home alone for nine hours every weekday was no big deal," Claire said. "I mean, maybe some dogs can handle that but it's not ideal. Given that she didn't seem a good match for Dempsey in most ways, I didn't recommend her."

"Well, I'm sure the right person will come along. Just like me for Hank."

She stared at him, and he wondered if she was applying that statement to herself, as well.

Tyler gripped Matt's ear and pulled with a squeal of joy.

"Ow," Matt said on a laugh. "Quite an arm you got there." He tickled the baby's belly and made funny faces at him, sticking out his tongue.

Tyler laughed that big baby laugh that was almost impossible to imagine coming from such a bitty body.

"You really have a way with babies," Claire said. "Ever think about fatherhood?"

His smile faded. "Of course not."

"Of course not?" she repeated.

"Claire. If I have nothing to offer a woman, I have nothing to offer a baby. I wouldn't inflict myself on an innocent life."

"You really don't see yourself the way others do," she said.

"Key word there is *see*. I know who I am. Others *see* an honorably discharged soldier. They don't look past the uniform and what it represents."

"Because it means so much," she said. "It speaks for itself."

"I didn't say I'm a bad person. Just that I have nothing to offer a family. So I'm not going there."

"Matt, you've been home only a couple of weeks. You expect to have your new life figured out already? I certainly don't expect that of you."

Once again, she just didn't understand. Making a baby laugh didn't mean he was cut out for fatherhood. Training a puppy didn't mean he was cut out for man of the year.

"Claire, do yourself a favor and stop trying to make me into something I'm not. I don't want a wife. I don't want a baby. I'm on my own. Me and Hank."

She stared at him. "I'll never forget you telling me that when you had a son, you were going to name him Jesse, after your brother."

His chest seized up and the back of his eyes stung. He pictured his brother, older by four years, the best person Matt had ever known. And his hero.

"Did I say that?" he managed to choke out.

"Yes, you did," she said softly.

He closed his eyes and got up and put the baby in the bouncer, latching the little harness. He pushed the On button and the bouncer gently swung side to side. He watched Tyler's eyes droop and droop some more until they closed.

"Magic," she said, moving closer behind him.

He turned around and pulled her into a hug. "I did say that," he whispered. A long time ago, but he'd said it.

"And his middle name would be Thomas, after my dad."

He closed his eyes again. He remembered saying that too. She'd lost her father when she was only nine, barely older than Ellie. Then her mother had died a few years ago; he'd heard the news through his sister. "I'm so sorry about your mom. I don't think I ever said that. When my sister mentioned it in a letter, I wanted to write you, but then I thought I should just leave well enough alone."

"I wish you had written," she said. "I wish a lot of things."

He put his hands on either side of her face, and she looked up at him. There was so damned much hovering between them. History and feeling. He lowered his face, and she tilted up even higher to kiss him.

"I'm leaving by the end of March," he said, taking a step back. "Sparkle will be ready for my sister's house. I need to be clear. There's not going to be any baby named Jesse."

She stepped back as if he'd slapped her.

A dog barked, then others chimed in. Matt went to the glass door and looked out, his chest tight, his heart racing. The dogs were standing under a tree, staring up at a fat squirrel racing across one of the branches. "I'd better get these guys out of the cold."

"We all need to be let out of the cold," she said. "The deep freeze."

He glanced at her, then walked over to Tyler. "Night, little guy," he whispered, and then fled outside.

On Sunday afternoon, Claire accompanied Bunny on a home check for a couple who had an approved application to adopt Pierre, a two-year-old black Lab mix they'd met at the adoption event earlier that day. The Changs had an adorable toddler named Mia and lived in a classic white Colonial with a red door. They had a fenced yard, and had already decked out the house with everything a dog could need—plush beds in a few rooms, food and water bowls, toys and two sets of leashes and harnesses, plus an assortment of poop bags. These people were prepared to bring a dog into their family.

"Mia's first word was dog," Camille Chang said, the little girl on her lap.

Bunny smiled. "Well, Mia, I'm happy to let you know that you'll now have a dog of your very own."

"So all is well with the home check?" Michael Chang asked.

"All is well. You can come pick up Pierre anytime." She added her card to Pierre's paperwork, which included the Chang's application. Claire watched her write *Approved to adopt Pierre—Bunny W.* across the back of the card. "Just show this at the desk and he's all yours."

They left the very happy Changs and headed out to Bunny's ancient car with the Furever Paws logo painted on the sides.

Claire got in and buckled up with a deep sigh. When she realized she actually sighed out loud, she winced.

"What's got you all wistful?" Bunny asked. "Spill it."

Claire smiled. "You know when you want something but the someone you want it with isn't interested in any of it, including you, but you want him, and so you're just spinning your wheels in what feels like gravel?"

"I assume you're talking about our handsome new volunteer?"

Claire nodded—and then found herself launching into every detail of her relationship, and lack thereof, with Matt Fielding.

"Ah, well, he's interested all right."

"He's told me flat out he's not. Attracted, yes," she added, thinking she probably should have left out the part about ending up in bed. But the Whitaker sisters were hardly shrinking violets, and she'd always felt she could get personal with them. "Interested in a future with me? A family one day? No."

Bunny turned the ignition. "My hard-won wisdom is this, Claire. He's interested. In fact, he probably just doesn't know how to get from here to there. You've just got to flip him."

Claire raised an eyebrow. "Flip him? What do you mean?"

"You've said he doesn't think he has what it takes to be a husband and a father because he has nothing to offer. But he's shown you time and again he most definitely is husband and daddy material."

"Right," Claire said. "But where does the flipping come in?"

"By spending time with him, not hiding or avoiding

him. The more he sees for himself who he is, the closer you'll get to your dream."

Her dream. Husband, children. Dogs. "Am I that transparent?"

Bunny grabbed Claire's hand and squeezed. "Sorry, but yes. You love that man."

Claire bit her lip. She did.

"So are you going to give up like you had no choice when you were eighteen? Or are you going to make that man yours?"

Claire smiled. "You make it sound so easy."

Bunny backed out of the Changs' driveway and headed toward the shelter. "He adopted Hank, Claire. He's halfway there already. He just doesn't know it."

"Halfway could go either way. Backward or forward," Claire pointed out.

"If you're a pessimist like Birdie, maybe." Bunny chuckled, then added, "Don't tell my sister I said that. She calls herself a *realist*."

"I think I need a dash of you to believe this relationship has a chance, and a dash of Birdie to keep my head out of the clouds."

And she wasn't so sure that adopting Hank meant Matt was setting down roots. Making something his. Creating permanence. Dogs loved unconditionally and didn't talk or ask for much. They were easy to love. People were much harder.

But Bunny was right—Matt's adopting Hank was a major sign of his commitment to love, honor and cherish that living, breathing creature. *A* living, breathing creature. It was a start, and all she had at the moment, so she was going to run with Bunny's dreamer ways.

"Oh, and Claire?" Bunny said as she pulled into Furever Paws' gravel parking lot. "He named his some-day son. I'm not sure you need more *sign* than that."

"That was a long time ago, when he was a different person."

"Was he? According to the broken record of Matt Fielding, he had nothing to offer you then and has nothing to offer now. So for him, nothing is different. If he could imagine being a father then, he could imagine being one now." She smiled and shook her head. "Men."

Huh. Bunny was absolutely right.

Except he was leaving by the end of March. "He's out of here in four weeks, Bunny."

"Or not, dear."

He'd left once. For eighteen years. Claire had no doubt the most stubborn man she'd ever met would do it again.

Chapter Nine

Was Matt really walking the dogs around the front of Claire's house to avoid running into her in the backyard with Dempsey? *Yes.* He sighed, hating that it had come to this. How could he want to be with someone so much and want to avoid her at the same time? What the hell was that?

The front door opened and Dempsey's snout, followed by the rest of her and then Claire, came outside. Guess Claire had the same idea.

Awk-ward.

"Oh, hi," she said.

"Hey."

Dempsey started pulling on her leash, something he didn't think he ever saw her do. Must be a particularly interesting squirrel nearby.

Sparkle started pulling too and barking up a storm. "Whoa there, pup," he said. The only dog not pulling was Hank, but he was staring at something across the road.

Matt glanced toward where they were staring. A small, gray, scruffy dog was half-hiding behind the wheel of a car parked across the street. "See that dog?" he asked Claire. "Sure looks skinny and bedraggled."

Claire gasped. "It's him! I saw him a few days ago and tried to lure him with treats, but he was scared and then a truck passed by and must have spooked him, because he took off running."

"I don't see a collar," Matt said. "Poor thing must be a stray from the looks of him."

"I think so too."

"Here, I'll take Dempsey. Maybe you can lure him over with treats now."

Claire handed over Dempsey and pulled a treat from her pocket. "Here, sweetie," she said, bending down a bit as she moved forward toward the curb. The mutt was still half-hiding, staring at the dogs more than her—or the treat.

"Ruff! Grr-ruff!" Sparkle barked.

"Shh, Sparkle," Matt said. "You might scare him away."

Claire stepped off the sidewalk and onto the street. But just then, a teenager on a moped came racing down the road, and the dog took off running.

Oh no.

Claire ran after him, treat in hand, but then she stopped, throwing her hands up before she came back.

"I lost him. Poor guy. It's so cold at night, especially. I called the animal warden when I saw him a couple of days ago, but she hasn't been able to find him."

"Well, we know he likes this road. So maybe he'll be back."

Claire bit her lip. "I hate the idea of that skinny, hungry little thing out there on his own."

"I know. But let's hope for the best. You'd bring him to the shelter?" he asked.

She nodded. "Our vet, Dr. Jackson—we call him Doc J—would check him out with a full exam, and we'd go from there. The little dog seemed to be in good enough shape."

"I'll keep an eye out," Matt said. "Maybe he'll be back later."

She nodded. "Me too. But little dogs are hard to catch. So many places to hide. I don't want you to be disappointed if we can't rescue him."

"I will be. I know what it's like to think you have nowhere to go." He froze. *What the hell?* He hadn't intended to say that.

"You'll always have somewhere to go, Matt. You have your sister, and no matter what, I'll always be your friend. Even if I'm really, really, really mad at you."

That actually made him smile. "Are you? Mad at me."

"Yeah, I am."

The snapping miniature poodle two doors down was storming down the sidewalk, pulling her owner, who kept saying "One day I'm going to hire a trainer."

"Dempsey's nemesis," Claire said. "I think I'll head back inside. Thanks for holding her."

"Anytime," he said.

The second the door closed behind them, he missed Claire. He really hoped they'd find and rescue that gray dog. Because somehow, in no time at all, Matt had become a dog person. And because he wanted to do something to make Claire happy.

With Dempsey at Doc J's main office for a dental cleaning, Claire's house sure was…lonely. She attempted to bake a pie, which came out lopsided and missing something vital, like sugar, maybe. Then she cleaned both bathrooms and vacuumed Dempsey's fur off all surfaces. She watched two episodes of a TV show, then tried to read a memoir about a woman who adopted a dog after divorce and it changed her life.

But she couldn't concentrate on anything. She kept lifting her eyes to the ceiling and toward the right, wondering what was going on in Matt's over-the-garage apartment. Part of her wanted to march up the deck stairs, knock on that that man's door and tell him straight-up how she felt, point out that he clearly felt something too, and that he was being ridiculous. And that he'd better fall in love with her *this minute*.

Well, maybe she'd just tell him how she felt. He was leaving soon. If his response was, *Sorry, I just don't feel the same way* or more of *I can't because of this-that*, at least she wouldn't be mortified around him for long. But there was a chance she could get through to him. Flip him, like Bunny had suggested.

She went upstairs to her bedroom and sat down at her dressing table, planning to doll herself up a bit, but frowned in the mirror instead. *Take me or leave me. This is who I am. A woman who teaches tweens all day and gets down and dirty with dogs all evening at the shelter. Accept me, dog hair and all.*

She got up, went to the kitchen for a bottle of red wine and a block of one of her favorite cheeses, put on her jacket, then went out the deck door and up the stairs to Matt's entrance. She knocked. *Please don't let me humiliate myself—again*, she thought.

He answered the door with a towel around his waist, damp from the shower and looking so incredibly sexy, she couldn't find words for a moment. Luckily, two sets of canine eyes were staring at her as Sparkle and Hank stood beside him, assessing the interloper. She cleared her throat and gave each a scratch under the chin.

He eyed the wine and cheese with interest in his blue eyes. "What are we celebrating?"

"A second chance for us." She held her breath.

He shook his head. "Claire, you dodged a bullet with me. Why can't you understand that? My life is completely up in the air right now."

"Really? Looks to me like your feet are solidly on the ground. You have a home, family nearby, a *dog*."

He tilted his head. "I *do* have a dog, don't I? Never saw that one coming."

She smiled. "Life is happening, Matt. You might be trying to stand still because being out of the military is a culture shock for you. But life is moving around you, and you're responding whether you mean to or not. Hence, Hank."

"Hence?" He laughed.

"I'm an English teacher. So *hence*. *Hence*, Matt Fielding, shut up and let what is going to happen happen instead of trying to fight it for reasons that aren't standing up to scrutiny."

He smiled and shook his head. "I guess I could use a glass of wine."

Thank you, universe! she shouted in her head. She went into his kitchen and took out two wineglasses from a cabinet and poured. They clinked. And that was when the towel dropped.

Oh my. She'd seen him naked not too long ago, but oh wow, oh wow, oh wow. Matt Fielding was magnificent. Tall and muscled and strong. She lifted up her face to kiss him.

He kissed her and kissed her and kissed her, and suddenly, he was walking her backward, his lips still on hers, toward the bedroom.

"I can't stop thinking about you," he whispered, his hands in her hair as they stood just inside the doorway. "Everywhere I look, there you are—my apartment, my dogs, my past. I spent an hour searching for that little gray dog mostly to see your smile when I found him."

She was speechless for a moment. She couldn't even process everything he'd just said, so she focused on the easy part. "Did you find him?"

"He slowed down a few blocks from here, and I thought I could stop my car and lure him over with little bits of a mozzarella cheese stick, but something spooked him and he took off. I couldn't find him after that."

"I appreciate that you tried, Matt." She led him by the hand to the bed and kissed him again, slowly sinking down to the edge of the mattress.

This is so right, she thought over and over. *Can't you feel it?* she silently asked him. *There's no way you can't feel this.*

"You know what I think is unfair?" he asked, one hand in her hair, the other undoing a button on her shirt.

"What?"

"That you're still dressed while I'm naked."

She grinned and got rid of her clothes, aware of him watching her remove every last piece of wool and cotton and lace from her body.

"You do, right?" she asked, running her hands over his glorious chest, all hard planes and muscles.

He trailed kisses up her neck, pausing briefly to ask, "Do what?"

"Feel this. What's between us." She could actually feel him freeze, his body just *stop*. "I want you to stay. And I don't mean just the night, Matt. There, I said it. No one's a mind reader, right? Now you know."

He sat up against the headboard, grabbing part of the top sheet to cover him from the waist down. "I can't stay, Claire. And I really don't want to talk about it."

She stood up and quickly dressed. "Let me tell you something, *bub*."

"Bub?" he repeated.

"Yes, *bub*."

"I'm listening," he said.

"What you might not realize is that you actually do have one thing to offer, Matt. And it happens to be the only thing I want from you."

He stared at her. "I can't possibly come up with anything you could be talking about."

"The one thing you have to offer is *yourself*, Matt Fielding."

He shook his head. "Matt Fielding is a shell, Claire."

Grrr! "A shell? Does a shell of a man adopt a senior three-legged dog and buy every treat and toy and dog bed for his comfort? Does a shell of a man foster a nutty puppy for his smitten niece? Does a shell of a man volunteer at an animal shelter and move furniture around the Whitaker sisters' house? You *love*, Matt. Whether you want to admit it or not. You're just choosing to avoid commitment."

"That's where you're wrong. It's not a choice. This thing in here," he said, slapping a hand over his chest, "is blocked by a brick wall. It's there all the time. The dogs, two sixtysomething sisters with nicknames, and an eight-year-old with a crooked braid don't threaten my equilibrium. I'm not looking for attachments beyond them."

She crossed her arms over her chest. "So you're just a lone wolf."

"Better than what you're doing with Dempsey. You're so attached to her, when you're just going to have to let her go. I saw the look on your face, the tension in your body language when she got that application the other day. Loving Dempsey means breaking your own heart."

"Bullcrap. Love is all there is in this crazy world.

Everything you've been through has helped build that brick wall in that chest of yours, but I can help break it down if you'll let me. You have to let someone in, Matt. May as well be me."

Please don't say Sorry *and turn away. Stop pushing me out of your life.*

"I am really sorry, Claire. But I'm leaving in a few weeks as planned."

She could use that brick wall over her own heart right about now. Because it was breaking again, and she was powerless to protect herself. So she did the only thing she could. She left.

After rushing downstairs from Matt's last night, Claire had kept busy by grading quizzes and baking and cleaning some more. At least her house was spotless. She'd spent the night tossing and turning in her bed, vacillating between giving up on Matt as the lost cause he said he was and being on Team Bunny and working on the flip. Which apparently she was no good at.

There was a rap at the sliding glass door. Matt stood there with Sparkles's and Hank's leashes dangling from his neck.

"Hi," she said, barely able to look at him.

"Hi. I just realized I forgot to bring down poop bags. Got two extras?"

Sigh. He could have run up and gotten some from his apartment. She supposed it meant he was trying, that he wasn't avoiding her.

"Come in out of the cold," she said. "I have some in the kitchen."

Just as she rounded the kitchen, her phone dinged with a text. It was from Birdie.

GREAT application just came in for Dempsey! Forwarding to you.

Goose bumps broke out along Claire's spine and arms. And not in a good way, she realized.

She went to her laptop on the kitchen island and opened Birdie's email and the application. Her heart sunk with every line. A single, middle-aged writer, who worked at home, didn't have a fenced yard but lived near wooded trails and would walk Dempsey at least three times a day, who "lost my furbaby last year to cancer and am finally ready to love another dog." She fell in love with Dempsey at the adoption event last week but had wanted to sit with her feelings, and yes, she'd love to have "beautiful, majestic, lovely" Dempsey.

Claire burst into tears, her hands darting up to her face. Her shoulders shook and her knees started to buckle.

"Claire?" Matt said, rushing over to her. "Hey, what's wrong?"

"I just love Dempsey so much. But this applicant... she sounds so perfect and just right for Dempsey. I know this woman will appreciate her as much as I do. I can feel it just by having read the application." Fresh sobs racked her entire body.

Matt pulled her into his arms. "Oh, honey. It's hard to let go. I know."

He didn't know. He didn't.

"I don't want to give her up. I love that dog, dammit."

"I know you do. Could you keep her?"

She felt herself go limp against Matt, grateful he was holding her. But then she remembered where she was, who was keeping her upright, and she sucked in a breath and stepped back, swiping at her eyes. "I go through this with every dog. I love them so hard, and it's my job to prepare them for their furever home. It's what a foster parent signs up for. I know there are 'foster fails' out there, those who do keep their dogs, but I feel like that would be wrong. I'm meant to take in dogs who can't find homes and work with them until they're so ready, they're irresistible. And now Dempsey is."

"She is pretty irresistible," he said, going over to Dempsey and petting her.

"You knocked for dog bags and got a crying Claire. Sorry you asked, huh?" She walked back to the kitchen, pulled two poop bags from the doggie-drawer and handed them to him.

"Never," he said, stuffing the bags in his pocket. "I'm here for you. You can always talk to me."

"Till the end of March, anyway."

He winced slightly. "I guess the key is not to love the dogs when you have to give them away. I mean, you know you're not keeping them. It's not a permanent arrangement. So why get attached?"

She gaped at him. "How could I not?" Was he seriously asking this?

"You just don't. You know what you're walking into, and you create boundaries. That easy."

"Oh, really?" she said. "Well, it's not that easy for

most people. Just you. I don't know one foster parent who hasn't gotten choked up about bringing their dogs and cats to their forever homes. Not one. And you know what, Matt Fielding? I don't think you'll find it so easy to let Sparkle go."

"Trust me, I will."

"Having Hank won't protect you from having to say goodbye to that adorable fluffy little dog that you trained for weeks."

"Boundaries. It's all about boundaries."

"I guess you'd know!" she shouted and ran into her bedroom and closed the door.

She closed her eyes and shook her head, wondering what had happened to good ole levelheaded, even-keeled Claire Asher.

The hot dude in the living room happened.

Dempsey's application happened.

Boundaries were for toxic people in your life. Not for the good ones. Not for the furbabies, who saved you as much as you saved them. Even if you were just their temporary foster parent.

She heard the sliding glass door open and close, and she breathed a sigh of relief that he was gone. She ran back out into the hallway, and there was her beloved Dempsey, staring forlornly at Matt's back as he went to get Sparkle and Hank from the yard.

"Oh, Dempsey," she said, lowering to the floor on her knees and giving the sweet boxer mix a hug. "Your new mama sounds wonderful. She even has trails behind her house that you can explore."

Dempsey licked her face. Good thing too, because the tears came crashing down.

"I love you, Demps," she said, placing her forehead on the dog's warm neck, her body shuddering with fresh sobs. "I'm going to cry my eyes out and recommend the application back to Birdie. Then when it's time to bring you to your new home, I'll cry some more and foster a new pooch, and the cycle will start all over again. Because that's what it's all about.

"I might be heartbroken to lose you, but at least I feel something."

Chapter Ten

"Where should I put this, Birdie?" Matt asked, picking up the huge fifty-pound bag of dog food that someone had donated to the shelter.

After what had just happened with Claire, he'd needed to get out of the house and, at the same time, feel connected to her, to what she was going through. He hadn't wanted to think too deeply about why. So he'd grabbed his phone and called the shelter, and Birdie happened to answer. He'd asked if she could use an extra pair of hands at Furever Paws right now, and she'd said *always*, so he'd driven over.

"We have a storage closet in the back hallway," Birdie said. "I'll show you. How's our Hank doing?"

Matt smiled. "He's doing great. He keeps that little spitfire Sparkle in line, that's for sure."

Bunny came out of the cat adoption room and smiled at Matt. "I miss his sweet face. But I sure am glad he's with you now."

He pictured Sparkle and Hank, who were probably curled up in the huge memory foam dog bed, Sparkle in her preferred napping position, with her head tucked between her front paws. *Would* he have trouble giving Sparkle up? He had a feeling he would if didn't have Hank. And if he didn't have Hank, he'd have to go get himself a Hank. So why didn't Claire have a dog of her own? Suddenly, it struck him as strange. He'd have to ask her the next time he saw her—if she was speaking to him.

"Oh, Bunny," Birdie said, turning to her sister as she stopped in front of the storage closet. "I meant to tell you—Gator texted earlier."

Birdie, Bunny and Gator. Their other brother, Moose, had passed away years ago. Since he'd started volunteering at Furever Paws, Matt had heard the Whitaker sisters talk about their family quite a bit. Birdie held Gator in high regard, and as the no-nonsense woman didn't suffer fools, he figured Gator had to be something special.

He'd learned, from overhearing many conversations between the sisters, that the Whitaker siblings had inherited the Whitaker Acres land from their parents, who'd lived in Spring Forest for generations. Gator and Moose had sold their shares long ago, but the sisters had hung on to forty acres, smartly selling small sections of their property and living off their investments.

Bunny smiled. "Oh, how nice. And what did our brother have to say for himself?"

Birdie bit her lip, something Matt didn't think he'd ever seen her do. Bernadette "Birdie" Whitaker could wrestle a crocodile, so when she seemed off balance, Matt noticed. "Well, he thinks we should sell off a parcel of the property, namely the large acreage we use as an outside dog run and training area."

Bunny frowned. "Really? Well, I don't know about that, Birdie. That would leave the shelter with little room for outdoor areas—especially if we expand in years to come."

"I know," Birdie said with a bit of a shrug. "But that was his recommendation."

As always, Matt tried not to eavesdrop but since the Whitaker sisters were talking right in front of him, he couldn't help but listen.

"Gator's never let us down with his investment recommendations," Birdie added, "but I'll talk to him about selling a parcel on the far side of the shelter instead."

"I thought the two of you owned the land outright," Matt said, looking from Birdie to Bunny. "Why would it be Gator's decision? If you don't mind my asking."

During one of their talks about Furever Paws, Claire had mentioned that most of the Whitaker land was undeveloped forest with some creek-front areas. But apparently the region was in the midst of a development boom, and the sisters had been getting offers to buy them out for years, especially by the neighboring Kingdom Creek housing development, where Matt now lived in Claire's house. According to Claire, the sisters had refused all offers; they intended to leave Whitaker Acres as a trust. Now, the Kingdom Creek development wanted to buy land right on top of the shelter. Gator seemed to think that was a good thing.

"Oh, we like to keep our attention on the furbabies and the running of the rescue, not on the business and financial end," Birdie explained. "That's Gator's specialty, and he's proven time and again he's a shrewd financial planner."

He nodded and put away the giant bag of dog food in the closet and shut the door. The rescue, surrounding area and the sisters' farmhouse were all in great condition, so it looked like the way the sisters had chosen to operate Furever Paws was working just fine. Besides, they had been living off their investments for years, so Gator Whitaker had to know what he was doing.

Matt envied what the sisters had built here. They had such rich, full lives, worked at something they loved and were so passionate about, gave back to the community over and over, and lived on their own terms. He admired the Whitaker sisters. They might not think of themselves as businesswomen, but they most definitely were.

"Bunny! Birdie!" a woman called out from the direction of the lobby. "Someone just dumped two dogs from a car and sped off!"

What the hell? Matt glanced at Birdie's and Bunny's concerned faces and followed the women as they rushed out to the lobby. Lisa Tish, one of the volunteers at Furever Paws, stood frowning in front of the door.

The young woman looked to be on the verge of tears. "I was manning the front desk when I saw the car stop up the road. A man got out and practically dragged both dogs from the car, then sped off. I saw the dogs run after the car, and then they ran back to the exact spot he'd left them. They're just sitting there!"

Matt's mouth dropped open. "He dumped them? What the hell?"

"Unfortunately, it happens all the time," Bunny said, grabbing two long rope-style leashes from the counter.

Birdie nodded and let out a deep sigh. "Twice last week." She took a handful of soft treats from the jar on the desk, put them in her pocket, and they all headed out.

Matt could see the two medium-sized dogs, one black and tan, the other mostly brown, standing up the road. That area could get busy, and he hoped the dogs would stay put until the sisters could get to them.

"Hey, pups," Bunny called in a warm, friendly voice. "Got some treats for you."

The two dogs, who looked like hound mixes, stared at Bunny. The mostly-brown one had floppy ears and seemed to have some beagle in him. The black-and-tan dog was possibly a coonhound mix, Matt thought. Two weeks ago he couldn't have told anyone the difference between a hound and a shepherd, and suddenly he could pick out breeds in a mutt.

"These treats are yummy peanut butter," Bunny added, slowly walking a bit farther as the rest of them hung back.

Matt wondered if the dogs would take off scared the

way that little gray dog had, or if they'd come running for the treats.

They came slowly toward her for the treats. Relief flooded him. He had no idea why he cared so much about two dogs that he'd never seen before two seconds ago, but hell, he did.

The sisters gave the dogs a once-over. "No collars," Bunny said, "but they do look to be in decent shape. Maybe old hunting dogs that stopped doing their 'jobs.'"

"I'd love to get my hands on that jerk," Matt said, shaking his head. "They weren't useful so he just abandoned them?"

"Like I said, it happens a lot," Bunny said. "I'm just glad folks know we're here and at least abandon them on our property." She turned to Lisa. "I'm glad you saw it happen and called us right away. Otherwise, they might have run off along the road."

Lisa nodded. "I'm with Matt. I just can't believe someone would do this. Dump dogs like that." She shook her head.

Birdie slipped a leash over the larger dog's head. The rope-like leash worked as a collar and lead in one. "Well, that's what we're here for, so all's well that ends well, right, handsome one?" she cooed to the hound. "What a majestic-looking hound you are," she said, patting his side. "Good dog. You look like a Captain to me."

Bunny put the leash over the other dog's head and secured it. She gave him a pat too. "And I'd say you look like a Major."

Matt smiled. "No Corporal?"

"Doesn't roll off the tongue as easily," Birdie said. "But the next cat that comes in will be named Corporal in honor of your service, Matt."

He laughed. "I wasn't fishing."

"Well, you've done so much for us in such a short time that you deserve it," Birdie told him.

He smiled, his chest tightening. How had he made all these connections in Spring Forest? He hadn't intended to. Was Claire right about him accidentally making a life for himself here?

"We sure owe Claire for bringing you into our lives," Bunny added as they started back toward the shelter building.

Matt frowned.

"Now, Bunny, Matt came here on his own, remember? He didn't even know Claire volunteered here when he came to look for a puppy for his niece."

Bunny seemed to think about that for a moment. "Oh, yeah."

"I guess I just associate you two with each other. Matt and Claire. Claire and Matt."

Had the temperature suddenly increased? It was barely fifty degrees today, and Matt felt feverish. There was no Matt and Claire.

Birdie smiled and patted his hand. "Why don't you go up ahead and ready two kennels while I call Doc J and let him know we have two new dogs for assessment?"

"Will do," he said, taking both leashes and bringing the dogs inside the shelter and down the hallway into the Dogs room.

"Hey, Tucker," he said as he passed the chiweenie's kennel. "Some new friends for you to sniff from afar."

Tucker ignored him, as usual, but Matt threw him a treat. The little guy ambled over for it. Someone was going to snap him up soon, Matt had no doubt.

Lisa opened the kennels for Matt, and he ushered each dog inside. "I wish I could take them both in myself, even as a foster mom," she said to Matt. "I used to have dogs, two that I adopted from here long ago, but now that I have young children and one is allergic, I have to get my fix by volunteering here when my kids are in preschool."

Matt smiled. "I get it. Before I started volunteering here, I had no idea just how much I loved dogs. Now, I can't imagine ever not having one. Or two."

She laughed. "Yup."

The door opened and Claire came in, saw him and frowned, then turned right back around.

How had things gotten so bad between them?

Because of you, idiot. Push, pull. Pull, push. You tell her no, then you're naked in bed together. And you wonder why she hates your guts.

Except she didn't hate him. And he was *hurting* her.

He felt like crud. Now he was making Furever Paws awkward and uncomfortable for her by just being here. This was *her* place, her sanctuary. And he was ruining it for her.

He loved it here too, and had only another few weeks to help out. Hell, maybe he should move out of her house. He probably should. But he couldn't go back to Laura's since Sparkle wasn't 100 percent ready. So where could he go?

His phone rang—an unfamiliar number. "Hello?"

"Matt, this is Jessica Panetta, Ellie's teacher at Spring Forest Elementary."

His heart stopped. "Is everything okay? Is Ellie okay?"

"Oh, yes! I'm sorry, I should have opened with that, the way the school's nurse does when she calls parents. Ellie is just fine. I'm calling because after I met you and Sparkle in the park a few weeks ago, I couldn't stop thinking about how wonderful it would be to have a show-and-tell about puppies and what goes into training them. Kids beg their parents for puppies, but they really don't know the work that goes into training a puppy and taking care of one. I've spoken to the principal, and she agrees it would be a great experience for the kids."

"Wait, you want me to come in and give a talk on training puppies?" he asked, completely dumbfounded.

"Exactly. I envision you bringing in Sparkle and giving a twenty-minute presentation on puppy training and what goes into it. If you like the idea, our principal only requests that you have someone from Furever Paws accompany you as a second pair of eyes and hands."

Oh God. Was this conversation actually happening? She had to be kidding.

"I just saw how good you were with that dog," the teacher continued, "the way she listened to you, how much work you clearly were putting into the training, and I knew it would be a truly special extra learning event for the kids. And to be honest, I think Ellie would enjoy a little spotlight."

His heart dropped. He remembered Ellie saying she didn't have a best friend when they first met Sparkle. Did she have friends at all?

If twenty minutes of his time would make a difference for Ellie at school, that was all he needed to know.

"I'm in," he said. "And I'm sure someone from the shelter will be happy to help me out for the presentation."

"Great!" Mrs. Panetta said. They set a date and time for the week after next, and when Matt clicked End Call, he actually had to sit down for a second.

Matt Fielding, talking to a classroom full of kids? About puppies and training them?

His life was sure taking crazy routes.

Someone from Furever Paws to be an extra set of eyes and hands... He could ask Birdie or Bunny, but Claire was a teacher and she'd be able to give him pointers on how to set up the presentation. Then again, she probably couldn't just leave her own school to help out at the elementary school, even for just twenty minutes or so.

He could ask. Because it would give him a meaningful reason to spend some time with her despite everything in him telling him to keep his distance. And no matter how he tried, he just couldn't keep away from her.

A couple of hours later, as Hank and Sparkle ran around in the enclosed dog run at the park, Matt sat on the bench near the fence with his phone, reading through the online classifieds from the free weekly newspaper's website, circling possibilities for rooms for rent. Ever since seeing Claire at Furever Paws earlier, the look on her face, the hurt and confusion and sorrow in her eyes—caused by him—he knew that moving out of the apartment at Claire's was the right thing to do. To give them both space, to keep them from constantly running into each other in the yard. This way, if she did want to work with him on the school presentation, she wouldn't be overloaded with his presence.

He read through the ads. There was a boardinghouse, and he could always move in there temporarily. Or even an inn or motel, but then again, they wouldn't allow two dogs.

All he knew for sure was that he had to let Claire be.

"Hey, Fielding!"

Matt turned around and smiled. His old neighbor, Zeke Harper, was jogging toward him. Several years younger than Matt, and tall and strong in his running gear, Zeke reminded Matt of how much he used to love to run. Maybe one of these days.

"Hey, Matt, how's the pup training going?" Zeke asked, pulling the wireless ear pods out and putting them in his pocket.

"So good, in fact, that I adopted a dog of my own," Matt said, pointing at Hank beyond the fence. The three-legged old guy was doing great keeping up with the younger pups.

Zeke grinned. "That's great! And I hear that PT I

recommended is working out too." He watched the dogs run. "You're really settling in, Matt. Glad to see it."

"Hardly settling in," Matt said. "In fact, the opposite. I'm in need of place to live."

"Didn't you say you were renting Claire Asher's apartment in Kingdom Creek?"

The sound of her name brought her face to mind. Beautiful Claire with the kind, intelligent green eyes and all that silky blond hair. "Yeah, but maybe it's better that we're not that close, you know?"

Zeke nodded. "Understood. A friend of mine has a small, furnished carriage house available right now. Not too far from my place. It's month-to-month, so since you're planning on leaving town, that might work out. And he has a dog himself, so I'm sure pets are welcome."

"Sounds perfect." He put the contact info in his phone. That was a call he'd be making very soon.

For the next fifteen minutes, he and Zeke caught up, Matt explaining that he now volunteered at Furever Paws and spent a lot of time studying up on dog training and dog psychology so that he could be even more helpful to Birdie and Bunny and the least adoptable dogs at the shelter. He felt a real kinship with those who were always left behind.

"That's really something," Zeke said. "You know I'm a psychologist and volunteer with Veterans Affairs, and I have to say I'm really intrigued by what fostering and training Sparkle and adopting Hank has done for you."

"What do you mean?"

"Well, last time I ran into you, you were saying your

life was up in the air and you felt off balance because of it. Sounds to me like volunteering at the shelter, training the puppy for your niece and adopting a dog for yourself have given you purpose. And more too—a real sense of meaning. We already know how much comfort dogs give, but the purpose side of things—that's something I'd like to bring up to my colleagues over at VA."

Huh. Matt had to admit it was all true. His life *did* have meaning now. Purpose. When the hell had all that happened? And there was something else too. Something that had shocked him when he first noticed it. "I'll be the first to say that I went from having a nightmare a night to hardly any, especially since I adopted Hank." He'd had no idea just how much comfort a dog could be.

"You know, Matt, there's someone I'd really like for you to meet. His name is Bobby Doyle, and he's one of the vets I work with at the center. He has an auto body business he's trying to get off the ground, and didn't you say your expertise in the military was with vehicle mechanics? I bet he'd value your input as a former soldier."

"He's all alone?" Matt asked.

"Actually, he has a devoted wife and two great kids," Zeke said. "Thanks to them—and *for* them—he's making great strides." He glanced at the dog run. "I've suggested that Bobby get a therapy dog who is trained to help vets dealing with PTSD."

Matt knew full-well what a great idea that was. "I could talk to Claire and the Whitaker sisters about that. Maybe they know of programs in the area that match dogs with vets."

"I'd appreciate that," he said. "And, in the meantime,

I'll give Bobby your contact info and let him know you'd be happy to hear from him."

They shook hands, and as Zeke took off running again, Matt thought about all the man had said. Matt had never paid much attention to purpose and meaning all that mumbo jumbo because his life had been chock-full of both during his army years. And here he was, a civilian, traces of the injury still dogging him every now and then, and he had purpose and meaning up the wazoo. To the point that he was actually asked—him, Matt Fielding—to present a puppy training show-and-tell to a bunch of third-graders.

Once again, how had all this happened without him noticing?

A rambunctious little terrier was being a pain in the butt in the dog run, so Matt wanted to get Sparkle and Hank out of there. Sparkle was a toughie who gave back what she got, but Hank was a gentle giant who'd let the bully nip his ankles, and he had only three to spare.

He quickly pulled out his phone and called the number Zeke had given him for the carriage house to rent. He made an appointment to see the apartment in an hour. He'd bring the dogs home, then head over.

As he was helping Sparkle up into his car, something occurred to him. If his life *did* have purpose and meaning, then he did have something to offer Claire Asher.

Whoosh! It was like getting a surprise left hook in the stomach.

So why was he still so set on keeping his emotional distance from her?

Chapter Eleven

"Well, Dempsey," Claire said. "This is goodb—" Tears filled her eyes, and she swiped them away. "I promised you I wouldn't cry, didn't I? And I'm a blubbering mess."

She sat in her car, Dempsey sitting shotgun in the passenger seat. The beautiful boxer mix looked lovely, all fresh from the groomer's and smelling slightly of lavender.

"We were only together seven weeks, and I feel like it's been forever, Demps," she said, her hands on either side of the dog's snout. "But your new mama? She really seems wonderful. She even asked me to meet her for coffee yesterday and tell her every detail about you so she could understand your every nuance. She wrote down your favorite food and treats, too, and your favorite places to trail walk."

The woman really seemed perfect, the best possible forever home for Dempsey.

"It's time, sweet girl," Claire said, getting out of the car.

Kelly Pfieffer came running out of the house. "Dempsey's here!" The woman was even planning to keep Dempsey's name to make things easier for the transition.

I've been through this before, and I'll go through it again, she thought, forcing herself to smile for Kelly. This was a big moment for both adoptive mom and Dempsey and she didn't want to make this about her.

She waved at Kelly and kneeled down next to Dempsey. "I love you, sweet girl. You're the best. And you're going to have a great life. And I promise we'll see each other at the dog park, okay?"

Dempsey put her paw on Claire's arm, and she almost lost it, but held it together.

Kelly raced over, fawning and fussing over Dempsey, thanking Claire profusely, and then soon enough, Claire was in her car alone.

She let herself cry for a good minute before driving right over to the shelter. Bunny sat behind the reception desk.

"I just dropped off Dempsey with her new mom," she said, tears still in her eyes. "I need a toughie. A foster dog who really needs me."

"Aww," Bunny said, coming around the desk to wrap Claire in a much-needed hug. "It's always so hard to give up the fosters. Especially when we bond with them.

But the bonding is what makes them so ready for that forever home. Right?"

Claire blinked back tears. "Right. Dempsey is special, and I know she's in a great home now. Letting her go was rough, I'll tell ya."

"I had one of those heart-wrenchers," Bunny said. "Remember Buttercup? Long-haired dachshund? I was crazy about that little gal. I almost kept her too. But then I remembered my mission—to prepare as many rescue dogs as I can for great new homes. Not to keep every one I fall madly in love with."

"It is really hard to let go of someone you're madly in love with," Claire agreed, her voice cracking.

"Oh, Claire, I'm so sorry Matt is a stubborn fool. A helpful one, but a stubborn fool when it comes to what's right in front of his face."

"Thanks, Bunny," Claire said. "So, who do you have for me? Distract me with a real needy one."

Bunny put her fingers on her chin. "Oh, have I got the pooch for you. Remember the black-and-white shepherd mix that came in two days ago? Doc J has him on medication for a bad ear infection, and he doesn't seem to know any commands. He's very timid. He's praise and food motivated, so I have no doubt you'll do wonders with him."

Blaze. For the white lightning bolt-like zigzag on his otherwise black head. "I'll go see him."

Blaze was in the far-left kennel. He was pressed up against the back of the kennel on a blanket, his head down, and looked pretty scared.

"Hey, boy," she said gently.

The dog lifted his green eyes first, then his head. She held out a treat, and he came padding over very slowly. Claire could have counted to twenty-five in the time it took him to reach the front of the kennel.

"Hi, Blaze," she said, giving him the treat through the bars. "Aren't you handsome? It's no fun to be in here, is it?"

The dog stared at her, and she could swear he was saying, *Please pick me to be your new foster dog. I need you, Claire.*

When she opened the kennel, he ran toward the back, flattening himself against the far side. "It's okay, Blaze. I'm all about love and treats."

"She's telling you the truth," a familiar voice said.

She whirled around to find Matt returning Tucker to his kennel and latching the door.

"I've been walking all the dogs," he said. "I even walked Blaze about an hour ago. Shy guy."

"I'm hoping to bring him out of his shell," she said, turning her attention to the dog as she leashed him and led him out of the kennel. His ears were back, which meant he was scared. "It's okay, Blaze," she said softy as she knelt down beside him. "You're coming home with me, sweetie pie. And I'm going to give you a ton of TLC as I get you ready for your forever home."

"Are *you* okay?" Matt asked as she stood up, and she was touched that he remembered today was the day she had to say goodbye to Dempsey. But of course he remembered and asked how she was doing—because he was Matt Fielding and a great guy, dammit.

She glanced at him and nodded, blinking back the

sting of tears that poked at her eyes. "It's never easy to say goodbye. But I'll tell you, it feels good to say hello. This sweetie already has my heart."

He smiled and shook his head. "I don't know how you do it. But I'm glad you do."

His tone was so reverent that she looked at him, and all she wanted to do was fling herself in his arms and be held. It would be a while before Blaze became a cuddler, if he ever did. And Claire could use some cuddling.

"I have a big favor to ask," he said.

"If I can, I will." She *could* start changing that motto. And just say no.

"Ellie's teacher called me and asked if I'd bring in Sparkle for a presentation on how to train and care for puppies. She thought it would give Ellie a little boost in the class too, which is why I couldn't say no, even though I have no idea how to present anything, let alone to kids."

"You're great with one third-grader in particular," she pointed out. "The class will love you. Plus, Sparkle will do most of the work for you by being adorable and keeping the kids' attention."

"I'm hoping so. But here's the thing. The principal says someone from Furever Paws has to be present as an extra pair of ears and eyes, just in case. I know your hours are probably the same as the elementary school's, though. We'd go on at two thirty."

She remembered Bunny's advice—not to run and hide from him. The more time they spent together— quality time—the more he might see that they belonged together. Unless she was kidding herself. "Actually, I monitor a study hall as my last period of the day. I can easily have someone cover that for me."

"Perfect. And you'll help me figure out what to say? How to structure the twenty minutes?"

"I'd love to. Dogs and kids are my two favorite things." *Add in being with you, and it's heaven.*

He smiled, but then the smile faded. Uh-oh. "Look, I know things between us have been strained and the push-pull is my fault. So, I thought it best if I find a new place to live for the next few weeks."

She didn't want him to go. Closer was better, as much as it hurt. "Matt, you don't have to do that."

"I already did."

It probably was for the best, but it still stung. Like everything these days. She shrugged. "Okay."

"Okay."

Except it wasn't okay. He was running away before he even ran away for good. This time, across town, probably near where he grew up.

"I'll miss Sparkle and Hank," she said, hoping her voice wouldn't crack.

And I'll miss you.

"I owe you a lot, Claire," he said.

"Well," she started, but what could she say? What was there to say at this point?

You need to replace Matt Fielding the way you have to replace Dempsey, her sister had texted earlier, when Claire said her heart was in pieces. New foster dog to dote on—new man to fall for.

Or maybe Claire should just focus on the dog. And the child she wanted. There were some options she could look into. Becoming a foster parent to a little kid. Foreign adoption. The ole sperm bank. She'd always wanted the traditional setup—spouse, at least two kids and dogs—but that wasn't what life had set out for her.

"I'd better get Blaze home before he thinks he's going back in the kennel," she said. "He seems almost excited."

"His tail is giving a little wag," Matt agreed.

"Guess I might not even see you leave the apartment," she said, "since all you have is a duffel bag. No moving van." She was rambling, she realized, and clamped her mouth closed.

"Don't forget the two dogs," he said with a killer smile. "Or the fact that I'd never leave without saying goodbye, Claire. I'll text you about getting together to work on the presentation."

She managed something of a smile, and watched him walk away and disappear through the door into the hallway.

"It's you and me, Blaze." The scared dog looked up at her, holding eye contact. She almost gasped, and gave the pooch a peanut butter treat. "Good dog!" she said, with a pat on his back. "And good sign."

For Blaze. And Claire's entire life.

Two weeks later, Matt looked at Sparkle, sitting very nicely after the *stay* command he'd issued, and declared her done. Her favorite treat, a chicken-flavored soft chew, was fifteen feet in front of her, and though she wanted it, she'd obeyed Matt's command and had for the past three days. She was fully trained. She knew *sit*, *stay*, *come*, *heel* and *drop it*, and a few others that Matt had taught her. Occasionally, she chased her tail, but now it was just cute.

He wanted to call Claire and tell her, to have her come give Sparkle the "Claire Asher, dog whisperer" stamp of approval, but since he'd moved out of her apartment and into the carriage house, he'd avoided her except to get together to structure the presentation to Ellie's class. He volunteered at Furever Paws only on days when she wasn't due in. He missed the hell out of her, but it was for the best, for both their sakes.

The doorbell rang and he answered the door, his niece Ellie flinging himself at him and wrapping her skinny arms around him.

"You're the best uncle in the world!" she said. "Thank you a million zillion times for training Sparkle!" She raced over to the puppy. "Come, Sparkle," she said very seriously.

The puppy padded over, wagging her tail.

"Good, Sparkle!" Ellie said, dropping down to her knees and petting the dog all over. "She is going to make everyone in my class wish they could have a puppy!"

No doubt. Or maybe not. "Well, tomorrow afternoon, when everyone sees how much work went into training her, how much picking up poop is involved..."

It *had* been a lot of work. And he'd loved just about every minute of it, despite the middle-of-the-night potty breaks in the freezing cold. And thanks to the presentation scheduled for tomorrow, he'd been able to get together with Claire twice over the past week. She'd kept the sessions short, making excuses to get home to Blaze, but he couldn't blame her for wanting to keep her distance.

Ellie laughed. "I don't mind picking up gross poop because that's what taking care of Sparkle is all about."

He held up his hand for a high five. "Exactly. So I'll see you at your school at two thirty."

Ellie beamed. "Yay! I'm so excited! Everyone will get to meet my great puppy!"

"Thank you, Matt," his sister said. "For *everything*. Come over anytime to visit Sparkle."

Ellie clipped on Sparkle's leash and headed toward the door. She turned to the dog. "I can't wait to show you my room."

A minute later they were gone, and it was just him and ole Hank. Matt dropped down on the couch, the big dog slowly sinking down on the rug, his head on his paws. "You're relieved that little pest is gone, aren't you?" Matt asked, laughing. Hank lifted his head. "No? You're not. Hell, I'm not either. I loved that little mutt."

The place seemed so empty without Sparkle. Even with Hank there. As the day wore on, he felt the puppy's absence so acutely that he wanted to talk about it with Claire. She'd understand exactly how he felt.

And he owed her an apology for the "you can't get attached" crud he'd tried to feed her. He'd gotten attached to Sparkle. He *was* attached to Hank.

Luckily, he couldn't go see Claire even though he thought it was a good idea. He had a job interview. His old friend Zeke had hooked him up with the veteran he'd told Matt about at the dog park. Bobby Doyle owned an auto body shop and needed some help—temporary was fine—because his best mechanic was out with a back injury. Matt quickly understood what Zeke hadn't said—that Bobby, who suffered from PTSD, could use a steadying presence like Matt around, a guy who'd been injured in a blast overseas and had come back and was piecing his life together. Bobby had built a good life for himself, but despite the family and the business, the man had trouble seeing what was right in front of him. The nightmares made it worse too. Matt had spoken to Birdie about hooking Bobby up with a program that matched therapy dogs with veterans, and Birdie was working on it.

Once Bobby's mechanic returned to work at the end of March, Matt would be leaving Spring Forest. A week, maybe ten days at most. He and Hank would hit the road and settle somewhere and start over. Matt was sure now he'd find work as a mechanic, and lately, he was thinking he might go to dog training school and become certified to work in an animal shelter, maybe even start his own business.

His life was moving forward in the right direction. He wasn't there yet, but maybe he'd get there. Then maybe there could be a chance for him and Claire.

Whoa. He'd had that thought and had always pushed it back down in the recesses where it belonged. But now it was up and out there. He could no longer deny that things were happening for him, that he was building something here in Spring Forest without ever having meant to.

Which meant he'd actually stay?

He looked at Hank. "What the hell, buddy? Why don't I know what's up from one minute to the next? Why is this so damned hard?"

Hank came over and put his head on Matt's thigh. He could swear the dog was saying, "I know, right?"

Eighteen third-graders, including his niece, Ellie, were staring at him as he stood at the blackboard in the front of the classroom, Sparkle on a four-foot leash beside him in the *sit* position. Mrs. Panetta's desk was to his left, and Claire stood just slightly behind him on his right, next to Sparkle's kennel. He'd walked the dog in on her leash, and the moment they'd entered the classroom, the kids had gone crazy with oohs and aahs, so cute, aww, throwing out tons of questions about how much she weighed and how old she was and if she knew she was a dog. Mrs. Panetta had gotten them to shush and explained that Mr. Fielding—man, did that sound weird—would answer all their questions after his presentation.

Ellie sat in the first row, just to the left of him. Next to her was a girl with her arms folded over her chest, who seemed to be sulking. Maybe her parents wouldn't let her have a dog. The boy on the other side of the sulker was grinning like crazy, and could barely contain his excitement about having a puppy in his classroom.

The teacher had introduced him and Claire, so he'd better get cracking.

"Hi, kids," he began. "About a month ago, my niece Ellie was promised a puppy for her birthday, which is coming up in just a few days. So I took Ellie to the

Furever Paws shelter to pick one out. Who did she fall in love with? A totally untrained five-month-old puppy that wouldn't stop barking or spinning in circles and chasing her tail, and had no idea that she wasn't supposed to go potty in the house."

The kids broke into laughter at that one. Ellie was beaming, and Matt winked at her.

"Well, my sister, Ellie's mom, wanted a trained puppy," he continued. "So I offered to turn Sparkle into just the right puppy for their house. It was a lot of hard work. Sparkle had to learn her name, to come when called, to stay when told to stay, not to chase birds or squirrels when told no, not to jump up and—very importantly—to do her business, if you know what I mean, outside only."

"You mean pee and poop!" the excited boy shouted.

"Exactly," Matt said, laughing.

He handed Sparkle's leash to Claire, then moved to the far end of the classroom. "Sparkle!"

The dog immediately looked at him.

"Sparkle, come!" She came trotting over, Claire more holding the leash than guiding her. He led her back to the front of the room, then put a treat down on the floor right in front of Sparkle. "Now, this is Sparkle's favorite treat. Peanut butter. Oh boy, does she love peanut butter."

The sulking girl in the front shot her hand in the air.

"Yes, Danica?" Mrs. Panetta said.

"If it's her favorite, why isn't she eating it?" the girl demanded, crossing her arms over her chest again.

"Because I didn't tell her she could," Matt explained. "Okay, Sparkle. Treat."

The dog looked at Matt and then gobbled it up.

Everyone clapped. "Ellie, your dog is so awesome!" someone called out.

Ellie was glowing.

"Sparkle, treat!" Danica said, holding out what looked like half of a chocolate bar.

"No, Sparkle!" Claire shouted. "Stay! Chocolate is toxic to dogs."

"Here, Sparkle!" Danica said, waving the chocolate.

As if in slow motion, Mrs. Panetta, Matt and Claire all rushed forward—the teacher to grab the chocolate before the dog could, and Matt and Claire to get ahold of Sparkle on her leash. But the puppy lunged, jumping up on the girl and knocking her lunch box all over the floor. Her sandwich went spinning—and Sparkle went flying after it.

"Sparkle, stay!" Matt commanded. The puppy stopped and looked at Matt. He scooped her up and put her in her kennel.

"Your puppy is so dumb!" Danica shouted, collecting her baggie-wrapped sandwich and putting it back in her lunch box.

"*You're* dumb!" Ellie shouted.

Oh no. Tell me this is not happening, Matt thought, his stomach sinking.

"Danica and Ellie, you're both going to the principal's office after the presentation," Mrs. Panetta said, directing a stern look at both girls.

Ellie had tears in her eyes. Danica looked spitting mad.

Great. The spotlight sure was on Ellie.

He'd blown this. He'd gotten smug, thinking he knew

everything about puppies and training, when he'd forgotten about how unpredictable things could get.

And Claire had reminded him when they'd last gotten together.

"Sparkle will be in an unfamiliar environment," Claire had said. "Lots of little hands will be poking at her, wanting to touch her. We'll have to be on guard and mindful that it may stress her, even though she's well trained."

He'd let Sparkle get too close to Danica, and now both girls were in trouble.

"Mrs. Panetta?" a boy asked, his hand in the air.

"Yes, Tom?"

"I wanted a puppy for my birthday, but now I don't," he said.

"Yeah, what if I got a puppy and it ate my Halloween candy and got sick?" a girl asked.

Sigh.

"That's a great question," Claire said, stepping forward. "And that's part of caring for a puppy. We always have to be really careful about what a dog can get ahold of. It's almost like babyproofing your house. Dogs can chew wires, they can eat things that are bad for them. Having a pet really does take a lot of work, but you know what?"

"What?" a few kids asked.

"Having a pet is also really great. You have an instant buddy, a friend to love and care for, and the rewards are worth all the hard stuff about having a pet."

"I have a dog and he's my best friend," a boy in the back said. "He sleeps next to my bed every night."

"My cat does that," another boy said.

"I hope my parents let me get a dog for my birthday. You're so lucky, Ellie," another girl said.

"Your dog is an idiot!" Danica hiss-whispered to Ellie.

"No, *you're* the idiot!" Ellie hiss-whispered back.

"Girls, that is enough," Mrs. Panetta said sharply. "Well, kids, that's it for today. Let's all thank Mr. Fielding and Ms. Asher from Furever Paws Animal Rescue for coming in today and telling us all about puppy care and training."

After lots of thank-yous, Matt picked up Sparkle's kennel and gave Ellie a quick hand-squeeze, then got the hell out of that classroom. The teacher followed him and Claire into the hallway.

"Please don't worry about things getting a bit out of hand," Mrs. Panetta said. "Claire will tell you—as a teacher, you just never know. But the presentation was great, and I think the kids got a lot out of it. Thank you so much for coming in."

Matt managed a smile and shook her hand. He needed air. Cold March air. Gripping Sparkle's kennel, he headed for the exit.

"Well, it was realistic," Claire said. "And Mrs. Panetta is right. You just never know what will happen. I hope you're not upset about the end."

He gaped at her. "Not upset? Are you kidding? This was Ellie's chance to shine. Instead, some girl tried to poison her dog, and now Ellie's in trouble for calling her dumb."

They reached the door and Claire pushed it open,

holding it for Matt who held the heavy kennel. "It happens, Matt. In third grade and in middle school and in high school. All part of learning to get along."

The cool air felt good on his heated skin, but his heart kept pounding with how badly it had all gone down. "I'd hardly call that getting along. Ellie is going to be really pissed at me, and rightly so. I didn't handle things right. Why the hell I did think I belonged in this environment? With kids and puppies? I knew better than that. But I let myself be talked into thinking I'm someone I'm not."

"Oh, Matt, come on," she said, glaring at him.

"I'm not Uncle Matt the puppy trainer, who can lead a classroom presentation," he snapped. "I'm a former army corporal with a slight limp trying to figure things out now that I'm a civilian."

"And you are," she said, touching his arm.

He pulled away. "I thought I was. But I don't belong here, Claire. This is your world. Not mine."

One thing was for damned sure. He *wasn't* staying in Spring Forest. Come the end of the month, he and his Mustang would be gone, Hank riding shotgun.

Chapter Twelve

"Claire, you know I'm not one to pry, but are you planning to get pregnant by a sperm donor?"

Claire almost spit out the sip of water she'd just taken. She straightened the stack of applications for tomorrow's adoption event and moved them to the counter. How on earth would Bunny know she was looking into options? Then she eyed her tote bag, which had slumped over on the desk. The big pamphlet for "Is Using a Sperm Donor Right for You?" was sticking out.

She sighed. A week had passed since the fiasco in Ellie's class. A week without a word from Matt, despite her texting and calling and even showing up at his place and knocking on the door. She'd peered in the windows, and he didn't seem to be home, so maybe he wasn't avoiding her. She'd heard Hank's nails scrape the floor as he'd come to the door to see who was there, and she'd been almost doubled-over with pangs of missing the old dog. Missing Matt.

She glanced around the lobby. The two of them were alone, thank goodness. Claire shoved the pamphlet back in the bag and hung it on the back of the chair. "Just looking into all possibilities," she whispered.

"I understand," Bunny said. "Believe me."

Claire was about to use the opportunity to ask Bunny about her personal life. She knew Bunny had been engaged in her twenties and that her fiancé had died tragically. Bunny often mentioned the man with a sweet, wistful tone, and Claire had always wanted to know Bunny's story—how he'd died, if Bunny had tried to find love after her loss.

But before Claire could think of a nonprying way to pry, Bunny rushed to say, "Guess things aren't working out with Matt?"

Sometimes Claire wasn't sure if Bunny wanted to be asked about her life or not. Her money was on the latter. "Nope. I tried everything, Bunny. But the man insists, once again, that he's not future material, no one's husband or father, and is planning to leave town at the end of the month. And March is almost over, so…probably Sunday night."

"Stubborn fool," Bunny said, shaking her head.

Claire couldn't help but smile. "Thanks."

Birdie came in from the back hallway, carrying a donation of stacked empty litter boxes, and Claire jumped up to take them from her. "Thanks, Claire. Would you mind logging these in?"

Claire was glad to be busy. She'd walked all the dogs, played with them individually and together in the yard, swept, sanitized, and now she was looking for things to do to avoid thinking about Matt. In fifteen minutes she'd be done here, and would go home to sweet Blaze. The noon dog walker reported that Blaze was a bit skittish on leash when other dogs were nearby, and that was something Claire was working on. She adored Blaze, but Blaze wasn't a cuddler yet. He might never be, and that was okay too.

"Oh, Bunny—Gator texted about selling that parcel of land again," Birdie said.

"I don't think we should, Birdie. It's prime Furever Paws acreage!"

Birdie shrugged. "Gator said he looked deeply into it."

Claire had begun to realize that Bernadette "Birdie" Whitaker had one weakness: her brother, Gator. Bunny, who tended to defer to Birdie in most things, also had one weakness: the animals. So when there was discord about something related to Whitaker Acres, Birdie and Bunny butted heads, which was a good thing. No quick agreements on what should be carefully considered— like selling the land currently used for training the dogs.

"Tell him we're thinking about possibilities," Bunny said, giving Claire a wink.

Claire blushed. She hoped Bunny wouldn't tell Birdie that she was checking out options for having a family. Ones that didn't include a husband. She wasn't quite ready to share that yet.

Because she also wasn't ready to give up on her dreams of a future with Matt Fielding.

The bell over the front door jangled and Richard Jackson, aka Doc J, walked in. The veterinarian, a tall, kind man in his sixties, had a thriving private practice but spent a lot of time at the shelter, offering his services out of the goodness of his heart. If Claire wasn't mistaken, he'd been in more than usual the past few days, fussing over the Whitaker sisters, complimenting their hair and outfits. Considering Birdie often wore paw-muddied overalls, and Bunny liked her Crocs with animal-print socks, Claire thought it was sweet.

"I like your rabbit pin, Bunny," Doc J said with a warm smile.

"Oh, thank you," she said, peering at it on her big blue fisherman sweater. "Birdie gave it to me for my birthday. A bunny for Bunny, she said." Bunny laughed.

"And I just happen to have a bird for a Birdie and a Bunny," Doc J said, handing Birdie a bakery box.

"What's this?" Birdie asked with a surprised smile.

"Open it," Doc J said.

Birdie opened the box and placed a hand on the region of her heart. She pulled out a big cookie in the shape and colors of a robin. "A bird for a Birdie."

"There were no bunnies, or I would have gotten one," he said to Bunny. "But I did get two robins."

Bunny laughed. "You're a peach, Doc J."

Claire watched the interplay between the three and was sure the doc had a little crush on one of the sisters—she just wasn't sure which one. Hey, if Claire had no love life, she wanted others to so she could live vicariously through them.

Her phone pinged with a text. Hopefully, it wasn't her sister with a blind date suggestion.

Nope. It was Matt.

Sparkle slipped out the front door and that moped spooked her and she took off. Ellie's frantic. We're searching on Holly Road. Help?

Oh God.
On my way, she texted back.
Oh no. Holly Road was busy with cars. *Please let them find her*, she thought, rushing out the door.

"Where could she be?" Ellie asked Matt, tears streaming down her face.

"We'll find her," he assured his niece, praying that would be true. "Let's keep looking. Remember to use a gentle voice if you see her and hold out the cheese stick. Sparkle loves those."

They walked down the sidewalk, looking under cars. No sign of the little dog.

A girl around Ellie's age stood on her lawn holding a Hula-Hoop around her waist. As Matt got closer, he realized it was the sulky one from Ellie's class. Luckily, Ellie hadn't been upset at Matt for what had happened. Instead, she'd given him an earful about how Danica was always mean to her and that the principal had given Danica a detention for "not being kind, and starting a problem," whereas Ellie didn't get in trouble at all.

Ellie ran up to the girl. "Danica? Did you see a brown-and-white puppy run past your house?"

The girl barely looked at Ellie. "Yup, I did."

"Did she go that way?" Ellie asked, pointing ahead toward the intersection. It had a four-way stop sign and not a light, thank God, but it was a busy junction.

Danica nodded. "Yup. Straight into traffic and kept going. Guess your only friend is gone, Ellie," the girl said, giving the Hula-Hoop a spin. It landed on the grass, and she frowned and picked it up, giving it another spin. "Maybe she got hit by a car." She spun the Hula-Hoop again, this time working it around her narrow hips. "Too bad, so sad."

Jesus. Matt's sister often mentioned the mean-girl drama among girls of Ellie's age, and he would have sworn eight was way too young for that crud. But he'd seen it firsthand at Ellie's school, and here it was again, right in front of him.

"Danica Haverman!" A woman came around the side of the house with a gardening tool in her hand. "I heard what you said. That was very unkind."

"Her own dog doesn't like her!" Danica said, looking like she was about to cry.

Suddenly Matt realized what was going on here. The girl was very, very jealous that Ellie had a dog.

"I'd rather have no friends at all than be the meanest girl in school!" Ellie screamed.

The girl froze, and then winced and burst into tears.

"We have to go find Sparkle," Matt said to Danica's mother. "I hope they can work this out."

The woman sighed. "Me too. You go inside and

straight to your room, young lady," she added to her daughter.

Matt took Ellie's hand, and they went running down the sidewalk in the direction Sparkle had gone. They looked under every car, asked everyone they saw if he or she had seen a little brown-and-white dog. No one had.

All of a sudden, he saw Claire's car coming down Holly Road. He waved, and she parked on the street and got out. "I have mozzarella string cheese," she said, handing one each to Matt and Ellie.

"We have them too," he said, holding up the five he'd stuffed in the pocket of his leather jacket.

"What if we can't find her?" Ellie asked, her tone frantic.

"Honey," Claire said. "Sparkle has a collar with her name and your telephone number on it. Plus, she's microchipped, which means if she's turned into a shelter, they can use a scanner to read the chip and find out who she belongs to."

Matt just hoped that if they didn't find her, someone had picked her up. If that little dog got hit by a car… He was supposed to be watching Ellie for his sister, supervising her with Sparkle. This was on him.

Great job, Fielding, he thought as he got down on his hands and knees to look under a low-slung car. "Sparkle? You hiding behind those wheels?"

There was no sign of her.

"We'll find her. Or someone will," Claire said.

Matt squeezed her hand, and the moment their skin made contact, he realized how much he'd missed touching her. Missed *her*. "Thanks for coming to help."

"Hey! Are you guys looking for a missing dog?" a woman called out from across the intersection.

"Yes!" Matt shouted, and they all went running to the stop sign.

"There's a brown-and-white puppy trembling behind the wheel of this truck."

Oh thank God, Matt thought.

"Sparkle! She's alive!" Ellie exclaimed.

"Let's let Uncle Matt go get her," Claire told Ellie. "She's very used to him, and I think she'll respond best to him in this scary situation she's gotten herself into."

Ellie bit her lip. "Okay. I know you can do it, Uncle Matt."

He put his hand on Ellie's shoulder. He was not returning without that dog safe and sound in his arms. He hadn't ever been able to find the skinny gray dog they'd seen a couple of times, but he was saving Sparkle. Hell yeah, he was.

He waited for a bunch of cars to pass, then ran across the road. He got down again, wincing at the jab in his leg. There was Sparkle, on the inside of the wheel on the far side of the car. Shaking.

"Hey, girl," he said. "Silly of you to run out the door when all the good stuff is inside the house. But I do have your favorite treat. Mozzarella string cheese stick." He ripped off a chunk and held it out toward her. He wished he could grab her, but his arms would have to be ten feet long. And he wouldn't be able to reach her from the other side. Plus, he'd no doubt get hit by a car himself.

Sparkle looked at him and tilted her head, then looked at the cheese in his hand. A big SUV went by, causing her to tremble again and flatten herself against the wheel.

"Yum," he said, taking a bite for himself.

Sparkle slowly moved toward his hand, and when she went for the cheese, he put one arm around her midsection. "Good Sparkle." The dog relaxed a bit, and he gave her another bite of cheese, then he scooped her up. He braced himself against the car to stand back up. "Got her!" he called to Claire and Ellie.

His niece broke into a grin. And seeing Claire smile almost made him drop to his knees.

He attached Sparkle's leash and walked the dog over to Ellie, who smothered her in kisses.

"All's well that ends well," Claire said.

"I blew it," Matt whispered. "We got lucky, but I almost lost that dog on my watch."

"Dogs slip out, Matt. It happens."

"It shouldn't." Just another example that he didn't belong in this world of kids and dogs and people depending on him. He had no experience as Uncle Matt. He'd been winging it, and he'd had no right when a little girl's heart was at stake.

And a woman's. *Stick to your plan, Fielding,* he told himself. *You'll help out with the adoption events, then you're gone Sunday night. Someplace where you'll feel…comfortable, in the right skin.* He just had no idea where that was.

She shook her head and turned to Ellie. "I'm meeting a couple girlfriends for an early dinner, but I sure am glad I got to see you and Sparkle reunited. That's all that matters. That you're back together."

"I'm so happy. Thank you, Uncle Matt!" Ellie said, flinging herself into his arms while holding tightly on the leash.

Man, it was going to be hard to say goodbye to this sweet little girl. And as he watched Claire hug Ellie and then dash off toward her car, he knew he was going to break his own heart again by saying goodbye to her.

As he and Ellie headed back toward his sister's house, Sparkle scampering on her leash just ahead of them, Ellie stopped and said, "Uh-oh."

"What's wrong?" he asked.

"Danica Haverman's back in her yard with her dumb Hula-Hoop."

Matt glanced over. She sure was. "Well, let's see what happens."

Ellie shrugged and they resumed walking.

Just as they neared Danica's yard, the girl dropped her Hula-Hoop and stared at them. She just stood there, not saying anything. Finally, she slowly came over to the end of her yard. "You found Sparkle."

Ellie tilted her head. "My uncle did. She was hiding under a car."

Danica bit her lip, looking at Ellie one second and the ground, the next. "Can I pet her?" she asked, looking sheepish. "You'll probably say no."

"I'm surprised you even want to," Ellie said, giving Sparkle a protective pat on the side.

Danica's eyes glistened with tears. "I wish I could get a dog."

Ah, Matt thought. He might not understand eight-year-old girls so well, but if he knew his niece, her next move would be kindness.

"Dogs are definitely awesome," Ellie said. "You can pet her. She's really soft."

Danica almost gasped. She bit her lip again and then both girls dropped to their knees, Danica petting Sparkle and Ellie staring at the girl in wonder.

Tears misted in Danica's eyes. "I'm sorry I said your dog didn't like you. Anyone can see she does."

"Well, I'm sorry I said you were the meanest girl in school. You're not. Because mean people don't say sorry and they don't pet puppies."

Danica beamed.

"Wanna come over later and play with her? I taught her how to fetch my socks."

Danica laughed. "Sure, I'll ask my mom."

And just like that, Ellie had a friend.

If only he and Claire could patch things up between them as easily.

Claire pulled open the door to the Main Street Grille, grateful for a little girl time. She, Amanda and fellow Furever Paws volunteer Mollie McFadden often got together for lunch or coffee after adoption events, but she was glad they'd set something up for today, just a regular ole day. Too bad her heart felt like it weighed thirty pounds.

She spotted the two young women sitting by the window. Amanda walked dogs on her day off from running the Grille, and Mollie was a dog trainer who assessed the shelter's newcomers when she had free time. Furever

Paws hadn't just brought furbabies into her life, but friends, as well.

"I hear you have a new foster!" Amanda said. "How are things going?"

Claire smiled just thinking of sweet Blaze. "So far, so good. He's on the timid side, but is slowly coming out of his shell."

"Guess who I saw in the park yesterday!" Mollie said. "Dempsey! She was with her new owner, fetching ball after ball. Oh, Claire, she looked really happy. And I heard her new owner say to her, 'you're the best dog ever, Dempsey.'"

Claire laughed, her heavy heart lightening a bit. "Good. I couldn't be happier about that match."

"I wish I could have a dog," Amanda said. "But I live here. One of these days…"

"Well, I know how much Birdie and Bunny appreciate that you come in to walk the dogs," Claire said.

Mollie leaned forward. "Speaking of shelter volunteers, my…friend Zeke is good friends with Matt. He mentioned that Matt now lives in a carriage house nearby. I thought he was living over your garage."

A waitress served the food just then, and Claire's hearty appetite for her turkey club waned. She still popped a fry into her mouth.

"Just didn't work out between us," she said, taking a bite of her sandwich to avoid having to elaborate. She couldn't talk about Matt or think about him without wanting to cry these days.

She knew he'd added the Sparkle-going-missing episode to the list of reasons why he wasn't meant to be a family man…when to her, how he'd handled it proved that he *was*.

"Sounds like you put 'friend' in air quotes, Mollie," Amanda said, adding a dollop of ketchup to her veggie burger.

They both knew that Zeke was Mollie's late brother's best friend. Zeke treated Mollie like a little sister, while she clearly had feelings for him. But she was gun-shy to act on them for fear of messing up the friendship.

Why was romance so complicated?

The door jangled and in walked Ryan Carter, the new owner and editor of the small local newspaper, the *Spring Forest Chronicle*. He headed straight to the counter, looking around for a waitress.

"Hey, Ryan," Amanda said with a warm smile and a wave. Claire knew that Amanda had developed a little crush the newcomer. "The counter waitress is just picking up an order in the kitchen. She'll be right out."

He barely acknowledged that she'd spoken.

"Chatty, isn't he?" Mollie whispered with a devilish grin. "Gotta love the brooding types."

"What's his story?" Claire asked. "Single? Divorced?"

"No one knows," Amanda said. "He's a man of mystery, apparently."

But Claire noticed how Amanda's gaze lingered on the very attractive newsman. Yup, romance was complicated.

"Speaking of stories, what the heck is this about the crazy thunderstorm forecasted for Monday night?" Mollie asked, taking a sip of her iced tea.

Claire had just heard about the storm this morning. People were already hitting the supermarkets to stock up on water and flashlights since losing power was a strong possibility.

Dempsey never minded bad weather. But Blaze was a scaredy-dog, and she had a feeling she'd be under the covers with him during the storm.

She picked up her sandwich to take a bite when she glanced out the window and saw Matt across the street, headed into a shop, Hank's leash around the pole out front. Her heart leaped at the sight of both of them, man and dog. She missed them so much.

What she wouldn't give to be under the covers with Blaze *and* Matt when the storm struck.

Chapter Thirteen

By late Monday afternoon, all anyone could talk about was how the thunderstorm forecasted for that evening had turned into a tornado watch. If there was a tornado, it was supposed to miss Spring Forest by a good margin, but you couldn't be too careful. Matt's sister's family had left for a planned vacation to his brother-in-law's parents' place, so they and Sparkle were far from harm. He was grateful he wouldn't have to worry about them. But all *his* plans to leave Spring Forest last night had gone out the window. No way could he leave knowing the town—and the Furever Paws shelter—could be hit hard by the storm. He'd rather stay put for a day or two and just make sure the people and animals he cared about were safe. Then he'd go.

Matt had done some online research on tornado

preparation, and apparently taping windows or even cracking windows to equalize pressure was no longer considered useful. Taking down mirrors from the walls and moving other glass items under chairs, creating a safe space in the basement—preferably with no windows—and having food and water for at least seventy-two hours were all listed as steps to take.

At five o'clock he headed over to the shelter to help batten down the hatches, but when he'd arrived, Birdie and Bunny had assured him their handyman and his assistant had it covered and had handled all the storm preparation for years.

Birdie seemed to be trying her best to be strong for Bunny, even chatting about their nephew Grant, who would be visiting soon. Matt had tried "shooting the breeze" about how he remembered Grant and his sisters coming to visit and staying every summer, and how they'd all—him included—go swimming in the creek behind the sisters' farmhouse. Bunny's face had lit up with the reminiscing, and Birdie had mouthed a thank-you to him for getting her sister's mind off the impending storm, even for fifteen minutes.

His research into helping dogs through particularly severe weather had had him up all night, and this morning he'd bought a few things from the big pet emporium two towns over, including something for Blaze, which he was planning on dropping off at Claire's. He wasn't so sure she would be happy to see him, but he also wanted to make sure she had everything she needed for the storm.

He rang the bell and was greeted by a short bark.

Claire opened the door, surprise lighting her pretty face. "Hey."

"I have something for Blaze." He pulled a package from the bag. "It's a thunder shirt. It's supposed to be comforting to a dog who's afraid of thunder."

Her face softened and she knelt down in front of Blaze. "See that?" she said to the dog. "Matt got you a present to help you through tonight. That sure was kind of him." She stood up, taking the package. "Thank you."

"You probably already have one, but I just wanted to make sure."

She laughed. "I actually have three, in all sizes."

He smiled. "Well, you can never have too many thunder shirts."

"I just spoke to Bunny. They're all set over there. She and Birdie and the staff moved all the dogs and cats to the basement, and two volunteers will stay with them overnight."

"I was just over there. They said they have everything covered. But what about the barn animals?" he asked, thinking of the sweet pair of llamas that Hank liked to visit whenever they went to the shelter together. "The pigs, goats, and geese?"

"The sisters will bring the geese with them into the basement of the farmhouse for the night. They say the rest of the animals will be safe in the barn."

He sure as hell hoped so.

A crack of thunder boomed in the gray sky, and they both looked up. Blaze ran back inside under a chair in the living room.

"I might need *all four* thunder shirts for him," she said. "Thanks again, Matt."

"By the way, I put up a bunch of signs in town about the gray dog we saw—I described him best I could and asked folks to call me or Furever Paws if he's spotted or found, but I haven't had any responses. If only we'd gotten a photo, that would have helped."

She nodded. "Well, I'm sure he'll find some sort of shelter tonight. Dogs have a good sense of weather and hopefully he'll find a safe haven at the first scent of thunder."

That made him feel better in general, but he still didn't want to leave her. "Well, stay safe," he heard himself saying.

She bit her lip and grabbed him into a hug. "You too."

He froze for a moment, then pulled her tighter against him, breathing in the scent of her skin, her hair, so in need of her against him that he'd lost all ability to think.

A streak of lightning lit the sky, followed by another boom of thunder, and Claire pulled away.

"You'd better get home," she said.

I don't want to leave you, was all he could think. If he had had Hank with him, he might have found a way to invite himself in for the night, just to make sure she would be safe.

He forced himself to his car. *I don't want to leave you* echoed in his head to the point that it was louder than the rain beating against the windshield.

By seven o'clock, the rain was coming down so hard, talk of the tornado watch on the TV news freaked him out to the point that he couldn't just stay home. He had to check on the sisters, on the shelter and on the barn animals, who were all alone on Whitaker Acres. He packed up a sleeping bag, Hank's favorite bed, food and water for both of them, his phone and charger, put on his trusty L.L.Bean raincoat and muck boots and headed out.

He drove over to Furever Paws first, the concrete building strong and sturdy in the beating rain. He'd called ahead to let the two volunteers know he was coming to check on them and to see if they needed anything. They said they'd thought of everything but extra batteries for their flashlights, and asked if he happened to have any, so he brought two ten packs that he'd had in his kitchen drawer. He found them safe and sound and playing cards in the basement. Some of the dogs were howling. The tremblers who were scared of thunder were in the farmhouse with the sisters. The cats all seemed okay.

Next he drove over to the farmhouse and found Birdie and Bunny hunkered down in their basement with the special-needs dogs and cats and any ones who'd been particularly frightened in their kennels, all in thunder shirts with extra blankets to cozy up in. The geese were in a large pen.

Three booms in a row were so loud that Matt felt them in his chest. "I'm going to stay the night in the barn," he shouted above the noise. "I'll watch over the animals and be close by if you need me."

"Oh, Matt, bless you," Bunny said.

Birdie grabbed him in a hug.

He raced out to his car, his raincoat soaking wet in just seconds. He drove the one minute down the gravel road to the big barn, the windshield wipers on their fastest setting unable to keep up with the pounding rain and winds. He covered himself with a tarp and grabbed the sleeping bag and Hank's bed under it, then darted into the barn, setting up their sleeping quarters on the far side where there were no windows. The rain beat down on the roof so loud he was surprised the llamas and goats weren't trembling in their pens. The crazy thing was that the worst of the storm hadn't even started.

He went back out to the car, backing it up as close to the entrance as he could, then opened the door for Hank to jump out. He ran inside, his fur wet, and gave himself a good shake.

Matt grabbed a towel from his backpack and dried him off, giving him a pat. "You can go lie down and try to relax, buddy," he said. "It's gonna be a long night."

Another crack of thunder exploded, and Hank lifted his head from the bed. The white noise machine he'd brought to try to counteract the thunder was useless since the booms were so loud. The llamas and pigs were a noise machine in themselves; no one would be getting any sleep tonight, that was for sure.

His phone pinged with a text—from the National Weather Service. This is a weather alert. The tornado watch is now a tornado warning. The alert repeated three times.

Matt gasped. "Oh hell."

Panic gripped him as the winds began to howl. Another boom of thunder hit so loud that Matt put his arms around Hank. The senior dog didn't seem afraid of the noise, but he'd let out a low growl indicating he sure didn't like it. *Neither do I, buddy.* Grabbing his phone, he sent up a silent prayer for cell service, relief washing over him when he was able to call the Whitaker sisters. They assured him they were fine, safe in the basement with their motley crew of dogs, cats and geese, and she and Bunny were playing cards and having those robin cookies that Doc J had brought. He didn't know Birdie Whitaker all that well, but something told him she kept her fears to herself. If she needed him, he had a good feeling she'd call right away.

Another crack of thunder hit, lightning streaking across the sky. He thought of Claire, alone in the house with the timid Blaze, and tried to call her, but the screen on his phone flashed No Service. *No, no, no.* His chest got tight and his heart started beating too fast. He needed to be able to hear that she was okay. He needed to be reachable for the Whitaker sisters. *Dammit!*

He checked his phone again a few minutes later. Same thing. No Service.

He thought he heard a car door slam right outside the doors to the barn. Hank stood up, staring at the doors. "It's okay, buddy. I'll go check it out."

He unlatched the doors and threw the left side open. Claire's SUV was there, the lights shining. *What the hell?*

He ran over to the car just as she got out.

"I have to get Blaze!" she shouted over the crashing sounds of the storm. "He's in his kennel!"

"I'll get the kennel," he shouted back. "You grab your stuff."

She nodded, and he hurried to the trunk and popped it open, grabbing the kennel, which was covered with a small lined tarp.

"I've got you, Blaze. It's gonna be okay," he said in what he hoped was a soothing tone. He felt anything but soothed. He rushed the kennel inside the barn and set it down, and when Claire dashed in with her bags, he closed the barn door and latched it again.

"Claire, how could you risk it?" he asked, staring at her.

She shoved off the hood of her raincoat, her blond hair dry in a low ponytail. "I couldn't sit at home knowing the barn animals were here alone. I just couldn't."

She knelt down in front of Blaze's kennel and opened it. The dog put his snout and one paw hesitantly out onto the barn floor, then slowly came out all the way and looked around. He saw Hank over on his bed and walked over, giving a sniff, then cautiously put a paw on the bed to see how Hank would respond. Because Hank was awesome, he lay his head on the far side of the bed to make room for the smaller dog, who stepped in and curled up alongside Hank's big body.

For a moment, they both watched the dogs settle, and Matt felt more at ease, knowing the timid Blaze would be watched over by Hank tonight.

"Me too," he said. "I should have let you know I was planning to come out here. I tried to call you a minute ago, but there's no cell service."

"I'm glad you didn't reach me," she said.

"Why?" He held her gaze.

"Because I might not have come. And then I wouldn't

be with you right now. And I need to be with you right now, Matt."

He unzipped her soaked raincoat and helped her out of it, then hung it up on a peg next to his. He got his jacket off, and then, before he could stop himself, he pulled Claire into his arms. "It's going to be okay. I checked on the shelter and the sisters. Everyone's fine. Did you hear the watch has turned into a warning? And that it's supposed to strike over Spring Forest?"

She nodded, her face draining of color. "I heard on the way over. Thank God I left when I did, or I wouldn't have been able to come at all. I would have been worried sick about the barn animals here all alone." She smiled and looked at him. "I should have known you'd come."

"I should have known *you*'d come. Want me to grab anything from your car?" he asked.

"I just brought my backpack with supplies for Blaze and some water and granola bars." She clunked herself on the forehead with her palm. "Oh no, I forgot my sleeping bag at home."

"Guess we'll have to share mine," he said, pointing at the rolled-up green nylon pack near Hank's bed. "If you want," he added. "Or you could have it, and I'll make do with the extra blanket I brought. I saw a stack of blankets on a shelf too."

She glanced to where he pointed. "They're for the animals. Those blankets smell like goat and llama."

"So you'll save me from that?" he asked with a smile.

She nodded. "Thanks for offering to share your sleeping bag."

She was thanking *him*? When he'd get to spend a scary, crazy night with Claire spooned against him, safe and sound? "Blaze looks like he's doing okay," he said, his gaze on the black-and-white dog calmly lying between Hank and the wall.

Claire smiled. "I think Blaze found his safe space for tonight. Thanks, Hank."

His heart was practically bursting with how much he cared about this woman, how much he wanted her, needed her.

Over the next couple of hours, the power went out, so Matt set up a couple of flashlights to provide illumination. There was little to do but listen to the rain pound against the barn. Both of them were too wired to talk much. At around midnight, Claire slid into the sleeping bag with a yawn.

"I don't know if I'll be able to sleep," she said.

Matt slid in beside her. They were so close. To the point he could feel her body heat. "Me either."

When a crack of thunder boomed and Claire almost jumped, Matt laid a comforting, heavy hand on her shoulder and then smoothed her hair back from her face. "It's okay, everything is going to be okay." Her eyes looked heavy, as though he was lulling her to sleep, and he hoped that would be the case. Her lids fluttered closed, her breathing soft and steady, and he realized she had fallen asleep. In his arms.

He closed his eyes, his chin resting against her head. He could stay like this forever. Without the tornado, of course.

A noise unlike any Matt had ever heard raged outside, and he started, bolting upright. He'd fallen asleep too. Claire popped up, disoriented, fear in her eyes as a strange howling wind raged outside. The dogs were standing pressed against the barn wall, Blaze trying to get between his protector, Hank, and the wood.

The tornado. *Oh God.*

The howling was downright scary—from the winds and the dogs now, both of whom were reacting.

"I wish we could do something," she said. "I hate that it has to run its course. Who knows what's going on out there? The damage it's causing." Her eyes were wet from unshed tears.

He reached for her and she melted against him. "We just have to ride it out. I'm gonna go check on the animals."

"Keep your distance, just in case they spook," she said.

"Birdie and Bunny warned me about that," he said with something of a smile. He got out of the sleeping bag, immediately cold and missing being so close to Claire. His flashlight guiding the way, he walked to the far end of the barn and turned into the corral area, immediately spotting the big pink pig with his head half-hidden under some hay. "Good idea, buddy," he said.

In the next pen were the four goats, and they were all huddled against one another in the tiny house a volunteer had made for them and given to the Whitaker sisters for Christmas last year.

The llamas, Drama and Llama Bean, were standing and looking like nothing got them down. They both eyed him and stepped to the edge of the pen.

"It's almost over," he assured them. "Just got to get through tonight, and tomorrow everything will be better."

A good metaphor for life and tough times, he thought. He sent up a silent prayer that Birdie and Bunny and the volunteers and all the Furever Paws animals were holding up okay, then he came back into the main area of the barn.

With the tornado roiling toward them, they'd just have to huddle together like the goats and hope like hell the damage was minimal.

Matt lay back down in the sleeping bag, and Claire did the same, this time facing the dogs. He spooned against her, his arm around her, and she grabbed on to his hand. Their flashlights were within reaching distance, next to their backpacks and water bottles, in case they needed to make a quick escape. He'd read that a tornado could last anywhere from a few seconds to an hour. He'd also heard on one news station that a recent tornado had lasted for *three* hours.

"It sounds like a freight train," she said, her voice choked.

He pulled himself tighter against her, holding on for dear life. He'd made a promise to himself and Claire—without her knowing it—that he wouldn't touch her, that he'd keep his hands and lips to himself. He wanted to break that promise right now, but he knew come morning, when everything was a wreck, he'd need to be strong for her, the sisters and for the animals.

Besides, he'd have to walk away soon enough. So keep his hands to himself, he would.

Claire's eyes popped open in the dark. Matt was silent and unmoving beside her; he'd stayed up well past

2:00 a.m., a fact she knew because that was the last time she'd jerked awake from the noise and he'd wrapped his arm around her, burrowing his chin into her hair. Every time he'd done that, she'd felt safe and secure enough to actually fall asleep, but she had a feeling Matt hadn't slept a wink.

Before she'd driven out to the barn, she'd put on her old battery-operated watch just in case the power went out, and she was glad she did. It was almost four o'clock now. The winds were howling. She'd heard crashes earlier, possibly trees falling, and she prayed the big oaks on the property wouldn't land on any of the buildings. The tornado had stopped, and she was glad Matt had finally fallen asleep. It was pitch-dark outside, the rain still beating down and the thunder still crackling.

His eyes opened, and he seemed to be straining to listen. "The howling stopped. Still pouring, though."

"We made it through."

He grabbed the smaller flashlight and shone it on the dog bed. Hank and Blaze were curled up tightly next to each other. "They seem okay."

She nodded. "I'm so glad they had each other for the worst of it."

"Like us," he said.

"Like us," she agreed.

She could barely see him in the dark, but she could feel him, breathing beside her, the very presence of him. They were just inches apart.

"I want to go out there with the flashlight and assess the damage," he said.

"In the morning," she whispered. "The flashlight

can't illuminate everything, and who knows what debris is out there or broken branches that could fall any minute."

He nodded. "I had a nightmare earlier. Not the same one I used to have about the explosion. This time it was about you."

"Me? I'm the subject of your nightmares? Great." She tried to inject some levity into her voice, afraid he'd turn away from her and go curl up with the dogs.

"You were running in the dark, thunder booming around you and lightning streaking above your head. Tree limbs were falling everywhere. I was standing up ahead and you were running toward me, but you never got closer. It was so strange. I couldn't move a step toward you. I was scared to death you were going to be hurt right in front of me."

"Was I?"

"I woke up," he said.

"What do you think the dream meant?" she asked. Because if he was about to read too much into it, she wanted to be able to refute his interpretation.

"It means what it is."

"What it is?" she repeated. "What is it?"

"That I'm supposed to let you go, even if I don't want to."

Now she was glad she asked. "You're not *supposed* to. You're *choosing* to, Matt. *You're* the one standing in our way. Your way."

"For good reason," he said.

"No, for no reason."

"I really love you, Claire," he said, his voice breaking. "I always have. But you've always deserved better."

"I don't get a say?"

He shook his head. "You're romanticizing the past. You always were a romantic."

"Me? Hardly. You're the romantic, Matt. Except in this case, you're turning our would-be love story into an almost-tragedy."

"I'll stay in town long enough to help Birdie and Bunny with any cleanup efforts, but then I'm leaving."

"Great. Hurt us both. Good going, Fielding."

"When you're married to a great guy who can give you the world, you'll be glad I was willing to walk away."

"I don't want the world, Matt. I just want you. I've only ever just wanted *you*."

He shook his head again, but she reached both hands to his face and kissed him so that he couldn't say anything else. No more talking. No more. He was leaving. Their second chance was a lost cause. She would have to accept it.

"Do something for me, then, Matt," she whispered.

"Anything."

"Give me a last night with you. Let's just have tonight and then you can go."

"I made myself promise I wouldn't touch you."

"You get to change your own rules," she pointed out. *Please let that sink into his stubborn head. You get to change your own rules.*

"You have no idea how much I want you," he said.

"Show me, then," she said.

He kissed her, peeling off her thermal shirt. His warm hands on her skin were electrifying. She reached down and undid the tie on the waistband of his sweatpants. And then he moved over her, his hands and mouth everywhere.

"Are you sure?" he whispered in her ear, trailing kisses along her collarbone.

"I'm sure," she said.

And then, after retrieving a little foil packet from his wallet, he made her forget all about the storm, all about his stubbornness, all about the fact that he'd be leaving in a matter of days, once again with her heart.

Chapter Fourteen

Matt opened his eyes, aware of only the silence and Claire's gentle breathing as she slept beside him.

Silence.

He gently touched Claire's shoulder. "Hey, sleeping beauty."

She opened her eyes, then bolted upright. "It's quiet."

"Exactly."

Well, it was quiet if you didn't count the pig oinking in his pen at the far end of the barn. Someone wanted breakfast.

"Let's go see what's going on outside, and then we'll check on the barn animals," she said.

They both shimmied out of the sleeping bag and rushed to the barn door.

"Wait," he said, Claire's hand ready to open the door. "We need to prepare ourselves. It could be really bad."

"I know."

The dogs padded over, Blaze looking much perkier than he had last night.

"Careful, guys," Matt said. "We'll go out first and make sure it's safe for your paws. Stay."

The dogs listened as Claire opened the door and sunlight poured into the barn. She looked out. "Oh no. Oh God. Matt."

She stood there, shaking her head, looking all around.

Devastation was the only word for the scene outside. Trees were torn from their roots and lying sideways across the property. One had even fallen on the roof, but luckily, it hadn't damaged the barn as far as he could see. The tornado had touched right down on Whitaker land, and had taken many of the huge old oak trees.

"Over here, Hank and Blaze," he said, allowing the dogs out in a safe area to do their business. The dogs seemed careful about stepping over branches and debris.

"Oh God, Matt, the shelter. What if—"

They could see the back of the building from where they stood, but not the front or the sides. They ran over, navigating through the downed tree limbs.

Birdie and Bunny stood in front of Furever Paws, their arms around each other's shoulders.

"Birdie! Bunny!" Claire called.

The Whitaker sisters turned around. Tough Birdie looked like she might cry. Bunny did have tears in her eyes as she shook her head.

"Somehow our farmhouse was barely affected," Bunny said. "We got darn lucky."

"The shelter fared worse," Birdie said. "Right in the path of those huge oaks. There's serious damage to the roof," she added, pointing at where a big section had been blown off and now rested against some trees in the forested area. "And a lot of fencing is gone."

"A few of the storage sheds were blown away—one slammed into a tree and seems to have half pulled it up from the ground."

"But you and the volunteers are okay?" Matt asked. "All the animals are okay?"

"All of us are fine," Birdie assured him.

"Same with the barn animals," Claire said. "And these two," she added, gesturing to where Hank and his shadow, Blaze, sniffed around.

"Well, we sure could use your help walking all the dogs," Birdie said. "Why don't we start with the ones in the farmhouse, and then we'll go see if the volunteers in the shelter basement are awake yet."

The four of them went into the farmhouse, Matt grateful the beautiful white home hadn't been hit. In the basement, they each headed for a kennel, Matt going for the little chiweenie, Tucker. As they stepped back outside, letting the dogs stretch and walk around a bit, he was amazed that so much sunshine could follow such turbulent weather. It was early, barely seven, and chilly, but the day promised to be warmer than it had been lately.

"The fenced play area is sound," Bunny said. "So

why don't we put these guys in there and go see how the dogs in the shelter basement fared."

"You two also," Claire said to Hank and Blaze, closing the gate behind them.

Once the dogs were secured, and Matt made sure that none of the trees were possibly near enough to come crashing down on the shelter or play area, they all headed inside the shelter. The section of the roof that had been damaged was in the lobby, toward the side where the gift shop had been. Thankfully, Birdie and Bunny had packed everything and secured it, so nothing was damaged, except the table where people would sit to fill out applications; it lay on its side, and there was some bad water damage from where the rain had come in. *It could be a lot worse*, Matt thought.

Just as they were about to head into the basement, the door leading downstairs opened, and two women stood there. "Boy, are we glad to see you all," one said. Matt hadn't met these women before yesterday, but he couldn't be more grateful to them for staying with the animals. There were five dogs down there, and they all trooped down the stairs to bring them up on leashes.

Finally, with those dogs settled in the play yard with the others, Birdie and Bunny hugged the two volunteers, who were anxious to leave and check on their homes.

With the volunteers gone, Matt, Claire and the Whitaker sisters stood in the fenced yard, watching the dogs play. Even Tucker, who usually kept to himself, seemed glad to join the reunion, sniffing at a gentle shepherd mix's ankles.

"Just based on the roof and the fencing alone, I'm

thinking we're looking at around twenty thousand in damages," Birdie said, eyeing the roof of the shelter.

Bunny shook her head. "Thank goodness for solid insurance. *And* that no one was hurt. Boy, did we get lucky."

Birdie nodded. "And we haven't walked the entire property—more downed trees might need hauling away."

"I hate this," Matt said. "Furever Paws and Whitaker Acres are so special and necessary, they should be untouchable. Even from acts of God."

Birdie put a hand on his arm. "This is how it goes, though, isn't it? Things get damaged and rebuilt, and life goes on."

He felt like she was talking about him. He *knew* she was. But some things were too damaged. Like himself.

Claire stared at him, as if hoping the wise Birdie had gotten through to him, just like she'd been trying to do for weeks now. Why did he feel so stuck? Part of him wanted to grab Claire and tell her he loved her, that he wanted to be with her, build a life with her. But part of him just couldn't. So he stayed silent.

"Let's go take a walk farther up," Bunny said. "See how bad it is up near the road."

So much debris, Matt thought as they surveyed the land. He saw lids from garbage cans that weren't Whitaker property, window shutters from God knew where. And so many tree limbs.

"Oh Jesus, is that a dog?" Matt said, his heart stopping.

"What? Where?" Claire said, looking at him, her beautiful green eyes frantic.

"Under that big tree branch," he said, pointing up ahead. A skinny black dog lay unmoving under the heavy branch. His eyes were open and he closed them every now and then, the only indication he was alive.

"Oh God, it is," Bunny said. "He's trapped. Poor thing looks like he gave up the struggle to free himself. Not that he could, given the weight of that tree limb."

"He's probably injured," Birdie said. "But how are we going to get the limb off him without bringing down the entire tree on him?"

Matt stared up at the rest of the tree, hanging in such a precarious position that could it could come toppling down any minute.

"I've never seen this dog before," Birdie said. "I sure as hell hope someone didn't abandon it before the storm." She shook her head, anger flashing in her blue eyes.

"Maybe the thunder or the tornado spooked him, and he ran off from his home and then got hit and trapped by the limb," Claire said. "I can't tell if he has a collar."

Matt couldn't see either. "I have to help him. Somehow, someway."

"I don't know Matt," Birdie said. "We might have to call in our tree guy with his heavy equipment."

Matt shook his head. "If he can even *get* here. We don't know how bad the roads are. And even if he could get here, the dog can't have much longer."

I'm going to help you, he said silently to the dog as he advanced slowly toward the downed tree, his heart beating a mile a minute.

"If you touch anything, that hanging branch could

come crashing down on both your heads," Bunny warned.

He stared at the injured, scared dog and saw himself. Claire, Sparkle, Hank, his sister and Ellie, the Whitaker sisters, Zeke and Bobby—they'd all reached out to him and brought him back to himself. Now he was going to help that dog.

Fear can't stop me, he thought. *Not from saving that dog. Not from life.*

Or from love. Because as Claire said, love is all there is. It makes everything else work.

He sucked in a breath and turned back to look at Claire, to drink in the sight of her for sustenance. She believed in him—she'd always believed in him. And she'd helped him believe in himself. He was getting that tree limb off that dog. End of story.

"I have some experience from my time overseas," Matt assured everyone, moving closer to the dog, his gaze going from the precarious tree limb to the dog's frantic eyes. "We were hit with all kinds of hard stuff in our path."

"Oh God, be careful," Claire said.

"I will," he said. He looked at the dog. "I'm coming for you," he said. "I'm going to get you out."

One wrong move and that tree limb would take them *both* out—permanently. *You can do it*, he told himself. Slow and steady. Then quicksilver. In a flash he thought about coming home to Spring Forest, the shock of seeing Claire. How a little girl's birthday wish of a puppy had completely changed his life. *What if I'd told my sister I didn't know anything about dogs and left it to*

*her to choose a pup? I likely never would have run into
Claire. I certainly wouldn't have trained Sparkle. Or
adopted Hank. Or volunteered at Furever Paws and
met the Whitaker sisters.*

I wouldn't be here right now.

Save that dog, he told himself.

"Matt," Claire said—from right behind him. "I'm
going to help you."

He was about to say *no, you could get hurt,* but he
could see the insistence in her eyes. She was determined. And Claire Asher didn't care about getting
hurt—she was front-line material.

Yes. She was.

He held out his hand and she took it.

They walked over as silently as they could, since it
was clear that any movement would topple the limb. He
kept his eyes warm and on the pooch, who was staring
at him, half-frantic, half-resigned to his fate—which
probably hadn't been all that great till this point.

He calculated where to best lift the limb pinning
the dog and noted a branch hanging precariously, just
barely attached to it. "I'll lift and you drag the dog
out," he said.

She nodded. "Got it."

"You might get bitten," he warned.

She waved a hand. "Hazard of life."

He stared at her and reached out a hand to her cheek,
then turned his attention back to the heavy limb trap-
ping the dog.

"We've got this," she said, holding his gaze.

He believed her.

"On my count, pup, okay?" he whispered to the dog. "One. Two. Three."

Before three had finished echoing in his head, he used every bit of strength he had—and a hell of lot in reserve—and lifted the limb up. Claire grabbed the dog under his front arms and pulled him clear.

His arms about to burst, Matt dropped the limb, and the hanging branch came crashing down right on the spot where the poor stray had been.

His heart was booming. He stood, his eyes closed, his legs buckling, his bad leg unable to deal.

"Oh, Matt," Claire said, rushing over, cradling the dog against her chest. "You did it. We did it. This sweet dog did it." She kissed the top of the dog's head, stroking its clumped, wet fur.

"I'll take him," Birdie said, stretching out her arms. "*Her*, actually," she added, as Claire transferred the dog to her arms. Bunny must have run to the barn for a towel, because she wrapped the poor thing up as Birdie shifted her in her arms. The dog looked so relieved to be warm and drying off.

"I'll call Doc J and see if he can come right away," Birdie said. "Her leg looks injured."

She and Bunny rushed the dog back into the shelter.

"You can take the man out of the army, but you can't take the army out of the man," Claire said.

He grabbed her to him and held her, relishing the feeling of her arms tightening around him. "We're all okay," he said, hearing the wonder in his own voice.

"We're all okay," she repeated, placing her hands on either side of his jaw.

His mind had gone as jelly-like as his legs, so he

let himself sit back and catch his breath, let his heart rate come back down to normal. But nothing was normal anymore. Not Furever Paws or the Whitaker land stretched out before him, devastation as far as the eye could see.

And not him.

Claire kept glancing at Matt as they all waited for Doc J to arrive to check on the injured dog. Matt had been very quiet since they'd gone inside to join the others. Now it was just the two of them in the shelter's examination room—and the dog, of course, a female mixed-breed that lay on a padded exam table.

Birdie had said it was a good sign that the dog had accepted a few treats from her, and her eyes did look brighter now that she was safe, though it was clear she was in pain. Right now, the dog seemed content to lay there without being pinned by the heavy tree limb, her rescuers cooing at her, petting her side.

Claire didn't know how she didn't melt into a puddle on the floor, her heart was so overflowing with love for this man.

Birdie and Bunny had gone out to the yard to check on the dogs, and make a plan for what to do with everyone until the roof could be taken care of and all the fencing restored.

"You're going to be okay," Matt said to the dog, gently patting its side. "You're in the best possible place now. Doc J will get you fixed up, and then someone will give you a good home. You'll be fine."

The dog gave Matt's hand a lick as he reached to scratch her ears.

Matt smiled. "No thanks necessary. Anyone would have done it."

"But you did," Claire said. "And whether you like it or not, Matt Fielding, you're going to have to listen to me tell you that you're more of a man than any I've ever known. And I love you. I know you're not a coward, so if you do leave Spring Forest and leave me, it's not because you're scared of commitment or love. It's because you don't love me. I get that now."

His mouth dropped open. He'd been a coward when it came to her. Afraid to let himself *feel* what he truly felt. Afraid to let himself have something so precious.

"I do love you," Matt said, looking into her eyes. "I absolutely do love you, Claire Asher."

"But…" she prompted, waiting for it. Bracing herself, tears poking her eyes and her heart so heavy she was about to drop to the floor.

"Not *buts*," he said. "I just love you. And you're right, I'm not a coward. So why the hell would I leave Spring Forest when everything I love is here? When you're here." He walked over to her and held out his arms. She rushed into them, closing her eyes, reveling in the feel of his arms around her, holding her tight.

"I truly thought I had nothing to offer you, and you showed me that I do," he said. "I'm just sorry it took me so long—and a tornado—to see it."

Claire smiled. "I call that the silver lining."

He reached both hands to the sides of her face and stared at her with so much love, so much intensity in his eyes, it was almost too much to bear. She'd seen that look before, when they'd been very young and deeply in love, no cares in the world. Now there were cares, but the look remained. She called that serious progress. "Eighteen years later, will you do me the honor of becoming my wife and sharing your life with me?"

Okay, now she was crying. "Yes. Yes, yes, yes."

"And, Claire, remember when I said a long, long time ago that if we had a baby I'd want to name him Jesse, after my brother?"

She held her breath. "Yes, of course I remember." She remembered what else he'd said too. *Not* that long ago.

"Let's have a baby," he said. "It's lucky that Jesse would work for a boy or a girl."

"Baby Jesse," she repeated, wrapping her arms around him. She put her head on his chest and stayed like that for a good minute. "Oh, Matt? I do have one request for our new life together."

"Anything," Matt said.

"If no one claims our new buddy here, I'd like to foster her—I'd like *us* to foster her—once she's given the okay by Doc J." Birdie had checked for a microchip and there wasn't one, but protocol meant alerting lost dogs websites and hanging flyers and waiting five days to see if anyone would come looking for her. Then she could be put up for adoption. But she'd need nursing back to health and training—and that was Claire Asher's specialty.

"Sounds like a great idea to me," he said. "I have a good name for her too, if the Whitaker sisters will give up naming rights. Hope."

She grinned. "Hope is a great name. A perfect name for her."

Just then, the black dog on the table let out a little

bark as if she agreed. Claire's eyes widened. "She likes the name!"

"Sparkle, Hank and Hope can be our ring bearers," he said. "And Blaze, unless he finds his forever home before then."

"Absolutely," Claire said, laughing. "And all our favorite dogs can be invited. Think they'll sit during the ceremony?"

He laughed. "I don't know about that, but I do know something." He put his arms around her shoulders.

She tilted her head. "Oh yeah? What?"

"That *I* found my forever home," Matt said, just as Hope let out another bark of agreement.

* * * * *

MILLS & BOON

Coming next month

SURPRISE BABY FOR THE HEIR
Ellie Darkins

'I'm pregnant.'

The words hit Fraser like a bus, rendering him mute and paralysed. He sat in silence for long, still moments, letting the words reverberate through his ears, his brain. The full meaning of them fell upon him slowly, gradually. Like being crushed to death under a pile of small rocks. Each one so insignificant that you didn't feel the difference, but collectively, they stole his breath, and could break his body.

'Are you going to say anything?' Elspeth asked, breaking into his thoughts at last. He met her gaze and saw that it had hardened even further – he hadn't thought that that would be possible. And he could understand why. He'd barely said a word since she'd dropped her bombshell. But he needed time to take this in. Surely she could understand that. 'I'm sorry. I'm in shock,' he said. Following it up with the first thing that popped into his head. 'We were careful.'

'Not careful enough, it seems.' Her voice was like ice, cutting into him, and he knew that it was the wrong thing to say. He wasn't telling her anything she didn't know.

Fraser shook his head.

'What do you want to do?' he asked, his voice tentative,

aware that they had options. Equally aware that discussing them could be a minefield if they weren't on the same page.

'I want to have the baby,' Elspeth said with the same firmness and lack of equivocation that she had told him that she was pregnant. How someone so slight could sound so immovably solid was beyond him, and a huge part of her appeal, he realised. Something that he should be wary of…

Continue reading
SURPRISE BABY FOR THE HEIR
Ellie Darkins

Available next month
www.millsandboon.co.uk

COMING SOON!

We really hope you enjoyed reading this book. If you're looking for more romance, be sure to head to the shops when new books are available on

Thursday 24th January

To see which titles are coming soon, please visit

millsandboon.co.uk/nextmonth

LET'S TALK

Romance

For exclusive extracts, competitions and special offers, find us online:

 facebook.com/millsandboon

@MillsandBoon

@MillsandBoonUK

Get in touch on 01413 063232

For all the latest titles coming soon, visit
millsandboon.co.uk/nextmonth